JEREMY MOON DREAMS

"I'm here," he said.

"You want this to end," the other replied, his voice hollow and distant.

"I wish it would."

"You can end it, you know."

Moon frowned. "I've seen you before."

"Yes. In the mirror."

"You're me?"

"In a manner of speaking."

"I don't understand."

"You don't have to. Just come through the door, that's all."

"And the dreams will end?"

The other smiled menacingly, teeth white in the brown beard. "I can assure you, you'll never be troubled by your own nightmares again. . . ."

MOONDREAMS

BRAD STRICKLAND

A SIGNET BOOK

NEW AMERICAN LIBRARY

This book is dedicated
with love
to my father and mother,
who always encouraged me
to grow, to learn, and to try

NAL BOOKS ARE AVAILABLE AT QUANTITY DISCOUNTS WHEN USED
TO PROMOTE PRODUCTS OR SERVICES. FOR INFORMATION PLEASE
WRITE TO PREMIUM MARKETING DIVISION, NEW AMERICAN LIBRARY,
1633 BROADWAY, NEW YORK, NEW YORK 10019.

Copyright © 1988 by Brad Strickland

Map designed by Thomas F. Deitz

SIGNET, SIGNET CLASSIC, MENTOR, ONYX, PLUME, MERIDIAN
and NAL BOOKS are published by NAL PENGUIN INC.,
1633 Broadway, New York, New York 10019

First Printing, May, 1988

1 2 3 4 5 6 7 8 9

PRINTED IN THE UNITED STATES OF AMERICA

ACKNOWLEDGMENTS

Setting out to write a novel is like embarking on an epic quest without benefit of weapon, supplies, or map; and those who choose to walk this path must always rely on the goodwill and assistance of the people they meet along the way. Before we set off on this particular journey, I want to pause to acknowledge the kindness of a few who made the trip possible.

First, my agent, Richard Curtis, was ready with advice and encouragement anytime I needed it—and he understood that sometimes he helped me best by allowing me to fight my way alone out of thickets of my own making. Thanks, Richard, for your patience with me. Similar appreciation must go to John Silbersack, my editor at NAL/Signet, whose gentlemanly advice, acumen, and quiet support were always more welcome than perhaps he realized or I made clear.

Next, my gratitude goes to the gang at SFWCC, in the shadow of the Big Chicken. This hardy band kept me going with monthly conferences, critiques, bull sessions, and brew: Tom Deitz, Thom Hartman, Mike Langford, Jack Massa, Greg Nicoll, Lamar Waldron, and Wendy Webb. Thanks, folks, for helping me fend off the monstrous Beast of Adverbia.

To Mark Stevens, keeper of volumes of mystic lore at the sign of the dagger and rocket, I give assurances of my deep appreciation. All writers covet bookstore owners as supportive and enthusiastic as Mark.

To my children, Amy and Jonathan, who stood guard duty over the word processor while Dad was "working on the book," I also give my thanks, though they deserve (at least) Thaumian medals of honor for being willing to forgo trips to the zoo or the beach on those days when Jeremy's adventures took up most of my attention.

Last of all, to the reader I treasure most of all, my wife, Barbara: Thank you, darling. The book is yours as much as mine. You helped me write it more than you know, and I hope you like it.

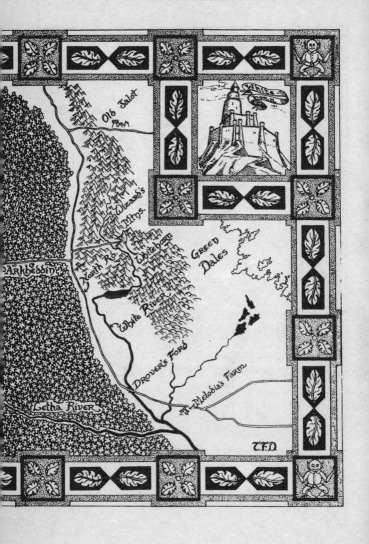

CHAPTER 1

THE ROOM HAD a 3 A.M. feel.

At the far end, past clusters of silhouetted heads, past drifting nets of silver cigarette smoke, the bartender stood in a rectangular fluorescent island, backed by hard-gleaming rows of bottles. Between him and Jeremy the blackness of the room was spotted with glowing red points of cigarette ends and broken by tiny green-shaded circles of light on tables.

To Jeremy's left, on a two-foot-high stage, a black pianist occupied a second island, a round spotlight island. His blind ebony face glistened in blue highlights, sweat-sheen, as he leaned back to let slow blues leak between his fingers and out into the bar.

Jeremy stared into the dark. *They* were there. He couldn't see them, but somehow he knew they were there.

They had come for him.

A baby cried somewhere in the dark, shushed after a moment. Jeremy frowned. A baby? In a bar? Where were its shoes?

Cassie had stopped by his office earlier that day. "You look terrible," she had said with the assurance of someone who knew she looked terrific, svelte and glowing in a russet business outfit. "Getting sick before Christmas?"

Jeremy shook his head. "Not sick. Just tired."

She stood over him, a warm blonde presence, her sheer vitality filling the little cubicle. "You're in luck. You get eight whole days off."

"And you're going to Florida," he said. "Lot of good the vacation does me."

"Hey, I won't be gone the whole time," she said, and having mentioned time, she checked her Geneve wristwatch. Three of the diamonds caught the overhead fluorescent light and flashed rainbows in Jeremy's eyes. They only reminded him that his eyes ached from lack of sleep. But Cassie didn't even stop: "Oops, gotta go. I've got to chew up an artist." In the doorway she paused, looking back. Jeremy regarded her opulent figure, one that made her sensible harvest-colored business dress somehow lewd and tempting. "Get some rest, seriously. Get some sleep tonight."

Then she was gone in an invisible swirl of Giorgio, but Jeremy said to her absence, "How can I get some sleep? I always dream."

Jeremy was cold. The air-conditioner outlet somewhere up among the fake black beams directed its breath on him, and his highball glass, lifted to his lips, offered no warmth. It was empty, though Jeremy's tongue and stomach bore no memory of its contents. The pianist took the melody down a staircase of sound, a graceful nude descending into the smoky room.

Movement, dry rustle, a skulking figure caught momentarily against the light of the far-off bar: coming toward him: one of *them*.

Jeremy darted a glance to his left. Crowded tables, no escape. No exit signs anywhere. The scrape of a chair, pushed out of a deliberately slow walker's way, close. Jeremy pushed away from the table, found his legs, stood. The stage was only a step away; he took the step, gained the stage, found the dark exit into the wings—

"Here!" A hiss, Escher's voice. Why was he here? "You wanted to be the star. Take this damn thing and sing!"

Cold, phallic shape of microphone thrust into his hand. "But I can't—"

"Taplan and Taplan doesn't have room for quitters. You do what I tell you. Light!"

Blue stab of a spot on him, pinning him, an insect on the card of the stage. He turned toward the obscured audience, seeing nothing but the slant of light, looping the mike cord with his nervous left hand. On that side of him the pianist, blind face grave, inclined his head sideways, away from his long black fingers, and teased fill music from his instrument. The light-purpled lips moved, the soft voice said, "Anything you wanna sing, man. Anytime you ready."

Stage fright clenched cold in his chest. The microphone

reared up of its own accord, a cobra of wire and metal ready to strike at his face. Nervous energy propelled Jeremy, and he paced, the light following him. "Ladies and gentlemen, I guess we all have blues in our lives. Yeah, blues from the time we stand up in baby shoes till they drop us barefoot in the ground." His voice. *His* voice? "So this is for all of us, ladies and gentlemen, 'cause we're all in the same damn boat."

He didn't know the words. Hell with it, his business was words. They would come. Bending his head low over the mike, he brought his voice up from deep in his abdomen:

> Driftin on the ocean, ain't no land in sight
> Said driftin on the ocean, Lord,
> Ain't no land in sight—
> Somebody tell my woman,
> Say "You man ain't comin round tonight."

He rolls in sweat-damp sheets, groaning, trying to wake up.

Jeremy felt a difference in the room, the press of attention turning on him, someone looking up here, a conversation breaking short there, whispers ceasing, heads turning. He caressed the mike, sent words through it and out into the smoky room:

> Ocean's mighty big, Lord, water black as coal,
> Say the ocean's big, baby,
> And that water's black as coal,
> And we all in the same boat,
> Ev'ry single livin' soul.

More words spilled from somewhere inside him, words about darkness and loneliness and the bleakness of souls alone, the feelings coming not from him but through him, without effort, the voice not really his own but a whiskey baritone, rich and sick and full of knowledge and the sharp smoke of weary sin. At the song's end a surf of applause rolled forward through the dark to curl, to break against the stage. The light went out

a city full of night and no lights showing, only the

wind's howl in the streets, a rattle and hiss at ankle height, a windblown paper trying to snag his leg. Around him loomed buildings, deeper black against the black of sky. Jeremy had never before noticed how much difference city lights made: they shut out the stars, but also threw into relief the street mysteries, banished night fears to the deepest alleys, cast the sodium-yellow or mercury-blue light of sanity on the river of passersby.

This is crazy, Jeremy thought. *I'm dreaming again. Nothing is chasing me.*

He was driving an unfamiliar car through the night city, his eyes on the rearview mirror. *They* wouldn't give up that easily. Somewhere they would be behind him. The mirror, a rectangle of city night, showed headlights, hookers, marquees, liquor stores, a manhole pluming steam into the darkness. No gaze turned toward him, no one seemed to mark his passage.

If I can only find the shoes, he thought.

"Tacky," Cassie had murmured beside him. They had been heading home from work on the day before Thanksgiving—Cassie's car was in for a tune-up, and Jeremy had put his Civic at her service.

"What's tacky?" he asked. They had stopped at a red light on Highland, not far from her apartment complex.

"Look to your left. The Mercedes."

Jeremy darted his glance sideways. A gleaming black Mercedes, driven by one of those cool, angular brunettes with swept-back hair, eyes concealed behind large sunglasses, the sleeves of her red blouse tight over tennis muscles in her arms. "I don't see—"

"Her mirror."

"Oh." A pair of baby shoes dangled from the mirror. "Kind of unusual," Jeremy said. The light changed.

"A trophy," Cassie said with a trace of smugness.

Jeremy's attention was on the Audi ahead, the one driven by an uncertain man who just couldn't choose which lane he preferred. "Hmm?"

"Trophy," Cassie repeated. "She's a cradle robber." Cassie giggled a little. "Snatched the poor little bastard right out of his shoes—what's wrong?"

"Nothing," Jeremy had said that afternoon almost a month ago. "Goose walked over my grave."

* * *

Jeremy sensed *them* somewhere in the neon maze of streets behind him, in a long dark car like a shark come to town. Its flat eyes, without mercy or knowledge, searched the night for him. He shivered, realized that he could take no more of this random driving. He pulled off the street, into the cramped parking lot of a small restaurant; one slot open, a tight one, he had to ease his door open to avoid dinging the Corvette next to him. He stood, took a deep breath of night air, and looked toward the restaurant entrance. It wasn't hard to make a decision. Better inside than caught out here.

The restaurant was absurdly tiny, no more than four tables. A topless waitress met him, escorted him to a table, seated him. He was the only customer. Her breasts stared at him like round pink eyes. Her face seemed unclear, a blur beneath mussed black hair. He waited for a menu, checked his watch: 9:14:32

she thrust a check into his hand. "Thank you, sir. I hope you enjoyed it."

Why do I have a check? I haven't eaten.

He turned the paper over.

"A hundred and thirty-eight dollars?"

"Is anything wrong, sir?"

"But I haven't had anything to eat."

"That's not my fault, sir." Breasts round, with faint blue veins, two moons in the dim restaurant. His brother Bill was two years older than Jeremy. In high school they had been the Two Moons, Billy and Germy.

"I won't pay for food that I haven't eaten."

"In that case, sir, I'll have to call the baby shoes."

Sour bile rushed cold into his mouth. "Here." He handed his MasterCard to her, seeing that the intersecting circles on it had become her breasts.

She took the card away

his watch said 10:47:05

and came back with a bearded policeman. "What's the trouble here?" the uniformed man asked in a genial voice.

"My watch—"

his watch showed 12:00:21, the same backward or forward

The policeman reached for the handcuffs dangling at his belt. They were small and white, tied together by the laces—

Jeremy shoved his chair over backwards, heard it bang as he ran for the door. The door had opened from the parking lot directly into the restaurant, but now it was at the far end of a long corridor. Shots reverberated behind him, the vibrations felt through the soles of his shoes as he thrust his shoulder against the door.

In his tangled sheets Jeremy whimpered.

The door burst open, and Jeremy pitched forward off a ledge. He held his breath. The water was cold but not deep; not far above his head he saw the mirror of the surface, surprisingly clear, reflecting perfectly his upturned face, his streaming hair, each rising bubble also a descending pearl. Those are pearls that were his eyes. He fought to keep from breathing, felt himself rising with an agonizing deliberation through the water. If only he could wait it out. He could use that big black piano as a raft—

Piano? He frowned. Above him, his inverted image frowned back, eyes flashing. Beware, beware, his flashing eyes, his floating hair. What was there about a piano? No, it was a boat, on a coal-black ocean. That was it. A car with eyes like a shark. Sharks.

Jeremy nervously looked down, at nothing, at fathoms of nothing, silver shading to dusty blue to far dim midnight, way down between his dangling bare feet. He was really in deep this time. If the coach criticized his diving form, he'd damn well quit the team. Who needed tower diving with finals coming up, and Christmas—

That was eight years ago. That was in college, *for crying out loud.*

—coming up. Coming up fast now. Jeremy looked up. He saw himself reaching down for his own outstretched hands, and on the reflected face (a bearded face! his own face!) a demonic grin stretched, a grin he could not feel.

Jeremy went cold enough to freeze the water, and suddenly he knew he didn't want those hands closing around his wrists. He bent at the waist, pointed his feet up, and dived down into the darkness, dived knowing he was dying, losing his air, already past the point of resurfacing, already

falling faster and faster, from miles above the earth. A toy landscape grew to be real, a small pond (the eye of God) benign and blue one second, expanded, ready to swallow him the next. If he hit the water, he might live. If he missed the rocks, he might make it.

But the wind in his face was like a knife, slicing his eyes, making tears flow like blood, forcing them back along his temples, feeling like wounds opening in the flesh, drying before they could be blown off, and he knew he could not hit the pond.

No.

He *must* not hit the pond. He would break it, break through, meet himself coming and going.

Somewhere there were baby shoes.

The only alternative was the rocks, and at the last possible moment he twisted, rolled, saw the pond water thrash in outraged disappointment, saw the rocks rush at him, pointed, deadly

"You'll be safe in here."

Beside his car, a stranger, holding the door open. Not the car door, just a door frame, a door ajar, door to nowhere? Jeremy blinked. Yes, a door frame, made of white pine, unfinished, set up on the asphalt of the parking lot. On the ground in front of the frame Jeremy could see a tuft of grass, green-bladed but red-streaked, a white flattened cigarette butt, the tab-pull from a beer can. And among it all a night beetle the length of the last joint of his little finger, a ridged blackish-green capsule, hurrying along like a miniature buffalo—all on this side.

On the far side of the frame, nothing. No thing.

The doorkeeper wore a faded purple robe. He was bareheaded, shock-haired, bearded. Teeth gleamed white through the whiskers. "Safe. Through here. Come on."

A hand closed on Jeremy's shirt, dragging him toward the doorway.

Jeremy grasped the wrist, felt its bones hard in his hand, felt the other's warm breath close against his cheek, looked into the other's face

it is *his* face, his own, but bearded

screamed, fell, screamed

he *wants* to go through

no, remember the shoes—

"—AAHH!"

"—God!" Jeremy Sebastian Moon found himself sitting up in bed, sweat-soaked and shaking. He gasped for breath, felt his heart leaping like something that wanted out of his chest. He ran a hand through his wet hair and said, "Oh, *shit!*"

The red digits of the bedside clock winked over to 3:02 A.M., the sigh of the heat vent overcame the thudding of his blood in his ears, and the dim outline of the bedroom windows registered.

He took a long, shaky breath. It was 3:02—no, now it was 3:03—dark in the middle of a workday morning. He had to be at Taplan and Taplan in just under six hours.

Moon swung his feet out of bed, pushed up, and padded barefoot into the bathroom. Standing on the cold tiles, he urinated, flushed, grabbed a still-damp towel off the shower-curtain rod, and rubbed his chest and belly. In the chill air he could smell the sour tang of his own sweat. He glared at his image in the mirror, wild-haired, thin-faced, pale, eyes thumbprinted by sleep, and he saw in it the memory of that other face, the bearded one. Gooseflesh made a relief map of his upper arms.

"Another late night special," he muttered to his reflection. It stared mutely back, offering no word of comfort or advice. Moon drank a glass of water, put his thumb on the light switch, hesitated, and finally left the bathroom light on. But he pulled the door almost shut, leaving only a wedge of light. The bed looked as if he had fought a battle in it—and in a sense, he supposed, he had. He tugged ineffectively at the covers, found an opening, and slipped in. The bedside clock said 3:09. His pulse rate, he guessed, was still above ninety.

Moon watched the minutes flick past. At four-thirty he decided he would get no more sleep that night, but sometime before five, he slipped back into slumber, this time, blessedly, one that brought with it no dreams.

The clock woke Moon again at seven-fifteen, and he got up with a dry mouth and the springy, drunk-like feeling of too little sleep in his head. His stomach lurched at the thought of breakfast. He settled instead for an extra-long and extra-hot shower and a new blade cartridge for his razor. He scowled into the mirror as he shaved. How many more nights like this could he take? But the hand with the razor was steady, the harrowed rectangles of skin visible through the lather showing no nicks.

He dressed and checked his pocket reminder before slipping it into the inside pocket of his jacket. December 21: Robinard, the wine people, today. Albert Robinard, despite the French pronunciation he insisted on for his

Christian name, was a Savannah yachtsman who cultivated a casual elegance and a taste for underage blondes. Moon considered his clothes. His dark gray slacks, pale blue shirt, navy-blue tie, and gray tweed blazer seemed all right, enough to put Robinard at ease without making it seem as if Moon were trying to outclass the yachtsman.

That should please Taplan, Jr., Moon decided. Moon's boss, the younger Taplan of Taplan and Taplan, was a great believer in putting clients at ease. Moon thrust the pocket calendar into his jacket, sighing at how Byzantine advertising was, sometimes as much so as the law, or medicine, or even politics.

The clock radio was still on. The announcer told Moon that this was the first day of winter and advised him to dress warmly, for there was an eighty percent chance of sleety rain. A brighter feminine voice was chirping the praises of Macy's lingerie department, to the background strains of "White Christmas," when Moon turned the radio off.

Taplan and Taplan was located, by any sane calculation, about twenty minutes' drive from Moon's north Atlanta apartment, but then no sane calculator would envision the traffic snarl of Peachtree Industrial Boulevard, I-285 East, and Thornton Bridge Road during rush hour. Moon prudently allowed an hour for the trip, and this morning, with the promised sleet snapping against the windshield, he needed every second of it.

At that, he was a few minutes late, for he had to find a parking slot at Taplan and Taplan, a quadruple-decked building of yellow brick within sight and hearing of the perimeter highway. He climbed out of the Civic, hunched a little deeper in his overcoat, and fished his briefcase out from behind the front seat. Just as he straightened, Moon became aware of Cassie—Cassandra Briggs, at twenty-four the youngest of Taplan and Taplan's department heads—close beside him. "Hi," she said in a voice that Moon had once, in a moment of moderate inebriation, compared to a distant silver bell. "Shitty weather, huh?"

"Awful," he agreed. Cassie slipped her arm comfortably through his, shielding them both with her umbrella, and Moon had to transfer the briefcase to the other hand. He asked, "What's the art department up to today?"

Cassie scrunched up her face, an arresting face, small-featured, elfin, with a faintly pointed chin, snub nose, and two tilted green eyes. "Easter bunny crap for the dime-store chain. I wish old Max'd drop these penny-ante accounts, but what can you do?"

"You can get his story about how he started in the business." Moon grinned as they walked past dripping rows of parked cars. "Just a pen and ink and some paper, and a fellow in the dime-store business took a chance on him—"

"Please," Cassie said. "I'm not even pregnant. I don't want to puke right here in the parking lot." Her hip gave his a soft nudge. "So what's up with you tonight?"

Moon opened the door for her and stood back as she folded her umbrella. He said, "Not much. The usual, you know. Got some copy to work on for the wine people, probably be sharpening that up. How about the weekend?"

Charlie at the front desk nodded to them over his morning newspaper. Cassie gave Moon a sideways glance. "Have you forgotten? Got to spend Christmas in Tampa with the folks."

Moon shook his head. "That's right. It slipped my mind."

"Won't even be able to attend the office party tomorrow afternoon. I have to be at Hartsfield at twelve for my flight."

Moon thumbed the elevator button. "Sorry."

"You don't need to be. Just don't get drunk and fall into the typing pool."

The elevator doors opened, and they stepped into an empty car. As the doors closed, Cassie reached up to plant a quick kiss at the corner of Moon's mouth. "Hey," she said, "I've got an idea. I'll catch you in between."

"In between what?"

She arched an eyebrow. "Christmas and New Year's, of course. Keep your mind on your work today, Jeremy."

"I'll try. If I could get some sleep—"

The elevator doors opened on the third floor, the art floor, and Cassie slipped a thigh against the rubber bumper to keep them open. "That reminds me. I told you yester-day you needed to get some sleep—" She rummaged in her purse for a moment, then produced a brown plastic phial. "Got it. Here you go."

Jeremy took the tube. "What are these—"

"Sleeping pills. I went through a rough spell a couple of years back. Take one and you'll sleep all night. No dreams. Guaranteed. Bye." Cassie's pixie face disappeared behind the closing doors.

Jeremy rattled the pills in the tube. The label told him they were 100-milligram Nembutal capsules, that the dosage was one capsule at bedtime, that originally there had been eight pills in the bottle, and that the prescription was not to be refilled. He popped the top off the tube and shook three yellow capsules into his hand. With a shrug, he put them back into the phial, replaced the top, and dropped the tube in his coat pocket as he stepped out of the elevator on the fourth floor. Here, in a warren of offices, was his own home base. He got there, shucked off his overcoat and hung it on a hook behind his desk, and settled into his swivel chair, ready for a day of work.

He spent most of that morning proofing a series of magazine spots he had done for a Miami Beach oceanfront hotel, and reading them reminded him of Cassie and her Florida Christmas. When the words began to chime meaninglessly in his brain, Moon occasionally allowed himself to daydream, fantasizing about sand and surf and a very tan Cassie. At least once his daydreaming crossed the line into a doze.

In a dream he recognized as a dream, Moon stood naked in the bathroom of a hotel suite—through the open door he could see a ceiling-to-floor window, and beyond that, the ocean shading from beachside white and green through brown over the sandbar to a faraway deep blue—while Cassie took a steaming shower. He was ready to shave, and looking into the mirror he decided he looked like a smiling lecher, Pan without horns, needing only some grape leaves in his tousled brown hair. But he'd have to get rid of the beard. Cassie began to hum, a nameless but cheerfully licentious tune, and he turned to look her way, her figure tantalizingly blurred by the frosted glass of the shower door as

his reflection lunged out of the mirror to grab his shoulder

"Hey, hey!"

Moon blinked. Bob Escher stood over him, hand on Moon's left shoulder. "Hey," Escher repeated. "What's wrong with you?"

Moon rubbed his palm over his face. When he took it down, he saw his own cubicle, ad ideas and roughs thumbtacked to the corkboard covering two of the three walls, computer terminal glowing green on the desk in front of him, the hotel ad proofs fanned out beside it. "Sorry," he said. "Guess I must've dropped off for a minute. What time is it?"

"Nearly time for the Robinard meeting. You want some water or coffee or something? You look pretty rough."

You're not so hot yourself, Moon thought. Bob Escher was almost two years younger than he, but with his baby face developing a double chin and his fine platinum hair thinning to show pink scalp beneath, he looked older. At least, Jeremy *hoped* he did. But aloud, he muttered, "No, I'm all right. We might as well run on down." He scooped up a brown folder and rose from the desk.

In the elevator Escher said, "Any ideas so far?"

"Nothing we didn't talk about last time. I thought we'd wait to see how Max decides to pitch it."

"Yeah, right. I thought that too."

Sure you did, Bob. Sure you did.

The group at the meeting was small, with Max Taplan presiding, Albert Robinard moodily looking out the rain-streaked window at the gray woods beyond, at the gray office towers beyond the woods. The art, broadcast, and copy departments had all sent reps, and they kept up a desultory murmur until Taplan called them all to order.

"Now, then," Max said, rubbing his hands as his father did, "let's settle in and take a look at what Robinard Wines needs. Minter, what about the magazine art?"

The room seemed stuffy to Jeremy. Too hot, or maybe it was just the influence of their fearless leader: Max Taplan was a nervous man in his early fifties, still seeking a way to impress his father, Taplan, Sr., with his acumen. Or perhaps by this point only with his bare competence. At the meeting Max was like an exceptionally jittery basketball player, passing the ball along as soon as it came into his hands, to the art department, the TV people, even to Robinard. Jeremy closed his eyes for a moment, and the moment extended.

Again Bob Escher jostled him awake, but this time he came merely from sleep, not from a dream. "Well, Jeremy?" Max said for what was evidently the second time. "What do you think?"

Jeremy tilted his head back, studied the rough-textured ceiling tiles, then dropped his gaze back to the walnut-topped table. His hands rested there, holding a pencil horizontally between them, and in the shiny table top he could see two pink blobs—his hands—and between them the fuzzy yellow bridge of the pencil. He cleared his throat. "Radio," he said.

Robinard looked at him with the indifference of a man dreaming of sun on Gulf waters. Max cleared his throat, and the sound was half a hysterical giggle. "But Bob has already talked about the possibilities of—"

Jeremy lifted a finger for silence. When it fell, he said, "Just one word: demographics."

A flicker of interest, like a marlin below the surface, showed in Robinard's eyes. "That's the stuff we need," he said. "What can you tell me about demographics?"

Escher murmured inanities for a moment before Taplan ordered a far-reaching demographic survey of potential radio markets. That should be ready, certainly, by the middle of January—

Robinard, Jeremy was sure, felt delight at the reprieve. Now he could get in a month of sailing before having to return to Atlanta. At any rate he beamed. "Good thinking, fella," the yachtsman said across the table to Jeremy. "I can see you earn your keep around here." He got up, terminating the meeting.

On their way back up to the fourth floor, Bob Escher glared at Jeremy. "Thanks a lot, guy," he said. "Demographics. You had to do that to me."

"You should've worked them up," Jeremy said. "That's standard for accounts like Robinard's."

"Yeah," Bob said, his voice still surly. "You wait till I'm department head. We'll see about demographics then." But a moment later he added, "Hell, I'm kidding. You know I'm kidding."

Yes, Bob, of course you're kidding. You've still got an ad campaign to blunder through. You'll need somebody's brain—you never use your own.

Jeremy didn't say that aloud. To Escher he said, "Sorry. I didn't mean to put you on the spot. But Robinard likes the idea, so go with it."

"Yeah," Escher said, turning into his own office.

By the time Moon got behind his desk again, his head was pounding. He kept aspirin in his desk drawer, but after he managed to flush them out from their hiding place among paper clips and printer ribbons, he found

the flat tin jammed shut. *Press red corners*, the instructions snidely told him. When he did, he succeeded only
in hurting the pads of his thumbs. Moon put the tin on
the floor and used his heel, crunching the aspirin con-
tainer twice before finally unjamming it. By then he had
powdered aspirin.

Grunting with disgust, Moon ripped a square sheet off
his notepad ("Taplan and Taplan," it proclaimed. "Ideas
on tap for you!"), veed the paper into shape between his
fingers, shook some aspirin into it, tilted his head back,
and dumped the contents into his mouth. Suddenly, forcibly, Moon remembered his grandfather, dead fifteen
years now, in life an overalled farmer on 120 acres of red
north Georgia clay.

His grandfather used to take headache powders, the
individual doses wrapped in waxed paper about the size
and shape of a band-aid wrapper. After his grandfather
had swallowed the dose, for some ungodly reason Jeremy
had liked to lick the last of the bitter, astringent dust
from the wrapper, following it with a nose-stinging gulp
of icy Coke. The aspirin was like that now, coarser but
reminiscent enough to make him long for a soft drink.

At noon he phoned the art department, but Cassie had
already acquired the harried manner of pre-holiday rush.
She was tied up with some last-minute changes, sorry,
sorry. He went to lunch alone.

For no reason Moon ate at a restaurant that Cassie
favored, a young professionals' haven. It was a trendy
little place hung with ferns, its menu given over to veggie
burgers, whole-grain breads, organic salads, and its service provided by waiters who seemed to have sprung to
life by means of asexual fission. The alfalfa sprouts in
Moon's salad got stuck between his third and fourth molars.

Back at work, Jeremy cleared his desk of the old
proofs, then worked for four more hours on prelims for
the wine campaign, ones that Robinard had casually okayed
before leaving the meeting room. He became aware of
the overtime he was putting in only when Glenda, the
division secretary, stuck her head into his cubicle and
told him that he could spend the whole Christmas season
at work if he wanted to, but *she* was heading home in
about two minutes.

Shaking his head, Moon finished typing a paragraph,
printed it, tucked it into a folder with the rest of the

ideas, and put the folder into his briefcase. He took his overcoat from the hook, and when it rattled, he examined the pockets. Of course. Cassie's prescription.

He got into the overcoat, hefted his briefcase, and arched his back. His spine crackled. On the first floor, Tony, the night security man, had replaced Charlie. Tony didn't look up from his newspaper, but grunted as Moon passed. Charlie and Tony, Jeremy thought. What would happen one morning if some evil being substituted the *Journal,* the evening newspaper, for Charlie's morning *Constitution?* Chaos, probably. The downfall of T&T.

The air outside was colder, but overhead the sky had cleared, showing a pale full moon already risen in the east, and in the early twilight it looked as if the world had never even heard of sleet. "Another day," Jeremy remarked to himself unoriginally as he unlocked the Civic. Then the difference between the fair blue sky overhead and the rain of the morning struck him more forcibly. "Another world," he added.

Might be a peg there, he thought, sliding behind the wheel. Might just be something to hang the Robinard campaign on. Robinard wines . . . take you to another world. Robinard, when the Old World needs a new look. Robinard, a new world of taste. Robinard . . . gets you drunk as all hell.

With a rueful chuckle Jeremy switched off his brain, or at least the part of it that was creative on demand. Time enough for the wine account later. After all, *he* wasn't exactly bound for a new world. He'd be right behind his desk tomorrow, and next year, same as always. Meanwhile, he thought, the Bob Eschers of the world would nail down their promotions and pass him by.

He, on the other hand, would be stuck in the same old world, stuck there forever.

Pulling out of the parking lot, toward the murderous traffic of I-285, Jeremy hoped, just for a moment, that he was wrong.

As a matter of fact, he was.

CHAPTER 2

MOON WENT TO bed at eleven tired enough to hope no dreams would disturb him and trusting enough in modern alchemy to believe that Cassie's magic pill would help to insure that. But sometime in the dark he found himself running again, fleeing through an ill-defined and shifting landscape something that he feared, though he did not know what it could be. From one part of his mind, some removed and objective part, Moon watched himself with sardonic detachment, knowing all along that this was all dream and illusion, that nothing real pursued him.

Even so, another part of him ran with heart-busting speed through a gray world, all slumping, runny cubes of gigantic size, twisting pathways between them, and a glaring gray-white sky overhead. Manhattan would look like this, he thought fleetingly, after the high-altitude bombs went off.

Slow down, the observer part of himself told the runner. *Slow down and think.*

Somewhat to Moon's surprise, his dreamed self did just that: pounded from a full run into a trot, from a trot to an exhausted shamble, and finally to a walk. Dry air, tasting of hot metal, rasped in his mouth and nose. His lungs ached. The slower pace was a godsend, but even so his muscles quivered in exhaustion. If only he could find a place to rest, to sit. . . .

But there was no such place, none that he could see. Indeed, when he looked ahead, Moon could see only the path before him. Dimly, peripherally, he was aware of the melted-candy land around him on either side, but whenever he looked directly at one of those colossal, sagging cubes, he found instead that the pathway had

24

turned and that he was following it through the place where, a moment ago, the obstacle had stood.

Finally he stopped, the thudding in his chest now diminished to something more like a normal heartbeat, and turned completely around, making a searchlight survey of his surroundings. "Great," he mumbled to himself. No matter how he turned, he seemed to be facing the pathway, with vague blocky shapes on either side. "Now what?" he asked aloud. It was a perfect time to wake up, if only Cassie's damn pill would let him.

Since it wouldn't, the observer part of his mind, that part that was comfortably aware of being snug in bed light-years away from this place, suggested with cool rationality that he continue along the path. Something was bound to be at the end. The part of him that seemed trapped in the gray netherworld told the observer to stuff it—but his body began to plod along the pathway nonetheless.

After what might have been an hour of walking, or a week, Moon perceived a reward of sorts. Ahead of him, like a wall running from horizon to horizon, was a dim gray barrier, one that did not dance away to nothing when he looked directly at it. He recalled a Jimmy Durante sketch he had seen on TV years ago: Durante and another actor were shipwrecked sailors lost on an empty ocean. He gave himself the advice that the Schnoz had given the other sailor: "Pull for the horizon," he muttered to himself. "It's better than nothing." Each step brought him imperceptibly nearer the wall. He began to count his paces, but somewhere past a thousand he lost count. Just at the point when Moon had decided that nightmares at least had the virtue of excitement and interest, unlike this endless trudge, he became aware that he had more than the wall as a goal: he saw a doorway.

A doorway and a guard, evidently. The wall seemed suddeny to loom overhead, the height of a skyscraper, featureless and gray. And set in the wall, dead ahead, perhaps only a hundred yards or so distant, was a man-sized aperture, with a figure visible within it. Setting his jaw, Moon made directly for the opening.

It grew larger, swelled into an oval perhaps seven feet high and, at its widest, three broad. The figure inside waited patiently, not budging as Moon approached. It was a man, bearded, wearing a faded purple robe—as

Moon came nearer, he could see that the garment once had been quilted and brocaded but now showed considerable wear, its quilting gone loose and baggy, the brocade threadbare and dull. Moon was, for the first time, aware of his own attire, the ridiculous red pajamas that Cassie had given him. That was all; he wore no shoes. The ground under his feet didn't feel like soil, but was rubbery and pliable, soft enough almost to allow him to grip it with his toes. He halted a step away from the stranger. "I'm here," he said.

"You want this to end," the other replied, his voice hollow and distant, as if coming through a long tube.

"I wish it would."

"You can end it, you know."

Moon frowned. "I've seen you before."

"Yes. In the mirror."

"You're me?"

"In a manner of speaking. Look, you won't stay asleep forever. Do you want to end this thing now, or not?"

Moon did not at first reply. The other man did look like him. The two had the same dark brown hair, the same brown eyes, the same lines of forehead and cheek. But Moon had never, not even in his student days at the university, worn a beard, and the other had a luxuriant growth, chest-long, curled a little at the ends. "I've dreamed about you before," Moon said at last.

"I know. I've been trying to make contact for some time now. It's very difficult, not knowing the times of exaltation, you see. I had only a rough idea of the best cusps of temporality for the attempt. Still, I think I did pretty well, all things considered. Now, do you want to stop these dreams or don't you?"

"How do I do that?"

"Just come through the door here. That's all. Let me cross over to your side, and you take my place." When Moon hesitated, the stranger said, "It can be done. I've made all the calculations, and it can be done with practically anyone. But the only way to make sure it lasts is to exchange those who have sympaths on the other planes, you see."

"I don't understand."

"You don't have to. Just come through the door, that's all."

"And the dreams will end?"

The other smiled, teeth white in the brown beard. "You'll never be troubled by your own nightmares again, I assure you."

Irresolute, Moon turned away. He stood at the base of the enormous wall, and on every other side of him, as far as he could see, gray desolation stretched. After a complete circuit he faced the stranger again.

"Come on," the figure in the purple robe urged. "After all, it can't hurt you, can it? This is just a dream."

"That's right," Jeremy said, though somewhere far-off a warning bell jangled in the mind of Moon the observer. "What the hell." He stepped forward.

For just a moment there was a curious sensation of going in two directions at once, of *oozing* simultaneously forward and back; and then he was through. He turned. The purple-robed man now stood on the other side of the oval. "Good," the other man said. "Excellent."

"And now my nightmares are over?" Moon asked skeptically.

"*Yours* are." The other grinned. "Before I go, one word of caution: beware of the storms. They can really kill you. Oh, and another thing: Tremien may look in on you now and again. Give him my best."

"I don't understand," Moon repeated in a plaintive voice.

"You don't need to. Good luck." He grasped the edges of his side of the oval, tugged—and the entire wall poured into a point at the oval's center, faded to a drifting dot like the point of light left after a TV is switched off, and then disappeared.

"Hell," Moon said. He stood at the center of a flat, featureless gray plain—wall, door, and stranger had all vanished. Overhead, empty of sun or moon, was the luminescent gray sky, and at equal distance all around was the scarcely distinguishable flat line of the horizon. "I'm not walking any farther," Moon announced to himself. Still grumping, he sat down on the yielding surface to wait for developments. Not at all to his surprise, after sitting there for what seemed like an hour, knees drawn up to his chest, boredom washing all around him, he nodded off and fell asleep.

As strange as it is to have a dream in which you are sleeping, it is stranger still to have a dream in which you are dreaming, but that happened to Moon sometime after he dozed. With an unnatural clarity he dreamed that he was hungry and that he had ordered out for Chinese food. With supernatural efficiency the delivery boy was at the door before Moon had hung up the telephone, and—even more wonderful—he refused Moon's proffered cash. In the dream within his dream Moon had just transferred the aromatic goodies to his dining-room table when he woke up.

For a second or two, Moon was disoriented and distressed. He lay on his side, almost in a fetal position, on a rubbery gray plain, with an opalescent gray sky luminous overhead. Then it came to him that he was still asleep, and had only awakened from the dream of a dream. With a grunt he pushed himself up on his left elbow.

The garlic chicken still smelled delicious.

Moon blinked at the improbable sight before him: four white cardboard cartons arranged at the corners of an invisible square, and in the center of the square a teapot and cup. His stomach growled.

Investigation proved that the cartons contained garlic chicken (wonderful aroma!), fried rice with bits of egg gleaming yellow, two eggrolls, and a dozen fortune cookies. The tea steamed from the pot into the cup and had an agreeable snap when he tried it.

"Should've dreamed of a fork," Moon muttered to himself. But he had not even a pair of chopsticks. He munched the eggrolls and found them good as he considered the problem. Inspiration finally struck, and he carefully tore and folded the waxed cardboard carton the eggrolls had come in to form a sort of primitive spoon, not as good as a real utensil but serviceable. With it and with some help from his fingers, he ate his way through the chicken (marvelously tender!) and fried rice. All the time he was aware of the most profound silence: nothing, not even a breeze, stirred across the great leaden plain. His own swallows sounded loud in his ears, and his satisfied belch at the end of the meal almost made him jump, it was so thunderous.

Only the fortune cookies were a disappointment. The slips of paper they bore were blanks, all of them. But Moon managed to eat the entire dozen and finish the last cupful of tea.

That done, he rose and stretched. "Better than the nightmares," he told himself. He tried to remember the last time he had felt so comfortably filled, so peacefully at home with the universe. It was beyond the reach of his recall, whenever it was. Now if only something would happen.

After a timeless interval of waiting that was probably ten minutes, Moon struck out on a stroll of exploration. He left behind the litter of his meal, empty cartons, pewter teapot, delicate china cup, and that proved his only bearing. He took a hundred steps and looked back. Only the debris from his picnic broke the monotony of the gray plain. With a grunt Moon turned his back on it and started to walk. After a while, locked in boredom, he began to sing.

He had gone through all the early Beatles, a considerable part of the Rolling Stones, and several Broadway musicals before he stopped to rest. "Wonder how long it's been?" he muttered aloud, to no response. If only he had his watch—but no, it was beside his sleeping body, on the bedside table back in his apartment. He tried to estimate how far he'd come but was stumped. It might have been a matter of miles. After a few minutes' rest Moon trudged on again, going in the same direction as before. He launched the second stage of his march with "Me and Bobby McGee."

By the time he was riding on the City of New Orleans, Moon was almost ready to scream. He was about to change his mind about the benefits of dreaming this weird place over the nightmares; at least the nightmares gave him reference points and didn't threaten to drive him out of his mind through sheer inaction. Grimly he sang his way through the song, all the way down to the Gulf of Mexico. While he was casting about for an encore, he became aware that finally he saw something different.

It was far-off, to be sure, but it was a feature of sorts: a mesa-like projection on the horizon, darker than the landscape, almost purple against the luminescent sky. With bleak determination Moon strode toward it.

The formation failed to gain solidity as he approached, but remained an amorphous, though growing, swirl of darker colors. It seemed to be the size of a circus tent. At least, as he approached, its shifting outlines appeared to

stay roughly in that size frame. It was more like a
coherent fog bank than anything else, though opaque;
when he came close enough, Moon stopped, wondering if
it was plastic or insubstantial. He swept a hand into the
periphery of the area and felt nothing. Emboldened, he
took a couple of steps forward and found himself actually
inside the fog bank.

It was a schoolroom, out-of-date and badly fraying at
the edges. Old-fashioned desks, arrayed in strict and
correct lines, bore faint carvings. At the front of the
room (for Moon had stepped in from the rear, from what
now appeared to be a solid wall of bookshelves), a tall
man loomed large over a smaller, seated, cringing figure. Behind the man was a chalkboard, and on the chalkboard were the arcane hieroglyphics of some unimaginable
mathematics problem.

"You know what I do to little girls who don't turn in
their homework," the man at the front of the room said
in a voice like a badly oiled hinge. "You *know* what must
be done, Jean Louise."

"Yes, sir," said a middle-aged lady in a flannel night-
gown from where she sat in the front row. She cringed a
little lower in the too-small seat. "Just don't tell my
daddy, Mr. Guest."

Moon blinked. With each breath the teacher was visibly inflating, his shoulders rounding, his brow protruding
more and more. Frothy saliva dripped from suddenly
grown fangs and drooled down his chin. His hands, holding a ruler as if it were a baseball bat, knotted with
muscle, became grossly hairy. "Get out of your seat, Jean
Louise."

"Yes, sir," said the woman. Timidly she slid from the
desk and turned to lean against it. Now that she was
facing him, Moon saw that she was about fifty, with
rumpled gray hair and improbable plastic-framed spectacles. She started as she saw him. "Who the hell are
you?" she demanded suddenly. Behind her, the terrible
Mr. Guest simply froze in mid-motion, one frame of a
movie seen as a still.

"I'm Jeremy Moon," he said, surprised into answering.

"Why are you wearing red pajamas? They make you
look like a tomato."

"Uh—they were a gift," he said. "What's going on?"

"What do you mean, what's going on?" The woman's voice was nasal and waspish. "Mr. Guest is about to spank me for not having my homework, that's what's going on. What are you doing here? You were never in this dream before. Do I know you?"

Moon had suddenly noticed something that shocked him, momentarily at least, into silence. The entire picture, the whole classroom, was in black-and-white, indeed like an old movie: the desks, the books, the chalkboard, even Mr. Guest, all had a solid three-dimensional look about them but no color at all. Only he and the woman exhibited any hue.

"Hurry up and answer me," Jean Louise insisted. "I want to get this over with before I wake up."

"Excuse me?"

She rolled her eyes, magnified behind the pink-rimmed spectacles. "Go away, will you?"

"Wait a minute," Moon said. He had the distinct impression of *pressure,* as though the woman were exerting a physical push against him, forcing him back. "Wait, I said! Why is everything in black and white?"

"I never dream in color," Jean Louise snapped.

"What about my pajamas?"

Her eyes narrowed. "That's right. They're red. How did that happen?" She backed away from him, her derriere gently swiveling the inert Mr. Guest aside as she did so. "You get away from me. This is scary."

"Perhaps," grated Mr. Guest, "the young man needs to be punished." He grinned, displaying teeth that had been filed to points, as he began to advance on Moon. The ruler, Moon saw now, was a ferrule made of steel, maybe an eighth of an inch thick and two inches broad. Mr. Guest whished it through the air and smacked it into his left palm with an explosive sound. "I think we need to teach this boy a lesson."

Jeremy gasped for air. As he retreated down the aisle, he *shrank.* Or the classroom—and Mr. Guest—grew. Moon was painfully aware of everything about him, of the smell of cleaning compound, of Scheaffer's Ink and chalk dust, of the hard, slick feel of the wood floor beneath his bare feet, and, at the end of the aisle, of the uncompromising press of the bookshelf against his shoulders. He could not back out the way he had entered. By now, Mr. Guest towered over him, the size of a bull walking erect, his eyes glowing a baleful orange, the gnarled hand brandishing the ruler more like a claw than anything human. "Turn around!" Guest bellowed, and the floor beneath Jeremy's feet vibrated.

"Whip his ass!" shrieked Jean Louise from the front of the room. "Beat him!"

Books tumbled off the shelves behind Jeremy. He caught one, a heavy textbook with the title of *Human Development*. With a surge of desperate strength he hurled it straight at Guest, catching the man square between the eyes.

"Bad boy! Bad boy!" screamed Jean Louise. "Now you're gonna get it!"

With a mindless roar Guest swept his arm back and arced the ruler. It slapped against Jeremy's upper left thigh, shockingly loud, and felled him like a lightning-blasted pine. He scrabbled under a desk, heard the steel ruler smash into the desktop, sending splinters flying, and tried to get to his feet on the far side. His throbbing leg wouldn't hold him. He crawled under another desk as Guest kicked aside the ruins of the first.

"Get him, get him!" Jean Louise giggled.

"Wait a minute," Jeremy protested. "Wait!"

But the behemoth was still coming. Jeremy had reached the wall and finally got to his feet there. He hobbled to the front of the room; Mr. Guest, now as big and implacable as Frankenstein's monster, lumbered after him. A flag stood beside the chalkboard, Old Glory, its black, white, and gray stars and stripes attached to a wooden staff that was supported by a knee-high wastepaper basket. The staff ended in a decorative sphere and cone, a stylized spear. Jeremy seized the flagstaff and fended off Guest with it.

"Ooh!" squealed Jean Louise. "Now he's gonna kill you!"

With all his strength Jeremy thrust the spear forward, striking Guest in the chest. The wooden staff splintered, and with a sweep of his arm, the monster knocked the flag aside. Jeremy, too late, realized that he was cornered. He sank to the floor, his back in the angle of the wall, knowing that Guest's next blow would surely kill him. The ponderous arm swept back and up, paused, and then began its descent—

—the school bell rang—

"Damn," cried Jean Louise. "I'm waking up."

—the ruler whistled down upon him, and Jeremy felt—

—a harsh, dry breeze across his face and cheek.

He had been holding his breath. He let it out now and gasped in another. Guest was gone. Jean Louise had faded. The schoolroom was dissolving into a bruise-colored mist that dissipated even as Moon watched. The walls behind vanished into insubstantiality, dumping him backward onto the level gray plain. In a few minutes all traces of the experience had disappeared under the even gray glow from the sky.

Except one. Moon unsnapped his pajama bottoms and shoved them down to his knees. There on his left thigh was the only remnant of the—dream?

But dreams didn't leave bruises behind. Especially not bruises two inches wide, four inches long, and shaped like an old-fashioned flat steel ruler.

The injury seemed real to Jeremy, more real every minute as he limped painfully along across the featureless plain. *That* had never happened to him before, not even in his worst nightmares: he thought hard and decided that never before had he actually dreamed pain. But this hurt like the devil and made it necessary for him to rest more frequently.

Twice more he slept, both times in brief dozes, but neither time did he dream within his dream. "This is getting alarming," he told himself after waking the second time. "It's really about time I woke up." He concentrated on waking up, to no avail.

"That damn sleeping pill," he decided at last. He had been sitting for some time, thinking about waking up, trying to make contact with the sleeping Jeremy back home in his bed. But it was no good. Just as he was about to get up and resume walking, the ground heaved beneath him and the lights went out.

For a dazed moment Jeremy thought he was actually awake and back home, but then something familiar in the swirling dark colors around him broke through. "Oh, no," he groaned, getting painfully to his feet. "Not Guest again!"

No, not at all. He was in a forest, or at least a glade, with birches abounding and a blue sky overhead. The air had the cool caress of early spring, scented mildly with the green smell of fresh new leaves. Moon reached out and rubbed his palm against a tree. It was solid, smooth, cool, and real.

Liquid laughter came from his left, from downhill, and he followed the sound. After a few steps he heard water, too, the gentle chuckle of a woodland stream. And after a moment he stepped into a clearing and saw—

"S-sorry," he muttered to the young couple on the beach. They continued in their activities, blissfully ignoring him. Moon turned away, hearing the man's gasps, the woman's cooed endearments, and made his way back uphill, thinking to himself that he was surely going crazy. By the time he noticed that the trees were thinning, they were also becoming insubstantial, and a moment later he stood just outside another dark swirl of fog. Other than that, he was on the gray plain again.

After a moment's thought Moon reached to grasp the topmost button of his pajama jacket—he never buttoned it—and tore it loose. He placed the button on the ground as a reference point, and began to pace the circumference of the dark, pulsating fog bank. On the eight hundred and thirty-second step, he saw the button again. He picked it up and dropped it into his breast pocket. Then, with a deep breath, Jeremy stepped back into the fog.

This time he was in a meadow, closer to the couple. No, same man, different girl. Their activity was one which left the man relatively unoccupied but which plainly took up the woman's full attention. Moon managed a diffident cough.

The man, propped on both elbows, opened his eyes and beamed. "Hi," he said. "Nice day, isn't it?"

"Uh, yeah, nice enough," Jeremy said, finding it hard to ignore the nude young woman and the incredibly energetic thing she was doing.

"I hate my damn job," the man said. "I shouldn't be locked up in a bank all day."

"You are?" Jeremy asked. The woman had discovered a whole new rhythm.

"Yeah, Dunwoody branch of First National. I should be an artist. I've got a real feel for the outdoors."

"Uh-huh." How in the world does she manage the whole thing, Jeremy wondered.

"Birds," the man said dreamily. "I'd like birds."

Birdsong filled the air. A light pressure on Jeremy's

left shoulder jerked his head around. But instead of Guest's grip—the thing he had first feared—his shoulder was held in the delicate pinch of a bluebird's feet. The bird, a rather idealized creature in the mode of certain animated films, looked back at him with a bright, intelligent gaze and whistled part of a Brahms sonata. The ruddy little throat swelled with the beauty of the music.

"I don't understand this at all," Jeremy said. When he looked back at the man, he found the first girl had been joined by a second, equally unclad and equally single-minded in the attention she gave the man.

"What's to understand? Just enjoy the beautiful day."

"But I don't even know you," Jeremy said. "Why should I dream about you?"

The man laughed. "You've got it wrong, friend," he said. "I'm doing the dreaming, not you."

"No," Jeremy smiled. "I'm aware of my own existence, thank you."

With a wicked leer the man said, "Yeah, but are you gettin' any? Think I'll change the landscape a little."

Again the earth heaved beneath Jeremy, toppling him in its unexpected writhings, and he tumbled sideways, but softly, onto a pliant surface. When he got his bearings again, he became aware that he was in a rubber raft, bright yellow and very roomy, bobbing gently on a recurring swell. The bluebird hopped from his chest to the edge of the raft, gave him a backward glance, and flew away.

When Jeremy got his chin above the edge of the raft, he saw the man and *three* girls some distance away, on the beach. He himself was riding out to sea on his raft. "Hey—" he yelled in dismay.

"Get your own girls" came the faint reply. In a few seconds the beach was lost in cloudy distance; in a few more, the rocking of the ocean subsided to nothing, and the raft itself dissolved away. Jeremy was again outside the swirling fog bank, sitting on the soft gray surface of the endless plain. He got to his feet, grimacing against a twinge from his injured leg. With a mental curse he turned his back on the man and his impossibly nubile attendants and walked away.

After what might have been an hour of walking, Jeremy had seen at least another dozen of the indistinct, swirling bands of colors that marked—what? Dreams, he supposed, though none of the three he took cautious looks at were remotely like anything he could recall having dreamed before. He found a black child in an alley full of rats and spiders (Jeremy backed out of that one quickly); a woman gorging herself on pies and cakes and growing visibly thinner as she did so (he took a slice of lemon meringue pie out of that one, only to have it vanish softly away once he was clear); and a thin, bald little man dressed in a tailcoat and white tie, though without trousers, on a dais in front of an impatient symphony orchestra.

None of them were recognizable to Jeremy, and none gave any sign of having recognized him. He had left the last one behind, had turned back to the endless walk across the infinite plain, when he became aware that someone here, outside the swirling fogs of dreams, had joined him: a man, running toward him from the right, with long, loping strides. Jeremy stood still as the fellow approached.

He was young, Jeremy saw, probably twenty-two or -three, with a shock of red hair in untidy disarray, and he wore the strangest outfit Jeremy had ever seen, in or out of a dream. The boots were lustrous, soft-looking, but a peculiar shade of blue, the iridescent blue of a skink's tail; the trousers were white, what there was of them, but slit from waist to mid-calf down each side, held together by an intricate webbing of gold lacework (the same material decorated and held in place a codpiece in the shape of a delicately whorled pink seashell). The shirt bloused out magnificently, a multicolored, shining garment like a mad costumer's idea of pirate garb for an especially gaudy production of *Penzance*. At the man's left hip a pouch, apparently of the same azure leather as his boots, bounced comfortably as he approached. The man came to a halt a dozen paces away from Jeremy. "Za Sabastin," he barked in a loud but thin voice. "Hai dsahdgen tel unteyinoth!"

Jeremy stared at him. "What?"

"Theganrah heddel coshtrato," the other insisted. "Besh pom mirganst."

Jeremy shook his head. "Hold on. I don't understand you."

The red head tilted to one side, its posture eloquent of suspicion. Finally the newcomer beckoned to Jeremy, walked off a few steps, stopped, beckoned again. A thin

finger pointed at the swirl of color from which Jeremy
had stepped just moments before. "Ka theganrah!" the
red-haired man said with great clarity and emphasis.
"Nizhanti felanit pishto zehn. Teshti, teshti."

"Hey, Dad," Jeremy said aloud. "I think Lassie wants
us to follow her." To the man he said, "Go on, I'm
coming." When he had taken a few steps forward, the
other seemed satisfied and set off at a trot over the plain.
Grunting at the throb and sting of his injured thigh,
Jeremy broke into a half-hearted jog after the man. Every so often the other would pause and let Jeremy catch
up, or at least come to within twenty feet or so; then he
would lope away again, leaving Jeremy cursing and limping along behind.

The trip seemed to take forever. "Damn it," Jeremy
told himself for perhaps the twentieth time, "I should be
awake by now." But he wasn't, and in the oppressive
dream he followed the beckoning man farther and farther. At last he became aware that the countryside had
actually changed: it was no longer completely featureless.
Ahead was a low mound, like a dome not quite finished.
It seemed at first to be smooth, but as they neared it, it
took on the appearance of rough stonework, with all the
stones as gray as the plain. Indeed, they seemed to be
pieces of the plain, with the same color and texture, but
cut into blocks. Jeremy's leader circled to the right of
this—it rose so gradually from the level that Jeremy
wasn't quite sure whether he was walking beside the
dome or on its fringe—and then ducked into a low-
arched passage leading into the dome.

Jeremy paused at the entrance, looking ahead with
caution. The redhead stood inside in a sort of arena.
Beyond him Jeremy could see the inner wall of the dome.
The man gestured with every sign of impatience.

Stooping to avoid bumping his head and holding onto
the right wall—the feel of the stones, Jeremy noted, was
the same yielding, plastic texture as that of the ground—
Jeremy went forward for five steps and came into the
circle of the arena. "All right," he said. "Now what—"

Something hit him from behind, hard enough to buckle
his knees. He landed on his stomach, felt someone on his
back, felt his hands snatched and the quick whirl of cord
around them. Before Jeremy was fully aware of what was
going on, he had been kicked over, so that he lay on his

back. A woman straddled him, her knees in his armpits, her buttocks on his stomach. Her dirty blonde hair was hacked indifferently short, and from her he caught the reek of sweat. "Wevelos inat, Sabastin," she said in a harsh caw of a voice. "Tilbet heddel kelantho!"

The grinning redhead appeared over her shoulder. "Kestah lomoch isdros," he said. "Visto ha'charra inzosh takira."

The woman slapped him, hard. "Ow!" he yelled. "Look, I don't know what you're up to, but get off me."

She scowled at him. "Centos destaba!"

Jeremy looked up at the man. His teeth were very bad, dead white next to gray next to black next to yellow. "Tell her to get off," Jeremy said. "I can't breathe."

The woman chanted something quickly and in a breathless tone. "Better now?" she asked abruptly.

"Uh—yeah." Jeremy said, surprised. "Look, would you please get off? You're kind of heavy."

She slapped him again, making his ears ring, and drew back for another blow. The man stopped her. "Here, enough. We got him. That's all we need worry about."

"Sebastian, you slime-born carrion eater," the woman said, "we have you at last."

"Wait a minute," Jeremy said, though he had the unpleasant sensation that his diaphragm was being forced up toward his Adam's apple. "I'm not Sebastian. I'm—"

Another slap exploded on the right side of his face. "Shut it!"

"Get off!" the man ordered.

"You too, Niklas," she said. "Shut it, now!"

The man spat something nasty and low at her, then grabbed her hacked-off hair and yanked back viciously. She screamed, whether in anger or fear Jeremy could not tell, and rolled off him. She aimed a kick at the redhead—she wore cut-off pantaloons too big for her and another shimmery blouse like the man's, but she was barefoot—and he easily caught her foot and dumped her back on her rear. She scrambled up again, stiff-armed his chin, and scratched his cheek. He hacked his arm sideways at her, caught her neck, and knocked her into a cartwheel.

Jeremy had gained his feet by then, though his hands were still tied behind him. "Hey!" he shouted.

She had risen to one knee and was cocked and ready to

spring on the man. He had thrust his hands out and wore
a snarling, bad-toothed grin of welcome for her. Both of
them looked at him. The tension flowed out of their
muscles, and warily the woman got up.

"What's going on?" Jeremy asked them.

"Save it for him," the man told the woman, and she
nodded.

To Jeremy she said, "Shut it, filth. Shut it now. When
we want you to talk, we'll make you talk. Then—"

She broke off and a kind of grim pleasure came into
her face. It wasn't a pretty face, narrow-chinned and
broken-nosed, with heavy eyebrows straight above washed-
out gray eyes, crowned by the untidy shock of dull blonde
hair, but it was a good face for showing grim pleasure,
Jeremy thought.

"Then what?" he asked.

Her whole body relaxed, subsided into an easy posture
like that of a woman who has just had a satisfying sexual
encounter. "Then," she said, and now her voice was
lower, with a chesty thrill in it, "then we will kill you."

CHAPTER 3

"I'M NOT GOING to wake up, am I?" Jeremy asked for the twentieth time. "I'm really *here*."

Niklas File—the man Jeremy had followed to the crazy fortress in the rubbery gray desert—bit a chunk from a particularly unappetizing slab of meat, wiped his greasy fingers through his red hair, and said while chewing, "Stop up, you. Cut you throat soon as think. Tell me the stuff we dream-snatched gone get us outa the Between, then sneak to take off on your own. Where that mirror, that other stuff?"

"I never had a mirror," Jeremy said, squirming to ease the rough vine biting into his arms and thighs. He lay on his left side against one concave wall of the enclosure, and, he noted, the yielding surface seemed hard as concrete after one had been forced to lie on it for some hours. He had no feeling at all in his left arm now. Except for one quick latrine call, scowlingly supervised by Niklas, he hadn't been allowed to move. Hadn't even been given a drink of water or a mouthful of food. Actually, considering the bizarre look of the victuals his captors ate, that wasn't too bad—but Jeremy supposed that the time would come when even the maggoty meat would seem appetizing. The thought was not a cheerful one.

Niklas growled to himself, gnawing at his meal. He had removed the blue boots, but the rest of his outfit remained in place, from the multicolored shirt to the pink codpiece. "Where's Kelada?" Jeremy asked, just to take his mind off the tingle in his arm.

"Never mind," the redhead muttered, but after a moment of chewing he elaborated: "Gone dream-hunting. Try to find a nearby whorl, then she call me, I go snatch us out some goods. Takes two to feed two, in here. What happened you? Get your brains knocked out good in one dream-whorl? You different. Not just—" Niklas slapped his own chin and cheeks, the sound flat in the still air. "Talk different, too. Kelada had to use an understand spell on you. You get brain-scrambled in one dream-storm?"

"I don't know what happened to me," Jeremy sighed. "Could you help me turn over? My arm—"

"Turn over, turn over. Hah. Kelada come back, we find where you stash stuff, we kill you, turn over soon enough then, huh?" Niklas grinned his bad-toothed grin at Jeremy. "Slice you right, drop you in one person's nightmare, hah? You bloody-scarey, one boogeyman all bleedy on somebody's nighttime dreamhead, hah?" Niklas scaled the last of the bit of meat over the low walls of the fortress, then sat back and laughed. After a spell of that, he wiped his nose—it was running freely—with the back of his hand, snuffed, and said, "You gone soft in one head, I think. I counterspell you, counter you good, kill your magic talk. But you not even try. Ought to try, Sebastian. Ought to try."

Jeremy sighed and closed his eyes. He was so damned tired. "I'm sleeping," he said aloud, knowing the words for the lie they were. No, he was *not* sleeping. This was, somehow, madly real. He was here, in this—this place, whatever it was, wherever it was. He was really here, really trussed like a turkey, and really the prisoner of blue-booted Niklas File, thief, and his helper Kelada North. And the vine ropes really cut into his wrists and his legs, and he thought he would really begin to scream in about half a minute from the insanity of it all.

But he didn't. Instead he fell asleep, for the first time since his trek across the barren plain. For a time, perhaps two hours by his old measure, he slept soundly but in oblivion, mind shut off, voluntary muscles lax, breath and heartbeat regular. He sank into the depths of sleep, all unaware. Then the electricity of his brain altered sharply: the long delta waves faded and jittery alpha waves began to perk along a little more insistently than they had before. Like a rising swimmer, he made his way up from the depths of unconsciousness. Beneath their lids, his eyes began to move, flicking left, then right, as if watching something. The movements became more and more rapid. Jeremy was dreaming.

In the dream he stood beside himself, moved with pity

at the wretch he appeared to be. All tied up, clad only in an unbuttoned, tomato-red pajama top and matching bottoms, stuck there against the wall, hands useless behind him—he really looked very pathetic to himself. What he needed was a knife, he decided. Cut the cords and free the arms, and then deal with Niklas and his helper. So—dream a knife.

That wasn't as easy as he thought. His first trial, a straightforward attempt to remember the big butcher knife from the set that his brother Bill had given him on the occasion of Jeremy's getting his first apartment, back in college, veered off somehow into a recollected day in high school, back when the other guys still called him "Germy" and taunted him with his failure to be as good a football player as his brother. Red Fowler danced in and out again, slapping Jeremy alternately on his left cheek and his right one, and laughing, "Cry. Go on. Cry, Germy!" He almost sobbed in frustration when he remembered the cords on his arms and legs. Red and the others faded away.

Jeremy, still asleep, considered how to go about the business of dreaming a knife into reality. He cleared his mind. All right, he told himself, I'll *construct* a knife. That should be possible. And somehow he knew, or at least he intuited, the way to begin.

One started with the shine of the blade, and it had to be just right. This knife had a curved shine, suited to the blade it would have, a crescent-moon shine a palm's breadth from tip to curved tip. Jeremy almost hummed to himself as he visualized the gleam of the blade, cool and brilliant, like the new moon of a crisp, deep winter's night, just as sharp and just as pitiless. And under the shine lay metal, good steel, hard, tempered. Jeremy tasted the blood-tang of iron in his mouth as he dreamed the metal beneath the shine, as he sensed the molecules clumping to form particles, the particles grouping to form the shape of the blade. Next he needed something to hold onto. At one end a round wooden handle, comfortable to the hand, smooth. And now the hard part, the edge.

For what seemed like ages, Jeremy tried to put an edge on his dream blade. He made the cutting part shinier, brighter, but to no avail: it still was dull, he sensed, and would not answer his purpose at all. He wondered if he had begun wrong. Perhaps the way to dream a knife is to begin with the cut and then move to the edge; perhaps the way there is backward, ending with the shine. No, he decided, he merely needed a closer look at the blade—a much closer look.

In order to get it, Jeremy allowed his dream-self to dwindle to a foot high, smaller, to Swiftian tininess. Then he paced off the perimeter of the blade, dreaming, shaping, making the steel thin and keen. The metal was so real by now that it resisted the reshaping, fought to keep its original form, but Jeremy, stubborn as the steel itself, forced it to take on the edge he needed. He had to be careful that the metal behind him, still malleable from the dream, did not sag or bulge back to unwanted thickness; at the same time, he had to look ahead, to concentrate on pushing the metal back evenly, trying not to ruin the curve or the thickness. It took a long while and all his attention, but at last the task was done. Then, exhausted, the dream-Jeremy tried to wake the real Jeremy up.

Nothing doing. The depths of sleep waited, cool and dark, and down he went again, slipping cool and vertical down into the welcoming oblivion. A nagging little corner of his mind, a remnant of the dream-Jeremy, knife shaper, cursed his stupidity and the weakness of his body, but still he went.

And only later, when he was kicked awake by an angry Kelada, who held in her hand the wicked, effective curve of blade, did Jeremy fully realize the mistake he had made in not waking up.

"You can't have dreamed it," Kelada insisted. "And I know you didn't magic it. Come on, Sebastian. Tell me or—"

"I did dream it," Moon insisted. "I went to sleep and knew I needed a knife to get loose, and so I dreamed this one. I dreamed some food earlier, too."

Kelada got up and paced back and forth, making long strides, more like a gangly adolescent boy than a young woman. In the cloudy-bright light of this strange land, her face was suspicious, pinched, and sullen. "You don't even talk like yourself anymore," she muttered. "And now you've gone crazy too."

"Just dreaming," Moon said. "Lord, I wish I could wake up. That's the last time I take pills."

Kelada squatted near him. "Why did you cut your beard, Sebastian?"

"I never had a beard. And nobody calls me Sebastian. It's Jeremy—Jeremy Moon."

"Sebastian Magister," Kelada corrected. She reached out with the knife, touched its sharp point lightly against Jeremy's cheek. "The great wicked magician. He of the empty promises." The blade bit, just a prick, but Jeremy winced away from it.

"Hey!" he cried when she again nicked him with the tip of the blade. "Stop it. I'm not Sebastian Magister. I'm Jeremy Moon—Jeremy Sebastian Moon, but I never use my middle name."

"Jeremy." The tone was mocking.

"That's right," Jeremy said. "But you can call me 'Germy.' All my enemies do."

Moodily Kelada began to chunk the knife into the strange, pliant ground. "I'm not your enemy, Sebastian. More your victim. Yours and that damned Niklas's."

"Well, let me loose and we'll be friends," Jeremy said.

She snorted with derisive laughter. "Let you loose and I'll be dead." She looked around her, rubbed her right arm with her free left hand. "Be dead sooner rather than later here, anyhow." Her voice was thick, and Jeremy saw with surprise that her eyes brimmed. A solitary tear spilled and ran down her cheek to her elfin chin, a chin very much like Cassie's.

"Kelada," he said softly. "What's wrong?"

"Nothing," she said, but her voice held heavy anger. "Nothing except being born without big magic to a poor family. Nothing except being taken apprentice by a bungling thief who gets us both banished to this hell. Nothing except a clever exiled magician who promises a way out and then goes loony. Oh, everything's fine, it is. Just wonderful."

Kelada had grown more agitated as she spoke, and the curved blade waved dismayingly close. "Watch it, watch it," Jeremy cautioned, worming away. "I still don't know what you're talking about."

"It isn't important anyway."

"It is to me."

The woman studied his face for a long while. "You really don't remember, do you? You must have been

caught in a dream-whorl of forgetfulness. It must have
been a terrible one to affect a wizard like you."

"I'm no wizard."

Kelada drew in a deep breath and let it out again.
"You know what I think is wrong? We can't dream in
this place, none of us can. Back when I had nightmares
about having my hands cut off I'd have given many a
silver not to dream, but we need it, don't we? Without
dreams we're nothing. We're only half of what we should
be."

"I dream."

"You're the first, then." Kelada looked around, taking
in the little burst bubble of their fortress with moody
eyes. "Look at this place. The stuff of dreams all around,
and it won't hold shape. We had the walls twice as high
when we first built them—and the building nearly killed
us. Now they're sagging back to the primal stuff again. A
really strong dreamer could come through the walls even
now, or over them. I wish I could dream. I wish any of us
could."

"I can, I tell you. I dreamed a meal back a ways, and
just now I dreamed that knife."

Kelada dug a furrow in the gray ground with the point
of the blade. It oozed apart, plastic, more like sliced and
bloodless flesh than earth. "No one who's in the Between
can mindshape this stuff. Like word magic barely works
here. Only the outsiders can work the dream-stuff, and
only if we steal it out of the dream does it last after their
minds go back to the worlds. So don't give me any more
about your dreaming, Sebastian. You can't do it here."

Jeremy had been holding himself tense on the ground.
The arm beneath him throbbed with the effort, and he
relaxed. "Okay, okay," he said. "Have it your way. But
I think next time I'll dream these cords on my wrists are
tissue. Then we'll see, won't we?"

"I like you better without the beard," Kelada said,
tilting her head to one side. "You look younger, not so
evil." She reached out a finger and touched Jeremy's
cheek. He saw when she took it away that the tip held a
drop of blood, drying already to a dull brown. "Sorry I
hurt you."

"I've done worse shaving."

She smiled, and somehow the smile transformed her
features just for an instant, made the pixie shape of her

face innocent, young, yearning. Jeremy was moved—moved in the same way, he thought, that starving children on TV moved him, stirring pity but not real concern or even understanding. But then she got to her feet and walked away, leaving Jeremy to try to squirm into a more comfortable position. He tried to twist to look after her, but the curvature of the wall behind him prevented that. "Don't go," he yelled.

The voice came from overhead, from his horizontal vantage point: "Why not? Don't you want to dream yourself loose?"

"I'm not sleepy."

She laughed, a mocking sound. "What did you do with the things?" she asked. "Niklas will kill you soon, you know, if you don't return them. Especially the speculum. That nearly cost both our lives."

"What's a speculum?"

She had been closer than he thought. Her hand twisted in his hair, painfully, and jerked his chin up. "The mirror," she said. "The damned mirror that was *supposed* to be our way out of this place. Remember it? It was hard enough to come by, the silver, the wood."

"Ouch," Jeremy said. "Please, that hurts."

She was looking down at him. "Do you suppose the lady ever dreams of you now? You once said you could go back to Thaumia through her mirror, as long as she dreamed of you. Of course, Tremien would sense your presence at once and probably would do something even worse to you than this, if he could think of anything. But I swear, if I really thought you could do it, I'd force you to leap us both back there. Without Niklas I'd be free, and I don't think the magi would even notice my return." She dropped his head. "No, forget it," she sighed. "I'm doomed to die here, I guess, and rattle my bones around in the nightmares of the thousand worlds. Lie still, Sebastian. If you move too much, I may bury this dream-steel of yours between your shoulder blades."

She left him alone then, truly alone. Jeremy looked across the compound at the featureless opposite wall, just as gray and without character as the ground in front of him. Might as well dream myself loose, he thought. Something to do.

He tried visualizing the tough cords that bound his wrists and legs, tried imagining them rotting away to nothing, but they still held just as firmly. Finally he determined to try to sleep—and of course sleep eluded him. After what might have been hours, Jeremy recalled an old relaxation technique he had occasionally used back in college. Matter of fact, he realized, Susie Barnes had taught it to him, Susie the psych major. He wondered what she was doing now. Probably shocking rats. She had had a cruel streak.

But she had taught him a method of relaxing by dividing the body up into zones. First you told yourself that your toes were loose and relaxed, and then you felt them becoming limp. Then the soles of your feet, your arches. It was amazing how loosening the tension there could spread relaxation up your calves and thighs—and that was the course he followed now, telling himself that each new group of muscles was relaxing, going to sleep. It worked: by the time he was telling himself that his jaw was no longer tense, Jeremy was already in the ante-chambers of sleep. Before too much longer, he was lightly dreaming.

It was very irritating for a long while, because Jeremy could not quite get hold of the dream. It was less a dream, in fact, than a reverie, filled with idle, erotic thoughts of Cassie. Unfortunately, they kept getting mixed up somehow with angry, erotic thoughts of Kelada, whose face was generally structured like Cassie's but who lacked all the beauty that Cassie had—no sooner was Jeremy turned on than he turned himself off again. But after a while he began to get the hang of directing the dream, and soon he could concentrate on his bindings.

Tissue paper, he told himself. The cords did not seem to change. Jeremy thought about dreaming the knife. Detail, that was the key—detail. He stepped outside his skull and leaned over to have a look at the cords. They were very crude, fibrous, more like unworked vines than real rope. He imagined the fibers swelling, becoming water-soaked and pliable. They actually seemed to change as he kept his eye on them, growing green and softer. Then it was easy to see them as tender springtime vines, as almost nothing. His wrists, distant as they were, actually seemed to feel the damp ooze of sap as the shoots broke under his testing tugs.

This time the dream-Jeremy took no chance. He slipped back inside his sleeping self quietly, positioned himself close to his own ears, and screamed as loudly as he could.

The shock brought Moon awake at once. He sat upright, gasping for breath. Across the compound, Kelada, staring moodily out over the gray plain, started at the sudden noise and whirled on him, bringing the knife up.

"Wait," Jeremy said, holding up both hands in a placating gesture. He blinked, disbelieving what he saw.

Kelada dropped the knife, her mouth making an **O** of surprise. "You did it," she said. "You dreamed them loose!"

Jeremy said, "I did, didn't I?" But his dream had not prepared him for the magnificence of the flower garlands that, torn as they were, decorated his ankles and wrists. The blooms were of no color that he could name, and of no fragrance he could recall having smelled before.

But both appearance and scent were intoxicating, maddening, beautiful beyond thought.

"Dream-twin," Kelada said, surprise lingering in her voice. "Sympaths, Sebastian called them. I've heard others speak of them, but I thought they were myths, legends. You're Sebastian's dream-twin from the mirror-universe."

"Whatever. Sebastian, I guess, is the bearded fellow who promised me my nightmares were over—" Jeremy broke off, blinking. "He was right, wasn't he? I can control what I dream in here, apparently. No more nightmares." He looked around at the barren prospects. "I suppose I could even dream up a little paradise of my own here. House, sports car, women—"

Kelada shook her head. "No matter what you dream, you can only control the things a little way around you, a few steps. And I don't know what would happen if a dream-whorl stormed across something you made. Kill you, maybe."

Jeremy ran a hand through his hair. "I think I'm beginning to get it. Finally. You come from a place where magic works—"

"Thaumia," Kelada acknowledged. "But magic comes hard. Only a few can master it. Once a great spell is spelled, it loses virtue. Nowadays, all the easy great spells have been spelled, so it takes an especially learned and talented man or woman to work the word bindings right. Of course the little spells everyone can do, make fire, understand speech, things that don't actually require great *mana*." She cocked her head. Her short blonde hair was ruffled up on the left side, giving her the look of a gamine. "You mean, magic doesn't work in your world?"

Jeremy shook his head. "No. Not the kind you mean, anyway. We have tricksters who pretend, but, no, magic doesn't work in my world. As a matter of fact, it doesn't work in my universe, as far as anyone knows."

Kelada shook her head. "I've heard of theories about other universes, but a place where magic doesn't exist—do you dream of magic?"

Jeremy picked up one of his dreamed flowers. He found it hard just to look at the thing, for its lovely complexity threatened to pull all his attention in, to trap him in contemplation. He closed his eyes. "We dream of magic," he said.

"The Between. This is where all the universes touch," Kelada said softly. "This is the stuff all was made from in the beginning. Some parts of it give magic; some do not, I suppose."

Jeremy opened his eyes. "This is the borderland," he murmured. "This is where we go when we dream. I can't believe it."

Kelada picked up his curved knife. "You have to believe it," she said.

"Oh, I *do* believe." Jeremy smiled. "It's not that I don't—just that I can't."

A shrill whistle split the calm of the soundless plain. Kelada leaped to her feet, her hand flying to her broken nose. "Niklas!" she hissed. "He's coming!"

They had been sitting against one of the bulwarks of the broken dome. Jeremy got up, wincing at the pain in his thigh from the metal ruler of Mr. Guest. "We'll have to tell Niklas that he's got the wrong man—"

"He'll kill you at once," Kelada said, and from her tone Jeremy knew she was right. He found himself shaky in the knees.

"I could pretend to be still tied—"

Too late. Niklas the many-colored had already vaulted one of the low walls, a lumpy bag slung over one shoulder, a staff in his right hand. Jeremy had not even time to speak before the thief took in the situation, dropped the bag, and charged him. The first sweep of the staff caught

Jeremy glancingly on the hip, spun him away. He tripped
on his own flailing feet, and that saved his head from a
blow that surely would have killed him. Niklas's face was
set in grim determination. Jeremy rolled and scrambled
away from him, toward the dropped bag. He heard Kelada
cry out wordlessly. Jeremy got his hands on the bag,
found it was made of thick canvaslike cloth, half the size
of a mailbag, and he lifted it as a makeshift shield.

Niklas, the first surprise of his rush spent, circled warily, looking for an opening, the staff balanced. His wild
eyes gleamed with more than a hint of madness. "Mighty
magick," he crooned, ending the word with harsh,
exhalative "k." "You more trouble than need, magick-
maker. Put you under, yes, for good."

The staff whistled, and Jeremy was barely able to fend
off the blow. The *whump* of the impact threatened to
knock him off balance, even through the insulating cush-
ion of the sack. He took two steps back. "Wait, Niklas!"
he shouted.

Niklas ignored him, circled to the right, feinting with
the staff. From the corner of his eye Jeremy saw Kelada
coming up behind him. "Out of the way," he shouted,
realizing only then how much his chest was heaving, how
winded he was.

"Hah," Niklas breathed. "Wench and wizard? Break
more than your nose this time, cow. Break you so you
can't be fix." Niklas leaped forward, struck out with
several successive blows, some of them landing painfully
on Jeremy's forearms, and suddenly crashed the staff
straight down. Jeremy brought the sack up just in time,
but the force of the blow brought him to his knees, and
before he could recover, a sideways swipe struck the sack
right out of his hands. He threw himself wildly backward,
collided with Kelada, and fell to his butt as she rolled off
to his right.

Niklas was pressing in, staff raised. Jeremy, trying to
scramble away, felt something hard behind him. He
reached—and found himself grasping the handle of his
curved dream-knife.

He had no time to think: Niklas already was cocking
the staff back for a skull-crushing blow. Badly balanced
as he was, Jeremy lunged forward, coming inside the arc
of the swing, and he brought the knife up simultaneously.

It slipped in under Niklas's ribs with dismaying ease.

The thief jolted as if from an electric shock, cried out, and fell away. Jeremy kept his hold on the knife handle.

The redheaded File clutched his belly with his left hand. Blood spilled through his closed fingers, spreading in a ragged stain over the silky, multicolored shirt, spattering onto the thighs of the white trousers, making pear-shaped blotches on the toes of the blue boots. Niklas's face contorted. Taking painful steps, holding himself with his left hand, brandishing the staff with his right, he advanced on Jeremy again. "Kill you now," he grunted.

Jeremy was appalled at his handiwork. He backed away. "I—I didn't mean—"

Niklas cracked the staff against his legs, knocking them right from under him, and Jeremy rolled on the ground. Again Niklas raised the staff for a killing blow, but this time his own knees gave, and he crumpled slowly forward. "Kill you, *kill* you," he rasped, trying to raise the staff again.

Kelada appeared behind him, grabbed the staff on either side of his head, and pulled it tightly back against his throat. Niklas thrashed, grunted, kicked. Kelada wrenched back even harder on the staff, nearly raising Niklas off the ground. She had a knee against his neck. The redheaded man thrashed, his breath wheezing in his constricted throat.

"Help . . . me," panted Kelada.

Jeremy couldn't move. The thief's face had gone purple, and his eyes bulged, bloodshot and rolling. His hands, the left one crimson, clawed impotently at the air. The man was dying.

But not yet. The right hand caught Kelada's tunic, held it, and the whole body bucked, pulling the girl up and over. Kelada hit on her neck and shoulder, the breath whuffing from her. Niklas, gagging and hissing, had the staff again, and he brought it down across her chest with a sickening smack.

Jeremy cried out, staggered forward, and kicked as hard as he could, intending to knock the staff out of the thief's hands, but his aim was bad: his bare foot caught Niklas in the lower chest, knocking the man back. The staff, swung wildly and with no aim, stung Jeremy's left arm, numbing it from halfway to the elbow downward. Niklas was on his knees, still bleeding, still holding the staff. "Kill you," he muttered in a weak, hoarse croak.

"You're hurt," Jeremy said.

"Kill you!"

If Niklas had had an ounce more strength, he might have done it. But he couldn't handle the leap and the blow too, and instead of striking, he merely slammed against Jeremy. They rolled down together, and Jeremy felt the thief's hands scrabbling for the blade. He brought it up, struck, cut himself pulling it back, and then flung it away. Niklas rolled off him and began to crawl toward the knife.

Kelada was on her feet again. She had the staff, and she brought it down in a resounding crack across Niklas's shoulder and neck. The thief collapsed.

Jeremy sat up. He had a cut, not deep, about three inches long on his left forearm. He was sticky with blood—most of it the thief's but some of it his own. "You killed him," he said.

"He was crazy," Kelada said. "He would have killed both of us."

Jeremy crawled over to Niklas, rolled the man onto his back. The left eye was closed, the right open but rolled up so only the white showed. The red hair, matted with sweat and blood, spiked out wildly in every direction. Jeremy pulled the tunic up. One slash, the first, began next to Niklas's navel and went up to the bottom of his ribcage. The second was higher, beside the sternum. Both still bled.

Breath rattled in Niklas's throat. "Oh, God," Jeremy said. "He's still alive."

"Dying," Kelada replied. "It takes awhile. Better tie up your arm. Some cloth over here for bandages."

She limped away. Niklas rattled again, horribly. Jeremy didn't know what to do. He wanted to run, but something—the knowledge that he was responsible for this man's death—kept him there fascinated. In a few minutes Kelada was back. "I don't think he broke anything," she said, holding her side. "He marked me, though. Here."

Jeremy raised his arm as she tied a quick bandage. She held his forearm under her left arm as she finished the knot. "You're cold," she said.

"Can we help him?"

"Cut his throat, make him die quicker."

Jeremy shuddered. "That's not what I meant."

She looked at him with flat eyes. "That's the only way to help him now." Disdaining to say more, Kelada turned on her heel and walked away. Jeremy backed off from the body. The thief took a great, wheezing breath, held it for ages, and groaned it out again. Jeremy wanted to follow Kelada away then, wanted it more than he could remember ever wanting anything.

But instead he dropped to his knees beside the body. "I'm sorry," he whispered, his soft words lost in the other man's repeated groan.

Niklas File was a long time dying. But at last the body twitched restively once or twice, the breath—coming now at agonizingly long intervals—rasped harsher and rattled, and then the body went limp. Jeremy, keeping vigil, had the unmistakable impression of something—soul, spirit, the breath of life—vacating the body, leaving a wreck of flesh and bone. He closed the mouth and eyes, stood up, and found Kelada just outside the semicircular walls, sitting with knees drawn up, eyes on the gray line of the immeasurable horizon. "He's gone," Jeremy said.

"So are we."

Jeremy eased down beside her. "I've never seen anybody die like that. It's different on TV, in the movies."

She looked at him, though beneath their heavy brows her eyes did not focus on his. "I don't understand."

"There it's quick," he said. "One blow and it's over."

She shook her head. "Death is seldom that quick, unless dealt by magic. Niklas was tough, too. Hard to kill."

"Did he hurt you?"

"Bruises and aches. Be better before long. You?"

"The one cut. Like you, I've got bruises. My legs and side." Moon paused, then blurted, "He would have killed us."

Kelada's laugh was dry and thin, and it held no mirth. "Oh, yes. Niklas has gone mad in here, in the Between. He was mean enough on the outside, but in here, with nothing to do but scramble to live—something broke in his head, I think. A thief dreams of power, of wealth. What are wealth and power in here?"

"But you keep going."

She lifted one shoulder. "I'm different. I stay alive because that is what I do—what I have always done.

Niklas had to have a purpose in life—to become rich, to outwit his enemies. All that is gone in the Between. He was living, the last while, to help Sebastian Magister find his way out. Wanted to get out with him. I think he knew you were the wrong one, knew Sebastian had tricked him. That was too much, that broke his mind." Kelada rested her pointed chin on her knees. "Now we die, too."

"Why?" Jeremy asked.

She shrugged. "Niklas was the master thief. He had the secret of getting in and out of the dream-whorls with the loot. I'm only the finder. My one talent, I'm never lost. Even where there are no landmarks, like here. But I can't keep the dream-goods from fading, as Niklas could, and I can't even steal from dreams without being caught. The dreams, you know, can kill you. While you're inside one, the dreamer can do anything to you, anything at all." She shivered. "Some things are worse than dying. I'm afraid to go in the dream-whorls alone. We'll starve."

Jeremy stared at her. "But I can dream," he said.

She blinked at him. "I forgot!"

All at once her arms were around him, her face pressed against his throat. He held her as she shook with crying, awkwardly patted her back, caressed her neck. Her tears flowed warm against his neck, her breath puffed hot and moist against his shoulder. He was himself shaking, breathing in deep gulps of air. "Now, now," he mumbled. "It's all right. Now, now."

"I—I'm glad we killed him," Kelada said, her voice throbbing.

"We had no choice."

She shook her head. Her short hair ruffled against Jeremy's cheek. "No, not because of that. He—he wasn't what he used to be. His spirit had already gone."

They sat holding each other for some time. At last Kelada pushed away and wiped her hands over her cheeks and eyes. Jeremy had been thinking. "There must be a way into my world," he said. "If Sebastian could do it, so can I."

Kelada snuffled. "No. Only a great mage could do such a thing. You have to have the ability of seeking dreams, of finding the right dreamer. You have to know the times of exaltation. You have to make and invest a speculum. In here, in the Between, magic hardly works.

It takes someone with a great store of it, with much *mana,* like Sebastian, to do such a task of magic. You have no skill for it, no training in it. You could not spell our way out of the Between."

"Didn't you say something about a lady and her mirror?"

"Oh," Kelada sniffed. "Her."

"Sebastian's friend?"

Kelada nodded, looking away. "Back in Thaumia, Sebastian was beloved by a great lady, Melodia. He gave her a present of a magic mirror—a travel portal, I think, like the one he built here. He could communicate with her through the mirror, when he was back in the real world. His image would appear to her, speak to her, through it. He hinted more—that he could physically pass through the mirror to visit Melodia."

"Ah. A forbidden love," Jeremy said.

Kelada half-smiled. "Not a politic love, let us say. But anyway, something Sebastian said once made me think that he might be able to use it to get back to Thaumia. It would be most difficult—he would have to find Melodia during one of her dreams, have her open the way. He lacked the ability to find her, and I refused to try."

"Try now. It may be a way out," Jeremy said.

"You would leave me alone?"

"No."

Kelada laughed. "I do not think Melodia would welcome another woman into her dreams."

"We'll find a way."

She looked back at him. Her broken nose made her face seem blunt and tough, but her eyes were those of a frightened fawn. "I could take you to the place where the Lady Melodia's dream-whorls appear, when she dreams. But how can I trust you not to abandon me?"

Jeremy found no ready answer. "I don't know," he said slowly. "I can only tell you that I wouldn't do that."

Her eyes studied his face for a long time—for almost as long, he thought, as Niklas File's dying. At length she said, "I think I must believe you. It will be a journey of some time, of several sleeps." She stood. "We will need Niklas's staff, the things in the camp. We should see what he brought back this time, too. Let's go."

They spent what on earth would have been several hours packing. Jeremy lashed together the effects Kelada and Niklas had ransacked from others' dreams—most of it cloth, or rope, or bits of wood and metal, some of it so bizarre that Jeremy wondered what alien dreams had been plundered. At last Kelada said, "We should look at the body, too."

"There's nothing," Jeremy said.

"Maybe you're right."

They had left the ring of the camp when Kelada paused. "I think," she said, "I should at least cover him. Maybe with the empty sack."

Jeremy looked at her. "All right," he said.

"I won't be long." She went back into the circle, out of his sight. He stood looking off into the meaningless gray distance. After a minute or so, he heard her come up behind him. "Here," she said. "You'd better have these."

She held in her hands a pair of brilliant blue boots.

CHAPTER 4

"**Y**OUR PART OF the Between," Kelada explained on the fourth or fifth leg of their march, "is better for dream-raiding. Your people and mine are very much alike in the things we eat, the way we are made. That is why Niklas and I came here first."

"But why didn't you just stay in the part—uh, owned by Thaumia?" Jeremy asked, edging away from the nearest dream-whorl with some apprehension.

"Be still," Kelada said. She sat very still herself, legs drawn up, her pack beside her. She looked little-girlish, a teenager waiting for a school bus. She kept a wary eye on the haze of the dream-whorl as she answered Jeremy: "Niklas wouldn't stay there. He has—had—too many enemies in Thaumia, too many chances of finding himself in the dream of one of his victims, and at the victim's mercy."

"And now," Jeremy said, looking with some despair over the gray landscape, broken in dozens of places with the purple mists of dream-whorls, "we have to march back to the part that belongs to Thaumia. Is it far?"

Kelada scratched her head, ruffling her untidy blonde hair. "Far? A march of two weeks or more, I suppose, back on Thaumia. Distance has little meaning here."

Wherever *here* is, Jeremy added mentally. There was some geographical consistency: at least, one of the dreamers whose dream he had invaded on his first arrival came from Atlanta, too. But the landscape, in addition to being featureless, seemed malleable, plastic in the large sense as well as in the small, and as far as he could tell it had no north or south, east or west. Yet Kelada stuck to a line of march—her talent, she insisted, gave her an unerring sense of direction—and they made, Jeremy assumed, some progress.

Right now they were in an eddy of dreams, all but surrounded by the dangerous whorls, the ungoverned, amoral nighttime realities of Earthly sleepers, and so Kelada had called a halt. Jeremy had not ventured inside a dream-whorl at all since meeting Kelada, and the more he heard from her, the less he was interested in doing so. The nearest fumed now perhaps sixty paces away, stationary but threatening. From it drifted choking acidic vapors that brought tears to Jeremy's eyes and a cough to his lungs.

"Can't we move away from it?" he asked.

Kelada shook her head. "Sometimes they follow and engulf you if you're moving," she said. "No sense taking a chance."

Jeremy sighed. "How was Niklas able to get in and out of the things so easily?"

"Not so easily." Kelada turned her gray eyes away from him. "He was found out more than once. I think some of the dreamers changed him. They do that, you know. When we first came—" She shivered and broke off abruptly.

After a long pause, Jeremy prompted her: "What happened when you first came?"

"We met someone," she said tightly. "Someone from Thaumia, another exile. It—never mind. I don't want to talk about it. That whorl's clearing up. Time to go." And she stood, hefting her pack. Jeremy rose, too, feeling every creak in every joint, burdening his already aching back with his own roll of dream-goods.

"At least our supplies are holding out," he grunted as they began forward again.

"All but the water. Are you sure you can get us some water?"

Jeremy nodded. "I think so. There doesn't seem to be any real trick to it, once I concentrate." He did not add that the concentration itself was the trick. *Dreaming,* he thought. *The only real magic we humans know—and it's too magical for us to control it fully.*

As Kelada led the way, Jeremy fell into the same mindless rhythm of stride he had known for what seemed to be days, and he let his mind wander to the times he had slept and dreamed here, in the Between. The knife and the bonds increasingly seemed like flukes to him, perhaps made possible by the stress he had been under.

At any rate, so far on the trek he had dreamed up nothing substantial. He had tried, a couple of times, to dream himself back home, back in his own bed, to no avail. Though he could see the room, could hear its sounds and almost smell its smells, something kept him away, apart from it: and when he awakened here, no trace of the bedroom lingered.

After these failures Jeremy had tried to dream himself up a comfortable nylon backpack and some hiking boots, but airy musings had taken him before the job was done, and again he awoke with nothing—although, to be sure, he had dreamed an alteration into the blue boots that made them more comfortable. But as for creation—no, that had been a failure.

And now their water was getting low.

Jeremy turned his mind to other considerations. With no water to spare, he had not bathed in—what? Days, certainly. Yet he didn't seem to get any dirtier, and though he sweated from the exertion of the walks, he wasn't aware of what one of his predecessors in the field of advertising had once delicately christened b.o. Probably because there were no bacteria here in the Between, he concluded. Nothing alive here, except the exiles from Thaumia—and possibly from other, more exotic magic-using worlds. Yet there seemed to be oxygen to breathe. Or was there? He had once, just from boredom, begun to hold his breath while he counted his paces. At fifteen hundred he had exhaled, more from panic than from a need to breathe, and had felt none the worse. Still, his lungs pumped as they always had, and he had enough wind to talk when he wanted. Jeremy had more than once had the giddy sensation that his physical existence here was next to nothing, a candle flame in a dark void, ready to flicker out at any time, to subside to the gray primal material of this world.

Primal stuff. The world itself provided the substance for the dreams. The dreamers shaped it, transmuted it at need or at whim, and ordinarily, once the dreamer's mind lost contact with the Between, the dreamed items slipped back into plastic gray anonymity. The matter could be cut and worked, true—witness the fortress Niklas and Kelada had labored over—but within a short time it sagged, slumped, melted back into the featureless, empty expanse that seemed to go on infinitely.

"We'd best swing wide here," Kelada said. "Very dark whorl ahead, maybe five thousand paces. We'll avoid it."

Jeremy grunted, shifted the weight of his pack from its old uncomfortable position to a new uncomfortable one, and swung his steps into the subtly curving path that Kelada took. The blue boots pressed into the gray world, lifted, swung forward, and pressed in again, endlessly. Endlessly.

A time in camp, and at Kelada's urging Jeremy quested in his dreams for a source of water. It slipped away from him, and, angry, he commanded it to *be still!*

He awoke shivering, sleeping on a round platform of ice, with more ice frozen on his covering like a white carapace. It crackled and shattered as he pushed the stiff blanket off, ice cascading to a pile of shards and fragments. Jeremy was so chilled that Kelada held him close to her, warmed him with her body heat until his teeth stopped chattering, until feeling returned with stabbing pain to his hands and feet.

The ice melted into the needed water.

Another time, Kelada stopped, lifted her chin, and considered. "We have crossed," she said. "We are out of your part of the Between. Thaumia's part begins here."

Jeremy saw nothing to distinguish this part of nothing from any other part. He took her word for it. "What happens," he puffed, "if we cross all the way and go on? What's after the Thaumia part?"

Kelada shook her head. "You don't want to hear about the other parts," she said. She walked on ahead, Jeremy following, musing on the sturdy roll of her hips, the assured stride of her long legs. Without looking back over her shoulder, she said, "The other exile we met here. He had wandered far. Into an alien dream. The alien dreamer reshaped him, made him into something the alien knew, was familiar with."

In the unchanging temperature Jeremy felt as cold as he had when encased in dream-ice. "And?"

"It had its old mind left, or part of it. It begged Niklas to kill it." Step, step, step. "It took three tries. Niklas couldn't tell what part should have been the head."

And finally.

Kelada dropped her pack. A few dream-whorls showed, dim and blue, off in the distance. "Here," she said. "Melodia's dreams will appear somewhere around here, somewhere within our sight. I don't know exactly where."

"How do we find out?"

"Go into the dreams."

Jeremy drew a deep breath. "I was afraid you were going to say that."

Kelada stepped away from him, tilted her head, studied him critically. "You won't do, really," she said. "We mistook you for Sebastian, and there is a resemblance, but your hair is too short, you have no beard, and your clothing is all wrong."

"What do you suggest?"

"Dream a disguise," Kelada said.

Oh. Of course. Nothing could be simpler.

When Jeremy finally fell asleep, he dreamed first about the hair and beard. He had some memory of Sebastian's appearance, and he worked with that, dreamed himself in front of a mirror again, dreamed Sebastian's reflection instead of his own. Then he reached up to stroke the beard, found it real beneath his fingers, and woke himself up from sheer surprise.

"Good," Kelada said. "I watched."

The beard was still there. It tickled maddeningly, and stray parts of the moustache found their way between his lips. He thrust his tongue out, scratched his neck. "How did it look, when it appeared?"

"You shimmered, going sort of purple. Small dream-whorl, I guess. Then when you were clear again, you had the beard. Sit up."

Jeremy lifted himself to his elbows. Kelada stroked his beard, arranging it, and then his hair. Her hands felt curiously gentle. "All right?" he asked when she stopped.

She looked at him for another moment, then nodded. "Very good," she said. "You are Sebastian now." Her gray eyes widened. "You're better," she corrected herself. "Sebastian's magic hardly worked in the Between, and his dreams held no reality. You have more magic now than he. In Thaumia such creations and transmutations would be the work of a master mage."

"But in Thaumia dreams won't do it," Jeremy said.

"No. Word magic there, or nothing. And one must study for years to perfect magic skills." She reached out again, and with a delicate probe of her forefinger she swept the left part of his moustache free of his lips. "This will be no good," she sighed. "Tremien will catch us. If Melodia thinks you're Sebastian, then Tremien will think so, too. We'll end up right back in the Between—or worse."

"We'll worry about that later," Jeremy told her. "Right now I've got to create a robe. Describe Sebastian's to me—and be very particular."

She looked away from him, into her memory, it seemed. "It is long and full," she said, her voice as distant as her eyes. "A deep purple, like the sky of three stars in the evening. Rich, thick fabric, with a sheen to it. The hood . . ."

Like a schoolboy facing an examination, Jeremy leaned forward, hung on every word, and occasionally scratched ineffectively at the tickle of his new beard.

The fifth robe was not satisfactory, nor the sixth. Something always was off, not right, about them—and the six came over a spread of at least as many days and nights, with other, different, darker failures in between. Jeremy tried on the seventh attempt to visualize the robe exactly as described, exactly as remembered, and instead found himself lost in the beginning of a nightmare, an old one in which he was late for an important examination in school. He knew what lurked at the end of that dream, and managed to wake himself up, trembling but otherwise whole.

He swept the long hair back away from his face. "That's it," he said to Kelada. "No more. I have less control each time. One of these will have to do."

They deliberated long over the choice of robe. The first was gossamer, insubstantial, clothing perhaps for a fairy prince but not for a mage. The second was the wrong color, the red of his pajamas. The third was the wrong shape, and too short in the bargain, though its color was better. They debated among the fourth, fifth, and sixth attempts, with Kelada pointing out the flaws in each, before both agreed, finally, on the fifth. Jeremy donned it, turned, posed, while Kelada clucked and doubted. "It will have to do," she said at last. "But there is something wrong with the way the hood falls, and the sleeves are not nearly full enough—"

"It will have to do," he said. He stood, at the moment, on a vast empty gray card of nothing. Thaumia, it seemed, had one major difference from Earth: the world was flat, and its sun circled it, bringing day or night simultaneously to the entire planet. Here the result was fear or famine: the number of dream-whorls was much greater than in a comparable section of Earth's Between, for at any given time of the night there were simply more dreamers in Thaumia; but during Thaumia's day, the landscape was much more barren, for almost no one slept and dreamed during those hours.

Kelada and Jeremy had no way, of course, to determine the passage of time, except to await events. While they did, Kelada spoke of Sebastian and Melodia. "Melodia is the daughter of a wizard of great talent," she told Jeremy. "When the travel spell created by the songs of the great bard Dylan had almost worn out its *mana*, Melodia's father found a way to alter the wording of the spell and replenish it. He grew very wealthy from this—"

"Wealthy," Jeremy interrupted, "from magic?"

"Of course. Anyone who wished to use the travel spell had to pay a small tribute to Walther—"

"Walther being Melodia's father."

"Yes, true, and of course everyone finds it much easier to use the travel spell than to transport themselves or their goods on foot or by cart. That was the only Great Magic that Walther ever performed, but it made him one of the most wealthy and influential of all the chief magi."

"All right," Jeremy said. "Melodia is rich and spoiled. Now tell me—"

"Please," Kelada said, but her voice was anything but pleading, "will you allow me to tell the story in my own way?"

Jeremy stroked his beard—a habit he had fallen into early—murmured "Sorry," and she began the story again.

Melodia inherited or learned a good bit of magical talent herself. Though her mother had died when she was still young, her father, Walther, doted on her and raised her himself, offering her anything she desired, indulging her whims, and trying to shape and increase her magical abilities.

Melodia, like the great Dylan, was a poet and musician, and her spells often were sung to the accompaniment of a lute. At ordinary magics, like bringing light or starting fires, she was no good whatever. She was better at minor creations, though hers were all inanimate. She could not conjure up so much as a living butterfly. True, some of her simulacra were real and delicate enough to fool an observer, but her talent clearly lay in another discipline.

She found her true forte in healing spells, and most particularly in the soothing and healing of animals. Before she was twenty, she had made her reputation locally as a great and powerful physician. Now—or at least when Kelada had been exiled from Thaumia, no telling how many Thaumian years ago—Melodia was about twenty-five, world-renowned, and a recognized talent.

But she was also still a spoiled and headstrong little girl.

Once, some three or four years ago, an insistent pounding on the door awakened Melodia late at night. She sighed, snuggled deeper into her rose-scented sheets, and waited for her father's servants to open the door.

None did, and the knocks resounded louder and louder. Melodia, irritated, hummed a little silence spell, wrapping each knock in quieting cotton, shushing all sound.

But when the knocks penetrated even her sung magic, she realized why no one else was answering the door: the sounds were themselves magic, meant only for her ears, and they summoned only her. Melodia rose then, threw on a filmy white robe, shook out her dark hair in front of the mirror, and went to the door, softly singing a grooming spell on the way so that she opened the door looking rested and beautiful, a tall woman with black hair curling to her shoulders, arresting blue-green eyes tilted up at the corners, and a full, red mouth.

She threw the door open to storm and night. A man stood on the threshold, not an exceptionally tall or broad man, but one whose stance bespoke strength. His face was hidden in shadow, his figure disguised by a dark wind-whipped robe. Still, Melodia had only to look once at him before bowing her head in respect. "My lord," she murmured. Lightning flared behind the stranger, and cold rain lashed his figure.

"I think," he said, "my horse is dying." He spread his cloak like a dark wing. "Come," he said, and to the exploding music of thunder Melodia passed into its shadow.

When finally the robe swept aside, the two stood in a dry, sandy-floored cavern illuminated by wizard-light. They were deep, so deep that the thunder from outside barely penetrated, became only a low-pitched grumbling almost too soft for the ear. Before the two of them the horse lay on its side, its raven flanks speckled with sweat and with patches of adhering sand.

Melodia knelt beside the stallion, ran her hand over the sleek neck, feeling taut muscle beneath the prickle of hair. "This is no natural sickness."

"No," the stranger agreed. "It was magicked on me. I diverted it to Nightwind at the last moment. There was no other receptacle about—but I would not have him die."

Melodia crooned a wordless tune, pulled some of the poison into the very tips of her fingers. She knew for a cold instant what death would be like when it came for her, and for that instant she knew despair and emptiness as few have done. Then the moment passed.

"I will do what I can," she said.

"Send it back," the stranger ordered. "Turn the spell on the sender."

"No. Not that. If I can pull the spell out, I will disperse it into this cave. That will make the cave an evil place for many years to come—but I will not destroy a living creature, no matter what it did to you or to Nightwind."

"Then that will have to serve."

An observer wandering into the cave would have thought it a strange vision indeed: a great black horse stretching its length on the ground, a dark-robed man standing with arms folded above, and between the two, kneeling, a white-gowned woman swaying and singing softly. It did not look like struggle.

But struggle it was, with the sorceress walking strange magical paths, tugging at strong lines of force and change, feeling the pain that is deeper than pain, the agony of touching the work of a great wielder of ancient power. The stallion's breathing grew shallow and desperate, and the great cords of its neck stood out stark beneath the flesh. The hooves stirred restlessly, and the dark eyes rolled wildly in their sockets.

And at last there came a time when Melodia stiffened, threw her head back, and cried out in discord. The wizard-light in the cave dimmed, the horse snorted, screamed, and wobbled to his feet, splaying its legs and trembling like a colt finding its stance for the first time.

"Ah, God," groaned Melodia, crumpling at last into her own pain, "it is done."

The stranger spread his dark wing over her, and for a time she knew no more.

When at last she recovered her senses, she lay in an upper room of some great house. A breakfast waited for her, and she fell to with an appetite. Only when she had finished eating was she aware that she was not alone. A man, dark-haired, dark-bearded, stood at the foot of the bed, arms folded, head bowed.

She began, "Is Nightwind—" at the same time he said, "Nightwind is—"

They broke off, looking into each other's face, and both laughed. The man sat easily on the foot of the bed. "He is well," the man said. "I have brought you to Mountain Keep. It was the only place I could think of where you would be safe."

"How long?"

"Three full days and nights. This is the morning of the fourth day. Your father seeks you."

"I must go to him."

"How shall I reward your for your work?" the man asked.

"With your name, to begin with," she said.

"It will not be a welcome one. I am Sebastian Magister."

"My father is not one of your enemies."

"Yet," he said, his smile wry. "I seem to sow enemies as a farmer sows wheat, and I fear the harvest is still to come. But my name alone is not a sufficient reward. What else will you have of me?"

Melodia twirled one strand of her black hair around and around her finger. "Your purpose," she said.

Sebastian's dark eyes burned. "To find the limits of words," he said. "To wring the last drops of magic from them, and then to squeeze again. To bind and bend the power of syllables, to work my will and wonders to the utmost of my power." The light in his eyes flickered. "That has earned me enmity enough, and I suppose it is a dangerous ambition. My mother told me long ago that if the world were balanced precariously on the point of a great mountain, I would tilt the balance, just to see what would happen, never mind that Thaumia would smash.

She was a wise woman. And yet, the words are there, and the power." Sebastian stood. "But you are playing with me, Melodia. My name and purpose are no fit recompense for your service to me and to my steed. Come, what may I give you that will be of value?"

Melodia stretched both arms, hands linked, high over her head and sighed deeply. Then she held her arms toward him. "A kiss," she whispered.

So it began. After three more days Melodia returned to her father's house to find him frantic with worry. The storm that broke then, the storm of disapproval, accusation, and recrimination, put the tempest in which Sebastian had arrived to shame. At the end of the scene Melodia had left her father's house for good—and, as he had all but prophesied, Sebastian had gained in Melodia's father a new and powerful enemy.

The story became widely known. Melodia moved to a far district, and a lonely one, where she continued her healing work. She was watched by unfriendly eyes, and so she remained inside, in the little cottage she took or in the adjoining stable, seeing the outside world only through windows or through doors quickly opened and as quickly shut. She lived a lonely life but a safe one, for ancient and very powerful magics made one's home inviolate save to those invited inside, and Melodia grew suspicious enough to be very careful indeed about whom she invited in, or what animals she chose to treat.

But the same prying eyes that kept Melodia in also kept Sebastian out. She heard about him from time to time, travelers' tales of the evil wizard and his companions, about the power-hungry outlaws led by Sebastian Magister. There were tales, some of them chilling, of the Hidden Hag of Illsmere, of the Life-Taker, and most of all, of Sebastian himself. Usually the tellers of the tales would spit and line themselves upon mentioning his name, an ancient and probably useless bit of folk magic intended to ward off evil influences.

The watch, not the ceremony, warded off Sebastian. Melodia lived alone for months, refusing her father's letters, admitting only those folk whose animals truly suffered, accepting payment in gold or in foodstuffs for the healing she wrought. Then, according to the tale, on a frosty morning a farmer showed up in an oxcart. An old and ailing dog lay in the cart, and the farmer, himself seemingly crippled with twisted joints, limped inside. After some time the dog came out healed and whole, followed by the still-limping farmer. From the cart the farmer took a man-sized flat package, carefully wrapped in the tatters of blankets and tied with the raveled cords of old ropes. This, a watcher would assume, was the farmer's payment to Melodia.

Except, of course, it was the mirror.

Magic is like a tricky fluid. It seeks always to run away, to disperse itself, to return to the nonmagic that preceded first creation. It takes a great mage indeed to freeze magic, to prison it in words and bend it to purpose. It takes a greater one to instill it in material things, to give it a fixed home and habitation. But Sebastian's talent was equal to the task. The mirror was his portal, and after that he was able to visit Melodia when he willed.

The watchers knew that they had been tricked, and they cursed their luck. Still, the old prohibitions held, and they could do nothing directly. But they wove spells of subtle strength, laid deep and hidden traps, and bided their time.

Of all those who opposed Sebastian, the greatest was perhaps Tremien of Whitehorn Mountain, an aged wizard but a very powerful one. Tremien no longer worked visible wonders. Instead he rested in his ancient castle among the white peaks, snowy in summer as well as winter, and sent his spirit out into the world to feel how it went. Like a wise harvest spider, Tremien knew every tremble of the web that was the world; no vagrant gust of wind could fool him, no false stirring of a footfall could move him. But such shaking and tugging as Sebastian made—well, that bespoke to Tremien danger for the web, and for the whole world as well.

Somehow—Kelada did not know the whole story—Tremien had tricked Sebastian and had trapped him. Melodia, too, was involved in the tale, and she appeared with Sebastian before the tribunal of magi who considered the case. She was guilty of nothing more heinous than love, and so she was released.

The magistrates exiled Sebastian forever, sent him to the Between. There, wild and wandering, he had met Niklas and Kelada, had told them the story—the story from his point of view, at least—and had used them.

"That's the worst of it," Kelada finished in a dull

voice. "Sebastian cared nothing for us, made promises he had no intention of keeping. And I knew it, even if Niklas would not believe what I said. Sebastian cares for only one person—and that is Sebastian himself." She shuddered. "There is no telling what evil he has brought into your world."

Jeremy took a deep breath. "He'll find the going hard there," he said. "His magic won't work, and no matter how smart he is, he'll have a tough time convincing everyone that he's me. I think he'll be safe enough—if we can get to him in time. Time. That's the key, isn't it?"

Kelada nodded. "Well, anyway," she said, rubbing her arms, "when Sebastian first came through, I know Melodia's dream-whorls always appeared near here. If her father hasn't reclaimed her, or if she hasn't moved away, this is the place we will find her."

"And convince her to open the way for us back to Thaumia."

"If we can."

"If she still has the mirror."

"If it still works."

"If—" Jeremy broke off. "You look cold," he said.

"Afraid." Kelada covered her face with her hands. "Niklas and I were banished by a tribunal of magi, but not by Tremien. Tremien is—he is supposed to be a good man, but he is very powerful. I am afraid of him. Afraid for myself. For us."

"Don't be," Jeremy said, wishing that he could somehow fight down the churning dread that rose in his own stomach.

Kelada took three long breaths. She lowered her hands and gave Jeremy a tremulous smile. "I don't know why I should worry about Tremien. We probably won't survive the dream-whorls we'll have to visit to find Melodia."

"Cheerful thought," Jeremy said. He sighed. "Now, I guess, we only have to wait."

"Hold me," Kelada said, and for a long time they sat together, each wrapped in thoughts and fears not spoken but there all the same.

Night must have come to Thaumia, for in the Between the dream-whorls began to appear, spinning from air into shimmering existence, very pale and gray at first, then becoming opaque and purple. "I ought to try alone," Jeremy said, though to say it he had to swallow his heart.

Kelada took his arm. "We should go together." She paused, then added, "If you die, I have no hope anyway."

"All right," Jeremy said. "Together, then."

But they agreed that, at least, Jeremy should go first. Melodia, after all, would not expect a battered-faced waif to trouble her dreams, and so Kelada would try her best to hide, to stay as long as possible out of the dreamer's sight and notice. They discarded their packs—what good would they be in someone else's dream?—and, after the barest hesitation, Jeremy strode into the twilight swirl of the nearest whorl.

At first he had hopes, for he encountered animals, cattle, horses, and goats browsing and growing fatter before his eyes. This looked promising for a healer of animals, but he found no human anywhere within the dream, only the placid gazes of the beasts. Fine-looking animals, to be sure, but still only animals.

"It's a farmer's dream," Kelada whispered to him, and immediately Jeremy knew she was right. Kelada took his hand and began to edge back—even in the altered reality of a dream her gift of knowing direction held true—until they stood on the gray plain beside the little clutter of their packs.

"Not so bad," Jeremy said. "If they all are like that—"

"They won't be," Kelada told him, her face and gray eyes grim.

Nor were they. The next they tried was inchoate, unformed, loud noises, bright lights, half-created things rearing and groaning from the surface beneath them. The very land turned into liquid, sucking, stinking mud, and the two of them floundered, splashed, struggled to pull one leg out of the cold grip of muck, thrust it forward, and then pull the other out. They were exhausted and gasping by the time they collapsed outside the whorl, but they crawled paces farther away. The noisome mess covering them, a slimy brownish-green filth that reeked of excrement and rot, seemed to dissolve as they crept on, until at last they lay panting but clean.

"Nightmare," Jeremy said.

"A baby's dream. Or a madman's," Kelada said, and with that it all fell into perspective for Jeremy: a baby's view of the world, huge things moving around him, frightening changes of light and dark, the discomfort and stench of one's own waste products—a baby's nightmare, more horrifying in some ways than purposeful evil.

A few moments' rest, and then back to the task. They successfully moved in and out of three dreams without attracting attention, two of them anxious and threatening, one—a farmer's wife's dream, it seemed—dull and boring. A woman merely sat at the center of that one, a slight smile on her face, and in the circle of the whorl nothing changed, all remained the gray emptiness of the raw Between. After they left, Jeremy said, "What's wrong with her? She dreams of nothing."

"Nothing wrong," Kelada snapped. "You try bearing five children in six years, arising before dawn each day, keeping the chickens and the cow, cooking for seven or eight, cleaning, mending, making. Try that for a week, and then if you dream of doing nothing for a little while, then say there's something wrong with the dreamer."

"I'm sorry," Jeremy said. "I didn't know—in a place where magic works, I'd think life wouldn't be so hard—"

Kelada tossed her head. "A man wouldn't. But everything must be bought and paid for, and no magic comes free. The universe is always the same; it all equals out in the end. And besides, she may be unlucky, like me, and have no talent or small talent."

"Sorry," Jeremy murmured again, not sure of what else to say.

They rested. Outside the Between, night on Thaumia must have been progressing. Some of the whorls they saw winked out, and others started fresh. All at once Kelada straightened, her very attitude electric. "We're near," she said. "I think we're very near."

Jeremy leaped to his feet, scanned their surroundings. "That one," he said, pointing. "Is that it?"

Kelada got up more slowly, trembling slightly. "Yes. I believe it is. Yes."

They edged into the newly formed whorl. It was quiet inside, dim and cool with the blue filtered light of a moonlit room or an underwater grotto. "Speak her name," hissed Kelada, somewhere behind Jeremy.

Jeremy tried, squeaked, got control of his voice, and called quietly, "Melodia?"

A feminine murmur called him farther in. Ahead was a glow, dim but growing stronger, and as he approached he saw that a woman lay at the center of the glow, a woman asleep on richly embroidered cushions of gold, scarlet, emerald, deep blue. She wore a silky gown of white, clinging and so nearly translucent that he could see the pinkness around her nipples, the darker triangle at the base of her belly. Her dark hair spilled like black ink across the cushions, and her eyes, when they opened, hit him almost physically with their blue-green impact. She smiled. "My lord. You've come."

"I—yes, I am here," Jeremy stammered. God, she was beautiful! Languorous, lazy, long-legged—and her sleepy smile was heated wine to his blood. "I have come, Melodia."

"I'm so glad."

"Uh—the speculum. Where is the speculum?"

"It is here," she said, and there it was, behind her, an oval full-length mirror, its border decorated with gilt carvings of unicorns, gryphons, grotesques.

"Melodia—my love," Jeremy said, his voice halting, "I can visit you if you will open the way." He spread his arms wide in a gesture of invitation, his purple robe rustling like the insinuations of silk with the movement. With his right hand he stroked his beard.

"I'm so glad you've come," Melodia said, and her voice, true to her name, was chiming music, soft, clear, and unutterably sweet. "I have something so important to tell you."

"Yes, well," Jeremy said. "If you'll just open the way—"

"Who is behind you?" Melodia asked.

With an involuntary spasm Jeremy's hand clenched in his beard. It hurt. "A servant," Jeremy said, that being the story that Kelada had suggested. "She will make us comfortable and see that we are not disturbed. The speculum, love—"

"Don't call me that," Melodia said, and her voice now held the plangent notes of sadness and regret. "Sebastian, it hurts me so to say this, but I don't love you anymore."

"If you'll just—what?"

The beautiful eyes, the emerald blue of the sea, brimmed with crystal tears, and for a dizzy moment Jeremy ached with the sure knowledge that he would surrender everything, Kelada, his own life, the whole world, to prevent just one tear from spilling. "I did love you, once, but that was wrong of me. I had no understanding, then, that you truly wished to destroy the world. I've thought about it, and I cannot love anyone so evil. I am sorry."

"Uh, right," Jeremy said. "Sure. I see. But, uh—I've changed, Melodia. That's why I came tonight. To tell you I'm different now, I've decided to be good. Really." Behind Jeremy, Kelada struck him sharply above his right kidney.

Melodia frowned. "I don't understand. How can you change?"

Jeremy shrugged and tried to smile. His beard got in his mouth, and he had to smooth it away. "These things happen. You know, you're banished to the Between, you have a lot of time on your hands. You sort of think over what you've done—what's happening?" For, without his moving, Melodia was receding, going away; so was the speculum.

"It hurts me still to think of you," Melodia said, her voice faint. "Farewell, Sebastian, for the sake of the love I once held for you."

"Wait!" Jeremy shouted. "Melodia! Wait! I—damn it, wait, I said. I'm not even Sebastian!"

Melodia, by now a tiny figure, near and yet distant, a drifting wisp of smoke about to dissolve, hesitated, grew slightly more solid. "What?"

"I, uh, Sebastian tricked me. I only look like—ouch!" Behind him, Kelada had pinched Jeremy, a vicious pinch in a tender place.

But at least Melodia seemed to be growing larger again, or else coming near; dream perspective was very tricky indeed. "Who are you? And who is behind you?"

"Please," Jeremy said, "open the way for us to use the mirror. I'll tell you all about it, I promise. But we have to get through before you wake up." After a moment he added lamely, "We mean you no harm."

"I dare not," Melodia said. "Even the ancient inviolacy of home-rights would not protect me if I did so. My father, Tremien, the other magi, none would show me mercy if I let you back into Thaumia. I—I am sorry, Sebastian."

Again she started to fade. Desperate, Jeremy leaped forward, but still she receded. "Wait a minute!" he shouted. "Wait a—damn it, what sort of woman are you? You'd help a horse, wouldn't you?"

Once more Melodia teetered on the very brink of leaving them. "A horse?" Her voice was so faraway, so tiny, like the gentlest whisper imaginable.

"Once a stranger came to you," Jeremy said, extemporizing for all he was worth. "A dark stranger on a night of storm. He told you his horse was dying, and you passed with him without question, without pause to consider perils or evils."

"That is true."

"Well, we need the same kind of help. We're more than horses," Jeremy said in his normal tone. "We're people. Two people. And if you don't help us—Melodia, we'll die."

He heard a gasp behind him, from Kelada. Jeremy felt it, too, a heaviness in the air, a sense of an immense, immaterial balance weighing, swaying with the problem of decision. The moment stretched into eternity before Melodia whispered, "I believe you, Sebastian Magister. Come."

And then it was so simple. Jeremy couldn't believe how easy it would be, couldn't understand how a moment before he hadn't known how to pass through the portal. Why, all you had to do was *this*, and *this*. He reached behind him, found Kelada's hand, grasped it, and stepped through, feeling an electric prickle, the brush of cobwebs against all his skin at once, the crawling sensation that his skin was independently alive and moving. For a moment things went dark. No, not dark; things just *went*, into some realm of noncolor, nonbeing; and then the cool blue light came, light that he was hungry for, that he ached for, as a swimmer in deep water sees the light of air above and yearns for it. He gasped in a deep breath of the light, of the air.

Disorientation. He saw the same scene, Melodia asleep in her bed rich with cushions, but now from a wildly different angle, the whole world had shifted, and now he stood where the speculum had been. But he heard something, a deep, regular sound, the sound of Melodia's breathing. Soft snoring, rather, he amended, a homely sound, as real as the—why, as real as the stone beneath his bare feet, as real as the lingering scent of sandalwood from an oil lamp on a little table beside the bed. It was all real, the bedroom, the moonlight streaming through the casement.

He was real, he recognized with a shock, knowing now that for the longest time he had not been real, he had been the stuff and substance of dreams, that his body had been thinner than mist, thinner than the gauzy veils of the matter between the stars, had been nothing more than a very special kind of dream-whorl, held perilously together by his own consciousness, by his thin sense of who and what he was. But now he was real again, *real*, warm flesh, surging blood, sturdy bone. Another wobbling step, and behind him Kelada stumbled into reality, too.

The woman on the bed moaned, stirred, suddenly sat upright, the coverlet falling from her bare shoulders, her eyes opening wide in the dim light. She screamed once.

"Easy," Jeremy said, nervously reaching to stroke his beard.

He didn't have a beard. He had only the same shadow of whiskers that he had gone to bed with back on Earth, all that time ago.

He didn't have anything else that he had dreamed, either. And, as a quick glance told him, neither did Kelada. Dream-stuff, it seemed, did not survive in worlds of reality.

Both he and Kelada stood in Melodia's bedchamber stark naked.

CHAPTER 5

MELODIA'S SECOND SCREAM broke apart into a silly—yes, silly, little-girlish, undignified—giggle.

Kelada moved faster than Jeremy: she lunged forward, tugged a blanket off the bed, scattering cushions as she did so, and wrapped herself in it. Melodia scrambled out of bed on the opposite side of them, carrying the rest of the bedclothes with her. "Oh," she gasped.

Jeremy crouched and retrieved one of the cushions from the floor. It was too small to do much good, but it was something. He clutched it in front of himself, shivering partly from the shock of finding himself suddenly, really *there*—but even more from the chilly air in Melodia's bedroom.

"Sebastian?" Melodia asked. "Is that really you?" Her voice had lost much of its dreamed music, was really a very ordinary sort of voice, feminine and pleasant, but not a seductive siren call.

"Yes—" Kelada started.

"No," Jeremy said at the same moment. When Kelada glared at him, he said, "No. I'm not Sebastian. I look like him, but I'm someone different, from another—another place."

"I'm going to make a light," Melodia said, and in the dim moonlight Jeremy saw her reach for something on the bedside lamp table.

"Wait," he said. "I'm, ah, I need something to wear."

Melodia giggled again. "Look in the cabinet behind the woman. I think there is a sleep robe of Sebastian's still in it."

"Move, Kelada," he said. The apprentice thief edged past him, brushing against his bare back. He took two sideways steps, then fumbled behind him to find the door of the cabinet. He tugged it open and got behind its protection, but the inside of the cabinet was very dark.

"Here," Melodia said. She did something quickly with her hands, and a bright spark leaped into flame. She touched the wick of the bedside lamp with it, and in a moment a strong yellow light, smelling of sandalwood, grew from the lamp. Jeremy was painfully aware that the open door of the chest barely provided cover for him, but in the increased light he was able to sort through the hanging garments and find a silky black robe. Slipping into it, he struck the door of the cabinet with his elbow, momentarily revealing himself and making Melodia laugh again.

"Uh—thanks," he muttered at last, having cinched the robe at his waist. It was short, coming only to his knees, and its thin fabric did nothing to warm him.

"You—you really look very much like Sebastian," Melodia said. Jeremy found it hard not to stare at her: tall, raven-haired, wearing the same translucent white gown he had dreamed her in. She tilted her chin, her sea-emerald eyes intent on his face. "Younger, without the beard. Somehow, I don't know—somehow softer, maybe."

Kelada's laugh was quick and scornful. "He's softer, all right," she said.

Melodia blinked at her. "Oh, my dear, what happened to your face?"

With a start that allowed the blanket to slip low enough to reveal her small left breast, Kelada shot her hand to cover her broken nose. Above it, her gray eyes glared at Melodia.

"I'm sorry," Melodia said. "I meant no harm." She smiled at Jeremy. "I'm not much of a hostess, am I? The kitchen fireplace has a fire laid ready. Take this"—she passed him a flat wooden box about the size of a paperback book—"and light the fire. Warm yourself by it while I get dressed and find some clothes for—what is your name, dear?"

"Kelada. Kelada the thief."

"For Kelada here. Go on. Through the door, turn left, and then left again. Not that door, that's the bathroom. Yes, that's right."

Jeremy, the box in his left hand, felt his way into the hall, turned left, and at the second turn found himself in a large, dim kitchen, its general features just visible in the moonlight that streamed through two narrow, arched casements. The fireplace was against the wall that adjoined Melodia's bedchamber. Jeremy opened the box, could see nothing, and took it to the window to sort through its contents.

He had to move aside a few small flowerpots with delicate plants growing from them. Then he was able to see that the box contained a smooth piece of metal—steel, he supposed—a rougher, elliptical stone that had to be flint, a little round metal saucer, and a quantity of dry, fluffy stuff. Tinder, he guessed. He put a pinch of the tinder onto the metal plate, then took everything but the box back to the stone hearth. He knelt there, the stone floor cold and hard against his knees.

Holding the flint in his left hand, Jeremy gave it a tentative strike with the steel. He succeeded in bruising his left thumb. His second try was more accurate, and a little spray of sparks leaped into the darkness and died.

Well, if Melodia could do it in one movement, he would be able to get it sooner or later. He struck more sparks, and more, and even managed to send some of them into the little pile of tinder, but not a one caught. It was cold in the room, wintry cold, and he was starting to shake from it. He fluffed the little pinch of tinder out a bit, giving the sparks more breathing room, and struck some more.

On the fifth attempt after that, one spark lodged in the tinder, glowed red, and began to smolder. Jeremy leaned so close to it that it went out of focus in his eyes and gave it his breath, blowing steadily but gently, very gently. The spark expanded, and in a couple of seconds a little lick of yellow flame sprang up.

With great care Jeremy transferred the pinch of burning tinder to the fireplace, where more tinder awaited it, and piled on top of that splinters of kindling. The fire touched the tinder, shrank for a second, then grew again. Fingers of flame found the wood and claimed it, and in less than a minute the kindling was burning, crackling as the fire continued to grow. Jeremy felt its grateful warmth on his face, and by its light he found a bin beside the hearth, stacked full of firewood. He selected some thin pieces from it and put them on the burning kindling.

The wonderful smell of woodsmoke struck him as he leaned over the fire, taking him back in time to his grandfather's farm. He and Bill had spent parts of Christmas vacations there, in the drafty old farmhouse. His older brother had never taken to farm life, had never once volunteered to get up in the blue-black cold of a winter's morning to start the fire, but Jeremy had. Billy had missed something very special: the feeling of accomplishment as the cold cracked, splintered, melted before the onrush of warmth and light from a fire well made. Jeremy, stuck in an alien universe, cursed in his dreamings by the memory of the man he had killed, felt himself relax now in the glow of the fire, his fire. After a quick trip to the windowsill to repack the flint and steel, he stacked more wood, serious firewood, on the blaze, and stood to warm himself.

With his back to the fire Jeremy could make out more of the room. A sink, very much like his grandfather's old sink, with a hand pump for water, shared the wall with the fireplace. In front of him was a wooden table with four chairs shoved up to it. To the left of the table were the windows, and beyond the table were three floor-to-ceiling pantries, their doors closed. To the right of them a sturdy door, also closed, probably led outside. On the wall to Jeremy's right a profusion of pots, pans, and cooking implements hung, and when he turned to toast his front, he noticed a medium-sized black cauldron hanging on a hook, swung out from the fire, and the metal door of an oven built into the stone chimney beside the fireplace. He also noticed some candles on the mantel.

He peeled a long splinter off a piece of firewood in the bin, lit it in the fireplace blaze, and then lit one of the candles. When the wick gave a clear light, he tossed his improvised match onto the fire and used the candle to light the other three on the mantel. In their light he could see even more, could see half a dozen potted plants in the corners and on the windowsills, and could see three candles on the table, five more in wall sconces. He lit these as well, relishing the warm golden light they gave, relishing the simple fact of color. Thaumia, whatever else it might hold, at least was a world of color, and he had missed that in the gray Between, had thirsted for it. He drank it in now.

The women came in arm in arm. "Well," Melodia said, "you started a fine fire. This will have the house toasty by morning." She had brushed her hair and had tied it with a gold ribbon, and she wore a simple green gown, satiny, undecorated, tied at the waist by a golden sash. The hem was weighted with tiny golden bells, and they shed melodious music with each step she took. Kelada, beside her, was actually blushing as she stared defiance in Jeremy's direction: she wore a white pullover blouse of some coarse, linenlike material, with elbow-length sleeves, and matching trousers. Her feet were in sandals that scuffed a bit on the stone floor as she walked. Melodia nodded toward her. "Kelada wouldn't take a dress."

"This is good enough for the likes of me," Kelada murmured.

"It's very pretty," Jeremy said, but he couldn't take his eyes off the way Melodia moved. She glowed with assurance, her tiniest motion unstudied, beautiful, elegant. Aristocracy showed in each gesture, in the tilt of her head, in the shape of her smile. Next to her Kelada was gawky, boylike, ordinary.

"I will brew some sleeptea," Melodia said. "I think I will need some after the excitement. Are you hungry?"

"Not very," Jeremy said.

Kelada lifted her chin. "I'm starving."

"Well, we'll see what we can do about that, too," Melodia said. She took a brass teapot off its wall hook, filled it with water from a wooden bucket in the sink, and put it on the grate to boil. While it did, she found a loaf of bread and a round of cheese in one of the pantries. She brought them and some plates over to the table. Jeremy was enchanted by the way she cut the bread, by the way she carved the cheese. Every homely action she accomplished with simple grace, with a quality of—what? innocence?—of *something* that almost stopped the heart.

The teapot whistled, and Melodia took it off the fire. She brought some aromatic leaves, spicy and exotic, smelling like spring gardens in early twilight, and from them she brewed tea. This she served to them in mugs, and she provided honey for sweetening. As she placed Jeremy's mug in front of him, she paused as if listening. "Did you hear that?" she asked.

Her face was serious, abstracted. Jeremy listened. "I can't hear anything."

"Me either," Kelada volunteered. "What did it sound like?"

"Nothing, I guess. Maybe only my imagination." Me-

lodia put down the mug and set a platter of sliced bread
and cheese on the table, but she seemed a little subdued,
and somewhere in his mind Jeremy felt uneasy, too. He
had sensed, not a sound exactly, but a presence. He
couldn't shake off a sense of foreboding.

"Where are we?" Kelada mumbled around her first,
gigantic bite of bread and cheese.

"Westforest Downs," Melodia said. "In my father's
domains of Blackriver Holdings. Farmlands."

Kelada nodded and slurped her tea. "I know of it.
Never visited it, though. I was raised in Ranfora Harbor."

"I am never comfortable in cities," Melodia said.

"And I am never comfortable out of them. Not enough
places to hide in the country. A thief needs hiding places."
Kelada drank again. "This is good."

"It will bring sleep. You will be refreshed in the
morning."

"Good. I need to start early. It's many days' journey
to Ranfora."

"But why don't you use my father's travel magic—oh."

Kelada grinned. A fragment of cheese clung to her
front teeth. "Outlaws and poor folk can't afford it," she
said. "It's foot travel for me, or else ride the back of
whatever beast I can steal."

Jeremy had drunk two cups of the tea and had nibbled
some bread. He found himself staring deep into the heart
of a candle flame, noticing for the first time in his life the
intricate layers, the onionlike structure: first a dark flame,
more like the border between fire and not fire than
something in itself, but there, tapering to smoke at its
pointed tip: then the bright yellow light-giving zone, seeming almost solid: then a blue teardrop of flame right at
the wick, but at its base, and much smaller, a valentine-
heart dark spot, filled, if you looked very closely, with
swirls of vapor. His eyes closed on the beautiful, complex
flame and opened in darkness. "Here," a voice, Melodia's
voice, said in his ear. "The straw is clean."

Jeremy became aware that he was standing on unsteady legs. "What? Straw? Where are we?"

"I walked you out to the stables. Here, I've spread a
blanket for you."

Her hand tugged him down. Too tired to think more
about it, Jeremy eased himself onto a mounded, yielding,
crackly surface. Melodia threw another blanket over him.

In a whisper she said, "I feel a shadow over my house, not a good one. Do you remember what I told you?"

"Mm?" he said.

She sighed. "Listen," she said. "Remember. Tomorrow morning, go back to the house by the passage, not across the yard. My house is watched. I think the ancient inviolacy of the homeplace will keep others outside, but if you stray in the open, outside of the walls of the house, they will regard you as fair game. Will you remember?"

"Mm." Jeremy slipped away from her, into the warm dark of sleep. One dream troubled him, a vision of Niklas File staring at him with accusing eyes. The thief appeared as he had in life, gaily dressed, lithe, tough, but he stood silent, merely staring at Jeremy, his face slack and without expression, his eyes empty as the Between itself. Jeremy groaned in his sleep. "I'm sorry," he said to the apparition. It faded away, and from then until dawn Jeremy slept deeply, visited by no dream that he could later remember.

Waking was slow and comfortable. The morning air chilled the tip of his nose and made his breath plume visibly, but beneath the blankets, snuggled into a hollow in the straw, Jeremy was warm enough. Pale sunlight came through the main door of the stables, really a slatted gate wide enough to accommodate the animals. Streaks of light slanted in shallow buttresses to the straw-strewn floor, and in the light yellow dust motes swirled and danced. The sun had a watery and washed-out quality, the kind Jeremy had often seen at home on winter days with high clouds overcasting and filtering the light. At any rate, the bars of sunshine brought with them no warmth.

A sound of breathing made Jeremy turn his head. He lay in a stall above the level of the ground and filled with loose hay, evidently a storage bin. To his right and below him, a dappled mare stamped occasionally and munched on more hay. He watched her, appreciating the fine movement of muscle beneath her hide, the delicate spattering of white against the light gray background of her back. She looked at him once, with large, dark, mild eyes. Then she ignored him and went back to breakfast.

Jeremy took a great lungful of the cold air and decided it was time he rose as well. He wrapped one blanket around him for warmth, shook straw and hayseeds from the rest as well as he could, and folded them over his arm. He looked at the slatted gate—the sun was wholly gone now, and outside was the soft light of a fully overcast day—and remembered Melodia's last caution to him. He climbed down from the hayloft. Between it and the first, occupied animal stall he found a door. That led into a narrow hallway, windowless and perhaps twenty feet long, dark except for cracks of light outlining a door at the far end. Walking down the hall, Jeremy could smell the dry, sweet smell of stored fruits and vegetables, and he sensed rather than saw the shelves and niches lining the way.

He tapped on the door at the end. After a moment Melodia, still wearing the green gown, opened it. "Just in time," she said. "Kelada has finished her bath, and I'm heating more water. When you're bathed and properly dressed, we'll have breakfast."

"Ah—thanks," Jeremy said. Melodia walked away from him, over toward the fireplace, the jingling of her hem bells accompanying her. Jeremy noticed that her feet, peeping out from the hem as she turned or began to walk, were bare and small. She dipped the back of her hand into the cauldron, which was swung over the fire now, and nodded. A large wooden tub had been drawn up close to the hearth.

"I've emptied and rinsed it," Melodia said, putting a folded towel down next to the tub. "When you finish, please do the same."

"Empty it where?" Jeremy asked.

"The sink," she said. "Where else? The pump is already primed."

"Uh—thanks."

"I've gone through an old trunk," Melodia continued. "If you'll give me a moment before you begin your bath, I'll bring some things of Sebastian's you may use."

Jeremy nodded. Melodia was out of the room and back in a minute or less. From the clothes she brought with her, Jeremy selected a set of underwear, pearly gray and silky, a tunic, trousers, stockings, and slippers. Melodia spread them over a chair and took the rest of the clothing and Jeremy's blankets away with her. From the hallway she called back, "Just shout when you've finished."

Alone, Jeremy dipped hot water from the cauldron

into the tub, then tempered it with a bucketful of cold water raised from underground by vigorous sweeps of the pump handle. He shed the blanket and black robe—on this cold morning the air in the kitchen was nippy despite the good roaring fire in the grate—and slipped into the tub. He had left half a bucket of cold water on the hearth beside the tub, and near that were the towel that Melodia had brought and a small pewter dish that held a jellylike soap. It lathered well, and smelled pleasantly (if femininely) of rose petals. He scrubbed away with enthusiasm, but once he halted, suddenly hit by an uncanny sensation of being watched. He turned his head, soap dripping over his chest and off his raised elbow, but the room still was empty, and no eyes pried through the lightly curtained windows. None that he could see, at any rate; still, Jeremy hurried as he soaped his back and legs, and he kept one eye on the windows. His bath finished, Jeremy stood in the tub, tipped hot water from the cauldron into the bucket, and poured the resulting warm water over himself. He toweled himself pink before the fire and sighed with pleasure. It had been a long time between baths.

The silk underwear, a pullover top with half sleeves and knee-length pants that buttoned to the top, made him feel decadent. But the gray trousers, with baggy legs of an Arabian cut, and the blue tunic, its seams embroidered in silver and black and a five-pointed silver star worked in over the left breast, fit perfectly and felt comfortable. The gray stockings were thin but warm, and the silver-buckled black slippers felt soft and light on his feet. Dressed, he dipped water from the tub and emptied it until he was able to lift the whole thing and tilt the remaining water out. Then he used the last dregs of boiling water from the cauldron as a rinse. He pumped more water to refill the cauldron, rinsed the sink, and called out, "Finished."

Kelada came to stand in the doorway. "Well," she said, "you look different."

Jeremy blinked. "So do you." The blonde hair, though still cut short, had been evened and washed. It shone now in the pale light from the windows, and, trimmed, it framed the tough little face in a way that softened it, that made the heavy brows and the broken nose less important somehow. The gray eyes seemed now to be softer, too, and more vulnerable. Kelada still wore the white clothes she had borrowed last night, but in the light of morning they seemed to fit her better, to accentuate her awkward charm.

Under Jeremy's scrutiny Kelada dropped her gaze and blushed. "I know how silly I look," she muttered.

"No."

"Don't worry, you won't have to look at me for long. I'm leaving as soon as I can."

"That isn't a good idea." Melodia had emerged behind Kelada. "Look out the window and you'll see why."

Jeremy went to the window. Outside he saw a landscape that looked very Earthlike, very familiar: gentle hills, covered in winter-yellow grass, rolled away into the distance, to the eaves of a forest black and bare of leaves. A few isolated nearer trees also stood sketched against the landscape, and little patches of ground under their protecting shade were white with frost or unmelted snow. Here and there a short evergreen splashed a little color into the landscape.

But the arresting feature was the sky: truly dark now, with ragged clouds shading from a luminescent white to charcoal gray and even purple, the firmament seemed to be spinning around an axis directly over the cottage. Kelada's breath was warm against Jeremy's cheek as she spoke behind him: "Weather magic."

"Someone knows you're here," Melodia said. "The house is watched. The clouds are like a warning sign. No farmer will bring an ill animal here today, and I fear that anyone who leaves the house will be noticed and followed, at the very least. Until the watchers decide to reveal themselves, I counsel you to stay."

Kelada turned away and sank into one of the chairs. "I am dead," she said. "If any of the magi capture me, they will exile me to the Between again. I cannot bear that. I will kill myself first."

Jeremy had drawn aside a curtain. He let it fall back into place and paced back and forth in front of the fire. "Would anyone have ways of knowing if Sebastian had returned to your house?" he asked.

Melodia, in her matter-of-fact way, had busied herself with the teapot, with a small cooking pot, then with a loaf of bread and a knife. "Tremien, perhaps. He is very sensitive to lines of magical force and to disturbances in them. If his attention were on my house, yes, he would know if Sebastian had returned. Or my father might know, but only if Sebastian were in Thaumia and used his travel spell."

"They may think I'm Sebastian," Jeremy said. "Everyone else seems to believe that."

"Possibly," Melodia agreed. She took a complicated, many-branched toasting fork from its place on the wall and impaled slabs of bread on it. "Please toast these for me," she said, giving the fork to Kelada. Without a word the thief rose and went to sit on the hearth, where she stared into the flames as she held the bread close to the heat. "Whatever happens," Melodia continued, setting the table, "we will need a good breakfast in us to be able to face it."

Breakfast, with the thick cuts of buttered toast, a creamy yellow porridge, honey, and a minty tea, proved more welcome than Jeremy anticipated. Munching the homely fare, he was struck with how insubstantial, how unreal, all his meals in the Between had been. They had *seemed* filling enough at the time, but now in memory they were tasteless and insipid, the dream of food and not food itself. As the three ate, they debated courses of action. Kelada was bent on leaving, on striking off on her own, heading south and east to the seaport city of her birth, where she could hope to lose herself in the teeming and transient population. Moon wanted more than anything to consult Tremien, the mysterious great magician, but Melodia assured him that no lesser mortal could hope to make his way to Whitehorn without Tremien's active interest and aid. She counseled waiting, for someone certainly knew they were there, and before long they would hear from that someone.

Over Melodia's objections Jeremy helped wash the dishes after breakfast as Kelada dried them and Melodia stored them away. Going to the window and looking out on her way back from the pantry, Melodia idly remarked, "You worked good fire magic last night. It's freezing outside, but the house is nice and warm. I hope Whisper is warm enough in her stall."

Jeremy laughed as he emptied and rinsed the sink. "No magic," he said. "I just used the flint and steel."

"But you summoned the elemental," Melodia said. "And you made the offering to his liking."

"What?"

Kelada was wiping the last crumbs off the table. "Fire elemental," she said. "You call them by striking flint and steel together, and you give them an offering of wood to stay and provide warmth and light. There's one in the grate now."

Jeremy pushed the sleeves of his tunic back into place and stood in front of the hearth. "It's a good fire," he said, "but just a fire. It's a physical process. There's nothing magic—"

His jaw dropped. In the wink of an eye the flames in the fireplace coalesced, solidified into the shining body of a dwarfish little being sitting cross-legged on the charred logs. Two eyes like burning coals glared at him from a bald, glowing head. With a voice like a fire roaring up a chimney, the creature hissed, "Call me a physical process, will you? I've a good mind to smoke up the place."

"Please," Melodia said, coming up beside Jeremy. "He is a stranger in Thaumia. He meant no insult."

"Let him apologize then."

Jeremy tried to work his mouth. "I—I'm sorry," he choked out.

"Watch it, then." And the little man broke apart instantly into dancing flame.

Jeremy whirled toward Melodia. "What was that?"

"A salamander," Melodia said.

"A *lizard?*"

Kelada laughed. "You'll have him smoking us out in a minute."

Melodia shook her head. "A salamander is the visible shape of a fire elemental," she said. "Ordinarily, they manifest as flame, but when they need to speak to humans, they must take on the configurations of a human-like being. A salamander is the manifestation of that. This salamander is Smokharin, by the way. I would have introduced you, but in his human form he finds cold weather unpleasant."

"You give your fires names?"

Melodia laughed. "Elementals tend to accompany one person. Though they won't admit it, they do grow attached to human company. I've know Smokharin since I was a little girl in my father's house. When my father— when I left home, Smokharin came with me. He and I often chat on lonely evenings."

Jeremy gave the fireplace a nervous glance. "And I suppose there are other elementals, too? For water and earth and air?"

"Yes, of course." Melodia turned to Kelada. "He is not as untutored as you believed," she said.

Kelada shrugged. "He doesn't know anything that counts," she returned. "I think I'll leave this evening as soon as it's dark."

Melodia frowned a little at that. To Jeremy she said, "If your world truly has no magic, where did you learn of the elementals?"

Jeremy raised his shoulders. "Don't know. Maybe 'The Rape of the Lock.' That's a poem I read in college. Or maybe just from the name of a rock group."

Melodia's gaze was as uncomprehending as Jeremy's had been a moment before. "You give names to stones?"

Jeremy laughed. "No, a rock group is made of people who—oh, it's hard to explain. But people on Earth know about elementals, or at least imagine them, even though they're not real there."

"I can't conceive of a place where there is no magic," Melodia said, crossing her arms. "How would you live in such a place? How would you heal illness, or manage the weather, or even travel?"

"We do things like that by science—by technology," Jeremy said.

"I think," Kelada said from her seat at the table, "I'll want to borrow some things, Melodia. Or take them and send you the money for them when I get it."

Melodia ignored her. "How? How do you, oh, how do you travel, for instance?"

"I have a Civic," Jeremy said.

"And what is that?"

"It's a car. A sort of, uh, a sort of carriage, but without a horse. It has an engine in it, a thing that makes it go."

"Some warmer clothes," Kelada said, counting items off on her fingers. "A knife maybe, if you can spare one. Some walking shoes."

Melodia's eyes held puzzlement. "This engine has magic?"

"No, just gasoline. It burns a kind of liquid called gasoline, and that makes some pistons move, and the pistons turn a shaft, and the shaft makes the wheels turn, and the wheels, uh, make the car go," said Jeremy, feeling uncomfortably that his explanation fell short in a few details.

"But what tells the car where to go? What magic directs it?"

"None. A person drives it."

"Then it cannot go very fast?"

"I'll need to take some food, too," Kelada said. "Enough for a few days, until I can scout out some places to rob."

Jeremy scratched his head. "Cars can go pretty fast," he said. "I've driven one over a hundred miles an hour."

"I do not know what that means."

"Well—how do you travel?"

Melodia shrugged. "We use my father's travel spell. Each person in Thaumia pays him a tribute, and in exchange he assigns each traveler a secret syllable. Or his assistants do, now that everyone uses the spell."

Kelada, still seated at the table, snorted in laughter. "Not everyone," she said.

Melodia blushed. "Well, some people are too—too poor to pay the tribute. And others, ah—"

"Some of us are outlaws," Kelada said succinctly. "We don't get travel spells. We have to rely on our legs and whatever animals we can steal."

Melodia took a deep breath. "Anyway, to travel, we just visualize our destination, repeat the syllable aloud, and that activates the spell. We are then at our destination." She paused. "Of course, since it takes about an ona and a half in transit, people still walk or ride for short journeys—or when some people do not wish their travels to be detected, they, too, may walk or ride."

"What's an ona?" Jeremy asked.

"Five hundred simi."

They then fell into a discussion of time. Finally, with the aid of a sandglass, Melodia managed to make Jeremy understand that an ona (plura hona) was a period of time that lasted seventy-two Earth minutes. A day had twenty hona in it. Further, to anyone not traveling, travel by spell seemed instantaneous: if Melodia, for example, spoke her spell in her bedroom while visualizing her kitchen, she would pop out of existence in the bedchamber and, to an observer, instantly pop into existence in the kitchen. But to Melodia herself, any trip, no matter how long or

how short, would subjectively take seven hundred and
ninety-six simi to complete.

Jeremy found the concept hard to understand, but no
harder than Melodia's difficulty with automobiles. "No
human," she said, "could control anything moving that
fast."

Kelada, for her part, got a large bowl, a paring knife,
and some vegetables and started to peel them. "I want to
have a decent meal in me before I leave," she growled,
"even if you two professors aren't interested in your
bellies."

Jeremy, seated in a chair pulled away from the table
and intent on his conversation with Melodia, who stood
to one side of the mantel, arms crossed and head down,
barely looked at Kelada. "We're trying to—" he began
just before he was struck by lightning.

At least he perceived the blast of light and the bone-
shaking roar as a lightning bolt that had scored a direct
hit on the house, if not on him. He was aware of his chair
toppling sideways, but before he could make a move to
catch himself his face cracked against the stone floor and
fireworks went off behind his eyes. He rolled free of the
chair and pushed himself to his hands and knees on a
floor that seemed to be spinning around.

Jeremy shook his head. Melodia, her back still against
the wall, was sliding down to a sitting position, her eyes
rolled up. Kelada had been thrown forward from her
chair and half-sprawled across the table. Past her, where
the outer door had been, there was a large rectangular
hole in the wall, and standing in it was a squat, bowleg-
ged figure like something in one of Jeremy's bad old
dreams. Round-headed, pointy-eared, it was only a
sihouette against the light. Its abnormally long and thin
arms were upraised, and at the end of the arms two
three-taloned hands were spread wide.

Before Jeremy could put two coherent thoughts together, Kelada had rolled off the table and had landed
with feet wide apart facing the door. She still held the
paring knife, and with a yell she lunged for the thing in
the door. It swept its hands together and apart, barked a
word, and blasted Kelada backward, her arms and legs
jerking forward from her momentum, the knife flying
wide and clattering across the floor. She hit hard on hip
and leg and cried out.

And Jeremy, to his astonishment, realized that the emotion boiling inside him was not what he thought. His mind told him he ought to be terrified, he ought to be running now—but what he felt wasn't fear at all.

It was rage.

With an inarticulate growl he pushed up from the floor and barrelled toward the intruder. In the black beachball of a head, orange eyes flashed, and a slash of a mouth opened to speak another word. The three-fingered hands shot forward in a snakelike magical pass—

—and nothing happened.

The orange eyes blinked once, then Jeremy had grabbed the collar of the thing's tunic with his left hand, had cocked his right fist at shoulder height, and, aiming down—the creature was a good eighteen inches shorter than he—Jeremy let fly. His blow caught the creature hard on the mouth, sent it tumbling backward into the yard to land *splat!* on its butt.

It also hurt like hell. Jeremy danced in place, shaking his hand and wondering if any single bone in it remained intact.

In the yard, the creature sat with its orange eyes crossed, its head wobbling loose on its negligible neck, its bare feet—three-toed as the hands were three-fingered, but blunted—thrust out before it. Despite its huge head, covered with short gray fur that glistened with the sheen of sealskin, the thing was really very spindly. It opened a mouth that stretched more than ear to ear—the corners actually reached a point on what should have been the monster's neck two inches past the ears—and showed Jeremy a headful of white teeth.

"Come on," Jeremy said, still shaking his right hand. "Try it again, sucker."

A pointed black tongue came out, pushed at what should have been the left upper canine. The conical tooth waggled and fell out. Blue-green ichor dripped from the opening onto the round chin. The creature blinked. "Oo broe muh toof," it complained. "Oo broe muh *toof* ow!"

"Get up, you—" Jeremy paused, jerked his chin up. There, in the yard, had he seen the quick flirt of a shadow, a man-shaped shadow? If so, it was gone now. The creature, holding its mouth and wincing, seemed alone.

Behind Jeremy, Kelada said, "I think Melodia's hurt."

The tide of Jeremy's anger had begun to sink. "Get out of here, you—you freak," he said, and spun on his heel.

Kelada, crouched beside Melodia, was chafing her hands. Jeremy stooped over the sorceress and pressed his thumb against her neck, probing for the artery. "I think she'll be all right," he said, though in truth he felt no pulse. Considering that his hand was numb, that didn't really surprise him. But her color was good, and her breathing regular. Indeed, as Jeremy spoke, Melodia moaned and turned her head so that her cheek caressed the back of his hand, making it feel better immediately. "Get her some water," Jeremy said.

"I get it," said a voice to their left. The—thing, monster, demon, whatever it was—had come inside and was working the pump. First it swished water in its own mouth, then it took a cup from the sink, rinsed it, filled it with water, and brought it over clenched in both malformed hands. "Here." It stopped a couple of paces away, extending the cup far from itself. It flinched as Jeremy reached for the water. "Don't hit me!"

Jeremy growled beneath his breath, took the cup, and held it to Melodia's lips. She inhaled, murmured, swallowed some water, and opened her eyes. "Ow," she said. "I banged my head against the—Nul, it's you. What did you do this for?"

Blinking its orange eyes rapidly, the creature shuffled backward. "She came at me with knife," it complained, pointing one hand at Kelada.

"You bruised me from hip to knee," Kelada countered, rubbing her thigh.

"Well, he broke my tooth!" the creature said.

"You blew the door out!" Jeremy snapped.

"Stop it!" Melodia sat up, winced. "Ouch," she said. "I have such a lump. Feel." She guided Jeremy's good hand to the back of her head. He rotated his fingertips, massaging her scalp. Somehow he felt a little indecent stroking her head and palping the lump like that right in front of everyone, but in a perverse sort of way he enjoyed it.

"Mouth hurts," complained the newcomer.

Melodia groaned. "Help me up." Kelada and Jeremy got her to her feet and steadied her. She promptly settled onto a corner of the hearth. "Come over here, Nul. I'll see what I can do."

"He'll hit me," the creature muttered.

Jeremy rolled his eyes. "Oh, for—"

"He won't hit you," Melodia said. "Come on. I can heal animals, and you should be close enough. Let me help you."

The creature shuffled forward slowly. Melodia looked at the gap in his mouth, asked Kelada for a dishcloth, which she used to wipe the chin clean of blood (if that was what it was), and held her hand over Nul's cheek while she crooned some soft, strange words. The orange eyes widened, then drooped in a foolish expression of pleasure. "There," Melodia said at last. "The pain will ease and a new tooth should begin to grow in a week or so. Now, Nul, why did you break down my door? It's freezing in here."

Indeed, a frigid draft whipped around their ankles. Nul dropped his eyes. "*He* send me. From Whitehorn. To bring Sebastian back."

"Sebastian isn't here."

Nul glared at Jeremy. "I know what he look like."

"No," Jeremy said. "I know I look like Sebastian Magister, but I'm not. I—oh, it's too complicated to explain right now."

The orange eyes had narrowed. "Not Sebastian? That why my spell not work!" The voice, which was high-pitched but gravelly at the same time, took on an aggrieved tone: "Powerful spell, and I even used the True Name. Waste of *mana!*"

Melodia was gathering plants from the windowsill and transferring them to the hearth. "If Tremien sent you, he'll want to know about Jeremy here. My advice to you would be to return at once to explain why you damaged the house of a sorceress and hurt an innocent thief."

"Tremien?" Jeremy took a step toward Nul, who prudently retreated. "I want to see Tremien."

The creature blinked. "You—you *want* to see—?"

"Go on," Melodia said. "Tell Tremien that we have a visitor from another side of reality. From one without magic."

"I go," the little being said. It waved its hands, muttered some quick word, and was not there anymore.

Jeremy had a sensation of pressure in his ears and

heard a soft *vap!* He blinked at nothingness. "He disappeared!"

Melodia came over from the window, her arms full of tiny flowerpots. "My herbs and simples are going to wilt."

Kelada got up, took a limping step, and grimaced. "I'm leaving."

"He just—he just vanished," Jeremy stammered.

Melodia left the kitchen for two minutes. She came back with a tattered blanket—from the hayseeds clinging to it, Jeremy supposed it was the one he had slept on—a handful of small nails, and a hammer. "Help me," she said. As Jeremy unfolded the blanket, she stepped into the yard, stooped, and picked something up. "Demon tooth," she said, tucking it into a pocket of Jeremy's tunic that he had not even noticed before. "Might be useful, magically speaking."

Kelada had spread a large towel across the table. She was rummaging through the pantry now, packing it with dried fruits and other foods. "Pay you when I steal some money," she said.

Jeremy and Melodia hammered the blanket over the open doorway. It flapped in the draft, and chilling swirls of cold air leaked around it. By the time they finished, Kelada was tossing some odds and ends of clothes on top of the food.

"Maybe that will keep us from freezing," Melodia said.

"These looked like old clothes," Kelada told her. "Could I take the carving knife?"

"How could he just disappear?" Jeremy asked.

"The travel spell," Melodia said. "There's an old coat in the second trunk in the room where we got Jeremy's clothes. It's not fancy, but it's warm. Dear, I wish you'd reconsider."

"Where did he go?"

"Tremien's, I expect."

Kelada pushed past them. Jeremy stepped aside for her. "Then he'll be back—"

"The same way. Instantaneously, less whatever time his interview with Tremien takes, of course."

Kelada came back in, muffled in an ankle-length quilted blue coat with an attached hood. "I'll be going now."

But before she reached the table and her improvised

pack, Nul was back, coming into existence with an audible *pop!* Jeremy gaped at him.

"Tooth better," the round-headed little thing beamed. "Pain all gone."

"Good," Melodia said. "Unfortunately, my house is still a wreck."

Nul held up a three-fingered hand—extra joints in the fingers, Jeremy noted this time—in a placating gesture. "I explain to Tremien. He think up fix spell." In two strides the demon reached the doorway. He grasped the blanket with both hands and ripped it free.

"Hey!" Jeremy protested in the blast of cold air.

Nul ignored him, tossed the blanket aside, and spread his hands. "Iron and wood, be whole once more, once again you be a door," he chanted.

Jeremy stared. The splinters of wood and scattered nails began to stir, and not just from the draft. The nails rolled tinkling over the stone floor, the splinters stood on end—

It was, impossibly, a reverse explosion. Everything leaped back into place, sound seemed to travel back into the door, and there it was, whole and closed. Jeremy blinked in the sudden dimness, found his mouth dry.

"Good, good," said Nul, dusting his hands. He felt inside his tunic. "Now," he said. "Pay for healing. Here, you have this." He clutched a gold chain, and from it dangled a round gold medallion. "Little charm Tremien gave me long ago. You wear, you see auras."

Melodia said, "Nul, I didn't intend to charge you—"

"Take, take. Good for business. You wear, you know if sick animal really sick or if suffering curse. I want you have it."

"Well—" Melodia extended her palm, and Nul dropped the chain into her hand.

"There," the little creature said with a sigh. "All done. We all even now."

"Good," Kelada said. She had shouldered her pack. "Now I'll be going." She reached to open the door.

"Lock!" barked Nul, and the door latch clicked. Kelada rattled it without effect, and when she turned toward him, Nul added without looking directly at her, "You not to leave. Nobody leave till I say go."

Jeremy felt some of the old anger. "Now look, you little—"

Nul smiled at him, a wide, sharp-toothed smile (except

for one gap where the left upper canine should be). It was not unlike being smiled at by a shark, and Jeremy paused.

"Good," Nul purred. "Everyone together. Very good. Tremien tell me what to do."

"And what," Melodia asked with suspicion in her voice, "did Tremien say?"

Nul clasped his hands, as well as he could clasp hands that boasted only six fingers altogether. "You," he said, "all of you—Tremien say you under arrest!"

CHAPTER 6

KELADA OBJECTED, MOST strongly, until Nul spelled her quiet. Then she stood until told to move, stared straight ahead, and said nothing. Jeremy objected to *that*, and Nul growled to him, "Council of magi gave me permission. Temporary spell, anyway. We go now."

Melodia took his arm. "It's all right," she said. "He hasn't harmed her, and she'll remember nothing of this when the spell is lifted. It's better for her if you accept the spell."

"Better for all," Nul muttered. "Tremien waits for us. Better we leave at once."

But they couldn't go right away. Melodia insisted on making sure that Whisper, the dappled mare, was cared for, and so Nul, tapping one three-toed foot in his impatience, said, "Call someone to care for horse."

The calling was impressive to watch, at least for Jeremy. Melodia sat at the table, folded her hands on her lap, and spoke a series of words, ending in the name "Fairborn." From thin air, or at least from a spot on the bare tabletop about two feet in front of Melodia, a gruff male voice suddenly spoke up: "Ya, Fairborn here. What is it, I'm milking?"

"Good farmer Fairborn, this is Melodia the healer—"

"Ah, ya. The sheep are fine again, Lady—"

"Good farmer Fairborn, I have a problem."

The invisible farmer paused just perceptibly before saying, "How can I help?"

"I must be away for a time. While I am gone, I need someone to look after my mare."

Relief at the smallness of the request broke through with the farmer's words: "Oh, sure. Nice little animal. I fetch her over to stay in the barn with my Bob-Tail and Stepper."

"Thank you, good farmer Fairborn. I will find some way to repay you for her feed."

"Na, na. Only maybe my little daughter Belle can ride her of an afternoon? She is a good rider, and she would make sure your Whisper don't get fat and lazy on you."

"That will be fine, good farmer."

"Good, good. I finish milking and come over in maybe one ona. The weather is good there?"

Melodia lifted an eyebrow at Nul. Nul grunted and said, "Cloud spell off now. Sun shining out."

"The weather is good," Melodia reported. "Thank you, good farmer Fairborn." She uncrossed her arms and stood up. "I am ready to go," she said.

Jeremy stirred. "I suppose that was a long-distance speaking spell?"

"Of course," Melodia said. "It works much like the travel spell. The wizard Dornadin devised it, and all who pay his family tribute may use it."

"Then why not simply talk to Tremien—"

"No," she said. "A great mage will not allow just anyone to speak with him. Tremien is one of the council, and the council control use of the speaking spell."

"Brother," Jeremy breathed. "AT&T thought *they* had a monopoly."

The demon fetched a charred stick from the fireplace—the fire had burned itself almost to embers, and Jeremy wondered if Smokharin were dozing there—and used it to scribe a black circle on the floor. "Now," Nul said, tossing the stick back into the fire, "everyone in circle. Thief, walk here."

Kelada, who had been standing in a corner, drifted unseeingly to the spot Nul indicated. Jeremy winced at the indignity while at the same time marveling at the girl's unsuspected grace: while conscious, Kelada contained so much fire, so much life, that she was like a grasshopper, all arms and legs and sudden movement. Now, under Nul's spell, she walked with the fluid, enchanting motion of the woman she might have become under other circumstances.

Jeremy and Melodia joined her, as did Nul: they stood with heels just inside the circle, all facing in, the demon frowning anxiously down to make sure everyone was in. Jeremy could smell the faint charcoal scent of the circle even as Nul scrutinized it carefully and closely. "Good. No smudges, no breaks. Now," Nul said impressively, "we travel to Whitehorn." Raising his arms again and spreading his six fingers wide, he intoned, "Four to-gether, four to speed, to Whitehorn Mountain, at Tremien's need!"

The sound was louder this time and the feeling of pressure more pronounced, but the effect was the same as Nul's earlier vanishing: they all disappeared at once.

All except Jeremy.

He stood feeling foolish and alone in the kitchen. "Ah—Melodia?" he called out, raising only the ghost of an echo. "Anybody?"

No one answered. After a minute or two, Jeremy stepped out of the circle and shivered. Again he had the impression of being watched, and somehow he knew that someone, something, a presence, was just outside the door. Gritting his teeth, he strode across the floor and flung the door wide open.

Cold noon sun came straight down on the yard. Two bare trees stood in scant pools of shadow. Away to his left, from the barn, he heard the whicker of a horse. From the yard he heard only the rustle of wind across bare branches. "Is anyone there?" Jeremy called. After a moment of silence he closed the door again. Closed it, and after a moment, barred it. He shivered once more. It was getting cold in the house, that was the problem; he tossed a couple of logs on the fire and sat on the hearth, considering. As the fire leaped up behind him, he had an inspiration. Turning toward the blaze, Jeremy said, "Smokharin. Are you there?"

The fire burned a little more brightly.

"Smokharin, please manifest yourself."

Flame and smoke.

"Smokharin—I think Melodia needs you."

That did it. The manikin, diminished now, possibly because the fire was smaller, stood with evident belliger-ence on one of the new logs. Squat and round-headed, it reminded Jeremy irresistibly of one of those soft-sculpture dolls come to life and glowing from within. "What about Melodia?" the elemental demanded in its smoke-rush voice.

Quickly Jeremy explained what had happened. "I don't know why, but when they disappeared, I was left be-hind," he said.

The elemental, dwindling visibly as the coals beneath it cooled, paced back and forth on its firewood, leaving little scorched, smoking footprints behind. "She is at

Whitehorn," it said. "If Tremien called her, that's where she will be. You"—the eyes burned at him for a moment—"you are immune to the travel spell, maybe. Or have you paid tribute?"

"Of course I haven't paid tribute," Jeremy said. "I'm new here. But Kelada, as I understand it, hasn't paid, either, and she went."

"True, I wasn't thinking. It must be that you are somehow immune, then. But Tremien's servant will be back for you, never fear. Hmm. You think the magi may be angry with Melodia?"

"I don't know. They have no reason to be. Everything that's happened is really Sebastian's fault—and maybe mine."

With a keen look Smokharin said, "You would tell that to Tremien? To his face? And stand the consequences?"

"It's the truth. Yes, I'd tell Tremien." Jeremy felt a tightness in his chest. "And," he added, "I'd stand the consequences. Whatever they might be."

The little salamander, now no bigger than eight inches high, nodded decisively. "Get the tinderbox," it said. Jeremy found it on the windowsill where he had left it the previous night. Smokharin, having dwindled now another two inches, said, "Open it and hold it close to me."

"What are you going to do?"

"I'm going along with you to Whitehorn. Keep the box with you. I'll be asleep in it until you strike the flint." The little being poised as if to leap, then looked up. "It will be cold in the house," it warned.

"That's all right. I'll find some way to stay warm."

"Good." Another false start, then: "You like Melodia, don't you, strange human?"

"My name is Jeremy. Yes, I think I like her a great deal."

"You hurt her, ever, and I'll roast you alive from the inside out." And then Smokharin did leap, became a sudden rainbow of flame, into the box. The fire on the hearth, even the embers, went dead and gray at once, and in Jeremy's hand the wood box felt heavier—or was that only imagination again? In the new darkness Jeremy slid the top of the tinderbox shut, hefted it thoughtfully, and dropped it into the same tunic pocket that held Nul's broken tooth.

Almost as soon as he did that, he felt the change in pressure in his ears that heralded Nul's return, back in the circle behind Jeremy. The demon was beginning to look a little ragged, its orange eyes now purple-rimmed with fatigue. "You not come," he growled.

"It wasn't my fault."

"Hold still." Nul had a sort of purse hung around his shoulder. He opened it and fumbled inside for a moment before producing a soft leather envelope that held a pair of round, black-rimmed spectacles. They were not made for his face, but by holding them by one temple piece and slightly crossing his eyes, Nul could stare through them at Jeremy. He grunted, carefully folded the spectacles, put them back in the case, and dropped the case back into the purse. "You have a strange emanation," Nul muttered. The little demon began to pace, muttering to himself. "Magic not working on you. Better try another spell. Try one of mine." The creature whirled, chanted some words, and then said, "How you feel?"

"Fine," Jeremy said.

"Damn." Nul sighed, then said, "We have to go on foot. Wait. I call Tremien." Nul sat in a chair, his three-toed feet dangling clear of the floor, and glared at Jeremy. "You in trouble," he said. "Tremien hate to be called like this." Then Nul crossed his hands on his lap, chanted briefly, and said, "Hello, Mage Tremien."

From the air came a deep voice: "This had better be important, Nul."

"It is. The Jeremy not pervious to magic. Not mine, anyhow."

An ominous pause, then, "Let me speak to him."

To Jeremy, Nul said, "Cross hands. Good. Now ready. Mage Tremien? The Jeremy ready."

"Young man," the voice boomed, now seemingly focused on Jeremy, "can you possibly explain why one of my strongest spells failed with you?"

"I don't know," Jeremy responded. "Maybe it's because I'm not even from Thaumia to begin—"

"Answer me!"

Nul blinked. "*Is* answering, Mage," he said.

The voice fell quiet again. "One moment."

It proved to be a very long moment. Then the deep, disembodied voice boomed out, "Transmute and ensorcel it, I read only Sebastian-sign! But everyone here assures me that isn't Sebastian at all. And I'd be able to *hear*

Sebastian." An ill-tempered grunt. "Very well, Nul. Bring the man here overland."

"Long march," protested Nul with some indignation.

"I can't help that. There's a war on, you know—wait a bit."

Nul glared hard at Jeremy. Jeremy shrugged.

The voice resumed shortly: "All right. Melodia has a horse, Whisper. She's arranged for you to ride him. What? Sorry, her. That's the best we can do. You should be here in three days."

"Three?" Nul squawked. "Four at least, Mage."

"Three, if you start now. Nul, guard the prisoner well."

Nul grunted.

"Answer me!"

"All right, all right! I see he hurt nobody."

"More to the point," the deep voice said dryly, "make sure nobody hurts him. Leave. Now."

After a moment's quiet Jeremy said, "Is he gone?"

Nul slid off the chair. "Damn," he said. "Have to ride all the way to Whitehorn. Three days. Hardly have time to eat or drink. Come on. Get horse ready."

"Uh—there's something else you should know."

Nul glared. "What?"

Jeremy shrugged. "I can't ride a horse, either."

Tremien had advised the two of them to leave at once, but preparations had to be made, and *at once* stretched into a couple of hours. Nul, for one thing, was unprepared for an outdoor winter journey: he wore a dark blue tunic and trousers, sturdy enough, but scant protection against the cold. And of course he wore no shoes.

Jeremy found the trunk Melodia had mentioned in a squarish, windowless room—hardly more than an outsized closet, really—across the hall from her bedchamber. He found for himself a fur robe, black but trimmed dramatically in white, that fit him perfectly. He had less luck trying to find something scaled to Nul's size, but he finally did dig out a short jacket (had Sebastian *lived* here, Jeremy wondered, or was he just uncommonly careless about where he left his clothes?) that swallowed Nul up from neck to mid-calf. The sleeves, because of Nul's disproportionately long arms, were four inches too short, but that couldn't be helped.

Sebastian seemed to have left behind no riding boots

or anything like them, only the black slippers Jeremy wore and a pair of carpet slippers with swirling floral designs worked into them. Jeremy solved Nul's footwear problem as well as he could by giving the little creature three pairs of socks to wear, one over the other. With them on, Nul padded around in high ill temper, looking like a grotesque toddler got up to play in the snow. Jeremy took from the trunk one other outfit and a change of stockings and underwear for himself. Then from a shelf in the room he took four blankets. With one of them he improvised a sort of bedroll containing the clothing.

Food, Nul said, was no problem. "Eat along the way. Plenty of inns."

"I have no money."

"I have."

The really big problem was dapple-gray. Whisper seemed gentle enough and willing enough, but beyond a doubt she was, as horses go, rather stupid. She was no help at all in getting the saddle on, and since Nul was so small, Jeremy had to bear the whole responsibility. He tried to follow the little demon's directions carefully, but somehow things got mixed. The blanket was wrinkled and the saddle had to be taken back off. Then the saddle was ill-placed and slid off the other side while Jeremy stooped to try to cinch it. Nul blistered the air with arcane curses. Whisper turned her head to give Jeremy a big-eyed gaze of commiseration.

Finally the horse was bridled and saddled to Nul's grudging satisfaction. The demon had found a small bin of grain and sat on it, taking handfuls out to munch on as he gave his instructions. Now he hopped off the bin and waddled over to the horse. He took a complete tour, circling Whisper with a critical eye. He tugged the girth, tightened it, and tested the knot securing the bedrolls behind the saddle. "That may do," he grunted at last. "Get on. Not from that side!"

Whisper shifted her footing as Jeremy climbed aboard, complicating the process, but he managed to swing his leg over, and before he knew it, he was sitting on the horse. Nul, far below now, stretched a hand up. "Help me."

Jeremy swung him up. The demon rode pillion, his right arm hooked around Jeremy's middle. "Now we go," he said.

Opening and the reclosing the barn door while on

horseback was only the first problem. In the stableyard
Whisper suddenly twitched her ears, neighed, and stamped.
"Whoa!" Jeremy cried in desperation, calling on the only
horse word in his vocabulary. "Easy!"

"Something bother her," Nul said. "She sense something."

"How do I—woop!—calm her down?"

But Whisper calmed herself down, stood a moment,
blew through her nostrils, and became docile. "Better
go," Nul counseled, and Jeremy goaded her with his
heels. Whisper fell into a gentle, slow walk. Jeremy wobbled from side to side precariously for the first few minutes. At last he found the rhythm of Whisper's gentle
amble, and then he had no immediate fears of falling off.

However, he was beginning to notice that the saddle
pinched his buttocks together and chafed the inside of his
thighs uncomfortably. He tried to ignore both sensations,
and for the first time really began to notice the countryside around them. "Which way are we headed?" he asked.

"North and west. Can tell from the sun," Nul said.
"Not much daylight left today. We get to inn at Drover's
Ford, though. Rest there tonight, then travel."

They rode along a grassy and level country lane, between hills of dry winter grass or rolling fields, furrowed
but bare under the winter sky. Birds sang in the trees
around them, and a small flock of them, straw-yellow
and the size of pigeons, took off from knee-high grass at
the edge of the lane as they passed. "Trouble-me-nots,"
Nul said as the wings whirred. "Too bad we have no time
to hunt. Good eating."

"Why are they called that?" Jeremy asked, just before
one of the birds called out in a clear treble and answered
his question for him. "Trouble-me-not," it seemed to
say. "Trouble-me, trouble-me, trouble-me-not today."

Jeremy merely said, "Oh."

The encounter led him to ask Nul the names of other
things they passed, trees and plants and small animals.
He learned the names of five trees: the spreading black-
heart, something like an oak but smaller; the tall, bare
tremble-leaf, graceful in the light afternoon breeze; the
evergreen quickthorn, low, with spiky, glossy-green leaves;
the pomminut, rough-barked and many-branched, with a
few nuts still clinging to a twig here and there; and the
windmurmur, another evergreen, very piney in appear-

ance but alive with the smallest puff of air. He learned
about grasses, the wayturf on the lane, the taller and
hardier sheafblade of the pastures to the sides. He learned
the name of the brownstreak, an animal smaller than a
cat that once dashed out of their path and into the
sheltering undergrowth.

Jeremy had the feeling that Nul was only humoring
him. His companion was distant, absorbed in something
other than the wildlife they met on their way. Once, at
least, Jeremy felt Nul twist backward for several moments. "What are you doing?" he asked the demon.

"Looking back."

"What do you see?"

The spindly arm with its three-fingered hand tightened
around Jeremy's stomach again. "Nothing."

"What did you *think* you saw?"

"Shadow. Nothing. Hope nothing. Move faster."

Jeremy tickled Whisper's sides again with his heels,
rocked back as she quickened her slow trot to a canter.
Behind him Nul squawked a protest, and Jeremy muttered, "Sorry."

And all the time his butt ached more and more.

They passed a few lonely farmhouses, made of gray
and white stone, most of them, with heavy thatched
roofs. Chickens pecked about in the yard of one, and
Jeremy asked about them. "We have the same kind of
birds back on Earth," he explained. "And we have horses,
too, and goats and sheep. Why?"

"How should I know?" Nul grumped, but by now
Jeremy had learned that the little creature enjoyed show-
ing off its knowledge after an initial show of displeasure.
Sure enough, after a few moments Nul said, "Hear
Tremien speak of it once. There some connection between
Thaumia and other worlds. Yours close, used to be closer.
Closer many, many cycles back in history. Thaumia beings
visit there, sometime. Bring animals back, I guess."

"We have legends of magical creatures," Jeremy said.
"I suppose that would explain them."

"Mm. Or it could be our worlds once were the same.
Thaumia went its way, your world went another. That
might have happened, too. Hard to say."

"I guess so," Jeremy said, trying without notable success to shift his hips in the saddle. They had been going
downhill for some time, and ahead across their path a

small river meandered, silver and red in the afternoon
sun. The lane led to a little arched stone bridge. Without
a murmur or sign of complaint Whisper walked steadily
toward it. Jeremy suddenly asked, "Nul, what are you?"

"Fool who thought working for wizard good job."

Jeremy laughed. "I've had the same feeling about my
job, from time to time. But what sort of creature are
you? You aren't human."

"Nah, nah."

"Melodia called you a demon."

Nul laughed his urfing laugh. "Not demon. Demons
mythical beings. Nah, I a burrower, a digger."

"Like a dwarf?"

"Huh-uh. Dwarf look more peoply. I a pika."

"Pika?" Imitating Nul, Jeremy pronounced it *PEE-ka.*

"Uh. Used to be tribes of pika, millions of pika. Not
so many now."

"What happened?"

"Time." Behind him, Nul sighed. "You want hear
this?"

"Sure," Jeremy said.

Their shadows grew long behind them on the right as
they rode north and west and Nul spoke. Jeremy, his
concentration broken by the uncomfortable saddle and
by his own burgeoning saddle sores, tried hard to listen
to the pika's tale.

Nul (as he explained to Jeremy) was a deep-digging
pika, one of a tribe of two hundred or so that once dwelled
far beneath the Bone Mountains, in the distant north.
They lived simple lives, fishing the underground rivers in
the caverns they favored, occasionally going out on the surface to raid the widely scattered human farms, practicing
their simple magics, singing their ancient songs, and shaping
the minerals and jewels they found to their own delight.

Nul, one of the younger pika and more adventurous,
perhaps, than most, liked to spend his free time above-
ground. Generally pika children liked playing tricks on
humans, but this usually wore off with adolescence, around
the age of a hundred and fifty or so. This didn't happen
in Nul's case; he spent long hona setting up elaborate
practical jokes on the farmers in the area, nothing really
harmful, but irritating little touches just to let them know
he was in the area. "Tangle skeins of wool left to dry in

sun," he explained. "Sometimes take one farmer's calf, put in other farmer's pasture. Sometimes cast illusion and disguise self as priest, give farmer penance like making tower of all rocks in his fields. Little things."

Inevitably, one farmer caught him with a powerful trap spell. Nul refused to talk much about that, or about what the farmer did to him, but he implied that the next several years he spent in slavery, doing the work of farm animals and treated worse.

"Then great battle came," Nul said. "I didn't know about war, even, but war was going on then. Came like storm in sky, came in fire and lightning. Great wizard battle all along Bone Mountains. Hobs came through, ugly, nasty things. Kill my farmer, kill the family. I hide, they not notice me. They eat all horses, everything."

Nul fell into a long silence. "I go back to caverns," he said at last. "Through passage only pika-folk know. No good. Empty, all empty. Family gone, tribe gone. Evil there. I come out again."

Hungry and afraid, Nul approached a camp of soldiers. "I not know what it was then. Just human men, but they have fire and food. And I cold and hungry."

For a few days Nul made sporadic, skulking raids for sustenance. Then, he was caught again, this time by a wizard. "He scare me," Nul admitted. "Say he turn me into something nasty. I fall on my knees, I beg. Wizard ask, 'Why should I spare you?' "

Another long silence fell before Nul continued: "I say, 'Don't spare. Family dead, friends dead. Kill last pika of Bone Mountains.' "

"Wizard look at me long time. 'No,' wizard say at last. 'Never waste life, for no magic can bring back a life flown away. You will work for me.' So now Nul work for Tremien." The little creature sighed again. "Look for friends, family, never find. Tremien try to help, but some bad magic had swept through caverns, he could find no pika trace either. We not know what happen, where they go. Nul lonely sometimes."

Ahead of him, rocking on the horse, aching in joint and flesh, Jeremy said quietly, "Man lonely sometimes, too, Nul."

Nul spoke little of the war, an affair of wizards, men, and other surface dwellers, but he did indicate that Sebastian had had no part in it. "Nah, nah, that long ago, before Sebastian born, probably. That war over long time back."

"But Tremien spoke of a war going on now."

"Going on in his head," Nul growled. "Down there is inn. We stop there for tonight."

After they had crossed the bridge, the lane had turned more westerly, and for some time they had been following the line of the little river off to their left. Ahead of them, where it joined a much broader stream, a cluster of houses huddled. "A town?" Jeremy asked.

"Drover's Ford. We cross river here tomorrow. Sleep tonight."

They found an inn, the Goose and Bow, where a young ostler helped Jeremy down. He found standing almost as painful as sitting, and after the hours on horseback, his legs hardly agreed to work. Still, he made no real complaint, and when the boy handed him the bedrolls he tried to look nonchalant, swinging them up to his shoulder with what he hoped was a little panache. Nul had already waddled into the inn proper, and when Jeremy joined him, he found the pika already hard at work bargaining with a great tub of a man. "You'll take up a whole room between the two of you," the fat man roared. "Has to be a silver at least."

"Without meals? Five coppers for the room, three for supper and breakfast," Nul said.

The fat man lifted his pudgy hands to the heavens. "Do you hear?" he asked of the ceiling. "Do you hear how they try to impoverish an honest innkeeper? Eleven coppers for the room. Meals extra."

Nul shook his head. "Too much by twice. Ten coppers all told, room and board."

"And my wife and daughters will be on the streets tomorrow, begging crusts of bread. A silver piece for food and room, drink extra."

They settled, finally, on eleven for everything but drink. Jeremy, who had not spoken at all through the exchange but had stood with the bedrolls on his shoulder, returning the stolid gazes of a dozen or so heavyset men sitting in little groups of three or four at scattered tables in the dining room, eating, drinking, or smoking long-stemmed pipes, was relieved to find that the room was just down a short corridor. He did not think his legs could manage stairs.

"What's wrong with you?" Nul demanded as Jeremy tossed the bedrolls onto a great, plain bed and groaned.

Jeremy put his hands against the small of his back and tried to stand straight. His back popped, but he failed. "I'm not used to horses," he grunted.

Nul rolled his orange eyes. "Let's eat," he said. "Then bed early. We have time to make up."

The innkeeper at least set a good board. Jeremy and Nul had huge bowls of venison stew, or stew with something very like venison in it at least, followed by a couple of flagons each of a pleasant, light ale. Nul seemed to elicit no surprise from any of the other customers, and not one of them spoke to the pika or to Jeremy. "Farmers," Nul muttered from the corner of his mouth. "Nothing to do this time of year but get drunk and tell lies."

Jeremy looked around. The jollity at the Goose and Bow was, to say the least, subdued. Here and there a voice would be raised in querulous comment—"I tell'ee, worm oil's the best thing for a stopped-up sow. Put'er right no time atall"—but there was little laughter and almost no curiosity.

Nul indicated that it was time to retire, and, following the pika down the corridor, Jeremy was surprised to find his steps a bit unsteady. The ale had given him a buzz. He wasn't really drunk, but he felt definitely mellow. That wore off a bit as the two undressed for bed. "You've got a tail!" Jeremy exclaimed.

Nul, with his trousers down around his knees, looked over his shoulder at Jeremy. "And you've got blisters on your arse," he growled. His tail was really pretty short, a furred stub the length of Jeremy's little finger, but it added to the overall impression of inhumanity about the creature. Nul slipped beneath the blankets on the far side of the bed. "Sleep now," he said. "Try your stomach. Might be less painful."

On his stomach proved to be the only way that Jeremy could sleep. He dreamed, though, of sitting on Whisper as she ambled along, and he felt again in his hands the tug of her bridle. He was just dreaming that she was brushing him against tree branches when he woke up smothering. A hand clamped down tight on his mouth—a three-fingered hand. When he stirred, a quick whisper came in his ear: "Someone in room. Quiet." Nul's breath was like a breeze off a compost heap. It brought tears to

Jeremy's eyes. The hand eased off, and next to him Jeremy felt the pika tense. Nul was whispering something very softly.

Light flooded the room, sourceless yellow light, and Nul sprang out of bed at the same time, crying "Ha!"

The empty room mocked him. Nul shook his great basketball of a head. "Thought something here," he muttered. "Something bad." He clambered back up into bed. "Just dream. Gone now. We sleep, leave early-early." Nul turned on his side, pulling most of the blankets tight around him.

"Hey," Jeremy protested, tugging them back. "What about the light?"

"Minor spell. It die in short time. Close eyes."

Jeremy did, certain that he would sleep no more that evening. Thanks to the enchantment of exhaustion, he fell asleep at once.

He woke next morning stiff and aching, and he did scant justice to the innkeeper's breakfast of milk, bread, eggs, and ham. Nul quibbled a little about Whisper's feed bill, but not much, and the two travelers set forth in the deep darkness preceding dawn. A waning moon, much larger than Earth's moon, rode blue and pale low in the western sky. The firmament was sprinkled with stars, in configurations absolutely alien to Jeremy. With good reason, he reflected.

They headed north and west that day, climbing into hillier country where the farms were even more widely scattered, the inns smaller and more cramped, the farmers more dour and taciturn. Nul brooded and spoke little, and Jeremy suffered from saddle sores. Only Whisper seemed to take the journey in stride, her steady pace never slackening.

After a second night at another inn and another early start, daylight caught them climbing a winding road among rising hills. Again Nul seemed uneasy, turning from time to time to crane back over the way they had come, and once or twice Whisper tensed or did a quick, skittish double-step before settling back into her normal pace.

"Don't know," Nul grunted. "Feel like someone watching us."

"I've had that feeling a lot," Jeremy said.

Nul laughed. "You? You with no magic, no spells? How you know, human?"

"Humans have their moments, pika."

"Mm." They jogged along quietly for a while, came to a place where the road made a sharp turn around the neck of a hill, and then Nul said: "Stop. We see."

The road had been narrow, with steep shoulders slanting up and down into evergreen forest, but on the far side of the turn the uphill shoulder had leveled. At Nul's direction Jeremy urged Whisper that way, behind some low brush and stunted trees. Nul hopped off easily. Jeremy groaned his way down. "Tie horse," Nul said. "Not like that! Here, I show you." The three-fingered hands made a quick and dexterous knot. "Follow. Quiet."

The two of them climbed the hill and, shielded by trees, came down the other side to a point where they overlooked the road. The hillside here was practically a cliff, and Jeremy felt safer clinging to the trunk of a spearleaf than trusting to his own aching legs.

Nul gestured for quiet. Then, without a word, he pointed ahead and down. Jeremy followed, at first saw nothing, and then realized what he was looking at: a shadow, a detached and ownerless shadow the size of a man on horseback coming slowly along the road. He looked up, but the sky showed no cloud.

Nul unslung the pouch from his shoulder. Keeping his eyes on the road, he felt inside, pulled out the spectacles, and looked through them. Jeremy heard the pika's quick inrush of breath.

The spectacles went back in, and a stubby black stick, thicker than a pencil but about as long, came out. The shadow was near now, and in a second it would pass them. Nul tensed to spring, the wand tight in his right hand.

The shadow stopped, wavered. A flash of light and heat—lightning, Jeremy thought, but it couldn't be lightning from a clear sky—washed over them, and Nul toppled backward, then rolled, tumbled to the road.

"Nul!" Jeremy snatched up the black rod from the spot where the pika had dropped it and leaped. He hit hard in the dusty road, his ankles and knees exploding in pain. The pika, orange eyes wide, had thrown up both hands. "Here!" Jeremy thrust the wand into the left hand.

Nul spat a guttural phrase and pointed the wand at vacancy. For a bare instant the whole visible world went black, replaced by the ghostly white sketch of a monstrous thing on a monstrous mount, a thing reeling back in anger and frustration—

And then it was gone and the world was back. In the winter sunshine, crouched in the road, Nul slumped. "Thank you," he said.

"What was it?"

"An evil thing."

"But what happened?"

"It hit us with shock spell." The orange eyes turned in speculation toward Jeremy. "You not feel?"

"I felt something, but—"

"Mm. It have no real effect on you." Nul got to his feet, brushing dust from his coat and trousers. "Not hurt. You?"

"Skinned my knees. The—the evil thing. Did you kill it?"

"Nah, nah. Revealed it. Travels in its own dark, cannot abide light of day." Nul extended a hand, and Jeremy pretended to use it to help himself stand. "We go now. Hurry-hurry. May be more of them." Nul shivered. "They may be more prepared."

Whisper awaited them, all patience. As soon as Jeremy had painfully remounted her and they had regained the road, Nul said from behind him, "Almost safe now. Over next hilltop you see Whitehorn. All that country protected by Tremien's spells."

Jeremy goggled as they topped the crest of the hill, for in the distance was a purple line of jagged mountains looming high above them. "We're going there?" he asked.

Behind him Nul grunted, "See the tallest? There, a little to the left. That Whitehorn. Castle up at peak. Can't see now, too far."

"We've got to climb that?" Jeremy asked.

Nul sighed. "Too slow. Little faster now. We late."

Jeremy thought of more evil "things" coming back, perhaps angry. He flicked the reins and Whisper picked up her pace a little. Looking ahead, Jeremy despaired. He didn't see how they could possibly reach the peak of Whitehorn in less than a week, if that. And—he shifted his weight again—by that time he expected to be dead of terminal saddle sores.

He felt a little better by midday. The lane had become a road, hard-packed and well-tended, and somehow they seemed to make much better progress than he could have predicted. Already they were on the flanks of the great mountain, going upward. At first they rode under boughs of evergreens, but the trees became sparser and stunted, and by mid-afternoon, they had left the last of them behind. Above were bare rock and snow, and at the crown of the snow they now could see the yellow walls and turrets of a fortress. "Home," Nul muttered.

At a bend in the road Jeremy looked back the way they had come, across a broad valley, watered by a wide, shallow river that rushed and chuckled over time-worn stones. "How can we be going this fast?" he asked Nul. "It must be miles across—" He fell silent for a moment. "An enchantment on the road?" he guessed.

"Tremien is a powerful mage," Nul told him. "Hard to put magic into small object. Harder to put magic in large one. Think of this: whole valley around mountain is magical. Tremien magicked it, put good speed there for friends, put peace, put healing. You still hurt?"

"Of course I—hmm. No. No, I guess I don't."

"Tremien."

Whisper didn't tire at all. Indeed, if anything, she picked her feet up a little higher as the road wound and climbed. The road remained clear of snow, even when it heaped up cold and white chin-high on either side of them, even when it piled even deeper and they rode between blue-shadowed ramparts of snow that frosted their breath and stung their noses. For what seemed a long time they rode blind. Then the walls fell away and they came out on a high plateau. Again Jeremy looked back, and he caught his breath. Far off to the left the red sun balanced on the rim of the world. Between it and the mountain fields rolled, and little hills, and rivers snaked, bloodied by the dying sun. The air was achingly clear up here, and to Jeremy it seemed he could see forever. The bleakness of the winter landscape, and the forbidding beauty, made him shiver.

Then Whisper turned a sharp curve, clattered up another short incline, and they found themselves outside a massive, closed gate, wooden and iron-barred, set into a thirty-foot-high stone wall barring their way. It was sandy-red, with hardly a join where stone was laid on stone. Two towers flanked the gate, crowned at the top by frowning, gigantic gargoyles carved from the same stone.

"Home," Nul said again.

Jeremy took a deep breath. The left gargoyle was stirring, stonily. "Who's there?" it asked in a voice like the rattle of pebbles falling down the mountainside.

"Open up," Nul called. "We tired and hungry."

"What," asked the gargoyle, "is the word of passing?"

The other one moved its head to look at its neighbor, its head grating on its neck like a turning millstone. "Oh, it's only Nul," it said. "Let's open up."

Stone eyes regarded stone eyes with great hauteur. "I am only following procedure. If you don't like it—"

"Upstart," the right-hand gargoyle snorted. It leered down in a friendly sort of way at Jeremy. "Fred there was quarried from a late Tertiary deposit," it confided. "Ah, youth, youth."

"If you're going to bring our families into it—"

"Open up!" roared Nul.

"Well, you don't have to get snippy," the first gargoyle sniffed. "Fellow just doing his duty, after all." The wooden gate groaned open on hinges that seemed to want oil badly.

Jeremy automatically twitched the bridle, and Whisper plodded through. They crossed a narrow courtyard—the gate boomed back closed before they made it all the way across—and paused in front of the great palace itself, a many-turreted fortress of the same stone as the wall and the gargoyles, enormous in the growing twilight, great mullioned windows already aglow. Nul swung off the horse. "This it. Come on. Someone will look after horse for us."

Jeremy swung his leg over the horse—wonder of wonders, the raw spots on the inside of his thighs seemed healed, and his barked knees, too—and stood beside Nul. In front of them was a door the size of Jeremy's living-room floor. "Nul," Jeremy whispered, "are there any more, ah, things inside? Like at the wall?"

"Nah, nah," Nul said, leading the way. "Nothing here to be afraid of." The sun was down, but in the twilight Nul's backward grin shone startling, white, and still gap-toothed. "Nothing but Tremien," he said.

CHAPTER 7

THE ENORMOUS DOOR swung open on ponderous hinges, and a woman, diminutive by contrast, welcomed them in. Jeremy shifted the bedrolls that he carried across his shoulder and stepped over the threshold. "Kelada!" he cried in surprise, for the thief wore a long white gown and a tiara of flashing stones.

She scowled at him. "Can I help it if Tremien's taste in clothes is two hundred years out of date? Come in, it's cold."

They stood in a vast arched entryway, the groined ceiling almost lost overhead in gloom and mystery. Behind them the door closed with hardly a sound. "This way," Kelada said, lifting the hem of her dress with her left hand.

"I know the way," Nul grumbled, but he plodded along beside Jeremy nonetheless. At a more human-sized doorway, the pika grunted, "Wait." He propped his rear against the nearest wall and bent to strip the three layers of stockings from his feet. "Ah," he sighed, letting the balls of sock drop. "Have somebody burn these."

Then Kelada opened the door. They walked into a room ablaze with cheery light, hung with thick, rich tapestries in glowing colors. Jeremy saw unicorns, dragons, gryphons, other beasts—imaginary or real in this world?—worked into the wall hangings. One wall, pierced by many arched, leaded windows, looked out eastward into the courtyard. At the center of the room was a great table already set with places for four and piled high with food. Melodia rose from the table as they entered. "So," she said, "we're all here."

Nul waddled straight for a specially built chair, its seat considerably higher than those around it, and clambered in. "Starved," he said. "Where Tremien?"

"He knew you would be hungry. He wants us to eat first. He'll see us all afterward." Melodia took Jeremy's hand. "Come, sit."

Kelada sat across the table from Jeremy. Despite her new clothing she ate in the same old businesslike way, not sloppily, but with no nonsense about extra refinement, either. "How is Whisper?" Melody asked.

"Good horse," Nul said. He was tucking into a platter of something light blue and lumpy, and licking his nonexistent lips with his black, snaky tongue. "Mare fine. Stable boys see to her now, give her rest."

"Tell me all about the trip," Melodia said, and so Jeremy did. He left out one thing—their encounter with the shadow-creature on the hill—when Nul surreptitiously tugged his arm under cover of the table.

"And then," he finished, "we reached the gate and the . . . uh—"

"Keepers," Nul supplied. "Fred and Busby."

"The keepers—Busby?"

Nul shrugged. "They pick their own names. Don't blame me."

"Anyway, they let us in, and here we are." Jeremy helped himself to another slice of roast turkey breast. "What about Tremien?"

"We've hardly seen him," Melodia said. "More wine?"

As she poured, Kelada said, "He wants you, Jeremy. Not us. We talked to him once, the day we arrived. Since then we've been prisoners."

"Hardly that," Melodia said. "We are guests."

"Try to leave this wing," Kelada returned. "Well, we should know all about it after supper."

"Where is everybody?" Jeremy asked. "This is an awfully big place. Does Tremien live here alone?"

"Nah, nah," Nul mumbled. He swept a finger around the rim of his plate, capturing the last few drops of blue gravy. After he had sucked his finger clean, he said, "Tremien have family here, retainers. Many, many people. They all in main halls. This guest hall here. You see later."

"The sooner the better." Jeremy drained the last of his wine. "Now what?"

"Now you and I clean up. Then Tremien call."

Nul showed Jeremy to a small room with a single bed and an adjoining bath. "A medieval motel," Jeremy murmured. "Better with a window, though." Instead of a window, there were more tapestries, twining vines, prancing stallions, brawny men with swords coming to the aid of distressed young ladies—and in one case, a young lady armed with a glowing wand coming to the aid of a distressed, brawny man.

The bathroom, like Melodia's, boasted running water and another luxury: a shower. True, the shower head, a round-bellied little brass monstrosity with the body of an obese monkey and the cranium of an eagle, perched on the wall and disgorged the water through its mouth, but at least it didn't speak to Jeremy, and the water it provided was hot. He found another surprise on a counter beside the sink (this sink, he noted, was equipped with two hand pumps—one for hot, one for cold, he guessed): a real toothbrush. He had been making do with his finger, and it was a welcome luxury.

Feeling much refreshed, he dressed in his change of clothes. He could have used a razor, for the real whiskers sprouting now tickled him almost as much as his dreamed disguise beard had, but he had none. Still, he felt more confident about meeting Tremien after the shower and change.

Nul knocked on the door almost as soon as Jeremy had finished dressing. The women waited in the corridor with the pika. "Come now," he said. "Tremien see you in lesser council hall."

They went west, as far as Jeremy could tell, through a thick door. As soon as they had passed through, the sound of music reached their ears, elaborate string music coming from somewhere ahead. "Have to pass great room," Nul grunted. "Don't speak to anybody. Follow me."

Through another door, and into a huge chamber, with perhaps a hundred or more people milling about, speaking together, sipping wine, laughing, listening to the musicians. Jeremy had time only for a quick glance around, at the men wearing gold-braided tunics and trousers and carrying swords at their sides, at the women sparkling in bright colors and jewels. Nul kept straight ahead, walking alongside one wall, and out through another door. The crowd had grown a little quieter, Jeremy noticed, as they passed through.

Down another short hall, then a pause as Nul rapped softly at the door.

"Come," said the deep voice that Jeremy recalled as Tremien's.

They passed into a study. Three walls of it were shelves, running from floor to ceiling and crammed with ponderous books, leather-backed and smelling of libraries. The third wall was curtained, but through a part in the center of the curtains Jeremy could see a tall, leaded window. The light in the room was soft and subdued, and he could not fully make out the figure seated behind the desk, its back to the windows. He could see a nimbus of white hair. "So," the figure said, "you are Jeremy Sebastian Moon."

"Tremien?"

The shadowed head bowed. "I am. More light?"

"Perhaps a little."

Tremien raised one hand, and the light intensified. He was an old man, stooped, with skin the color of saddle leather. His white hair bushed out around a pate bald on top, and he wore a beard even longer than Sebastian's had been. His face was lined with age and care, but determination showed in his carriage, and his eyes were sharp and knowing. He wore a loose, simple robe, faded purple. For a long moment he inspected Jeremy with a close, critical scrutiny. "The resemblance is remarkable," he said at last. "You might almost be Sebastian."

Nul padded around the desk and held something out. "Better take a look."

Absently Tremien took the leather case from Nul, extracted the spectacles, and put them on. "Astonishing," he said.

"Mage," Nul murmured, "shadow-man attack us. His magic not work on Jeremy."

"I am not surprised." Tremien gazed at Jeremy over the tops of the spectacles. "Young man, you have a great deal of *mana* about you—of a type I have never seen before. I daresay no one else in Thaumia has, either."

Kelada, standing between Jeremy and Melodia, fidgeted. "You said you would decide what to do about us as soon as he got here," she said.

Tremien's eyes did not leave Jeremy, but he nodded. "Patience," he said. "I have to know all about Jeremy first. Nul, have someone bring chairs in. Bring one for yourself, as well."

Nul hurried away. Jeremy took a step forward. "Sebastian took my place in the real world—"

The wizard smiled and took off the spectacles. As he folded them he murmured, "Real world? This world is as real as yours, Jeremy Sebastian Moon, and as real as billions upon billions of other realities, in other universes. Pray don't insult us with unreality."

"Sorry," Jeremy said. "But the point is, he's in my place, doing God knows what. I have to get back there."

"Hmm. Yes. If that can be managed. Ah, here are the chairs."

A young man, taller than Jeremy but thinner, brought them in, two at a time. He gave them a curious glance, but did not speak as he arranged the four chairs in a semicircle before Tremien's desk. He left, still without having spoken. Nul climbed into one of the chairs and sat with feet dangling.

"Make yourselves comfortable," Tremien said, waving the others into their seats. "This may be a long evening."

It turned out to be very long. Tremien, all patience, insisted on hearing the entire story from the beginning, and each of them had a part of it to tell. Jeremy went all the way back to his nightmares, to the time of the exchange—Tremien, thumb and forefinger pressed against his eyelids, nodded at that and murmured, "The time of exaltations. That tells us when the transfer took place: six weeks and three days ago now. Continue."

Kelada took up the thread then and spoke of Niklas File's exile, and her own, and of how they met Sebastian in the Between. At one point, as she spoke of Niklas and how he had changed, Tremien frowned. "I thought his exile was a hasty decision," he told her. "True, he had murdered in the course of his thievery, and his victim was the son of a mage. Still, this wanton shuffling of people into the Between—it has to stop." Kelada continued the story, telling of Sebastian's disappearance with the mirror he had created, of Jeremy's coming.

And then Jeremy had to tell of the death of Niklas File. He did it levelly, with no adornment. A silence fell as he reached that point. Tremien stirred. "If it is consolation to you, Niklas File was a man already condemned. And if what I suspect happened to him in the Between did in fact happen, his death was a release, not a tragedy." The long old fingers waved. "However, that is nothing to you. You must work out your own remorse. Pray continue."

Jeremy and Kelada together told of their attempt to travel to Thaumia, of the mirror in Melodia's bedchamber, and of their final success. Melodia joined the tale then, explaining the way that Sebastian had brought the mirror to her and the way he had used it in the two years before his exile. The wizard listened quietly, and when she had finished, he said only, "Do you still love the renegade, my dear?"

"No," Melodia said. "At least—no, I don't think so."

The old eyes were penetrating. "But you are not certain." Tremien stroked his white beard. "The ways of the heart are hidden even to a wizard's eye," he murmured. After a short silence he added: "I sensed a change in the magic of Thaumia that night. I sent Nul to find out what was afoot—as you know, my first thought was that Sebastian Magister had somehow returned—and he brought you all here."

"There is something else," Nul said. "Something that happened on the way here." He explained about his and Jeremy's feelings of being watched, pursued, and about the shadow on the road.

Tremien picked up the spectacles in their case and toyed with them. "I feared as much. I am not the only one who felt the change in the lines of force. Someone else pursues our friend."

"Who?" Jeremy asked.

"That I cannot tell you. But it is bound to be a servant of the Great Dark One, for no one else would send such a messenger." Tremien slowly pushed up from his chair. He was stooped and slight, and his head would barely come up to Jeremy's shoulder. With hands clasped behind him the magician turned to look through the barely parted curtains. "Monstrous evil is shaping," he said. "The dark is growing stronger. I wondered about the source of that strength." He turned slowly, as if bearing a weight on his shoulders. "I think," he said, "it may be in your world now. One end of it, at any rate."

"What is that?" Jeremy asked.

Tremien pushed a curtain aside, looked out into dark night, and let the curtain fall back into place. "The others on the council will be here tomorrow. I fear we can do nothing more tonight, except try to sleep." Turning away from the window, Tremien permitted himself the suggestion of a smile. "I have not answered your question. You wanted to know the source of magic that is in your world. Have you not guessed? Sebastian was always reckless. And always fascinated by duplications and reflections. He seems to have made a hobby of creating mirrors." The old wizard came around the desk, his faded robe billowing around his legs, and stood over Melodia. "He left one with you, my dear. I know of at least two others now, and I suspect a third. One, of course, he carried into Jeremy's world. That, I think, is somehow increasing the power of our enemies. Another mirror is in the hands of the Hidden Hag of Illsmere."

Into a silence deep as dark water, Nul dropped words like four heavy stones: "Where is the third?"

Tremien sighed and leaned back against the desk. "I fear," he said, "it is in the hands of the Great Dark One. And if it is"—the old eyes suddenly seemed haunted and weary—"if it is, God help us all."

Jeremy was full of questions, but Tremien dismissed them all. "Tomorrow," he said. "I can do nothing without the council, anyway. Jeremy, I am sorry to have to isolate you tonight, and you, my dears, but that is an unpleasant necessity. Go now. I promise that your curiosity will be satisfied."

Nul escorted them back—in the Great Hall, only a few men were left awake, standing in front of a low fire and chatting, and they gave the newcomers sharp glances as they passed—but the pika stopped at the doorway that led to their hall. "Go now," he told Jeremy. "Rest and sleep."

"How did I do?" Jeremy asked.

With a frown Nul said, "Hard to tell. Think he liked you, though. You not a frog, anyway."

Jeremy stared at the closing door until Melodia said, "It was only Nul's joke."

Melodia had the first room on the hall, Kelada the second, and Jeremy the third. The black-haired sorceress entered her room without saying more than "good night," but Kelada paused outside her door. "I have to get out of here," she muttered. "This is no place for a thief."

"Especially one," Jeremy said, "who faces possible banishment."

Kelada's smile was rueful. "True. But I fear that less than I did. Tremien speaks in the council with the loudest voice, they say, and he at least is not in favor of exiling me again." She rustled the white gown around her. "These clothes are driving me insane. I must look a fool."

"No. You look—you are very attractive."

"With this face?"

"There's nothing much wrong with your face," Jeremy said. "Only in how you think about it, that's all."

Kelada looked away from him. "Melodia is beautiful."

"Yes."

"I wish—"

"What?"

"Nothing. Good night." And she was gone. Jeremy went into his own room thoughtfully. His travel clothes lay draped across a chair, where he had taken them off. He straightened them, and in doing so felt the heaviness of the tunic. He had forgotten about the tinderbox and Smokharin. He took it out of the pocket, took, too, the broken tooth of Nul, and put both on a round table beside the bed, making a mental note to give the tinderbox to Melodia in the morning. An oil lamp, this one scented like balsam, burned on the table, its flame clear and friendly. Wondering if he were sending some other fire elemental into a doze, Jeremy turned the wick low, undressed, and climbed between the sheets. They were so soft against his bare skin that it almost hurt, and it occurred to him that this was the first time in weeks— more than six weeks, if time here agreed with time back on Earth, and if Tremien were right—that he had slept between sheets.

Six weeks. Christmas over and gone, and New Year's, if six weeks had really gone by. Brown-needled trees piled at curbside, forlorn aluminum icicles stirring in the exhaust of passing cars. Paper-cone hats in the gutters, stepped on and flattened, their colors bleached out, no merriment left in them now, no wishes for a happy new year. The new year, if it ran true to form, was already tarnished, all the new worn off, rubbed off under the friction of the same old problems. By now even Cassie would be writing the correct date on her checks, instead of backdating them a year as she did every January. January was gone, dead and gone.

Atlanta was into February by now, a dull month and

usually a gray one. February tended to bring flurries of snow by night, sometimes gracing the city with as much as three inches of transforming magic, but more often dusting it with a powdery white coating like confectioner's sugar doled out by a stingy baker. February brought other delights, too. If it brought ice, it usually arrived in the early afternoons, ice that would turn the new overpasses and off-ramps of I-85 and I-75 to glass, that would tie up traffic bound homeward to Sandy Springs or Marietta or Peachtree City after a long day's work. Just one of February's little surprises, a thoughtful gift to fray tempers, ruin carefully tended trees, and cut electric power just in time for the cold of evening.

Or if the temperature happened to be above freezing, the precipitation would be rain, rain that lasted so long you began to think it had been raining forever, would go on raining forever, would rain until you drowned, then would wash your body away down the gargling storm drains. Rain would dance on your grave. Lawns became quagmires in that rain, side streets became tributaries, the main drags dirty brown rivers. Umbrellas were no good, for it was a cold, slanting rain that came at you horizontally, or lay in wait in flat brown puddles until a car helped it jump on you like a fond and foolish Saint Bernard to muddy your coat and ruin your day.

Flu, that was what February brought to Atlanta, aching joints and aching head, the world's worst hangover without benefit of the good time you deserved to feel this bad now. Runny noses, inflamed eyes, chests that felt as if vises were tightening inside them. Hoarse voices croaking frog calls over the phone, a chorus of coughs in the Fox auditorium, empty desks at work. Stomach cramps and diarrhea, pounding heads and soaring fevers. Illnesses to kill you and weather to make you happy to go, that was what February brought.

February in Atlanta was a bitch.

God, how he missed it.

Jeremy woke the next morning puzzled to find it so dark, remembered it was February, and figured the morning was overcast and—no digits shone red on the bedside table—the power was out. Yawning, he threw the covers aside, got up to visit the bathroom, and ran into the wall. Only then did he remember where he was. He felt along the wall to the bathroom door, then came back by the same braille system. In the dark of the windowless room, he fumbled with the tinderbox until he had a small flame going, and with this he managed to light the lamp.

He turned the wick up and started to get dressed. The light died down, and a tiny, hissing voice said, "Where are we?"

Smokharin was a mere mite, a fingernail-sized creature balancing on the blackened edge of the lamp. "Tremien's castle at Whitehorn," Jeremy said. "Melodia's here."

"Take me to her."

"I'll give your box back to her if you'll give me enough light to get dressed."

"Hurry, then."

The light flared up again. In its warm glow Jeremy saw his outfits, both of them, hanging neatly on pegs in the wall opposite. Somehow during the night they had been cleaned, sorcerously, he suspected, and they were both once again fresh and ready for wear. He donned the first one, the blue tunic and baggy trousers, opened the door for light, and held out the tinderbox. "Here you go." Smokharin arced into the box, and the lamp went out. Jeremy closed the tinderbox, slipped it back into his pocket, and went in search of Melodia.

She was at breakfast, her hair done up and a tiara winking there like a constellation of stars on the darkest night of the year. She, like Kelada, had new clothes: she wore a subdued blue dress that shimmered with tiny jewels. Kelada, a later riser, was not yet up. Melodia accepted the tinderbox with amused surprise. "Smokharin has never before expressed any concern for me," she said. "But I suppose we have grown close over the years, for a human and an elemental." She snuffed one candle, struck a light from the tinderbox, and in a moment an even more minuscule version of the elemental stood on the tip of the candlewick, balancing precariously and essaying a clumsy bow.

"You are well?" it asked in a voice so small it was almost not there.

"Very well, thank you. You are kind to come at my need."

"I will be ready when you call on me, Lady."

"Thanks, gallant elemental."

Another bow and Smokharin was gone, replaced by a

clear yellow flame. Jeremy shook his head. "I'll never get used to a place where fire talks back to you. What has Tremien prepared for breakfast?"

"It's good," she said. "Berries and melons from Southerland, brought here by magic. Brown cakes and butter, cheese and honey, and sweet milk."

"No tea?" he smiled.

She returned his smile. "No, alas. I miss my morning tea." She looked at him, the smile lingering, and she reached out to stroke his hair. "Your beard is growing in," she said. "You look more like—like him than ever."

He reached up to clasp her soft hand against his cheek. "You don't love him anymore, remember?"

"I remember," she whispered. Her eyes gleamed with tears, and she turned away from him. "Sebastian was not an evil man," she said.

Jeremy still held her hand. "He wasn't a good one. Look what he's done to me—to all of us."

Her face averted, Melodia nodded. "Yes, I know. He was ambitious, even driven. But he felt so weak—"

"Weak? Tremien and all the others seem to regard him as a great wizard, a powerful magician. How was he weak?"

"Oh, I don't know." Melodia sniffled, picked up a spoon, toyed with a few bright orange berries that remained in her bowl. "He was not born with sorcery. He had to earn it through hard study. He fought for every bit of knowledge, Sebastian did. I think—I do not know—I believe that Sebastian struck a bargain with the Great Dark One, that he became a servant of the evil, not evil himself. Is that possible?"

Jeremy let go of her hand. "I don't know. I do know that he's taken my place at home, and that I have to return there. Good, evil—I guess I don't really think in those terms very much. It's hard for me to decide."

"Sebastian talked like that, too. What difference did it make if Tremien wielded great power or the Great Dark One? Power was power, an end in itself, neither good nor bad. I don't know if he believed it."

Jeremy reached for a plate, helped himself to bread, butter, and honey. "Who is the Great Dark One?"

"A force," she said.

"Like a demon or a devil?"

"No, a real person. Or someone who used to be real."

As Jeremy munched his breakfast, Melodia tried to explain. Thaumia, it seemed, was a disk floating in space, its sun and moon circling around it. It was only one of billions of other worlds, all with their own suns, for these could be seen in the night sky as stars; but Thaumia, so far as humans knew, was the only inhabited world in all the universe.

Thaumia held four continents, two in the north and two in the south. The Great Dark One had risen more than fifteen hundred years ago in the more easterly of the southern continents, a land called Relas. From the beginning he had been obsessed with testing the limits of magic, and from the first flowering of his sorcery there sprang a terrible war. The Dark One lost that struggle, and most thought him dead as well as defeated, but this was not so, for he had retreated, wounded but living, to the icy fastness of the most southerly mountain range in Thaumia.

There he healed, brooded, and increased his knowledge. A generation after the first war—a generation of ordinary men and women, for through some hidden sorcery the Dark One lived an incredibly long life, even among wizards, who as often as not saw their two hundred-and-fiftieth birthday—the Dark One began to move once more, this time by stealth. On the continent of Relas were fifty-odd kingdoms, really colonies that had grown to independence over the years. First one, then another, fell to the Dark One, not by war this time but through subtle cunning, intrigue, and simple fear.

Before the magicians of the north became fully aware of his existence, the Dark One had made himself a habitation and a fortress in the continent of Relas, and for many centuries now it had folded into itself, a land unknown to others, wrapped in its own darkness and its own mysteries.

There the Great Dark One reigned still. And from there he reached northward to trouble the peoples of this continent, Cronbrach-en-hof, for in the council of magi who oversaw its magics the Dark One saw his greatest enemies. Their massed power, on their own grounds, would be too much for him; so the Dark One worked by proxy, corrupting and beguiling such wizards and sorceresses as he could, and probing always for a weakness. Even so, twice, once in the dim past when even Tremien

was young in age and power, and then again about forty
years ago, the Great Dark One had indeed sent armies
into the north, only to meet defeat. Nowadays he worked
in secret. The Five Countries of Cronbrach had always to
guard against rebellion, their leaders to beware of assas-
sination; and in the wild and unsettled outlands of the
continent, places like the Northwest Shore or the Meres,
the Great Dark One found willing aid.

What did he want, the greatest wizard of the south? "I
do not know," Melodia confessed. "Domination certainly,
sway over all the world and all its magics. But that, I
think, is in itself only a means to a greater end. What
that might be I cannot guess." She rose from the table,
her gown rustling. "This only I know: the Great Dark
One is evil. He brings with him despair and death and
night without hope of end."

"They say he eats souls." Kelada, wearing yet another
new dress, this one pink, had come in. "A thing which I
cannot do. I'm hungry."

"Help yourself to breakfast," Jeremy said, rising. He
pulled out a chair for her. She took one on the other side of
the table, and he sat down again. "And how did you sleep?"

"Badly." Kelada broke a chunk of bread, buttered it,
and took a voracious bite. "Can't wait to get home again,"
she mumbled around the food. "Place is too quiet."

"I find it peaceful," Melodia said.

"You would. No meat?"

"Excuse me." Melodia left with a swish of her skirts.

"No meat," Jeremy said, "but three kinds of cheese.
What's wrong?"

"Melodia," Kelada said. "I upset her."

"How?"

The little thief scowled. "My mouth. I should have
remembered about her. Didn't you notice at her home?
Of all the food she had, she kept no meat at all. And
here she eats none."

"I don't see—oh."

Kelada nodded. "She is a healer of animals. I'm so
stupid. I'm not fit for such company." But her appetite
was not affected, for she took four great pieces of cheese
and poured herself a pint of milk. "Better for all if I am
banished. Or imprisoned."

Jeremy toyed with his mug. "I will speak for you,
Kelada. If you think it will help."

She shook her head. "Who's to say?"

Nul came not long after breakfast to tell them the magi had assembled from all corners of the land and were in consultation already. They could expect to be called at any time. Jeremy sat bored and alone in his room for possibly an hour. Then, not knowing what to do with himself and not willing just to sit, he went to knock on Melodia's door. She did not answer, but next door Kelada came out. "She's probably walking in the courtyard. She does that."

"Are you afraid?"

Kelada crossed her arms and leaned against the door frame. "Yes."

"Good," Jeremy said. "I hate to be alone."

A crooked smile came to Kelada's face. "Then come in."

He sat on the foot of her bed, and she took the chair. Around it was a litter of rags, vials of oil, and an unstrung bow somewhat taller than she was. "Like it?" she asked, taking up the bow. "I had to have something to work on."

Jeremy took it. The wood was light and blond, lithe and springy, smooth under his hands. "You carved this?"

Kelada nodded shyly. "Most great archers have them done by magic, or at least make them and then have them blessed. I'm an amateur. I like to do my own work. Besides, it occupies my time."

"I had archery lessons in college."

"Oh? What is college?"

Jeremy handed the bow back to her. "It's a place to make friends, learn a little, and drink a great deal of beer."

"Oh, I see. Like a tavern."

Jeremy laughed. "Very much like a tavern, at times."

"Then you are a good archer?"

"Not even passable. I took the course for only one quarter, twice a week, and got a 'C' out of it." As he watched Kelada pick up a cloth and begin to work oil into the wood, he added, "I'm not much good at any activity, I guess. I run. Used to run, that is. I was up to seven miles a day, every other day. Had some karate in college, too, some weight training, fencing, swimming. I was pretty good at swimming, though."

Kelada's face held a puzzled smile. "You swam at a tavern?"

"Well, a college isn't exactly like a tavern. It's a school, really, for adults. Or people who think they're adults. Wise men and women gather there, and the younger people sit in rooms, and the wise ones teach them things."

"Then a college is like apprenticeship."

"Yes, something like that."

"How many years did you have college?"

"Five in all. Four for my A.B., then another four quarters for my M.B.A."

"Then you must be an adept."

"A what?"

Kelada left off working on the bow. "An adept. That is one of the seven degrees of magical ability: talent, apprentice, journeyman, adept, magician, wizard, mage. It takes four years of apprenticeship for a talent to become a journeyman, then at least another year for the journeyman to become an adept."

Jeremy laughed. "I suppose I am an adept, in a way."

"What do you do, back in your world?"

"I use words to make money for other people," Jeremy grinned. "There's magic for you, huh?"

"You are not so different from us, after all," Kelada said. The bow lay across her lap, incongruous against the delicate pink of her dress. She ran her thumb over it. "I like the beard," she whispered to the bow.

Jeremy felt his jaw. He had a beard, sure enough, a short and stubbly one. "Thank you," he said. "I like the way you look, too, Kelada."

"This isn't me."

Jeremy leaned forward. "Kelada—"

"Where the hell did I put the emery cloth?"

He took the bow from her hands and kissed her. "No," she said against his throat. "I'm ugly."

He held her as she cried. They sat together on the foot of the bed like that for some little time. Nul opened the door without knocking, stared at them for a moment, and said that the council awaited them. His orange eyes went a little pale, and Jeremy wondered if that were the pika's way of blushing.

The Great Hall had been made ready for the council meeting. No dancers, musicians, or soldiers lounged there now: instead, a great, heavy round table had been put in the center of the room, a roaring blaze had been made up in the fireplace, and the enormous curtains had been drawn to let daylight stream in through a window facing north, facing a vista of snowcapped mountaintops and far purple distances. The day outside looked cold and almost clear, with fogs shrouding the farther mountains and a few streaks of gray cloud low on the horizon. One further change had been made in the room: between the table and the fireplace a great oval mirror stood on its stand.

In the light from window and fire, the magi of Cronbrach-en-hof had gathered: Tremien in a high-backed chair, his back to the windows; to his right a diminutive man, completely bald, long of nose and chin, puffing intently on a long-stemmed black pipe; to the right again, a tall woman, fair of skin and hair, wearing a hooded cloak, hood thrown back over what seemed to be a coat of mail; then a man about Jeremy's height but older, with an incredible mane of untidy gray hair, an impenetrable gray beard, and eyebrows like ragged birds' nests; a motherly little woman in a simple blue shift and tight-laced black bodice containing an ample bosom; and a younger man, perhaps forty, or at least appearing so, with curly dark hair just beginning to show gray, a short curly beard, and gaunt cheeks. Four chairs had been left empty. Nul, Melodia, Kelada, and Jeremy took these.

"Kelada," Tremien said without preamble, "I think you will remember the council. Melodia, Jeremy Sebastian Moon, permit me. Altazar of Green Dales." This was the bald little man, who nodded carelessly. "Wyonne of Triesland." The tall woman inclined her head, giving them a brief smile. "Barach Loremaster." Barach separated a section of orange, somehow found his mouth in that wilderness of beard, and popped the fruit in. He did not look up. "Mumana, keeper of the heartlands." The motherly little woman tucked a lose curl of gray hair under and beamed at them. "And finally, Jondan, newest of our group." The dark-haired man looked steadily at them, the hollows of his eyes and those beneath his cheeks dark with shadow.

"We have been discussing the case," Tremien said. "It is a most unusual one. Indeed, we can recall nothing quite like it."

"There was," Barach said in a rusted-hinge voice, his eyes still on the orange he was devouring piece by piece, "an instance in the ancient writings of Metterin of Finarr—"

"Yes, yes," Tremien said. "But that was legend, Mage Barach."

The shaggy gray eyebrows lifted. "And we are not?" Another orange slice disappeared into the beard.

Tremien sighed. "We have considered," he began again. "Kelada, your case is first: from the beginning some of us doubted the justice of your banishment. Now, on second thought, we believe the punishment was too harsh, since you were innocent of the blood of Niklas File's victims. However, you still must earn your freedom.

"Melodia, you were guilty of nothing more serious than unwise love. But we cannot permit you to hold this mirror any longer, for it is a dangerous thing. It must be destroyed." Tremien paused, looked hard at the young healer, and then continued in a gentler tone: "It may be that you too will wish to make some form of restitution for the evil which, unknowing, you helped to foster. But that will be your decision."

The old wizard sighed deeply. "That brings us to you, Jeremy Sebastian Moon. The hardest decision of all." Looking around at the other council members, Tremien demanded, "Is it not as I said?"

"His aura," Wyonne murmured, "is indeed strange. I have seen nothing like it."

"Great power," growled bald Altazar beside her, "but untapped. Perhaps uncontrollable."

Tremien said, "Great spells do not seem to affect him—only small ones, like minor healing or language." A buzz of interest arose as the others added comments, none of them intelligible to Jeremy. A silence fell. It went on so long that Jeremy became conscious of the light sound of the wind against the windows, of the tangy scent of the orange across the table from him as Barach devoured the last piece. At last he said, "Well?"

Tremien looked hard at him. "We have a great need," he said. "Ours is to destroy the unholy mirrors created by your double. All of them, you understand. This one, and the one held by the Hag, and most of all the one in your world. That is our need. Yours is to return to your former home."

"Yes?"

"The two are hard to reconcile. The one who destroys the last mirror must remain in your world forever, a world without magic."

"I'll do it," Jeremy said. "Just send me there."

"No," Barach murmured. "A bird does not fly through the seas."

Jeremy blinked at him. "What?"

Mumana tutted. "He is trying to say that only a magician could hope to pass through from Thaumia to your world. A magician of mage level, one whose powers have been used and tested. Not a young man with no magic whatever."

"Then I'm a prisoner here?"

Tremien leaned forward. "Not quite. There is a chance. But we have little time. We all feel the increase of the Great Dark One's powers; they grow moment by moment. In less than a year he will be invincible. But if in that time you could master the great potential you have—if you could become magician enough to make the transference—then you have some hope, as do we." The bony hands spread, brown as the walnut wood of the table. "But we shall have to do something soon. If you cannot learn the magic by the next time of exaltation, one of us will have to attempt to destroy the mirror. That will put two Thaumian magi in your world, Sebastian and whoever makes the journey. It is a great imbalance in the worlds, and very dangerous for both. We fear even trying it."

The old man leaned back in the chair, the light from the window making his cloud of hair glow almost like a halo. "You must know this: using magic changes a man or woman. You have a talent, the most intense I, or any of us, have ever seen. What that talent will do for you, or to you, none of us can predict. Then, too, you will have to work hard, harder than you have ever worked in your life. It takes most people an ordinary lifetime to reach mage status. You would have to do that in months."

"What is the alternative?" Jeremy asked.

"To reconcile yourself to a life here in Thaumia. To pray that one of us can indeed destroy the mirror in your world, and that the results of the destruction are not catastrophic for both our worlds. If you choose this course, you cannot, you must not, use the *mana* we sense within you. You would have to be a mundane in a world of magic, an exile and an outsider forever."

"It's that dangerous?"

"Magic can burn a man up," Altazar said in his high-pitched, querulous voice. "I fear that you, an outsider, stand in more danger than one of us would. And I would not dare use such power as I sense in you. You must know, young Jeremy Sebastian Moon, that should you undertake to learn it and tame it, you will never again be the same person, not in any measure or in any way."

"A pomminut tree," Barach murmured behind his beard, "does not grow backward into seed."

For some reason Jeremy's throat was dry. "Could I"—he croaked—"die?"

An uneasy glance went around the table. Tremien bowed his head. "Yes," he said. "Or worse."

Jeremy looked from side to side. Melodia, her wonderful eyes wide and deep and green, sent waves of sympathy to him in a rush he could almost feel. Kelada gave him a ghost of a smile, wry beneath her ruined nose. Nul winked one orange eye at him.

He took a deep and unsteady breath. "Teach me magic," he said to Tremien, "and I will try."

Across the table, the mirror cracked from top to bottom. Shards and tinkling spears of glass clashed to the stone floor. Melodia stood, unsteady on her feet.

"Thank you, my dear," Tremien said to her.

"But I did nothing!" she protested.

"Search your feelings," Tremien said.

Melodia blinked. "Oh!" She turned and rushed from the room.

"What happened?" Jeremy asked.

Mumana smiled at him. "As long as Melodia held any love, however small, for Sebastian still in her heart, the mirror could not be broken."

"Yes," Tremien said. "Melodia no longer loves Sebastian." His old eyes regarded Jeremy steadily. "She has just realized that she loves you."

CHAPTER 8

"TWENTY-TWO . . . TWENTY-THREE . . . while you're doing this, you could be reciting the laws of thaumadynamics."

Jeremy, naked to the waist in the cold, thin air of Whitehorn, gritted his teeth, pulled his chin over the bar a twenty-fourth time, and grunted, "I might, if you'd ever told them to me."

Barach, warmly swathed and comfortably seated, said, "Once a fisherman caught a very small fish."

"Please," groaned Jeremy.

"Twenty-six, good. The fish was too little to eat, but instead of throwing back the only thing fate had given him that day, the fisherman used it for bait instead. On the next cast he caught a fish big enough to feed his whole family. Twenty-eight. Two more, I think."

Jeremy's upper arms screamed at him in pain, but he dragged himself up a twenty-ninth time, then, just barely, a thirtieth one. He dropped from the bar—it had been set up between one wall of the stables and a stanchion—and reached for his tunic. "I don't understand," he said. "About the fish."

"One day you will. Do you mean you've never heard of the three laws of thaumadynamics?"

Jeremy's head popped through the neck of his tunic. His beard, now more than two weeks old, had stopped tickling him, but the individual whiskers still had a distressing tendency to get caught in buttons and painfully extracted while he dressed himself. "Never heard of them," he said.

"I always forget your background." Barach smoothed his own beard, without visible effect: it still looked like the ruins of a singularly uncomfortable mattress. "Let me tell you a story— "

"Please," Jeremy begged, collapsing to the courtyard. He sat with legs bent, back against the stable wall, protected from the icy breezes off the mountaintop, trying to soak in a little heat from the afternoon sun. "No story. Just tell me the laws."

Barach, leaning back in his chair, made a tent of his fingers. "Very well, apprentice. But you must understand that these laws came late to the study of thaumaturgy. They were first formulated nearly two hundred years ago by a very great mage of Belimor Island, and they were the first truly systematic expression of the nature of magic. We have modified them since, but still we must recognize their importance in magical thought—"

Jeremy nodded. "I understand. But what are they?" His tolerance for absorbing lectures had worn thin since college.

"So impatient." Barach held one finger up. "The first law of thaumadynamics is that all energy and all matter are simply different forms of magic."

"So everything is made of magic."

"In a manner of speaking. Magic may not be created or destroyed, only transformed. Since matter is merely a form of magic, it follows that, with the proper approach, matter itself may be transformed. All this grows out of the first law." Barach scooted his chair around a bit to take advantage of the stable lee. "The second law is somewhat frightening if one dwells on its implications. In any closed system, magic tends to decrease and mundanity to increase."

Jeremy frowned into the distance. Since the curtain wall of Tremien's stronghold was only yards away, the distance did not amount to very much; still, his gaze was absent. "I've heard something like that before. Entropy? I think that's what we call it. The tendency of things to run down?"

"It could be expressed that way, yes. One corollary of that is that magical lines of force tend to dissipate after use. Fortunately, they are all but infinite; still, one can foresee a time when the universal magic has been utilized, when the universe will starve, figuratively speaking, of a dearth of enchantment. Practically, that means that great spells will work only once. In primitive times a person could, oh, move a mountain by looking at it and saying, 'Move, mountain.' But the next person could not move the mountain back by repeating the words. Some variant had to be found—'Take a walk, mountain,' or 'Be out of my way, mountain,' or some such. By now, great spells are arcane, difficult, and taxing. All a result of the second law."

"When do I learn magic?" Jeremy asked. "Kelada off somewhere, Melodia back in her cottage, me stuck here—I thought time was important."

"It is, apprentice. But time without knowledge is like a song without a bird. Or a bird without a song. Or—"

Jeremy groaned. "The third law?"

"Perhaps it would be better stated thus: time and magic are images of each other. Without the one, the reflection would not exist."

"Master," Jeremy said, "the third law?"

"Master," Barach murmured. "I like that better. Yes, 'Master' is very nice. The third law, apprentice, is that nothing in the universe can ever be made absolutely mundane. At least, as long as the universe endures. Some magic, however small, however latent, must forever exist in any disenchanted object; for without that tiny quantity of magic, the object itself would cease to exist." Barach leaned forward in the chair, arms crossed, and said, "Let me ask you a question, apprentice."

"All right."

The wind lifted tufts of Barach's beard, stirred his eyebrows. With a twinkle he said, "A man lies in a room with his eyes closed tight. He sees only darkness. The man knows if he opens his eyes, either one small candle will be lighted, or the room will be utterly dark. The man cannot move. It is vitally important for him to know whether the candle is lit or not. Indeed, it is a matter of life or death for him. The question is: how does he know without opening his eyes?"

Jeremy thought hard. "He smells the—"

"Odorless wax."

"He feels the—"

"The room is too warm."

"He calls out to the—"

"The elemental would only ignore him."

Jeremy shook his head. "Then I give up."

Barach rose from the chair. "Too bad. When you can answer, we will begin tutoring you in the use of magic.

Now, run from here to the front gate and back again. Twelve times today, I think."

Glaring at Barach, Jeremy took off his tunic. "This is more like football practice than a magical apprenticeship," he said. "This and the diet you have me on—nuts and berries. I must have lost ten pounds."

"To work great sorceries, one must be strong in body and serene in spirit. Twelve times. Go now."

And Barach wasn't satisfied with an ordinary jog. Oh, no. Jeremy had to sprint full-out, the whole distance and back, a matter of a quarter mile or so. By the eighth lap his lungs were afire and his legs beneath him were dead. But he stumbled through another, found his second wind partway through, and finally collapsed after the last leg, gasping and wheezing. Barach prodded him with a toe. "No. Get up. Walk it out, or you'll cramp."

They ascended a stone stairway to the parapet of the curtain wall and began to stroll the wall walk. The wall reached all the way around the mountain, running a distance of something greater than a mile, Jeremy reckoned. On it he was dizzily aware of the height of Whitehorn: in every direction the mountain walls fell away from him, and the nearest neighboring mountains, seeming close in the thin air but really miles away, barely came to Whitehorn's shoulders. Today the western horizon fell under the shade of thick clouds, their forerunners already dimming the sun. "Snow later," Barach said. A guard standing in one of the western machicolations of the wall gave them a brief glance as they passed.

"What is the answer?" Jeremy asked when he had enough wind to talk.

"It is my task to think of the questions," Barach reproved. "Yours is to think of the answers. Tell me, Jeremy, do you know how to read?"

"Yes, of course."

"Good. I think it time you began to study some basic books of magic. I will give you one to read this afternoon. We will discuss it tomorrow." They paused at the westernmost bend of the wall. Far away the hills rolled into deep shadow beneath the clouds, and the wind bit their faces with bitterly cold teeth. "Tremien is working a great wonder for you."

Jeremy gave his teacher a look of surprise. He had seen little of Tremien, and had assumed that the old mage had turned over the whole of Jeremy's education to garrulous old Barach. "What is it?" he asked.

"You will find out this evening. Tremien is no longer a young man, Jeremy. Such an act will greatly exhaust him. I want you to appreciate it."

"I'll try."

Though the mouth was invisible, the eyes, brown as two shiny acorns, crinkled in a smile. "That's what I like about you, apprentice: you are always willing to try. Come."

They moved on, completing their circuit. "Where is Kelada?" Jeremy asked.

"Why should I tell you?"

Jeremy stifled an irritated answer. Instead he said, "Let me tell you a story. A baby eagle lived on a mountaintop, and the old eagles fed him. Once the baby eagle was very hungry, and a grandfather eagle landed nearby, making sounds as if he were feeding. The baby eagle approached and found the old bird had been teasing him. The baby eagle pushed the old bastard right off the mountain. Now. Where is Kelada?"

Barach chuckled. "You are not entirely without hope. Kelada is doing a part of her penance. Far to the north and west of here, in a cold land, is the countryside of the Meres, thousands of still, cold, deep lakes. There dwells a great sorceress, the Hidden Hag of Illsmere. She is one of the Great Dark One's chief lieutenants, and, as you know, she is thought to possess one of the mirrors fashioned by Sebastian. Kelada, Nul, and a few others have gone to test the way. They seek to learn if the shadow-shapes actually are her servants, and how much they know of you. You see, it may be that with you dead, the mirror in your own land will become unbreakable. We don't know. Kelada, though, is a good thief, and she should be able to bring back some intelligence of how things stand."

"She's been gone a week."

"And should be gone for many more. She is well, don't worry."

"How do you know?"

The eyes this time held no mirth at all, but a great weight of care. "We do know. Trust what I tell you. We do know." Barach wore a heavy cape, but as clouds slid across the face of the sun, he huddled a little deeper in it and shivered. "Let's go inside now. I want to give you a book."

The book was in the study, centered neatly on Tremien's bare desk. Barach picked it up, opened it at random, and handed it over. After an initial puzzled glance, Jeremy closed the book, studied some golden hieroglyphics on the cover, and looked up in despair. "I can't read this. I don't even know the alphabet, let alone the language!"

Barach raised his bushy eyebrows. "Of course you know the language. You speak it!"

"I'm speaking English—" Jeremy broke off. "No, I'm not," he said, surprise raising the pitch of his voice. "I haven't been since I first met Kelada."

"Of course. The other world would have a strange speech. That may be an advantage, you know. Often a great spell will repeat itself if merely translated to another tongue. Tell me, did Kelada use a spell on you?"

Fleetingly, Jeremy recalled being held down as Kelada sat astride him, as she snarled down at him. "Yes. I think she did."

"Ah. Devalo's understand spell, no doubt. Very minor spell—that may be why it affected you when major magics do not. Can you speak some of your original tongue?"

In English—which *felt* strange in his mouth after so many weeks—Jeremy said, "Hello, folks, I'm Jeremy. Testing, testing, testing. What's your sign?"

Barach nodded. "Not an unpleasant language, though one unknown to me. Devalo's understand spell, beyond a doubt. A high-level spell would have erased your old language from your memory. But I find it intriguing that even such a common enchantment worked. May I try another?"

"I suppose so."

Barach's enchantments were not rhymed or sung, but rather stated in a quick, barely audible whisper. He ran through a longish sentence, then said, "Now look at the book."

Jeremy blinked. The compact little book, perhaps eight by five inches and half an inch thick, now bore a clear title in gilt on its blue cloth cover: CONJURATIONS: A BOOK OF BEGINNINGS. Jeremy opened it to the first page and began to read aloud: "The beginning student of magic must recall that his is a task of both ease and difficulty.

Magic is everywhere; that is the easy part. The student must learn to harness it; that is the difficulty."

"I thought so," Barach said. "A simple corollary to Devalo. Very minor, but once you know the language, the reading comes easy. I'll expect you to have finished that by tomorrow morning, now."

Tremien had given Jeremy the freedom of the palace and had moved him from his original guest room to quarters in the sunrise tower. His room here was half a circle, with an adjoining bathroom like a wedge of pie, and it had two narrow windows, loopholes almost, and its own fireplace. Otherwise, it was if anything a bit more spartan than the guest room. Cold baths, for example, proved the order of the day. Still, Jeremy enjoyed the view from the windows, and the added light.

There was little enough of that as he lay on the bed and began to read his primer in magic. Before long a sound, an insistent, whispery tapping, drew his attention away from the book. He rose and looked out the window. Snow, huge, heavy flakes of it, was pelting down, flying so thick that the valley already was invisible behind the drifting curtains. Jeremy shivered a little, gave silent thanks that here at least he didn't have to worry about driving home in the stuff, and went back to the book.

It was simple enough. Acts of magic, the text said, could be broken down into three stages (Jeremy, thinking back on other schoolbooks he had known, wondered what activity could *not* be broken down into three stages), each dependent on a separate act of will by the magician: first, formulation, second, visualization, and third, realization.

Formulation seemed to be nothing more elaborate than the creation of a spell (a "word path" the writer termed it with neological smugness), unspoken at first but well-planned. This spell would be the trigger, as it were, to the completion of the magical act. It had to be personal, complete, and new, and the book had three subchapters under those headings.

The second stage, visualization, meant the establishment of a clear, complete, and vivid mental apprehension of the effects the spell would have. A spell alone had no virtue in it, and no power. The mind responsible for the spell had to know exactly what effects were desired. Incomplete visualization meant uncontrolled magic, which

could prove most unpleasant, judging from the caution-
ary notes abounding in the book's second chapter.

The final stage, realization, really was the bringing
together of the first two parts. In it the magician spoke
the spell aloud while externalizing his or her apprehension of the spell's effects. This process somehow trig-
gered the latent magic into sudden action. Jeremy thought
of a sound setting off an avalanche: not the words themselves but their meanings, their intent, set off the flow of
magic, and only when the loosed magic hardened again,
set along the new lines of the visualized result, would the
spell be complete, its ends accomplished.

Some further notes on great spells interested Jeremy.
These very often, the book told him, were deliberately
left incomplete. For example, the travel spell (the book
mentioned Melodia's father Walther with some defer-
ence) had been formulated to include all the billions
upon billions of unborn citizens of Thaumia who some-
day would want to use it. Each pronunciation of a private
cantrip helped the spell towards its completion and even-
tual exhaustion, and so each individual pronouncing his
or her cantrip was rewarded by instantaneous travel.
Walther and great magicians like him did not so much
share the magic as spread speaking parts for its activation
among thousands, perhaps even millions, of others; in
the grand scheme of things, the spell was no more com-
pleted by a person's traveling across the world with it
than the MARTA system was used up by Jeremy's occasional bus trip downtown. Eventually all the riders would
wear out the bus, and eventually all the travelers would
use up the potential magic (or *mana* as the book helpfully
added) of the spell; so entropy and mundanity would
finally hold sway.

The first three chapters were easy enough. After that,
the book began to relate magic and mathematics, and
Jeremy soon found his attention wandering. He yawned,
stretched, and put the book down on his bedside table. It
was quite dark outside now, and the leaded panes of his
windows had collected little ledges of snow. Jeremy swung
out of bed, put his slippers on, and went out to see what
was going on.

The circular staircase of the tower led down to a passageway that in turn led to the Great Hall. As always,
the people in it—a subdued group this evening of thirty

or forty men and women—fell a little quieter as he passed through. Several spoke to him, for he was becoming a familiar face around the palace now, as well, he suspected, as an object of gossip. He returned their greetings, smiled, and passed on.

Tremien's study door was ajar, sending a streak of firelight across the corridor floor and up the wall. Before Jeremy could knock, Barach's voice called, "Come in."

Tremien sat on one side of the fire, hands on knees, chin sunk on breast. On the other sat Barach, less bulky now that he had removed his winter cloak, but still wild of hair and whisker. Barach held an admonishing finger somewhere about the place where his mouth should be, and Jeremy came in quietly. "I told you he would respond to a summons," Barach said. "You owe me one minor spell, Tremien."

The head came up slowly, firelight gleaming on the bare brown pate. "So I do, Barach. So, apprentice, you felt our call?"

Still at the door, Jeremy said, "I don't know. I thought coming was my idea. I just felt—restless. I thought of you and wondered what you were doing."

Barach laughed. "One minor spell, Tremien."

"It seems so." Tremien's manner was much more subdued than usual, less brusque and imperious. "Come in, young man, come in, and close the door behind you." Jeremy did close the door, softly, and crossed to the two older men. Standing between them, he had the feeling that he was the subject of their scrutiny and evaluation. Tremien had his spectacles in his left hand. He put them on and squinted at Jeremy. "Some shading at the edges now," he said. "Your aura is changing, I think. Have you tried any magic yet?"

"No, sir."

"Hm. It will come." Tremien took off the glasses, folded them, and tapped them against his cheek. "I fear that as you begin to use your talent, you will find yourself more and more susceptible to magical attack. Right now your immunity to great spells is almost as much a miracle as any I could create. I wonder if we do more harm than good in educating you."

When Barach didn't speak, Jeremy said, "I learn by my own choice, Mage Tremien."

"Very good answer, boy," Barach murmured. "Very

good indeed. Now, Tremien, if you're ready, I'd advise you to begin your display." To Jeremy he added, "The old rascal intended this for later, for after dinner, but he's a lot more spry than he looks. He has the spell all ready to go, and frankly I'm eager to see it. That is, if you can forgo dining for a while."

"Certainly," Jeremy said. "I would fast for a week to see one of Tremien's major magics."

"You are certainly becoming well-spoken." Tremien's voice was dry as he dropped the spectacles into a pocket of his robe. "Very well, we shall have it. What I have been working on, Jeremy, is a means of looking into your world. It is a difficult thing to do, but proved easier than I anticipated. Sebastian, I think, has but little *mana* left. The mirror, however, is highly charged with it. Having one magical item in your universe makes the connection easier."

"He also thinks," Barach added, "that your universe may have a little magic in it."

"Oh, I'm quite sure it has some. Just a little," Tremien said with a weary, indulgent smile. "Perhaps not enough to move a mountain. But a bit, lurking here and there. Perhaps that too helped me. At any rate, what I am going to do is to conjure up some visions of what your counterpart has been up to. They are shadows only; you will be able to see and hear, but not to converse."

Jeremy drew up a chair. "Good. I've been wondering about Sebastian. I hope the bastard hasn't had it easy."

The old wizard's eyes flashed. "Apprentice, you will control your anger. I do not work wonders for fools."

Clenching his jaw, Jeremy nodded. He took a deep breath and tried to relax. "I am sorry, but he has done me great wrong."

Tremien did not rise, but he gave the impression of drawing himself in and up. He began to chant words in a strange tongue, and the chant went on for quite a long while. Jeremy felt a prickle on his arms and along the back of his neck: something was happening. Finally Tremien grew silent, his breath shallow and rapid.

"Well?" Barach asked, putting one hand on the arm of the older wizard.

"It is done. You may look, Jeremy."

Jeremy blinked. "Ah—shouldn't there be a crystal ball or something?"

"At my age? Nonsense. Just look."

"Excuse me, Mage—but look where?"

"Anywhere you wish. Think of Sebastian and your world and look!"

Jeremy thought, for some reason, of the elevator at Taplan and Taplan. The fireplace became a vision of the elevator doors, closed, startling him so much that he blinked. The vision was gone.

"You must concentrate," Barach said. "A man once asked a rufflebird why the bird looked so hard at the ground—"

"Barach!" Tremien did not sound angry, exactly, but definitely peevish. "Apprentice, clear your mind and concentrate. Don't try to look too closely at details—just think of what you want to see."

Without a process of clouding or shimmering, the fireplace again became a screen, and on it Jeremy saw Cassandra in the act of getting into her car. She shivered. A voice—Jeremy's voice—no, Sebastian's—said, "What is it?"

"Goose walked over my grave," Cassie said, and she slid behind the wheel. "Gonna invite me in for drinks after we get to your place?"

"If you like." Sebastian for sure, clean-shaven and wearing Jeremy's raincoat, but Sebastian for all that. Jeremy could see him too slipping into the passenger seat of Cassie's car.

"How much longer before your Civic's fixed?" Cassie asked as she started the engine.

"Don't know." Sebastian grinned at her. "Does it matter? It's nicer riding with you anyway."

"Hm. People are beginning to talk."

Sebastian slid back in the seat. Jeremy now saw both of them in profile. The magician grinned again and said, "Let them."

"You've changed since Christmas," Cassie said. "Since you were out with that bug. Did it do something to you?"

"Changed how?"

"I don't know. You've got a temper now, for one thing."

"Is that bad?"

"Oh, hell, no. It was high time you told Escher off. I like seeing you stand up for yourself. Frankly, I'd started

to wonder a little about you. And then all that stuff
about your brother—what's wrong?"

"Same goose." The face turned toward him. Jeremy
shivered. No doubt Sebastian was really just looking out
the passenger window, really seeing only the traffic down
on the Buford Highway interchange—but he seemed to
be glaring at Jeremy. The picture abruptly died.

"You cannot allow yourself to be distracted! Try again,"
Tremien said.

Barach broke in, sounding worried: "Mage, are you
certain that—"

"It's all right. I'll let both of you and Jeremy know
when I've grown tired."

Alone, Jeremy thought. Let me see the son of a bitch
alone.

There he was, behind the wheel of a car—an unfamiliar car. From his vantage point, which seemed to be
the rear seat, Jeremy could tell that Sebastian was driving, badly, near Stone Mountain east of the city. But the
car—he had it: a mad, red Porsche, one that he recalled
Cassie coveting. How had the magician come by it? Jeremy could think of only one explanation, and it involved
Sebastian's rifling of Jeremy Sebastian Moon's account at
the C&S Bank.

Sebastian, intent on the expressway ahead, pottered
along at forty and evidently had some difficulty in steer-
ing: the hood wavered uneasily between the center line
and the shoulder. With some little pleasure—but with
greater apprehension for his savings account—Jeremy recalled the difficulty *he* had encountered on his first day of
horseback riding, and with mordant spite he hoped Sebastian got carsick. That wasn't as good as saddle sores,
not by a long shot, but it would help. The day outside the
car was dull and overcast, a typical day for late February
or early March, and from the sparse traffic Jeremy guessed
it would be a Sunday. He concentrated on Sebastian,
willing to see him.

Sebastian's eyes flicked to the rearview mirror, then
back to the road. "Tremien?" Sebastian asked softly.
"Someone's there, I feel it. Tremien? There's something
you may not know, but you ought to. Take a close look
in the Between. The person who's there isn't the one you
think."

The picture vanished, leaving only the fire. Jeremy got

up, stood before the hearth, glaring into the flames. "He's taken my place. Everyone believes he's me."

"Do you want to try again?" Tremien asked, his voice faint.

"No. I want to go there and send the bastard back. Maybe not even in one piece."

"I shall end the spell." Tremien muttered a phrase or two, and Jeremy felt something pass from the room, a sense of presence, as if someone there had left. But the three of them remained before the fire, Tremien with his head down, Barach with his eyes on his friend, Jeremy standing before the fire.

At length Barach spoke: "That was a great wonder, Mage Tremien. I have never heard or dreamed of looking into other realities before. Had you worked no other magic, that alone would gain you immortality."

"It cost enough," Tremien said, lifting an unsteady hand to shade his eyes. "Did you read his aura?"

"Pale," Barach said. "Weak. He must have carried some *mana* with him, but it is not being replenished."

"I anticipated that," Tremien said. "He is calling upon his dwindling magic to learn about your world, Jeremy, to carry on his deception. That will make your task easier, when it comes."

"How?"

"He will not be able to oppose you with sorcery. I believe the mirror is beyond him in a way; he created it, but even if he unmade it, he would gain no advantage, find no *mana* left over to use in other forms. I sensed no protection spell about him. I think if he had put one on the mirror, some trace would remain; it was certainly strong with Melodia's. No, breaking the mirror should prove easy. If you survive the passage, of course." Tremien settled back in his chair. "Barach, how goes Jeremy's training?"

"I think we are ready to begin, Mage."

"Good, good. There is much to do. Tomorrow, Jeremy, you begin in earnest."

"I'm ready."

"I hope you are."

First ona began at sunrise, but each day Jeremy was up before that, for half an ona of calisthenics, then another of running. He then had a few minutes to bathe, a few more to eat, and two hona of instruction in theoretical and applied sorcery. After that, specialized instruction in the crossbow ("I'd make a real archer of you if I had five years," Captain Fallon told him, "but in three months you should be a pretty fair crossbowman") and in swordsmanship; a short rest and luncheon, then one ona for reading; two hona of other instruction (Jeremy thought of it as history, literature, geography, and current events, all rolled together), an ona for horseback riding, supper after the sun had set, and then conversation with Barach, one or two members of the court, and, rarely, Tremien. Reading and study then followed until bedtime. Barach insisted that he be in bed by fifteenth ona, which gave him, he estimated, about six hours of sleep. Jeremy rarely found it difficult to follow Barach's wishes.

This was his routine for six days of the week. The seventh day was a holy day (Jeremy wondered if God had rested at the same interval in all the created universes) which he usually spent in more reading. He did attend morning services in the chapel, partly out of curiosity, partly because he liked the chaplain, Brother Thomas, a wispy little man quick of tongue and dry of humor. Thomas had once told him that the Faith (for it appeared Thaumia had only one religion, though that one did indeed have numerous sects) held sacred certain ancient scriptures, all of which were written on one page, the Holy Commandments. These consisted of "Learn. Grow. Seek truth. Find Me," and nothing else.

"No 'thou shalt nots'?" Jeremy asked with a smile.

"Plenty of them," the cleric said. "Probably hundreds of thousands by now."

"And who came up with them, if God didn't?"

"Ah, well," Brother Thomas had replied easily, "God wanted us priests to have something to do, you see."

Despite this, Brother Thomas's sermons were more directed toward what to do than what not to do, and the choir sang lovely hymns, most of them celebrating the goodness of creation, a few recalling the deeds of good men and women of the past. The service was usually over by the end of second ona, and it put Jeremy into a good mood for improving his knowledge.

But despite his application and industry, for several weeks Jeremy was not allowed to undertake a spell, even a minor one, of his own. He learned about protections and hedges, about diversion and redirection; he studied mental shields and physical ones, insulation and removal. Still, Barach insisted that his theoretical knowledge simply was not strong enough to deal with such magic as he had latent within him.

Late one night toward the end of winter, when the valley below the castle had turned into a bog, brown with mud and silver with standing water, on the rare days when it could be seen at all through the low rain clouds that hung over it, Jeremy decided to try a spell on his own.

One of the books recommended a levitation spell as a good test for a beginner. Jeremy, his eyes on another, larger book across the room on his desk, tried the three-stage process: formulation ("Rise, book!"), visualization (he imagined the book floating up to the ceiling and then back down), and realization (he held onto the picture while saying the phrase). He concentrated hard on the volume, a weighty compilation of transformation spells, bound in brown leather. Nothing happened, which didn't surprise him too much. Surely some exhausted student—or librarian!—had used the floating book spell long ago.

Jeremy tried again, this time creating a rhyming formula. After a few moments of thought, he came up with:

> Heavy tome that daunts the eye,
> In the air, I command you, fly!

Pretty lame stuff, he thought, but maybe it would do. He went to work again. This time he felt *something*, a kind of electric tingle, but the book didn't move.

After ten minutes or so, Jeremy was sure nothing more would happen. He sighed, turned down the lamp, and went to bed. He tried to picture, once again, the book rising. The problem, he decided, was that he really didn't believe in magic. At least not in his own. Oh, he could see the results of Tremien's spells, or Barach's, or Walther's (these people had all the advantages, he thought, of personal cellular phones, and all the disadvantages as well), but Jeremy simply could not believe that he personally could travel to the ends of the earth in the twinkling of an eye, or speak to strangers miles away out of thin air, or make a book fly.

As the lamp flame burned low, Jeremy lay with his

hands behind his head, thinking, incongruously, of automobiles and magic. He didn't really understand what made a car go, but he could drive one—a hell of a lot better than Sebastian, he thought. Magic should be the same way: he should be able to turn on the ignition and go. Except of course magic was magic.

He almost fell asleep, but something roused him. He lay wakeful, listening, straining his nerves to catch it: a sound? Yes, a whisper of a sound, a kind of—

A flapping.

A red rim of flame remained on the wick of the lamp. He turned the wick up carefully, and the flame grew long and yellow. He sat up in bed just in time for the book to catch him over the left temple. He saw stars and fell sideways—it was a *big* book. Half in and half out of bed, he found it easier and perhaps more prudent to slide down than to try to scramble back up. From the floor he looked up with considerable caution. The book, spine toward the ceiling, pages dangling, covers flapping, orbited the room like a gigantic frightened bat. "Whoa!" Jeremy cried, to absolutely no effect. The book, if anything, sped up.

Jeremy stood and tried to catch it on its next circuit. Though the covers were at best inefficient wings, they flapped almost as rapidly as a hummingbird's, and the book was going fast now. It banged painfully off his hands, then careered off, its flight pattern becoming crazed: it crashed into the wall above his desk, swooped under the bed and past him at knee level, cracked a pane of the window, then found its bearings and whizzed around at what would have been about eye level, if he had dared to stand. Though it seemed to lack vertical stability, it gained velocity at every moment.

The door opened, and the book splatted against it, pages flying loose. After sliding to the floor and leaping up with desperate heaves of its cover, the book took off again, swooping in a blurred series of sine waves. Barach, eyes wide, edged into the room and closed the door. "What have you—agh!"

The book had caught him a good clip on the shoulder. He dropped to his hands and knees. "My heavens, boy, what did you *say* to it?"

Jeremy was too busy trying to evade a kamikaze dive to answer. The book missed him, grazed the floor, and flapped up, shedding more leaves. They flew thick now, trying to achieve flight on their own, revolving around the room as if caught in a whirlwind, and the book seemed thinner by almost half.

"I just told it to fly!" Jeremy said. "I didn't think that—umpf!" A leaf of the book had plastered itself against his mouth. He ripped it away.

Barach edged to a window, threw it open. "Think about it flying away into the night," he said.

Jeremy tried. The book, which had resumed its whizzing circles, responded almost at once and did indeed go out the window.

Unfortunately, it did not go through the window Barach had opened. The crash as it burst through the leaded panes was deafening. A flock of loose leaves followed it out in a swirling funnel of white. A couple of them even found their way to the open window. One went up the chimney. Barach shooed out the few that were left, except for one which had risen high up to the rafters and which fluttered back and forth with a rattling rustle. Finally Barach seized the poker from the hearth and managed to snag the leaf. He tossed it out the window, and it whirled away.

The wizard blew out his breath, ruffling his moustaches. "What book was that?"

"Hesselvin on Transmutation."

"Hmpf. Not a very rare book, fortunately for you. You'll have to replace it, you know."

Jeremy gave Barach a shamefaced grin. "I thought that—"

"Hush." Barach looked hard at him, whether in anger or estimation Jeremy could not tell. "Some weeks ago I asked you a question. Do you recall it? The one about the man in the dark room and the candle?"

"I—yes, I remember."

"What is the answer?"

In exasperation Jeremy said, "Oh, if a tree falls in the forest and there's no one around to hear it, is there any sound?"

Barach's eyes twinkled. "That," he said, "is a fair answer. Tomorrow we begin real magic."

"We do?"

"You should see your aura. It's changed tonight. I don't know if you're still immune to magic or not, but you've got a flame around you the size of a giant. No more practicing tonight! You'll get quite enough of that in the next weeks. I think I will enjoy watching you work. It should prove interesting."

Barach turned to go, and Jeremy said, "But I didn't really answer the question."

The wizard smiled from the doorway. "Like the man in the story, sometimes you have no way of knowing what is what. You simply must make up your mind and try to do something."

"That's no answer!"

"So who said every question has to have an answer?"

Jeremy turned down the lamp, lay back in bed, and fell asleep grinning.

But he awoke with a start well before dawn. He got out of bed—the room was icy, what with the broken window, and the stone floor froze his feet—and dressed without bothering to light the lamp. He clattered down the circular stair and through the sleeping palace to Tremien's study.

Tremien was there, slumped behind his desk. Barach was just turning from the hearth, where he had started a fire.

"Did you call?" Jeremy asked.

In a slow voice heavy with grief, Tremien said, "He is indeed becoming a magician. No, Jeremy, we did not call."

"But I thought—"

Barach turned away from the crackling fire. "You felt a cry for help, Jeremy. A movement in the lines of magical power. Not many young magicians are so sensitive."

Jeremy looked from Barach to Tremien. Both men were grim and shocked. "What happened?"

"The Hag," Barach said. "She has Kelada."

"Nul is on his way to report now," Tremien said. "He will be here any moment."

"Kelada—captured?"

"And by a servant of our enemy," Barach added. "It is a heavy loss."

"We've got to get her back!"

Tremien glared at him. "Young fool, you do not know what you say! The Hidden Hag is a formidable foe, as steeped in lore as I am, and younger. We have no one to send!"

"Send me," Jeremy said.

A weak voice came from behind him: "Mage, I think you must send him."

Jeremy turned. Nul stood there swaying, one orange eye swollen closed, a great gash in his shoulder trickling blood. Barach started forward, but Jeremy reached the pika first, caught him as he fell. "Nul—"

A three-fingered hand waved him off. "Must report. Mage Tremien, it is worse than you feared. Shadow-men are strong, strong. Must rescue Kelada."

"You need a healer," Barach said, kneeling beside Nul. "I'll send for Melodia."

"Yes," the pika agreed. "Need her. Need Jeremy. Must face the Hag now—or we lose all."

"I'll go," Jeremy said again.

Tremien put his hands on his desk and pushed himself up as if he were raising the weight of the world. "I think you may have to. Apprentice—Jeremy—we'll do what we can." The old wizard closed his eyes. "Dear God in heaven, boy, I am sorry for you."

CHAPTER 9

MELODIA CAME OUT of Nul's room exhausted. She embraced Jeremy, put her weight softly against him. "I have missed you."

"And I you. Nul—?"

"Weak, but mending. Exhaustion is his main problem. He will rest a long time now. After that he should be better." She pushed away from Jeremy, looked up at him with her sea-green eyes, her enchantress' eyes. "What happened?"

"Tremien doesn't know—or won't tell me. Nul and Kelada were in the country of the Meres, and somehow they were found out. Kelada is prisoner there now."

"The Hidden Hag," Melodia said. "I might have guessed."

"Who is she?"

"Not here," Melodia said. "Take me back to my room and I'll tell you." He put his arm around her, and together they descended a stair and crossed into the wing of the palace they had first occupied when Tremien brought them there months ago. Melodia's room was cold, dark, and cheerless. "I guess I wasn't expected," she said with a wan smile.

"Let me see what I can do." Jeremy considered for a while. Then he stared into the indeterminate distance and recited:

Let this room grow warm,
Let a good light show.
From warmth shall come no harm,
From light but gentle glow.

Melodia gasped. The room had become lighter, with a soft yellow light, and the air was springlike. Jeremy exhaled. "Good. I had visions of setting the palace afire."

"You shouldn't use a spell for something as simple as

light and warmth," Melodia said. "Magic is limited, you know."

"That's why soldiers here battle with bows and swords," Jeremy said. "Magic is too expensive to waste in warfare."

"Oh, it is used, when sorcerers are involved. But the spells normally are directed against other magicians. Of course, small magics are used, to direct the flight of an arrow, or to make a sword surer of striking its mark. But defensive ones are used, too, and unless one soldier is much more adept than the other, they cancel each other out." Melodia had worn a traveling cloak. She removed it and hung it on a wall peg. Underneath she wore the belled green gown that she had worn at their first meeting. She sat with folded hands looking a Jeremy. "You are thinner."

"And healthier. But you were going to speak of the Hag."

"Yes. You must know about her."

Jeremy pulled up a chair. "She is a magician, I gather. How powerful is she?"

Melodia toyed with a lock of her dark hair. "Very strong. If she were not a renegade, her power would be of mage level at least. But it has turned in dark ways, and her name is one of fear in the north countries. They say that many years ago she was only a country girl with much talent but no training. She grew to adulthood without realizing what lay within her. She was—is ugly. As a girl she was badly treated because of that. A wizard recognized her potential and began to educate her in the use of magic; at first she cast about her the illusion of great beauty, they say. But a spell of illusion cannot fool its caster, and she saw a different face in the mirror from the one others saw. They say she became obsessed with a transformation spell, to reshape her flesh and make it what she wished to be, but such spells come hard. The changing of living beings is a very great magic, one that only the greatest wizards can use or control. Her failure maddened her. She struck out at the wizard who was her teacher and killed him. They speak of her returning to the farmland where she was born and taking her revenge there too, by disease and disaster. How much is true I don't know. Some must be.

"At any rate, the farmers fled from the Hag. Wizards from the south, Tremien among them, banded together to drive her out—her power was already so great that

they could not destroy her. She fled to the desolate
country of the meres, a broad, swampy valley of little
notice or account to anyone else. There she built her
palace, by magic they say, and there she broods. Her
delight is only in another's woe, her only purpose revenge against all the world for what she is."

"And her magic?"

"They say she raises the dead and makes them her
slaves. That is why she spreads death: in doing so, she
increases her domain."

Jeremy was silent for a long time. Finally he said, "The
shadow-riders? Are they dead?"

"No. They are creatures from the swamps and fens,
hidden by her illusions from the eyes of men. But they
are mortal. They can be killed."

"That's some hope, anyway. You are tired. Sleep now."

"Stay with me."

"I shouldn't."

"Not to—I know that you don't feel—will you sit with
me?"

"Yes," Jeremy said. "I will do that."

He sat in a chair beside the bed as Melodia pulled a
blanket over her. The room was not terribly bright, but
when Jeremy sought to diminish the light spell he found
it hard to do. The light did not obey his commands, and
finally he had to use more magic to countermand the first
spell altogether. The room grew dark, and Jeremy sat
with his heart pounding, his breath shallow, as if from
great physical exertion. For some time he sat holding
Melodia's warm hand. The sound of her breathing grew
regular and deep.

Jeremy sat in the darkness pondering the Hidden Hag
of Illsmere, whose minions were monstrous creatures
from the swamp, whose servants were the dead, and he
wondered what lay in store for him. He recalled his
nightmares of old, the sense of being pursued, the feeling
that out there in the dark someone or something waited
for him, thirsted for his blood, hungered for his flesh. In
the quiet room he felt the old fears again.

Only this time they were real.

Barach wouldn't hear of Jeremy's leaving that day, and
so he spent the time chafing and worrying. Nul grew
stronger as he slept, as Melodia had said he would.

Tremien spoke briefly with him toward evening, and told Jeremy that next morning they would learn exactly what had happened. That night Jeremy slept only a little, and he was up and impatient for the sun an ona before dawn.

After breakfast they gathered in Tremien's study: Barach, Melodia, Jeremy, Tremien, and Nul himself, now looking much more fit. He even gave Jeremy a smile, and Jeremy saw that the tooth was more than halfway in now. "Sorry for bad news," Nul croaked in a voice still not quite his own.

"It couldn't be helped," Tremien said from behind the desk. "Best now that we hear the whole story. Begin at the beginning, please."

"Yes, Mage. Kelada and I go to find out about Hidden Hag. We use spell to travel as far as end of Arkhedden Forest; that as close as we dare, lest her magic detect us.

"There we ask foresters about magics. They say bad things coming out of the meres; speak of night things that steal children, suck blood. Many moving south, even in winter; hard time they would have of it, but not want to stay.

"We travel north and west, over hills. Land turn bad; trees all dead, black, no grass underfoot, only mud. No game. We run low on food, turn back to south again until we come to place where trees still grow. This, oh, week's march. Then we hunt, gather food until we have enough. This time go farther west, then north, into valley beside stream. At first stream clear; then water begin to grow cloudy. Finally it stink of dead things, run white like little milk poured in lots of water. We stop drinking.

"On fifth day, one of shadow-things come. Very dark day, many clouds. No shadow to see, but Kelada sense thing. It fight her, no see me. I scouting ahead, hear fight, come running, see Kelada fighting air. Kelada hurt a little, cuts on arms, but she use knife. Thing die, then it visible and we can see. It like a man, big, ugly, but not like man, too." Nul spent some time trying to describe the creature. Listening to him, Jeremy finally decided that the shadow-rider had looked amphibian, with a warty, brownish-green skin, large eyes, no nose, and an enormous mouth; but the most disturbing feature to Tremien was Nul's mention of a third eye.

"An amulet, you mean?" Tremien asked. "Something shaped like an eye?"

"Nah, nah. In forehead. Here." Nul touched his own brow above and between his orange eyes. "Glowed while thing dying. Then go dark. Little round eye, small like berry. Red first, then cloudy brown."

"That is not natural," Tremien said. "I fear some deep magic."

Nul shrugged. "We take body, dump him in one of the lakes. Many of them now, ground all soft and marshy. We camp three, four days for Kelada's arm to heal. We have to retreat then. Food low.

"Weather bad for week, two weeks. We hunt when we can. Finally we cross some mountains, come to wide deep water."

"That would be Lankas," Barach said. "A bay of the sea."

"Yes, snowbay. Lots of ice in it, lots of snow then. We cold. We go north to place of men, fishers. Place in Langrola."

Barach nodded. "Yes, a fishing town at the northern point of the bay."

"We stay there long time. Rest, eat, grow stronger. Talk to people about Hag. They not care—mountains between them and Hag's valley. Only one, two people talk of her. Some have heard that ships come in once, twice a year, have things for her. Strange men come to carry things over mountain passes. They not talk, not eat. People afraid of them."

"I don't wonder," Tremien said. "How long did you stay in Langrola?"

"Weather begin to change: rain, not snow, then some sun. We buy provisions, fish, fish, fish." Nul made a face. "Town stink of fish, nothing to eat but fish. Not want to eat fish again ever."

"But how long did you stay?"

"Until three weeks ago. Then we start again. Climb mountains this time, come in from west. But Hag ready. We come down mountains, into valley. Mud very thick, hard to walk. Come to dryer ground after many days, rest, go forward. Start to see plants, bushes, then trees. All just growing, just coming to life, like spring here.

"Then we find house. Little house in woods. Fire burning, smoke coming out, smell of cooking. Woman and man there. Say they live there many years, now bog surrounds them; they no get out. But little piece of ground good, they grow food there, fish still live in nearby lakes, they take them. Offer us food. Talk to us of Hag. Say they hate her for driving other folk out. Say it good if we kill her. Tell us way to her palace, deep in swamps. Talk until late at night. Kelada fall asleep."

Nul heaved a great sigh. "I sick of fish, not really eat. They think I sleep. I awake. They change. They under spell of illusion. Not man, not woman, but things, creatures like frogs, like toads. Kelada not wake up when I push, I pinch. They come to pick Kelada up, nasty flippery fingers all over her. I grab sword, attack. They fight back. Kelada finally open her eyes, try to stand. One grab Kelada, disappear—travel spell. Then two, three, more come. I wounded. They ready to kill me. I use travel spell. Now I here, Kelada lost."

"And the Hag knows where you went," Tremien said. "She would be able to sense your destination if you used the travel spell within her domain, even as I sensed Kelada's being taken to her palace. Well, no harm in that; the storm has been brewing for some time, and better for us if it break early. Jeremy, I fear this means you must begin your quest before you have begun to be ready, but your quest it is, without doubt, and I will not stay you from it."

"I go with him," Nul said.

"Thanks, good pika," Tremien said. "You have done far better than many others could have hoped, and your reward has been small. May you be better rewarded by a greater power than magi! Yes, I think you must be one of the number, to guide and advise."

Barach heaved a theatrical sigh. "I cannot allow my young charge to go off all unprotected. There is a story of Durelianus the bridge maker. Whilst he stood on the bank of the great River Sengasan, north of the town of Hest, casting a spell of power which heaved great stones into place and held them there, a swarm of gnats galled him and his helpers. 'Master,' one of his assistants cried, 'cannot you use some of your power to rid us of these pests?' Durelianus is supposed to have replied, 'Great magics are best not wasted where a slap of the hand suffices.' True, such magic as Jeremy possesses would hardly disturb a gnat; still, I think while mine would serve, his is best saved for time of need. I shall make one of the party."

Melodia put her hand through the crook of Jeremy's elbow. "My life and my nature are not meant for adventure," she said hesitantly. "Yet for my father's sake and my own, you did not punish me as you might have another who aided Sebastian. I will go, and such magic as is mine will serve our cause."

"No!" All eyes turned to Jeremy. "The quarrel is mine. I shouldn't bring my friends into danger. I'll go alone."

Tremien shook his head. "You have not been listening. The quarrel is not yours alone; it is all Thaumia's, whether folk realize it or not. Though none of us are wholly good, and none, I think—not even the Great Dark One—wholly evil, still this is a struggle between the dark and the light. I will not forbid these companions to go, for I feel their decision is right. Yet the four of you shall not travel alone, either. I will send some soldiers to do what they can and to go as far as they are able; and a part of my magic will go to ward you."

"But that will weaken the guard about Whitehorn," Barach cautioned. "Already the Dark One probes and tests on the hillsides beyond the valley."

Tremien flexed his hands and clutched the arms of his chair. "He will not find me altogether ill-prepared, should he venture his forces into our valley. Though my years are a child's span compared to his, I have abided here long, and Whitehorn has received a deal of my power. Not the Dark One, or any foe who breathes the air beneath the sun, will find it easy to overthrow the mountain and the mage together."

Nul stirred. "We must leave quickly."

"The day after tomorrow," Tremien said. "You shall have a travel spell like none other; Walther has promised me that." At Melodia's startled look Tremien added kindly, "Yes, my child, I have been in touch with him. Do not wonder, for in these times the wizards of power in our land must work together. He loves you very much, Melodia, and would forgive you were it not for pride. A foolish pride perhaps, but one stronger than any magic you could work. Yes, Walther has agreed to assist us, and for more than a month he has been planning a very special travel spell. Now go, prepare yourselves. Nul, Jeremy, I would speak with you."

Melodia looked into Jeremy's eyes, reached up quickly

to kiss the corner of his mouth, and left with Barach. Tremien got up from his chair and went to the tall window. "A wet spring," he said, looking out at ragged gray cloud and steady, light rain. "The wettest in my memory. I doubt not that the Great Dark One hurls storms at us. Well! He will not wash away Whitehorn, not even were he to live another lifetime as unnaturally long as this."

"Mage Tremien—Master," Jeremy said, "do not allow Melodia to go."

Tremien turned slowly to face them, the gray light of the sodden dawn turning his bush of hair silver. "Allow? Some things, Jeremy, are foreordained. I cannot see the end of this venture, and I do not know what your destiny shall be, but trust an old wizard's feelings. She shall go, because she must. I do not know the why of it, and my heart misgives me for her safety, but it feels right. You must watch after her as best you can, but never mistrust her own strength, for it runs deeper than you think."

"But—she says she loves me."

"So she does."

Nul shook his head and went to warm himself before the fire. Jeremy lifted his hands. "If we succeed, we'll rescue Kelada and break the Hag's mirror. Then I must try to break Sebastian's, in my own world. And if I succeed in doing that, I'll never see Melodia again, or—"

Tremien waited, but Jeremy had broken off. "Many things in our world, and in yours, I think, must be done. Few, perhaps, lead to happiness, and none to happiness that lasts forever, for the universes themselves do not last forever. Whether love is for a day or for a lifetime matters little, really. We take what happiness we find, for that is the nature of our beings, and it is our nature to love where we must, even when our love is not wise or prudent."

Jeremy smiled without warmth or mirth. "It doesn't take much to see the problems of two little people aren't worth a hill of beans in this crazy world." When Tremien looked at him without comprehension, Jeremy added, "That's from what Barach might call a parable of my people."

"Yes. That's as it may be, but you must accept this: Melodia will go with you, and not only because she wants to go. In some sense she *must* go, for she has a part yet to play, as do you. If it were left to me, I would not send her, but some things are beyond my powers and beyond my decision."

"I'll talk to her," Jeremy said.

"Yes, by all means, but do not expect to persuade her." Tremien opened a drawer of his desk, took out the round spectacles, and fitted them over his nose. "You have indeed changed, Jeremy," he said, his brown eyes sharp behind the lenses. "I pray you, do not practice your magic again, save at utmost need. You have some defense left, I think, against magical attack. Nul, try."

The pika, beside the fireplace, grabbed an iron poker and with one quick overhand motion threw it at Jeremy's face. Before Jeremy could flinch away, the poker swerved three feet from him and tumbled through the air toward the window. It halted inches from the glass, quivered in midair, then swept back to the hearth, where it clattered back into its stand. "Sorry," Nul grinned at Jeremy.

"What was that about?" Jeremy demanded.

"A test only. I enchanted the poker before you came in, specially enchanted it to strike a user of magic. Not my strongest spell, certainly, but a good one. Your power diverted it."

"And if it hadn't?"

"I was ready with a counterspell. Still, you might have gotten a lump on the head. But the power should have been stopped, not just diverted, if your emanations were still as strong as when first you arrived. I wonder if the transportation spell will work. Shall we have a test?"

"All right," Jeremy said. "How do I do it?"

"Nul," Tremien said, "do you feel well enough to accompany Jeremy?"

"Feel fine."

"Good. Jeremy, I don't know how much you've been told about the transportation spell. It works across any distance, and to those not affected by the spell, the time of transportation is instantaneous. For those who are traveling, the time seems always to be exactly seven hundred and ninety-six simi—a little more than one and one-half hona. I shall send you to your quarters, together with Nul. I think now that you have used magic, now that your aura has altered, the spell will work; if not, Nul will vanish and you will be left behind. If that does happen, we must seek some remedy, for overland travel between here and the Meres is difficult at best and now dangerous. Are you ready?"

Nul stepped to Jeremy's side. "We ready."

"Yes, I guess so," Jeremy said. "What do we do?"

"Simply wait." Tremien pronounced a sharp syllable—

And then was gone. Jeremy reeled, for he stood on nothing; Nul caught his arm. "Easy. Cannot fall."

They stood in a dimly lighted, ill-defined swirl of light and color. Jeremy was reminded of the dream-whorls, but this was of a different intensity and coloring, amber, red, cream: it was as if they were inside a soft, moving balloon. "I guess it worked," Jeremy said, his voice shaky.

"Worked," Nul agreed. "Ask question?"

"What?"

"You love Melodia?"

Jeremy was silent a long while. "I don't know, Nul. I—I feel something for her. And for Kelada too."

Nul nodded. "Too bad. Pika-man have many wives. Too bad you human."

"But I can't take any wives! I have to get home!"

For a long time Nul was silent. Then he said, "When I first lose my family and tribe, my heart hurt. I think my heart hurt again when you go."

Jeremy looked down. The great beachball of a head had drooped forward, the fur on it sleek and smooth as a mole's. "I'll miss you too, Nul."

"Well, well." Nul's high-pitched voice had grown a little gruff. "We do what we must."

For some moments they stood together in silence. Then Jeremy cleared his throat. "I think," he said, "I'd better know more about the Hag if we're going to face her. And about the Great Dark One."

Nul heaved a great breath. "We have lots of time. Might as well tell you." And there, in the luminous nothing of the travel spell, he began to speak of dark and deadly things.

The Hidden Hag of Illsmere was an old evil—not as old as the Great Dark One by many hundreds of years, but ancient nonetheless, well-known and well-feared by the folk in the northwest. None knew where and how she lived exactly, for common folk had not dwelled in her domain in living memory, and she herself had turned away from her fellow wizards to pursue her own hidden paths. These had led her into the valley of a meandering river, once called the Serpent River after the manner of its course, but now known by all as the Mere River.

In the broad valley were many pools, still, deep, cold, and mysterious. From the beginning the land was too marshy for farming, and fishermen who had toiled to the pools found to their disappointment that the fish who lived in them were small and of little account; so the valley had never been a haunt of humans, even before the coming of the Hag.

She fled there, pursued by the anger of those she had harmed, generations ago. At that time she was young in villainy and weak in the full light of day. Those she had wronged tracked her until the pools became a miry swamp; then, concluding that the Hag must have been sucked down by the quicksand and muck, they retreated.

But she lived, though injured, and in the depths of the swamp she made her abode. At first this was probably a rude hut she pulled together out of brush and mud, in the days before her evil magic grew strong enough to create works of wonder. How she lived no one knew. Perhaps she fished the meres and ate the bony, shriveled fish she caught; perhaps she found water-loving plants that were good to eat and subsisted on them. Nothing was heard of her for many years, at any rate.

Then the farmers on the southern slopes of the hills below the swamps began to be troubled in the night. This was the country where sheaf, a hardy grain, grew in great abundance, and root crops were raised on large farms. Those who lived here were resigned to the ways and weather of the land; long springs and autumns, short hot summers, and bitterly cold, dark winters with howling storms sweeping in from the west. They were not people easily frightened.

But the night raiders disturbed them. Animals secured in stalls would be killed and partially butchered between dusk and dawn, with no sound or warning. Guard dogs would disappear without having sent up an alarm, or they would be found dead where they usually slept, their necks broken, and in the barns half the family cattle would be lying stiff and cold. This happened at farm after farm, in widely scattered fashion, for some time, perhaps for a whole year together. Never was there any noise or disturbance, and never did the dogs find a trail to follow after the carnage had been done.

The farmers did not move then, for they had dealt with marauders from foxes to wolves before, and at first this did not seem like a problem so very different. Some took to laying ingenious traps, enhanced with a bit of magic; others kept watches going all night to catch the raiders in the act. Neither worked. The animals died and the traps remained set; nothing happened where men stood guard all night. Finally some of the farmers, angry at their losses, pooled together to hire a magician to investigate. He came and cast his spells, felt strong, deep, magic there, and something else that he could not name; but for a price he sold the farmers spells to lay about their houses and barns.

All went quietly for some months. Then one morning a neighbor discovered one magically protected farmhouse wrecked, pulled to pieces, as if smashed by an enraged giant, and all the family within it dead. Not an animal was left alive in the barns, nor were any whole. That was the beginning of the true terror.

Before it was over, before the last farmers had abandoned their lands and fled southward, it was rumored that the animals were not the only things butchered for meat by the night raiders; the magician himself, recalled in desperation, had fought *something* one midnight, something that in the end killed him. Still, it was said that he did not perish without striking a blow, for left in the yard with his corpse was a hand, scaly, with long, webbed fingers, like nothing any human had seen before, torn off at the wrist and still oozing blood.

They sent that hand to a great mage, but the farmers lived on the very fringes of settled lands, far out of thought and mind of most to the south, and the magi at the time were engaged in a struggle with other evils. Soon the farmers were moving to safer fields, and the countryside became wholly deserted of men. The last farmers had migrated forty years or more ago, and now the fields had become blasted and bare, gashed by deep gullies where the winter snows and spring rains had washed away the soil. Now the land that once was rich farmland was dust and hard-caked mud in the summers, sucking, sour ooze in the springs and winters. The Hag's hand had reached far.

No one really knew about her, but the rumors were that she had built her palace deep in the swamps and had fenced it about with magical spells and wards to keep her secure. Rumor also said that she had learned necromancy and called the spirits of the dead to be her servants and her army, but that, Nul believed, was no talent of her own but the doings of the Great Dark One.

That was hard to prove, even for the magi. From his stronghold, the great, enigmatic southern continent of Relas, the Great Dark One stirred and strove to interfere with the rest of Thaumia. Already he had won the fifty kingdoms of Relas, and already what happened there had fallen out of the knowledge of the rest of the world. Indeed, it was said that some peoples of the other two continents, the tropical Hadoriben and Finarr of the northeastern quadrant, paid tribute to the Great Dark One. Some, mostly islanders whose homes were in the southeastern part of the world close to Relas, were even whispered to worship him. But the dark mage knew that his main foes were here, in the northwestern part of the world, in the continent of Cronbrach, and it was toward here that he most turned his will and his anger.

Once, long ago, the Great Dark One had tried to take Cronbrach-en-hof by force of arms. On a misty morning great ships had materialized from the sea fog, and from them armies had come, soldiers armed with cruel magic and marching under the protection of black banners. They had caught the magi of Cronbrach unawares, and only after a desperate struggle, led chiefly by a younger Tremien, was the Great Dark One's power broken and with it the spirit of his warriors. The war went on for many months, but without the support of the Great Dark One, the soldiers lacked direction and were pushed back into the sea or hemmed up into pockets of resistance. Not one was taken prisoner. All fought to the death, or if captured, simply died. Tremien said they were less the Dark One's men than his property, and the evil magician refused to allow others to possess what once he had called his own.

It was a terrible struggle, and part of it was the battle in which Nul's people had utterly vanished. For long years the lands of Cronbrach showed the scars of war. Even now there were blasted places where little grew, where piles of rubble and charred wood marked places where once towns had been: Jalot, Tereskas, Barhalam, all dead places now. Tremien himself had suffered, for he had pitted his will and his power against the Dark One's, and such warfare demanded much even of a great and learned wizard. Since then the Dark One had not attacked, at least not openly, and as the land healed itself, so the children of Cronbrach's armies had come to regard the battles as something remote and not their concern.

"But," Nul added, "Dark One still lives, down in Relas. Tremien think more and more he work through others. Think the Hag come under his dominion. Maybe others he not know yet."

But certainly Sebastian. The Dark One offered many rewards for those he would make his servants and his property. Sebastian, a young talent, first in the wizard schools of Vanislach in the pleasant parklands to the south and west of Whitehorn, was a man of little patience and an unquenchable thirst for knowledge. All had expected him to rise rapidly to mage status, for his potential was great and his abilities already strong. That changed seven years ago.

That was when Tremien first sensed an alteration in the magical field surrounding Thaumia. He did not know what had happened, only that it was powerful and that it boded ill. Later, he and the other magi determined that Sebastian had rashly attempted a conjuration spell beyond his age and control, and the spell had put his mind in touch with that of the Great Dark One.

Yet the Dark One, perhaps still smarting over his losses in the great war, did not attempt to possess Sebastian or to warp his will; that surely would have been felt by Tremien. Instead, the sinister mage offered to teach Sebastian ways of increasing knowledge, special methods of capturing magic that only a very great and very ancient magician would know. Sebastian, eager as he was, accepted the offer. That was the seed; the mirrors were the fruit.

"Pika-people not have mirrors," Nul said. "Tricky things. Doubles always dangerous; maybe after you leave mirror, they stay inside there, thinking of evil." But humans used mirrors, and Sebastian's mirrors became creations of wondrous magic. For one thing, they were means of communication, tied to Sebastian himself. By using the mirrors, Sebastian could speak with others and never alert Tremien or any mage of the fact; more, he could travel bodily and not be detected. But what was worse, the mirrors could be conduits of magic, taking it from one place, transferring it to another, so that the Great Dark One could, if he chose, send his power into another place, and all without Tremien's knowledge.

Tremien believed, however, that the Great Dark One had sensed in Sebastian someone whom he could not control, and so could not possess, for Sebastian's natural talents were already highly developed and largely shaped by his teachers; though he was ambitious and vastly curious, Sebastian had nothing in him of the tyrant, no great will for evil.

The Hag was another matter. How he did it Tremien did not know, but certain the old mage was that Sebastian visited the Hag, gave her a magic mirror, and that through the mirror the Great Dark One had even further corrupted that already evil mind, had made the Hag his tool and her country his stronghold. That, at last, was what brought Sebastian down; for first he was declared outlaw (his meeting with Melodia had come not long after that), and then he was captured, tried, and banished. So great was his power already that Tremien feared the event: the mirror he had given Melodia had forces about it that the magi detected but could not understand, save to know that in breaking it they risked killing Melodia, whose only crime had been an unwise love.

The forces in the Hag's mirror they could only guess at, and those in the mirror that Sebastian had created in the Between they could only fear. Whatever the Hag's powers had been before the Great Dark One caught her in the mirror, they were bound to be greater and more evil now; whatever difficulty Nul and Kelada had had in approaching her country, it was certain to be more since the Hag knew that someone was interested in her and her doings.

When Nul fell silent, Jeremy asked, "But what does the Great Dark One want from all this? Power over the whole world?"

Nul shook his head. "Death over whole world. Darkness. And him alone to watch the stars and ache to eat them."

A sudden pressure on the soles of his feet, the dying of the light, and Jeremy found himself standing beside Nul in the tower room, no longer cold from the broken window, for that had been mended, but gray in the light from the two casements. "It worked," Nul said. "We go back to Tremien now."

"Where will he be?"

"Still in same place. No real time pass for him."

Jeremy shook his head. It would be hard to get used to this mode of travel, when each trip took what seemed to him to be nearly two hours but "really" took no time at all. He followed Nul down the stairs and back to the study. Tremien looked pleased but tempered his pleasure with a warning: "You are no longer fully immune, Jeremy, to magical assault. You must remember that at all times. Magic takes many forms, not all of them as obvious as a poker flying at your face. I will give you what warding spells I can, and will advise you on creating some of your own, but no spell in existence will take the place of a watchful mind and simple native caution."

"When will we go?" Jeremy asked.

"As soon as possible. You must equip yourselves, and I wish to confer with Barach about the magical difficulties you may encounter. While you are on the way I will call together the sorcerers and magi of Cronbrach, and we will do what we can to occupy the attention of the Great Dark One. But there is more to think of than magic, and I will have many other things to consider before you leave."

One of them proved to be arms. Captain Fallon would not join the expedition, for he was getting old and stiff in the joints, but he had some presents for Jeremy. "Take this," he said, handing Jeremy a bulky something carefully wrapped in soft cloth. Jeremy unwrapped it to find a crossbow, heavier than the one he had trained with, and a quiver of black-shafted bolts. The wood gleamed with age and loving care, though the footstrap was new and stiff. Fallon looked as if he were about to weep. "Used it myself," he muttered, "back when I was younger than you. Fought the invaders to a standstill, we did, even without magic, on the downs east of Fennian's Ford. Always meant for my son to have it. Well, well, he's a builder of houses, not a soldier, and maybe he'll live the longer for it and be the happier. But you take care of it, you hear? And bring it back whole to me."

"I will," Jeremy said. "And thank you."

Fallon wiped his nose with his fingers. "Another five years and I'd have made a real bowman out of you," he muttered. "Still, you're not too bad with a bolt. Never mind the speed, now. Speed don't enter into it with a crossbowman. A longbow archer will shoot ten arrows for your three, but that's no matter. What you have to worry about is accuracy. If two longbow arrows hit true to three of yours, you're still ahead in the game, understand?"

Jeremy nodded. He had been hearing the same thing every day for weeks now. Fallon also had a sword for him, broad and short, like the blunted one Jeremy had trained with for hours until his arms felt as if they were about to fall out of their sockets. No sentiment went with the sword, but a handsome belt and scabbard did. Tremien's quartermaster, a taciturn woman named Bial, rounded out Jeremy's military equipment with a light, close-fitting helmet, studded leather gauntlets, and a coat of mail. He expected to stagger under its weight, but to his surprise found it no heavier than a thick wool coat, and even more flexible. "Magic, what d'ye expect?" Bial had asked sourly at his expression of surprise.

Jeremy considered himself ready to go, but still Tremien tarried. First the old mage cast a series of spells over Jeremy, all designed to give the younger man some arcane protection. Then Tremien and Barach were closeted fast all day. Nul told Jeremy that their military guard had been chosen: six young men of the palace force, all of them well-skilled and each, to one degree or another, talented in military magic. Still they were not ready; backpacks had to be prepared, and rations to go in them.

Melodia looked singularly out of place in her own armor, another helmet and coat of mail like Jeremy's. The steel rode incongruously over her softness, and the distress in her eyes all but broke Jeremy's heart. "I bring life, not death," she wailed. "Look at me."

"Stay, then," Jeremy said. "You shouldn't even think of going away."

"No. I do not know why, but I must see this through. I must."

Nul, who wore his own mail under a leather tunic, was in the courtyard, busy at work with his short sword (even shorter than Jeremy's) and a small, whizzing grindstone. "Put edge back on it," he grunted, running his thumb critically over the sword. "Then put pika-magic in it, stronger than before." He stepped back and whished the blade through the air, back and forth. "Let damn swamp-hoppers come now. I show them!"

Jeremy asked a question he had saved with dread: "Do you think Kelada will be all right?"

"Don't know. Think so. She smart, tough. Hag not know what to do with her; think Hag be little afraid to hurt her, for a while at least. Sometimes hard to deal with those who have little magic."

"Why?"

Nul grinned his ear-to-ear grin, and his orange eyes flashed. "Have someone who looks like she has no magic. Yes or no? Only two kinds of people like that. One is kind that has no magic. Other is the kind that has *much* magic. Hag not sure, she not in a hurry to make Kelada desperate. Think she be all right for a while."

"I hope you're right," Jeremy said as Nul leaned back into his work, making sparks fly from the grindstone to dance and skitter in the hard-packed dirt of the courtyard.

Alone, ready to go but fearing to go, Jeremy wandered the palace. Few spoke to him, for he had kept to himself during the long days of his training, but the chaplain had some kind words: "Good is rarely unmixed in this world, Jeremy, and evil seldom wholly dark. Yet the Hag and the Dark One are evil and workers of evil, beyond doubt, and in this battle you will stand on the side of the good. Let that thought be strong with your strength, and that comfort be warm in your distress, and know that our blessings go with you wherever you fare. I do not know if the God of your universe and that of ours is the same, but in my heart I feel there is but one God, and that one is the creator of all universes and is the source of all good. To that God my prayers for your safety and success will go, and to that God's care I will commend you."

Jeremy thanked him and—something he had not done in many years—himself said a little prayer then. Whether or not it reached the ears of any deity he did not know, but it heartened him a bit and helped him through the long day of waiting and through the sleepless night that followed it.

At last, well before dawn, all was ready, and the travelers assembled in the Great Hall. Only when Jeremy saw weeping women embracing their sons and husbands, the soldiers who would accompany them to the Hag's country, did he fully realize that the expedition meant as much (and perhaps more) to others as it did to him. The young men, for their part, looked indistinguishable from Jeremy: armored, wearing swords at their belts, and (four of them) bows at their backs, they remained quiet and solemn. One of them, perhaps a little older than the rest, was the dark-haired Captain Gareth; he at least gave Jeremy a smile and a wink. He was the only other traveler equipped with a crossbow.

The floor of the Great Hall had been cleared, and on it traced in lines of glowing gold a huge circle, and within the circle a star. Jeremy, Nul, Barach (who alone wore no armor but a dark-green hooded cloak, and who carried no weapon but a chin-high walking staff), Melodia, and their guard of soldiers all stood within the circle, and indeed within the heart of the star.

A high-backed wooden chair, almost thronelike, had been brought out for Tremien. He sat with head bowed as the group assembled, and when he looked up his eyes held compassion for them as well as determination. "You go forth," he said, "to meet evil. You carry with you the strength of good. May it serve you well! Our thoughts will be bent toward you, and our hopes will go with you. Be resolute, be strong, and return to us whole and victorious."

The chaplain stepped forth then with a short prayer of blessing; next, to the audible sobs of some clustered around the edges of the room, Tremien began his incantation.

Almost before he knew it, Jeremy found himself again encased in the luminous, swirling bubble of the transportation spell. Only then did he realize he had been holding his breath. He exhaled and gasped for air.

Captain Gareth grinned at him. "Well," he said, "we're on our way."

CHAPTER 10

"**I** USED TO know this country," Gareth said. "No more."

"Hag has killed it," grunted Nul.

Jeremy, standing behind him, had to agree. The party stood on the summit of a low hill, a misty rain in their faces, and looked to the west. The hills rolled away and down, each hill bare or stippled with the black trunks of a few dead trees. Here and there tussocks of wiry grass thrust out of the soil, but most of these looked dead or dying. Between the hills lay sluggish, turbid streams of mud-colored water. An oppressive smell of stagnation and decay hung heavy in the air, and the rain was cold against their skin. Barach, his staff in hand, shook his head, his eyes sad beneath their great tufted brows. "Vengeance and death," he sighed. "So it ever is with those who walk the dark paths. They seek power, and they make a desert. They seek more life for themselves, and make of their country a charnel house."

They had materialized three hours earlier under the eaves of a great forest, Arkhedden. Behind them trees of ten-foot girth or better grew thick enough to cast the ground beneath in perpetual twilight; at first they stood under the protection of smaller and more widely scattered trees. Interspersed were huge old stumps, some of them still whole, most splintering into decay and oblivion, telling the story of foresters who harvested the wood long ago. Here, too, the rain came, whispering into the small, light-green spring leaves high overhead, dripping softly to the leafmold underfoot, but the canopy prevented the clammy touch from soaking the travelers.

The ten had walked west at a good march, the trees becoming sparser as they went on until for a time they passed over grassland, last year's brown growth beginning to give way to new green blades. Here the trees

172

were still more scattered and mostly evergreen, and the land began to break into low hills. As they walked, Nul explained to Jeremy that they were somewhat to the south of the Arkhedden Forest Road, an ancient road-way that passed through the northern extremity of the old forest before crossing the hills, then the Mere River, and finally climbing to the Hyspar Pass in the Wolmas Mountains before turning to the north, eventually to the fishing town of Langrola, the Ap River, and beyond to the Lofarlan Shore and the Northwest Sea. "We have to turn north soon," Nul had said. "Try to get as close to Meres as we can along Dinsfaer Hills, then turn west to find Illsmere. But hard going."

Now they stood among the Dinsfaer Hills, the chain that made up the eastern boundary of the low valley of the Meres, and Jeremy could understand the difficulty. Stripped of growth as they were, the hills looked soggy and slippery, with the sodden land at their feet as treach-erous as a quicksand bog. Yet this was their path and their best hope, for the rocky eastern face of the Wolmas Mountains provided a much more rugged terrain, and the Mere River valley was all but swamp.

"Let's be off," Gareth said in a voice not cheerful exactly but at least one not ready to give in to doubt so early in the game. He led them down the hillside, then found a way that put them on the shoulder of one of the sluggish streams—really just runoff from weeks of rain, Jeremy decided—and they squished their way to the north. No one talked much in the persistent drizzle, and the day wore on as they trudged along. Presently the land sloped up a little more, and they climbed a ridge that turned out to be the embankment of a broad road running east and west and cutting directly across their path.

There they rested for a few minutes, and as they set-tled down on the broad shoulder of the road, the rain ceased for a while. Overhead, low gray clouds swagged dark and ragged, but here and there a hole in them lightened to silver, and once or twice they even glimpsed blue sky and, far off, the slanting rays of sunbeams broke through, like ramps leading up to heaven. Gareth de-cided they might as well eat while in camp. "I wish we could make a fire, and have something hot," he said. "Plenty of deadwood about for one, but all this rain has soaked it to the core."

"I think," Melodia said, "I can remedy that, if you'll collect the wood."

Gareth sent two of the soldiers down the embankment to a hillside, where they picked up a couple of armloads of fallen branches. The captain was right, for when they brought the wood back, it was slimy and black from weeks of rain. Pieces of bark clung to their arms after they dropped the wood, and it was a most unpromising pyre.

But Gareth didn't question Melodia. He snapped the smaller branches across his knee—many were so wet that they merely bent like green shoots—and Nul broke out a little hatchet to chop short lengths of thicker wood. "Really wet," he grunted to Jeremy, holding up a freshly cut stick. The cut end was just as dark as the outside, and it oozed water.

Soon Garth had built a rim of stones and within it had laid out the wood for the fire. "Now, Lady," he said with a grin, "if you have magic, use it. Though I have never heard of magic that could burn water!"

Melodia took from her pack the tinderbox. Barach's eyebrows rose in interest, and he leaned forward with the air of an interested professional. "It isn't my own magic, Captain Gareth, but that of an elemental." With flint and steel she quickly struck fire to a pinch of tinder. No sooner had the flame appeared than it coalesced into the minute form of Smokharin. In a few words Melodia explained what they needed, and Smokharin agreed to try.

She spread more tinder, and in the form of flame Smokharin leaped into the midst of the soaking wood. The smaller branches steamed and whistled for a few moments; then flame, blue and weak at first, but growing brighter and stronger each second, began to gnaw away at the kindling. Before long the ends of the larger logs hissed and bubbled as the water was driven out, and within a few minutes the party warmed itself before a good blaze that burned almost without smoke.

Captain Gareth bowed. "Lady Melodia, you have powerful allies in the world of magic."

"A domesticated elemental!" Barach said. "Rare indeed is a friendship between one of their race and a human man or woman. A story is told of a fisherman who appealed to the elemental of water for a catch: 'I am so weak and you so strong. Pray give me fish as an act of kindness!' The element agreed and began to fling fish into the boat, so that within a few moments the fisherman's boat sank, drowning him. Beware the kindness of an elemental, for it is a blade that cuts the unwary hand! Captain, I believe you have wronged the Lady Melodia; this is not magic exactly, but it is a power even greater: simple friendship.''

With a cheerful grin Gareth said, "If I did wrong you, it was through my ignorance, which is my own and honestly come by. But I apologize for my doubts! Now, let's see what we can do about a meal."

They managed a sort of stew, which Jeremy found very bracing. Melodia, though, refused to eat any. She contented herself with a cup of steaming tea, another of a sort of gruel made from sheaf, and some dried fruit. They lingered perhaps longer than they had intended, for the fire was gratifying after the chill of the rain, but at last Gareth declared that it was time to make more progress. Smokharin, by now a little humanoid creature a foot high, materialized, dwindled, and leaped back into the tinderbox, leaving behind glowing embers that immediately began to send up billows of blue-gray smoke. Cosk and Prechet, two of Gareth's men, bent to scatter dirt over the fire, and within a few minutes all trace of it was gone.

The land was higher, the hills more like ridges running north and south, on the other side of the Arkhedden Forest Road. Far to their right, they could see pine trees, dark green against the yellow-brown background of last year's vegetation, but away to the west on their left hand, the land dropped and dropped until it lost itself in the winding toils of a river. Here were no living trees, indeed no living things at all, unless the green scum on the face of the river lived, or the dry stalks of sedge that sheltered in a few places yet held life. Melodia looked down into the dismal valley and shuddered. She reached for Jeremy's hand, and they walked holding hands for a long time but exchanged no words.

The sun sank low, obscured by the thinning cover of cloud, breaking out at last just before evening. Nul, swinging along on his long legs just ahead of Jeremy, turned his head to the west. "Sun red. Maybe good sign; maybe rain stopping."

"Day is stopping," Gareth said, "and so must we. But I don't like the idea of a camp up here on top of the ridge. Let's see if we can find a more protected spot, and one that we can defend at need."

The sun was halfway below a distant jagged horizon when they found a place that satisfied Gareth: the ridge they were on curled around, first to the west, then to the north, then back to the east again, and in the crook of the curl was a broad ledge where grass yet grew. It was a little below the crest of the ridge, and it faced east. They descended a few feet to a point where the ledge was perhaps twenty feet across. The grass was long, narrow of blade, and very springy. In good weather it would have been dry and pale gray, but after all the rain it was a dull yellow, except for the places where new shoots were working through.

Gareth's men quickly prepared the site. Dalom and Wessowin, complaining good-naturedly about the task, went around the shoulder of the ridge to dig a latrine trench. Cosk, away up the hill, kept watch. Syvelin and Prechet went to work to provide a place to rest and eat. They spread groundsheets and broke out the provisions. As soon as the latrine detail came back, they all had a quick meal and then talked quietly in the early part of dusk. Gareth arranged a rotation of the guard, using his soldiers only. Jeremy objected, but Gareth pointed out that these men had had some little experience in keeping watch, that Nul had earned a rest, that Melodia and Jeremy, the magicians of the team, were to be protected. Finally, and without really regretting it, Jeremy let Gareth have the point.

He, Melodia, Barach, and Nul slept in the center of a circle of sleepers. Despite their nearness to the Meres and to the Hag, despite the danger everyone seemed to feel they were exposing themselves to, Jeremy, exhausted, fell quickly into sleep. When Gareth awakened him only a few minutes later, he began to protest; then he realized the sun was up already and it was time to resume the march.

So three full days passed. Their progress north was slowed as the ridges began to heel away to the west, and Gareth began to seek landmarks. "There is, or used to be, a little stream that leads almost directly west from these hills," he said on the morning of the fourth day. "It joins the river before long and so turns south, but just beyond the river is Illsmere. That is the most direct route to the Hag's homeland."

"Best-guarded too," Nul muttered. "She know we coming before we reach river."

"Yes," Barach agreed. "Though she could not sense Smokharin's magic—at least, I have never heard of a mage who could detect that of an elemental—she will certainly become aware of us as we descend the western slopes of these cursed bare hills. Sooner, if we dared use any magic other than that of the fire."

"That may be," Gareth said. "But her power has grown great, and we could not long keep our approach a secret in any case, no matter what direction we attempted. Still, we will do what we can. We have not much cover anywhere, either here or in the valley, but such as we have we will use, and we will do our best to make speed our cover, too."

At least the rains had eased. On the second day they had only intermittent misting rains, and after that none at all. A few days even saw bright sunshine, still wan from a sun that had not the strength to climb all the way to zenith at noon, but giving them heart and reminding them that to the south of them, the land already was turning green in the height of spring. Jeremy wondered, from time to time, about Tremien. Barach, unusually quiet, advised Jeremy not to worry. "Tremien is an old fox, and he knows a trick or two that will puzzle the Hag and even the Great Dark One. Still, I too wish we had his counsel. I would use the communication spell, but we are much too near the Hag's domain; she would be certain to detect it. Cover or no, I think it would be unwise to fly banners as we come into her influence."

Finally, early on that fourth morning, when the valley below was lost beneath a shining mist which they saw from the ridge as the top of a ground-hugging cloud, Gareth found what he had sought: a deep cut in the hillside led away to the west, and down in the bottom of the cut a clear stream leaped gurgling from stone to stone. "Here is the stream," the captain said. "Now, if I remember right, we can climb down into this bed a little farther on, and that will give us some cover until we come out into the valley."

Nul looked uneasy. "What if Hag's soldiers come? They on top, we caught in crack."

"It's a chance," Gareth admitted.

Barach laid his hand on Nul's shoulder. "Nul, my friend, once a man encountered a great hungry longtooth. The cat scented him and gave chase, and the man fled. Finally he found himself on the very edge of a steep precipice, with the longtooth crouching to spring. In desperation the man threw himself over the precipice and barely managed to grab a little tree that grew out from the side of the cliff. There above him, he could see the snarling face of the longtooth, just far enough away so that the cat could not get him. Then, hanging by his arms, the man looked down between his dangling toes. On the ground below, just far enough down so she could not spring up to him, was the longtooth's mate."

Barach finished and for a long time Nul stared at him with his great orange eyes. "That not make any sense at all," he said.

"It's a parable," Barach explained. "It's meant to show that—"

"Why was man walking around without weapon?"

"Well, I don't know. It's just how the story—"

"Everybody know you don't run from longtooth. Climb tree maybe, but not run."

"But there weren't any trees!"

"Then it not a longtooth. Longtooths—" Nul broke off and looked puzzled. "Longtooths or longteeth?"

"Longtooths," Barach said, "but—"

"Why longtooths if it tooth and teeth? I break out my tooth, but new one grow back among my other teeth. Tooth, teeth. Longtooth, longteeth. Human talk not make sense!"

"But 'longtooth' is the name of an animal. One longtooth has two long teeth—"

Nul put his hands to his head. "Why mate of longtooth at bottom of cliff?"

"I don't know! That's not the point of the story!"

"What point?"

"The point is that sometimes one cannot choose between dangers!'"

"Then why not just *say* that? Why story about man in first place?"

"Because it's a parable!"

Nul blinked. "Look. One foot, two feet, right?"

Gareth burst out as if he could stand no more: "This way. Follow me."

But all the way down the draw, Nul kept muttering to himself, "Tooth, teeth, tooths. Foot, feet, foots. Rock, rocks. Reeks?" Barach rolled his eyes to the heavens. The hillside was still slick and muddy, and they slipped a bit. Jeremy and Melodia both took falls, neither of them serious, while two of the soldiers assisted Barach over the worst places. Finally, though, they stood beside the stream, on a rocky bed of smooth-worn stones.

Gareth suggested they fill their canteens. "This water is good," he said, "and I doubt if any in the valley can be trusted. We may have two days' march before we come to the river, and then perhaps another day before we reach the Hag's abode."

"We can't carry enough water to see us there and back," Jeremy said.

Gareth shrugged. "If we succeed, you or Barach can use a purification spell. If we fail, well, we won't need the water." Which was true enough, so Jeremy offered no more complaints but filled both of his large canteens with water. He felt considerably heavier as they resumed their march westward and downward.

One of the soldiers, the taciturn, blond young man named Syvelin, ranged ahead as a scout. As they descended, the mists closed in, and before too long Syvelin was out of sight. Nul grew increasingly more uneasy, swiveling his shoulders as he turned his head on his short neck to peer through the thickening fog, almost pricking up his small pointed ears as he listened. Jeremy, for his part, felt safer; if the mists made it harder for them to spot enemies, it made them equally hard to see. But the countryside was changing as they moved on and down, and not for the better: again, the rank, sour smell of stagnant mud was in their nostrils, and underfoot the rocky bed of the stream began to grow muddy and clinging, sucking at the heels of his boots when he made a misstep, making each foot weigh a hundred pounds.

The others moved more silently. Syvelin suddenly ran back toward them, not making a sound, and Gareth held up a hand to call a halt. The young soldier panted up, then gasped, "Some creatures, Captain. A patrol, I think, making their way across the mouth of the draw. Coming up from the south, maybe six of them."

"At least the wind, what there is of it, is in our faces," Gareth said. "Well, there's no place to hide, and I'll not go back. There's nothing for it but to try to take them by surprise. Wessowin, you take the rearguard with Barach, Nul, and the lady. The rest of you, forward, and as quietly as you can foot it."

Jeremy unslung his crossbow. He began to cock it, noticed the brand-new leather footstrap that Fallon had put on, and carefully wiped the mud from his boot sole before slipping his toe into the loop. Then he pulled the string into place, locked the trigger, and had a bolt ready to fire. He went forward with the others, but very cautiously, looking where he placed his feet with every step.

He was looking down when the creatures first came into view, but Gareth's sudden cry jerked his eyes up. They had taken the patrol by surprise, for the manlike things were just going for their weapons. Four bows sang almost at once, and one creature screamed and fell sideways.

Jeremy was frozen. The creatures were indeed like enormous frogs or toads, but with a manlike build to their bodies, with swollen arms and legs. They roared at the attackers with deep voices, and in their hands they swept short swords through the mist; as a group, the five of them still on their feet charged.

The other bowmen had gone for their swords. Gareth met the first onrush together with Syvelin, and their blades rang against those of the creatures; then Jeremy was faced with an attacker of his own, a pop-eyed horror whose mouth was wide open, showing no teeth but an arc of what looked like white bone. In reflex, he fired the crossbow, and a black bolt sprouted as if by magic in the thing's throat. It stumbled, gurgled, dropped its sword, and clawed at the protruding shaft; its momentum carried the thing right to Jeremy's feet.

It looked up at him with huge eyes rolling, pawed at his boots, and a fountain of blood jetted from its mouth. It made gobbling sounds deep in its throat. Jeremy was transfixed.

From behind the creature a man thrust a sword suddenly and hard into the skull. The whole body stiffened, jerked, and went limp. Syvelin pulled the sword out, grating it against bone, and grinned at Jeremy. "All down," he said.

The battle had ended almost before Jeremy was aware it had begun. One of the soldiers had a cut on the arm, and several had minor cuts across their knuckles, but none was really injured. All of their foes had been struck down. The one first hit by Gareth's crossbow bolt had not been killed, but had dragged his body several yards away. Gareth followed the trail of blood and killed the thing. "Two-eyes, all of them," he said, wiping his sword. "If Tremien was right, if the three-eyes are the Hag's spies, she is not yet aware of us." He rolled over the creature at Jeremy's feet. "Pretty things, aren't they? The Hag raised them out of the creatures of the swamp, gave them just enough intelligence to be her slaves. Get your bolt, Jeremy. You may need it later."

Jeremy looked down in revulsion. The being's eyes were still open, the right one flecked with mud. Below the shelflike chin the shaft of his arrow protruded perhaps a hand's breadth. "How do I do it?" he asked.

Gareth gave him a look of surprise, then put his boot on the thing's chin and pressed it back and down. The captain reached for the arrow, worked it around in the wound, and pulled it free. He took a few steps to the stream, stooped to rinse the shaft clean of blood, and brought it back. "Here you are."

Jeremy took the bolt and dried it on the tail of his tunic. Then he dropped it back in the quiver. Gareth clapped him on the arm. "That was a good shot," he said. "Never mind, Jeremy. The thing wasn't human, and it would have cut your heart out had you given it the chance."

"I know," Jeremy said. "But it suffered."

"It doesn't suffer now, at any rate. Let's get rid of these bodies, men! The rest of these beauties will be looking for us when this batch fails to report at sundown. We may as well make it hard for them to find us!"

The six bodies were quickly buried in shallow graves, the bloodstained earth turned over. Then the soldiers collected the rearguard and the party hurried on into the mist and into the valley. Jeremy walked mechanically, distant and abstracted. He had killed a second time now, and he found it disturbing.

True, the creature he killed looked more animal than

human—but then, so did Nul, for that matter. And there had been anguish in those great eyes, and a plea for mercy. But that was not what bothered Jeremy the most.

For, in truth, in the instant when he had loosed the bolt and knew it would hit its mark, in the moment before the creature jolted, stumbled, and fell forward, gagging on its own blood, Jeremy had felt a sense of excitement, of power.

And he had loved it.

As they went farther into the valley, the mounting sun thinned the fog to a haze that opened before them and closed behind. Jeremy estimated their range of visibility at perhaps a quarter of a mile or a little more. The walls of the streambed fell away and behind, and at last they squelched along on the bank of the stream, occasionally crossing miry rivulets that fed into it. Jeremy found the silence unnerving, realizing only now how much he had really heard while they were still up on the high ridge: the cries of birds passing overhead, the rustle of little mouselike things in the dry grass, the soft voice of the wind in his face. All was silence down here, silence and treacherous, trembling mud underfoot. It was hard going, and by midday they were sweating and weary, their boots heavy with clots of clinging muck. Still, they paused only long enough to eat a quick meal while standing up; then they started forward again.

Melodia struggled especially hard, and so did Barach. Finally Gareth decided that the way was just too muddy, and he struck away to the left, heading for what seemed to be higher and drier ground. They followed this path for a while until it turned to the south, and then they plunged down into the muck once again. They had left the stream behind, and here the footing was a little better. At length Prechet, who was taking his turn as advance scout, came into view out of the haze, standing quietly. Without turning, he beckoned them on.

Jeremy could see now that Prechet stood on the margin of a round pool of water, its far side hidden in the mist that rose in ghostlike swirls from the dark surface, but from the curving border that he could see, the pond must have been several hundred yards across. "One of the meres," Barach puffed. "Deep they are, and treacherous."

The party made a way through brittle stands of reed. The water looked foul, scummed with green, still and dark; it would have been a mirror had there been anything but haze to reflect. Greasy clusters of bubbles rode on the surface, but no living thing disturbed the water, no breeze of wind rippled the surface. "Dead," Prechet said as they came up. "The Hag's work."

"There are small fish, at least," Gareth said, nodding toward a clump of reeds growing from the edge of the water. Shadowy little torpedo shapes clustered there, riding as if at anchor in the tideless pool. "And perhaps larger things, out where the water is deep. I do not like this spot. Let's see if we can make our way around this."

They turned back to the north, skirting the mere, and at last its margin curved away from them. They walked on through a dim landscape, and Jeremy, for his part, thought the air became a little fresher away from the slimy, rotting water. At least the land underfoot became firmer. For some time they made good progress. Toward evening they climbed a gentle slope and found themselves on the domed top of a little hill like an overturned boat almost submerged in mud. Tree stumps, not cut neatly but rotted where they stood, still jutted from the hill, and some exceptionally wiry and tough grass still grew there. "This must have been a pleasant place, many generations ago," Gareth said. "Think! Once birds nested and fruit grew here in the warm sun of spring. And now it's nothing more than an island of dirt in a great sea of mud." The hill was perhaps a half mile north to south, an eighth of a mile across from east to west, but it was relatively dry, and there they decided to pass the night. This time, though, Gareth ordered two guards posted.

So gloomy was it as the shadows lengthened that they chanced a fire. Melodia summoned Smokharin and explained to him what was needed. The salamander understood at once and produced a low blaze, hardly more than a glow, certainly not visible at a thousand paces, and wholly without smoke. Still, it provided warmth and cheer, and over it they cooked more stew. Gareth took cups of it around to the guards before he squatted to eat his own rations.

Later, the coals reduced to a few friendly embers, the party sat on ground cloths around the campfire. "A song would lift my spirits now," Gareth said, "but the sound would carry. Let us have a story instead."

Prechet, reclining with elbow bent and supporting his head with his right hand under his chin, said, "A story! And a new one. Let the outlander Jeremy speak of some matter that we've never heard before."

The others agreed. Jeremy, embarrassed, protested, but Melodia leaned softly against him and added her entreaty to the others. "All right," he laughed. "Give me a chance to think." He wondered what tale might please these warriors, what magical story might amuse these users of magic. A notion struck him. Well, why the hell not? "I'll tell you," he said, "the story of a young prince of my world. Now, he had been away from home, studying, when word came that his father, the king, had died suddenly. He left for home, but no sooner had he arrived than he learned that his mother had already married his father's younger brother, Claudius.

"The prince—his name was Hamlet—"

"H—Hamlet?" Nul asked. He had some problems with *h*'s.

"That's right. Hamlet was dismayed that his mother had remarried so soon after his father's death."

"He should have been," Syvelin muttered. "Something unnatural about that, I'll warrant."

"Yes, well, anyway, while Hamlet was staying in the palace, he heard that a ghost had been seen walking the battlements—" And Jeremy was off into a condensed version of the play, as much as he remembered of it. To his surprise, his audience became entranced. At one point, there was a hot little debate going on the sidelines as to whether or not Hamlet should have acted immediately upon being told to punish Claudius. Syvelin was all for immediate action, but Barach urged the virtue of waiting.

"Revenants are tricky things," Barach offered. "A cousin of mine was once visited by a ghost that claimed to be her uncle's. It looked and sounded like him. But later it was discovered that her uncle was alive—"

"Sssst!" shushed Nul, who was absorbed in Hamlet's soliloquy on suicide, rendered in butchered fashion by Jeremy. All the audience paid close attention, and at the sanguinary end, with most of the cast being taken off stage in a death march, they broke into enthusiastic approbation.

"You should write the tale down," Gareth urged. "It would make a fine long ballad too!"

"Or a play," Melodia suggested. "I think mummers could present the story very well."

"Why Hamlet not kill Claudius after mummers trick him?" Nul asked.

"I told you. Claudius was praying. Hamlet didn't want his soul to go to heaven, so he waited."

"Should have sent soul to heaven, body underground," Nul growled. The story had really stirred the little pika's indignation. "Captain right, you write all down when we get back to Whitehorn. You good storyteller."

Jeremy grinned self-consciously. "I don't know if I could do justice to it," he said. "But if we get back, I may try to write down what I remember of the tale."

" 'To be or not to be,' " growled Nul, rolling the words with his round black tongue. "That the question."

"The question now is who will be the first asleep?" laughed Gareth. "A fine tale, nobly told, and all new, Jeremy. You could make a rich living as a maker of stories."

"I did that, sort of, back in my world," Jeremy said. "But the stories were very short ones. Usually they were about how one kind of sweetened water was better than another kind, or how one soap made clothes cleaner than any of the other kinds."

"Those stories no good," Nul told him. "You make more Hamlets. Blood, revenge, love—that what people want in a story."

"I'll remember, good pika," Jeremy promised. That night, as he lay rolled in his blanket, the sky dark except for the luminous smudge of the waxing moon somewhere above the fog, Jeremy thought of the proposition. If he only had the books from home, he could indeed make a good living as a teller of stories. He wondered which ones he could bring to Thaumia. Shakespeare, certainly, and Sophocles. And the magic lovers should delight in Spenser. Tolkien. How about some more mundane selections? His audience tonight had found the most wonder in the ordinary parts of *Hamlet:* the clever trick of using the play to catch the conscience of the king, the heartbreaking madness of Ophelia. Would Faulkner go over here? Jeremy fell asleep musing on the possibilities and smiling to himself.

* * *

He awakened early the next morning, another day of heavy fog, and stood an hour's tour of guard duty together with Gareth. They talked but little, and when the others arose, they ate a hasty breakfast and resumed their westward march. Soon Jeremy looked back at the little firm hummock of an island with considerable nostalgia, for increasingly they waded through nearly liquid mud, mud that found its way even through their well-oiled boots, that clung to their feet almost like an importuning live thing, that stank and bubbled and steamed into the already foggy air.

They made only a few miles before coming upon another mere, this one much larger than the last and with less definite borders: here the lake gradually blended with the mud around it so that one could not be sure whether one walked beside the lake or actually splashed in its waters. Syvelin got badly mired at one point, going in up to his waist, and it took three of them and considerable tugging to free him. This day the fog did not burn off but rather seemed to thicken as time wore on, until the travelers, marching two abreast, could scarcely see the backs of those going before. Gareth cast about for an easier route, but none was to be found. Poor Nul floundered, for though he was the lightest of all the party, his stubby feet sank easily into the mud and came out again only with the greatest difficulty.

Still they toiled onward, skirting yet another stench-heavy mere, splashing through sluggish winding knee-deep streams, tending, as far as Gareth could judge, westward. "We could use Kelada's talent now," Jeremy puffed to him as they tired to negotiate a stretch of particularly sticky mud. "She's never lost."

"Would we had her with us already! But the general line of our travel is clear. We will soon reach the great river, the Hagsmere, and then I fear our true difficulty will begin."

"Mine started some five thousands of paces back," grunted Barach behind them. "What difficulty do you foresee, more than this?"

"The river is too wide and deep to ford," Gareth explained. "And if it is as foul and noisome as these cursed meres, I doubt that any of us would wish to swim it."

Nul shivered. "Ugh. No, thank you."

"Then how do we cross?" Jeremy asked.

"There must be bridges. There used to be a good road through these parts, the Market Road, back when some farming was done in the valley, and it crossed the river over a good sturdy rock bridge. Unless some mischance has wrecked it, the bridge should still stand. Yet I do not know where it is exactly, and finding it in this weather will cost us much time."

"Will the Hag have left it?" Melodia asked.

"I think so. Her creatures are born from things that love the water, but they could not swim the river fully armed. But let us worry about what the Hag has done to the bridge after we find the river. Onward, now."

They came suddenly to the river not long after that: a sullen, dark expanse of water that at first they took for a new and larger mere until Nul noticed that the bubbles on its surface floated slowly toward the south. The fog still had not lifted. Two of Gareth's soldiers were exhausted from helping Barach along, and the old wizard was in even worse shape. Melodia found a fallen tree and sat on the trunk, staring sightlessly ahead, her whole body trembling. "Now," Gareth said, "we need to seek the bridge, but whether it is to the north or south I have no idea."

Prechet spoke up: "Send parties north and south to look out the land. The rest of you stay here and rest."

"I see you are one of the party." Gareth smiled. "Thanks, good Prechet! You and Syvelin go to the south, and—"

Nul stood. "I go north," he said. "Jeremy, you come?"

"I'll go with you."

Gareth hesitated, looked from the pika to the man and back again. "Well, why not?" he asked. "Each party to go no more than two thousand before turning back. Keep good count!"

Jeremy unbuckled his pack and shrugged out of it. "No sense in carrying so much weight," he said. "Will you keep the crossbow as well for me? In this fog I'd have no chance of using it anyway. The sword will have to do."

"I'll keep it safe, storyteller," Gareth said. "You do not have to go, you know, but I see you wish to go, and I will not stop you. Take with you the thanks of those of us who will rest."

"We'll be back as quickly as we can," Jeremy told Melodia. Stunned with weariness, she merely nodded.

Nul too had stripped himself of his pack, and together they made their way northward, Nul counting under his breath. A *thousand* meant a thousand double paces, a distance approximating a mile or a little bit more back on earth; Nul was shorter than a man, of course, but his spidery long legs made up the difference, and Jeremy was content to have him do the reckoning. The mud didn't improve, and their strides were not exactly strides, but still they made painful and slow headway. More than an hour passed by, Jeremy estimated, before they came to the end of their two thousand. "No bridge," grunted Nul, shaking his round head in doleful regret.

"No. Pity the whole way wasn't like this last little ridge," Jeremy said, for the last few steps of the way had taken them onto a narrow ledge of firm footing.

Nul grunted and kicked at the ledge, then made a noise of surprise. "Look!"

Jeremy stooped closer to the surface. It was rock—no, not rock, dark bricks, evenly laid. They were on a straight line of brick perhaps two and a half feet wide. It looked like a wall of some sort or—"A foundation," Jeremy said.

"Yes! Yes! Place where man-house used to be. See, there ahead, on bank?"

Something jutted into the water. Not a bridge but some handiwork of humans, certainly: a crumbling brick rectangle, slimed with mud now, but once long ago, it must have been a pier. Nul almost danced in his excitement. "Market town! This is River Market on old maps, place where valley farmers brought crops, sent them south on river boats! Bridge should be north of here, not far."

Jeremy said, "Well, let's go!"

They trotted along the line of the wall until it gave out, then found other traces of the older world: hewn beams, soft and rotten now but holding their shape still; scattered brick, mounds of rubble, and once a square, slimy pool where the basement of some building had been dug ages ago. The ground became cluttered with broken brick and masonry. It was firm underfoot at any rate, and they made good time for perhaps a quarter of a thousand paces. At last Nul stopped short and hissed in pleasure. "There!" he whispered, pointing ahead. "Bridge?"

Jeremy squinted into the fog. A great, dark, humped shape loomed ahead, arching out toward the river. They came a few steps more, and he said to Nul, "Yes! Bridge!"

It alone of all the works of human hands seemed whole. They walked out a little way onto the span, saw that the arch soared up and then down on the other side in one piece, and grinned at each other. Jeremy walked to the side and peered over a waist-high balustrade, but fog hid the water below. Nul came up beside him. "Not far now," the pika said. "Illsmere maybe two, three hona past bridge. We go back for others."

They started back, hating to plunge back into the mire at the end of the first wall they had come to but making the step anyway. For a time they trudged along in silence. Then Nul suddenly checked and looked back. "Hear something?" he hissed.

Jeremy listened with all his being. "I don't—yes." It was a flapping sound, the sound of flat feet pounding through the mud. Nul drew his sword, and Jeremy followed suit, his heart beating faster.

"Sound like only one of them," Nul whispered. "You go off to side, I stay here."

"Good luck," Jeremy murmured before he slipped away. He kept the little pika in sight, but went somewhat ahead of him and tried to steel himself to face their pursuer.

The creature burst upon him before he was ready, and it would be hard to say which of them was the more surprised. The frog-thing gaped, then swung its sword hard at him in a vicious backhand slash. Jeremy tried to parry, but the sheer force of the blow caught him badly off balance, and he felt the sword ripped from his grasp. He tried to dive inside the creature's swing, missed his footing, and sprawled in the mud. Just as he turned over, he heard his sword splash into the river. The creature had spun on him, its eyes glaring (three eyes! three eyes!) madly as it drew back as if it were a woodsman about to split a stump. Jeremy cowered back from certain death—

Nul came howling at the creature's flank. One chop of his sword bit deep into the creature's leg, staggering it. Its death blow came apart as it tried to turn on the new assailant—but too late. Nul, with a shout and a leap, chopped again, this time striking the thing's neck. Its head reeled back, spraying cold blood, it stumbled, and then it fell facedown in the mud beside Jeremy. It bubbled once, shivered, and died, its head canted at a crazy angle, its neck half cut through, only the spinal column holding it in place.

Jeremy pushed himself to his feet and for a long moment stared at the thing: manlike, froglike, it wore a helmet shaped like a turtle's carapace, a short, kiltlike garment of leather, and a scabbard. Otherwise its warty, gray-green skin was bare. Long bones showed through the flesh of the legs, a splayed and flattened rib cage through the skin of the torso. Its huge feet were webbed, as were the hands, one of them hidden beneath the body, the other clutching the hilt of its sword.

"Filthy swamp-hopper," Nul growled, his chest heaving. He was splattered with mud and blood, the fur on his face matted with it until he was all but unrecognizable, but his orange eyes burned vividly when he turned them toward Jeremy. "Where your sword?"

"I lost it."

Nul wrenched the monster's sword from its outflung hand. The fingers, really the supports of the webbing, twitched, opening and closing spasmodically. "Head already dead," Nul advised it. "Time for you to die, too, stupid." Hefting the sword, he frowned. He wrinkled his nose at it as he took a few experimental swashes. "This is a bad blade, old, rusty. But better than nothing. Here."

Jeremy took it. It was longer by a few inches than the one he had lost, but it fit the scabbard well enough. Nul was already tugging at the monster's arms. "Help me."

Jeremy took its feet and together they dragged the thing to the river. They tumbled it in. Nul shoved its slack buttock with his foot, and they watched it drift out and spin lazily in the current, its nearly severed head hanging forward, underwater, a dark stain spreading slowly from the hacked flesh. Nul's ears twitched. "Another," he said, peering northward through the gloom.

Jeremy drew the unfamiliar blade, finding its balance awkward, its hilt unfamiliar to his palm. The sounds were coming again, less regular but more frantic, it seemed, and again from somewhere to the north. They had no time to prepare a plan of battle, for it was already on them.

A shape burst from the fog, head low, running full-tilt through the mud. Nul leaped forward, but the intruder dived nimbly around him, struck out at Jeremy with no weapon but a handful of stinging nails. The body crashed hard into him, not allowing him room to maneuver his blade, and Jeremy felt himself borne down. He grappled with the attacker, rolled in the muck.

"Jeremy! Get head out of way!" Nul yelled, dancing beside them.

"Jeremy?" the thing asked in a familiar voice.

They had rolled into a broad, deep puddle, and Jeremy had pinioned the creature. At second glance, the head *did* seem more human, and the body—Jeremy dropped his sword and began to scoop handfuls of water into a face obscured under a thick layer of mud. His attacker coughed and spluttered.

Two gray eyes glared angrily up at him. "Glad to see you, too!"

"Good God!" Jeremy said, scrambling up. "Put away your sword, Nul." He extended a hand to the figure in the mud. "We've found Kelada."

CHAPTER 11

"LET'S GO," Kelada said as soon as Jeremy pulled her up. "They're after me."

"You armed?" Nul asked.

"No. I barely escaped with my skin, let alone a weapon. Let's go!" Kelada was caked with mud, coated with it: it was difficult to tell that she wore any clothing other than the thick black goo. Nul drew a dagger from his belt and handed it to her.

"This way," he said, taking the lead south.

"Go," Jeremy said, pushing Kelada ahead of him. A fair amount of the swamp ran into his mouth as he shouted, gritty, bitter, tasting of rot and ashes. He spat as he ran, and with his free hand tried to wipe his mouth. In the other hand he kept the sword out this time, held at the ready as they raced along the river's edge. The fog still clung thick to everything, distorting proportions, masking distances. They had not gone far when Jeremy heard a booming, drumlike call behind them and to their left. Another, closer, answered from ahead of them.

Without a word Nul veered off to their left, and Kelada and Jeremy followed. They plunged into a cold standing pool of waist-deep water, and Nul desperately lifted his chin as he waded even deeper; then he was out the other side and loping into the fog. They climbed a rise and found themselves on another islandlike hill, this one lower and smaller than the one of the camp. A jumble of boulders broke through its crown, roughly rectangular moss-grown stones the size of automobiles, lying as if dropped there by the hand of a careless giant. Nul scrambled around these, then froze. Sounds of pursuit came from that direction. "Back!" the pika barked to the other two.

But too late, for already running foes had reached the

foot of the hill. The three of them retreated to an angle of stone, their backs protected, pressed into a thick, springy layer of moss. "Jeremy," Nul whispered, "use magic."

"But Tremien said—"

"Forget Tremien! We dead unless you—there!"

Eight or nine of the frog-creatures were scrambling toward them from the fog. Kelada cursed and brandished her dagger as, using both hands, Nul menaced them with his sword. The monstrosities hesitated for only a moment before coming on, more warily but with the evident purpose of attacking. "Use magic!" he pleaded again. "Make weapon, something!"

The monsters, without pausing, chattered to one another in a language that seemed mainly pops, clicks, and guttural gasps. They charged now in a group, swords out and swirling. Nul clashed with one of them, got in a good blow that spun the thing away with a deeply gashed leg, and then had to take a step back as another closed. Kelada, between Nul and Jeremy, retreated: her dagger was simply no match for the swords. Three of the beasts came toward Jeremy, their mouths gaping, their movements wary, perhaps because of his greater height.

His brain was frantic with formulation, visualization and realization. Words of power, the strongest words he knew—damn! A creature had struck out with a vicious hack that he barely managed to catch—and his sword was broken two feet from the hilt. The spell had to be strong, strong, the best he, anyone, could do. The others were closing in—

Forgetting himself, Jeremy yelled in English, "My sword is NEW and IMPROVED!"

What happened next he could never accurately recall. Certainly a fierce light blazed on that barren hilltop, like a white-hot burst of lightning that went on and on without end or thunder, and certainly the source was the sword he held, no rusted short sword now but a veritable Excalibur, nearly man-long and so ponderous in seeming that he lifted his left hand to the hilt. Not that he needed the other hand, for in his grasp the blade held no weight. It leaped with a life of its own, seemingly, and Jeremy watched the three creatures go down in a tangle of limbs, wounds, and weapons before he fully realized he was fighting them.

One had reached for Kelada. It drew back hissing, leaving its forearm behind, the hand on the ground still clenching and unclenching. Another screamed when its sword was broken—no, not broken, shattered, *exploded* to flying fragments no larger than grains of sand as Jeremy lashed out again; another two he skewered, just like that, and suddenly the three companions stood alone atop their hill amid the fog and the retreating moans of the wounded monsters.

"Kazazz," breathed Nul.

Jeremy blinked. The bright blade glowed with wondrous splendor, and the sword seemed to thrum with the desire to find more enemy throats. "Huh? What?" he asked Nul.

"Nothing. Kazazz. What pika says when surprised past words."

"Oh," Jeremy said. "You mean 'wow.' "

"Wau," agreed Nul.

Kelada had hefted and rejected two dropped swords. She picked up a third, nodded, and handed Nul's dagger back to him. "Come on. There are more, and they're getting closer!"

They stepped over the fallen bodies and descended the hill. "We need to go south along the river," Jeremy panted, the breath hot in his lungs. "Tremien's sent some friends there. Once we're all together, we can use the travel spell."

"This way, then." Now they followed Kelada as the thief led the way. Off to their right, from somewhere in the direction of the river, they heard still the rumor of pursuit, gabbling voices and the slap of running feet. Kelada led them away from the sounds, but in the slippery, clinging mud they had a terrible time making any progress, and their pursuers were built for just this kind of travel with their flat feet and their indifference to water. The fog, roiling heavy and dark, helped not at all. Jeremy was just thinking they had surely gone more than two thousand when once again shapes appeared before them, as if materializing from the swamp itself.

For a heart-lifting moment Jeremy thought they had found the others, but then the newcomers stepped forward, and he saw they were once more beleaguered, and this time by more than a patrol. At least twenty of the frog-creatures came forward, heads lowered, eyes glowering. "Behind us, too," Nul groaned. "Any more magic in your head?"

None was, desperately as he tried to conjure some new spell, but the magical sword was in Jeremy's hand, and once more it shone with a harsh, pure light as it leaped and struck as of its own accord. Six of the creatures he hewed down nearly as quick as thought, while Kelada and Nul each accounted for one as well. Then the survivors drew back but not away. "They've ringed us in," Kelada said. "They're all around us."

It was true. Others had come out of the fog, and now the three seemed to be surrounded by a small army of the things. But they kept their distance, glowering, hissing among themselves. "Look," Nul said as one stepped forward.

This one, no taller than the rest and no more distinguished in equipment or dress, had one badge of office: a small eye, red as a berry, blinking in its own socket in his forehead. The creature paused ten steps from them and swayed. Its own bulging eyes seemed to go vacant and blank as the huge mouth worked to shape words breathed rather than spoken: "It isss you! I thought you eksssiled and probably dead!"

"The voice of the Hag," Kelada whispered to Jeremy. "She sees through the third eye, and her will can possess those vilorgs who have it. She thinks you're Sebastian."

Inspiration came with Kelada's voice. He stepped closer to the swaying thing, hoping the tiny eye could not see sharply. "Yes," he said. "I have returned, through many difficulties, and look! your servants attack me. Is this the way the Mistress of the Meres repays friendship?"

"Friendsssship?" hissed the swaying creature. "We knew no friendsssship, ssssave that thrussst upon usss! Ssstill, your sssspeculum hasss increasssed my power, even asss that Dark One promisssed."

"And now," Jeremy said, "I have captured one I found running from your palace." Turning, he whispered, "Drop the sword, Kelada." She glared at him but complied, and he reached to drag her roughly forward. "Is this your captive?" he demanded.

"Yesss, the one we sssought—but othersss are in the valley."

"Then let me help with the search, Mistress of the

Meres. Take me to your palace, so we may confer—and without these servants of yours."

"How many of you?"

"My helper here, the woman, and me. That is all."

"Very well, Sssebassstian Magissster. It isss done."

For a moment it seemed to Jeremy that nothing had happened, aside from the fog's thickening. But then he realized the travel spell, or one very like it, was in effect. He, Kelada, and Nul stood in the dimly lighted void, and the monsters of the swamp were nowhere to be seen.

"Wonderful," Kelada said. "I spent days escaping from that place, and now you're bringing me right back to it!"

"We've got something to do," Jeremy said. "Nul, can the Hag hear us or see us?"

Nul, his sword still out, shook his head. "Nah, nah. We in no-time, no-place now. Whole 'nother reality from Thaumia. Why?"

"We've got to make plans."

The pika gaped at him. "Plans? You mean we going into Hag's palace and you have no plans?"

Jeremy shrugged. "It was that or try to fight a hundred of those—what did you call them?"

"Vilorgs," Kelada said. "Damn. My sword didn't come with us."

"A hundred vilorgs. And even with my new and improved sword, I don't think we would have stood much of a chance. Now the Hag thinks I'm Sebastian—"

"It's the beard," Kelada said. "What you can see of it through the mud."

"You're lovely yourself," Jeremy returned. "She thinks I'm Sebastian, and that gives us a little time. Kelada, what happened after you were caught?"

"I don't want to think about it."

"You have to. We don't have all that much time."

Kelada took a deep breath. "The creatures that grabbed me used a travel spell. They held me as tight as they could the whole time we were in it. They're nasty, these things. Their flesh is cold and clammy, and they smell of rotten fish. Anyway, I couldn't move, and they never let go, not for the whole time of the travel spell. We materialized in the corridor of a stronghold—it's away over the river, by the way, and probably where we're heading now—and they threw me into a room and locked the door. There was one small window, high, and from it I could see I was up in a tower. The door was iron, closely woven bands of it, and very heavy. Nothing in the cell but a pile of dirty straw, a few stiff blankets, a pisspot, and a drain hole about as big as my fist cut into the floor against the outer wall and leading down and out. I could see through it—probably it ended in some kind of spout. It seemed to be about an arm's length, but it was no good to me. A mouse might get out that way, but I couldn't.

"Anyway, they left me there for a fairly long time, the better part of a day at least, and I slept, on and off, through most of it. I think the damned things poisoned me when they pretended to be an old man and woman—but Nul will have told you that. Finally, about nightfall, I did wake up. Then someone hit me with another travel spell, and I was alone in one of these damn bubbles for an ona and a half. This time when I came out of it, I was with the Hag."

Nul growled, and Jeremy said, "Hush. What is she like?"

"Ugly." Kelada absently put her finger to her broken nose. "Uglier than me, even. And puzzled by me, I think. She asked me questions and at first I pretended to be stupid. Didn't everybody going from Langrola to Arkhedden travel this way? I think she was growing angry with me and might have done me harm if she hadn't been, well, *summoned* away."

"Summoned?" Nul asked. "How?"

"I don't know, and I can't put it any plainer. She got a *call* of some kind, and even I felt it. I've been around magicians, and you know how the air gets sort of ticklish—oh, I don't know—how you *feel* the magic working? This was like that, but so strong it was painful, like millions of needles pricking into your skin. The Hag straightened on her throne—she has a throne made of iron cast into the form of skulls and bones, did I mention that?—then got up, very stiff, and just walked out. There were three passages opening off the room, and I tried to go down one right away, but there was a magical ward there, a strong one, and it held me. The same with the other I tried. The only other one was the one the Hag had taken, but any chance seemed worth it by then. I could get into the corridor, all right, but it was blind. It led to a little room at the end and no farther. The Hag stood in the room, in front of a mirror, and she swayed like one of the vilorgs does when she possesses its mind. *Something* was going on, something with a lot of magical power behind it, but what it was I do not know."

"I think I do," Jeremy said. "The Great Dark One was speaking to his servant."

"I don't know," Kelada said again. "I went back to the throne room, but there was nothing there, no way of escape. Nothing even to use as a weapon to hit her with—just a big empty stone room with a heavy iron throne, three passageways leading north, east, and west from it, and a ball of wizard-light hovering away up twenty feet above my head. I sat on the floor and waited.

"Presently the Hag came back. 'I'll deal with you later,' she said. 'There's no reason he should know about you,' she said. And she sent me back to the cell with another travel spell. I was stuck there for the rest of the night. Not long after I found myself back in the cell, a vilorg came to bring me water and food. Maggoty cheese and stale bread, that was all. But when he came, I heard him use a key; so the door was kept by lock and not by magic. And I'm no thief if there's a lock anywhere I can't pick, if I have only something to work with."

"Did you have anything?" Nul asked. He was getting swept up in her story, even as he had with Jeremy's tale of Hamlet back in the swamps.

"Nothing. The vilorgs ripped everything metal away from me, even my buttons. I had to tie my shirt together with strips I tore from the hem. But the next time my supper came I had a good look at the lock. It was an old one, though it sounded well-oiled when the key turned, and there was a tiny hole, just the smallest hole, for the butt end of the keyshaft on my side. Now all I needed was some tool to work with.

"Several more days passed, and I began to think I would never get it. Once a day the froggy thing brought my meal. One time I hid, or tried to, in the pile of hay, but the thing simply stood there shaking and said in the Hag's voice, 'I sssee you, my dear. Be patient. I will have time for you sssoon.' That was when I realized that the three-eyed vilorgs were the Hag's special servants, somehow in touch with her so that she could see and speak through them. Anyway, I waited and thought, and all the time I had that same feeling that some deep magic was working in the place. The throne room was to the north of the tower and below it—"

"How did you know—oh. Your direction talent. Sorry," Jeremy said.

"Anyway, that seemed to be the focus of the energies. Finally, just yesterday, in fact, the Hag sent for me. This time she didn't use the travel spell. I didn't know why until I saw her, but then I realized that she was exhausted, worn out. Whatever she'd been doing had left her all but dead.

"She questioned me again, and still I refused to answer. Somehow she had it in her mind that I was a spy from Tremien, but she seemed to hesitate about torturing an answer from me. I think something frightens her even more than Tremien. This Dark One is up to something—and if I'm right, somewhere in the back of the Hag's mind was the notion that if the Dark One's plot failed, she might somehow throw in with Tremien and escape destruction."

"Tremien sensed that the Dark One was moving," Jeremy said. "She must be helping him in whatever he plans."

"Tremien not afraid of her," Nul snorted. "No, or of Great Dark One either."

"She's raising something terrible," Kelada said slowly. "Something dark and without substance, but fearful all the same." She shuddered. "After half an ona or so, she ordered the vilorgs to take me back to the cell. Only this time two two-eyes were my guards, and the three-eyes remained behind.

"We went back the way we had come, through a long passage, up some stairs, along another passage, then up more stairs. There was precious little along the way— some carpeting trod into muck, a few rotting tapestries, nothing useful. But I had seen something that interested me on the trip down from my cell, and close to the second stair on the way back, I saw it again: a door roughly boarded up, with planks already hanging loose and rotting. I pretended to stumble there and fell against one of the vilorgs, and the other tried to drag me upright again. I floundered against the wall, went to my knees, and put my hands on the boards to pull myself up. The guards grabbed me and jerked me upright, but I had what I wanted: a rusty nail that I tore from one of the crumbling boards.

"After that it was easy. I waited until night, then went to work on the lock by feel. I had to file down the nail against the stones, and that was weary work. But at last I had it thin enough, and the tip of the nail bent at just the right angle, and when I pushed on the lock tumblers, they moved. Slowly, but they moved, one by one. Sometime past midnight the door was unlocked. I opened it and looked into an empty corridor, lit by one smoking torch in a wall sconce. I knew that I couldn't get out the way I had come, so I took the torch and explored the other direction. There was another room a little past mine, this one not in the tower but in the main body of the fortress, and it had a window big enough for me to wriggle through. Then I had to let myself down without breaking my neck. Then I was in the courtyard, and all that was left was to slip past the guards and out into the open. I did it, by the way, by finding a sewage drain. I don't know whether I'll ever be clean again. Anyway, once outside the fortress, I sensed the quickest way back toward Whitehorn and took it. I found a bridge and crossed the river, and then I was headed out when I came across your trail. Of course, I had no way of knowing it was you, but since I had no weapon, I thought I might raid a vilorg party for something to fight with, and came at you before I recognized you—and you know the rest."

"Then you can show us how to get to the Hag's mirror."

"Yes. What are you going to do with it?"

"Break it."

Kelada's lips tightened, and she shook her head. "It's protected by spells, I think. There's great magic in the room, anyway."

"I'll find a way." Jeremy held up his great flashing sword. "I think first I'll need to disguise this. Nul, is there danger in my working a spell while we're in the travel spell?"

"Who knows? Pikas don't use this kind of magic. Maybe yes, maybe no."

"Well—let's see." Jeremy concentrated. "All right," he said after a moment. "Maybe the two of you had better get behind me, just in case." Kelada and Nul moved, and then in English Jeremy half-chanted: "It's a whole new sword! It's a fabulous sword! But it looks just

like any other sword until YOU use it—and only YOU
know the SECRET!"

The temperature in the shifting bubble of the travel
spell seemed to plummet twenty degrees, and Jeremy
heard an electric crackling sound. At the same time the
sword seemed to shrink in on itself, to dwindle, and to
lose its luster. Jeremy turned, holding the weapon horizontally in front of him. "How does it look?"

"Like your old sword," Nul said. "You ruin it?"

"I hope not." Jeremy slipped it into the scabbard. The
fit wasn't perfect, but the sword would ride acceptably
well at his belt and would come free easily when he
pulled the hilt.

"What language did you speak?" Kelada asked.

"My old tongue. Spells seem to have more power
when I use it."

"It sounds strange."

"Even to me, now," Jeremy agreed. "Let's get our
stories straight. I'm Sebastian, and somehow I've escaped
from the Between—"

"Came through Melodia's mirror," Nul suggested.

"Yes, or through another mirror. One no one else
knew about."

"Ah! Sebastian had stronghold down on Kyrin Island.
Say you came back there."

"Is there such a place?"

"Yes, certainly," Kelada put in. "Kyrin is almost due
south of the Markelan Peninsula, on the southwest corner of Cronbrach, many hundreds of thousands from
here. The island used to be a vassal state of the Markelaners,
but the islanders revolted, oh, long ago. They're known
to be stubborn and independent."

"And Sebastian did hide there," Nul said. "Was from
there he would come and visit Melodia."

"All right. Kyrin Island," Jeremy said, trying the sound
on his tongue. "And I must travel overland because if I
used a travel spell—"

"Any magic," amended Nul.

"Yes, good, any magic at all, I would alert Tremien of
my presence back in Thaumia. So I'm using Nul as my
guide—"

"Some of vilorgs saw me," Nul warned.

"Three-eyes or two-eyes?" Kelada asked.

The pika frowned in concentration. "Two-eyes only, I think."

The thief looked at Jeremy. "We should be safe. I don't believe they have much intelligence of their own."

"Then Nul is my guide, and you are my prisoner. Now. We have to keep you safe."

"I'd feel safer with a sword in my hand."

"Here," Nul said, offering her the dagger again. "But where you put it?"

Kelada glared at him, turned, and slipped the dagger somewhere in her muddy clothing. Turning back to them, she asked, "Does it show?"

"Everything else does," grinned Nul, eyeing her clinging shirt.

"It's fine," Jeremy said. "We have more planning to do."

And they spent the whole remaining time of their journey in plots, in schemes, in private fears, in expressions of hope.

The throne room was alive with vilorgs. Jeremy, Kelada, and Nul stood in the center of a circle of them, the focus of their bulging eyes. The very air seemed rank with their breath as the creatures' pouched throats ballooned and pulsed rhythmically.

The Hag herself, swathed in a cloak that once had been white but now was an aged and bitter yellow, her head covered by a hood and her face hidden behind a veil, sat on the throne, which was indeed cast of black iron in the shape of dismembered and piled skeletons. Two skulls grinned from beneath her hands. "Welcome, Sebastian Magister," she purred in a rusty voice. "You have traveled far?"

Nul, by agreement, had his sword unsheathed and was holding Kelada's right arm tight in his three-fingered grip. Jeremy, his sword still secure in its scabbard, spread his arms wide, displaying his filthy garments. "Far indeed, Mistress of the Meres. All the way from the Between to here."

The eyes, all that showed of the Hag's face, glittered deep in dark hollows scored by a thousand wrinkles, but bright and sharp. "And so the enemies failed in their attempt to exile you forever?"

"Yes, and I made good my escape at last, though the

way was hard. The tales told of the Between are true, Mistress. It is a place of dreams and nightmares, of madnesses we hardly know. I fear that in some ways the Between has changed me."

"You must tell me about the Between," the Hag said.

"Yes—but first I should like to cleanse myself, Mistress. Your domain is hard to travel by mundane means."

"You could have spelled your way to me—or is loss of magic one of the changes you speak of?" The deep eyes glittered like a serpent's, as if the Hag were hungry to devour an unprotected Sebastian.

"My power is as great as ever. But surely you know why I must not yet use it. Tremien, old spider that he is, senses the least trembling of the web of magic. None of the enemy yet know that I have returned. I think it best for me—and for you, and for another I could name—that the secret remain a secret yet awhile longer."

The Hag did indeed seem tired. She thrust her body back in the throne with two hands that, braced on the skulls of the armrests, themselves seemed little more than skeletal bones, and for some moments she regarded him, her thin breast rising and falling with her breathing. "True. You may be right." To one of the vilorgs the Hag said, "Take Sebastian Magister to one of the human rooms, and see that he has hot water and fresh garments. Throw the female into the deepest pit we have, and keep a guard over the trap."

"Hold," Jeremy said. "I captured the woman as you see her, covered over with filth. I think I should be glad of a chance to find what is under the mud." When the Hag merely looked at him, Jeremy tried a lascivious and leering grin. "I have been alone in the Between for a long time, Mistress, and my journey here was long and lonely, too."

"She cannot be trusted."

"Mistress, the day has not yet come when Sebastian Magister is no match for a girl."

Kelada spat at him, and Nul wrenched her arm. "Not nice!" the pika snarled as Kelada feigned a cry of pain.

"Very well, very well," said the Hag, impatience in her voice. "But I will have guards in the corridor, Sebastian—just in case your magic or your . . . strength should fail you. And the guards will put you in a room without a window."

Jeremy bowed. Again the Hag spat orders at the guards, and this time three of them, one on either side and one following behind Nul, marched them down the west corridor. All Jeremy saw was stone, dark gray, square-worked, each stone fitting its neighbors so closely that even a thin blade would not find a lodgement between them. Here, unlike the corridor Kelada had described, were tall, pointed windows, though too narrow for an escape by any but perhaps Nul, and through the windows Jeremy caught glimpses of a garden of sorts, half hidden in the persistent fog, a green square lush with huge, leprous leaves and a few fleshy-looking flowers, but all was overgrown and ruinous. He could make no judgment of the time, other than the impression that afternoon was probably at least half done. The guards opened a door on the right and saw Jeremy and Kelada inside. Jeremy turned in the doorway to Nul. "Stay and help keep watch," he ordered.

"Yes, Master," Nul said, overacting enough to make Jeremy grimace at him.

Jeremy closed the door behind him. "Now, slut," he said loudly, "as soon as we have the means, we will see what lies under the crusted dung."

Kelada quickly scanned the room. "You pig! Would that my blade had tasted your blood!" She took a quick look behind the wall hangings. "Your death would be delight beyond my dreams!"

"Do people really talk that way here?" Jeremy hissed to her in a quick whisper.

She frowned at him. "My body you may take, but my spirit you cannot touch, dog!"

God in heaven, Jeremy thought.

The room was a cube perhaps twenty feet on an edge. The hangings here, though ancient, were in one piece: one showed an armed party in pitched battle with a rearing dragon, and the other, through layers of dirt, depicted a harvest scene with reapers and wagons loaded with sheaf. A hanging iron circle held ten oil lamps, though only seven of them burned. The stone floor was bare of carpeting or cover, and the room's only furnishings were a simple, narrow cot with no pillow or blankets, two chairs, and in the center of the room an enormous wooden tub at least six feet across with walls coming to

Jeremy's waist. He looked in and saw the tub was half full of water, and that the water was not too dirty.

"I think it's all right," Kelada said. "There's nothing here to be the Hag's eyes or ears."

"Good. 'My body you may take . . .'?"

She gave him an exasperated look. "That's the way all the princesses talk in the stories!"

"Never mind. What now?"

"They're supposed to bring us hot water and clothes, remember?"

"All right, then. We wait."

They didn't have to wait for long. The door opened—no one knocked—and a succession of vilorgs filed in, the first twenty or so carrying two buckets each of steaming water. They dumped these into the great vat until Jeremy, his arm plunged in, told them the water was warm enough. Another vilorg had towels and soap, which, after looking vaguely around, it put on one of the chairs, and yet another left two sets of tangled clothing on the bed. The froglike creatures filed out, and from the open door Nul gave them a quick look. Then the door closed, leaving them alone again.

Jeremy sorted through the clothes. "I guess this is mine," he said, holding up a large gray tunic made of coarse homespun cloth and a pair of trousers that looked for all the world like jogging pants. Kelada's outfit was the same but smaller. No underwear was provided. "You go first," Jeremy said. "I'll turn my back."

"Why?"

"Well, I—look, just go ahead."

Jeremy turned away and heard the wet slaps of Kelada's clothes against the stone floor as she undressed. Then there was a splash as she settled into the tub, and more splashes as she began to wash. "Soap," she said happily.

The soap was an irregular cake that felt gritty and smelled like lard. Jeremy backed toward the tub, holding the soap out. "Here, take it."

"Well, give it to me! Oh, turn around so you can see what you're doing."

Jeremy did turn. Kelada was submerged up to her shoulders, the rest of her body a pink blur under the water. She held her dripping arm up out of the bath. "Here."

Jeremy gave her the soap and retreated so that he

could only see her head. She scrubbed herself in businesslike fashion, washing her hair with the soap first, then turning her attention to her face, arms, and legs. "Come do my back," she said.

He scrubbed her shoulders and back until they were shining pink. "There," he said. "You rinse, I'll get the towel."

He again turned his back as she stepped from the tub. He heard her rummaging behind him. "All right. Ready." When he turned, she was standing barefoot and damp-haired, dressed in the rough gray outfit. She was thinner than ever, but to Jeremy she looked healthy, with the old, wiry toughness still showing in her stance and her movements. "Your turn," she said. "And I'm going to look."

Kelada pronounced him fit for company after she had scrubbed his back almost hard enough to take the skin off. He put on the clothing furnished by the Hag—Kelada, as she promised, watched him, grinning the whole time—then toweled his hair and beard again—they still held drops of water. "How about the mail shirt?" he asked. The rings were clotted with grime.

"Rinse it," she suggested. He did, shook as much of the water out as he could, and donned it. Then, using the cleanest part of his old tunic he could find, he wiped the mud from his belt and scabbard and put them on. The boots were hopeless, filthy and soaked. He would go barefoot. "Got your dagger?" he asked.

"I have it," Kelada said grimly. "Why wouldn't you look at me?"

"Because I don't want to be distracted."

"I distract you? With a face like mine?"

"Kelada, there's nothing wrong with your face. You look in the mirror and see ugliness where no one else does."

She shook her head. "No. I know what I look like."

"Damn it," he sighed. "If we ever get out of here, I promise I'll—I'll create a magic potion that will make you beautiful."

She blinked at him. "You could do that?"

"Sure I could. You saw what I did with the sword."

Kelada's eyes went wide. "But transforming living human flesh is high magic. Only a mage could do such a thing. Even the Hag cannot alter her appearance to make herself less ugly."

"I can do it. But save that for later. Right now I have to get close to that mirror."

"All right. It's down the northern corridor from the throne room, as I said, in the only room that opens from it. It is in the center of the room, facing the eastern wall. It's almost the same as the one Sebastian created in the Between: as tall as you are, oval, in a wooden frame that stands alone on the floor."

"Let's see if we can get there," Jeremy said.

He opened the door. Nul stood with his back against the opposite wall, two vilorgs against the wall on either side of the door. "Servant," Jeremy said, "do you wish a bath?"

"I can live without one, master."

"Still—" Turning to a vilorg, Jeremy said, "See that my servant has hot water and towels."

The creature goggled stupidly at him. Nul said, "Forget it. Only Hag can give them direct orders. They understand nothing else."

"Oh. Well, come inside."

Nul pushed off from the wall and waddled through the door. He grinned at Kelada. "You looking better," he said. "Still human, but improved."

Kelada returned his grin. "Thanks, pika. And thanks for bringing help. Even if the rescue put me right back in the trap again."

One of the vilorgs had left a bucket nearly full of hot water. Nul made use of that and a spare towel. He had no clean clothing, but he had not taken a serious spill and was in somewhat better shape than Jeremy had been. He got the worst of the filth off himself and then rubbed his head with a towel until his short fur bristled all over his head, giving him the appearance of an alarmed cat. "Better," he growled at last.

"Then let's go see the Hag," Jeremy said. "Take Kelada prisoner again, and be ready for anything."

The guards flapped along behind them as they went back down the corridor. This time they found the Hag alone in the throne room, propped in her throne, her eyes brooding and distant. "You look refreshed, Sebastian Magister," she said. "Now tell me of your journeys."

"There is not much to tell. I came back into the world

weeks ago, in a secret place I have on Kyrin, away to the south. Then I came by boat to Markelan; by nights I journeyed on foot north along the Korthon River, through Vertova and to the eastern edge of the Arkhedden Forest. From there I passed northward again along the Dinsfaer Hills until I entered the Meres from the east, knowing that to be the fastest way by foot to your castle."

"And you did not stray east of the Arkhedden? Say, to the Whitehorn regions?"

"And risk coming within Mage Tremien's ken? That would have been folly indeed."

The Hag's eyes flashed. "And yet one of my messengers felt something very like your presence. At the very edge of Tremien's domain he was stripped of his protection and struck dumb and blind by some force of magic."

Jeremy recalled the shadow-rider. "If he traveled that close to Whitehorn, I am not surprised," Jeremy said. "As to my presence, no doubt what you sensed was a mirror of my making, a very powerful magic, as you know, and partaking somewhat of my essence. Tremien had discovered it and was taking it to Whitehorn."

"There are more than the two, then?" the Hag asked.

"Certainly."

"Then you lied to me!"

"And have you been always truthful with me, Mistress? I doubt it! We all seek to protect ourselves. Yes, there were more than two mirrors: one I kept in secret on Kyrin, and one I had—in another place, for reasons of my own. But I say 'were': Tremien, curse him, has destroyed one of my works."

The Hag leaned back. "Yes. I felt it, through my mirror, back in the dark days of winter. A pain that seemed to rend through me as well, and one from which I was long weeks recovering."

"But as long as yours, and one other, remains whole, you are safe enough."

"True." The Hag's voice held a bitter note of sarcasm. "It is strange, is it not, that the one thing that has brought me increased power also shows me *this?*" She reached to her face and moved the veil aside. Jeremy took a deep breath, for the Hag was indeed spectacularly ugly: her cheeks jutting cliffs over sunken chaps, her mouth lipless, a deeply seamed horizontal gash showing malformed, brown teeth, her nose a gaping hole between her eyes. "That is your curse, I suspect, Sebastian. Others have always amused themselves at my expense. But your gift has brought power, and things are happening that you have not dreamed of."

"What things?"

The Hag rose from her throne. "The girl will be safe under his guard?"

"Very safe, Mistress. And if she were not, do your wards not hold strong as ever?"

"They do. Come, Sebastian Magister. I will show you a wonder." With a dry rustle the white-clad witch stepped down from the throne. The vilorgs made way for her.

Jeremy's heart pounded a little faster in his chest, for she led him into the north corridor. Involuntarily he fingered the hilt of his sword. The corridor, an arched and gloomy passage, led into a windowless room. In the center, shrouded under a frayed blanket, was the muffled oval shape of the mirror. The Hag swept the blanket aside.

Jeremy, behind her, was startled despite himself, for in the mirror he indeed was Sebastian, beard and all. The Hag studied him for a moment. "You cannot draw that in here," she said.

His grip on the sword hilt tightened, but he could not budge the blade in its scabbard. "Wards?" he guessed.

"Very strong ones. Your mirror must be protected."

"I am glad you look after it so well."

The Hag smiled. Turning to the mirror, she pronounced a quick activation spell, and the surface clouded. "Now you will see what the Dark One has taught me to do," she said. Her voice grew faraway and moody: "Ever did I love the dead more than the living, for the dead have no wills of their own, and they, at least, do not shrink from my face. Among the dead I can be queen or empress. But I can raise appearance only, not substance: ghosts that are powerless to do aught but look on without comprehension or understanding. The Great Dark One has taught me how to strengthen my powers. Look! Behold the hills outside of Whitehorn Valley!"

The dark mirror wavered into a picture. Jeremy recognized the hillsides just west of Whitehorn, now green with springtime. But as he watched, shapes began to ooze from the earth, dark shapes, transparent in the sun. Stooped they stood, but each bore a weapon, and all had a fell and grim look. Like wisps of smoke wafted away by a breeze, the forms moved from their place of origin, and there others grew, hundreds of them. The picture changed, became a panorama of the whole countryside, and everywhere the creatures appeared, armed, apparently solid, and implacably advancing. "Tremien is besieged?" Jeremy asked.

"Not yet. But he will be, by an army of the dead; and so will the other magi of Cronbrach. And this army cannot be defeated, even by magic, for it will be shielded by the power of the Great Dark One himself, power stolen from another world."

"The Dark One wishes to kill the magi," Jeremy said.

"No! Not to kill, but to corrupt; to bend to his own uses, that this land might fall to him, as long ago Relas of the south fell. With their magic added to his own, his might will be invincible. And almost all is ready."

"And you?" Jeremy asked. "Why do you help him?"

The Hag gazed into the mirror. "For power, after. For Whitehorn itself, from which I will rule all the northeastern parts of the land. For the ability to torment my tormentors, to work my will instead of theirs, to mold the countryside as I see fit."

The picture shimmered, darkened, and died, and then the mirror was only a mirror once more. The Hag threw the blanket back over it. Jeremy took half a step forward—and felt himself stopped short by an invisible wall. "Come," the Hag said, turning again to the corridor. Jeremy followed her. "The woman," she said, "I thought at first to be the one you were once enamored of. She is not?"

"No. I think she might know something, though, of the magi and their plans."

"Then we will have it from her. I am weary, Sebastian Magister. Summoning the dead from hell is dangerous work, even with the Dark One's aid. But we will have it from her."

Just in the doorway the Hag froze suddenly, her head jerking back on her thin neck. An instant later, Jeremy felt it, too, like a cold fist closing around his heart. He shuddered.

"Magic in my realm," the Hag hissed. "Magic in the Meres!" She stiffened, swayed a little, and her voice changed register: "Yesss, yesss. I sssee. It isss the old fool Barach. But it is hopeless! The wards are too ssstrong for him—" The witch jerked, and Jeremy realized that her mind had literally been elsewhere, that she had been seeing through the eye of a vilorg somewhere in the swamps. She turned on Jeremy suddenly. "I knew there were more!" She gave a shrill call and hurried into the throne room, Jeremy close behind her, his hand still working the hilt of his sword.

Vilorgs poured in from the east corridor, filling the room, surrounding Nul, Kelada, and Jeremy. "We will have them here in an instant," the Hag said from her throne. "Fools that they are!" She howled an incantation. "Back, Sebastian! Here they are!"

With a noise like a thunderclap, Barach, Gareth, Syvelin, and Melodia appeared, weapons drawn, back to back, in the center of the room. Barach had already begun an incantation when Melodia cried out, "Oh, Jeremy, you're safe!"

The Hag's eyes blazed at him. Gareth and Syvelin, their swords swinging and flashing, leaped forward. Nul spun to face the vilorgs, and Kelada brandished her dagger. Jeremy, his hand on the hilt of his own weapon, discovered that in the throne room the ward no longer held. With a shout he drew his sword, shining like daybreak.

But already the Hag has leaped to her feet and was crying a dire spell in a voice like rolling thunder.

CHAPTER 12

THE PAIN HIT like a toppling wave.

For a moment the whole world went red; then Jeremy fought his way back up—he had fallen to a kneeling position—and wrenched his sword free. Dimly he saw that the others, Nul, Kelada, Barach, all of them, had collapsed, but the sword in his hand seemed to leap at the vilorgs with a force that had nothing to do with him, and he merely followed it, wading in behind its slashing blows.

"Stop him!" the Hag cried. Jeremy cut his way through, saw an opening, and dived for it. In the arch of the east passage, invisible hands held him back, dragged at his body. He lowered his head, strained, and tumbled through the ward, rolling forward, scrambling again to his feet. Behind him confusion yammered as the vilorgs piled in the passageway. Then the Hag's spell snapped, or was broken, and they spilled in after him.

But by that time Jeremy was up and running. A closed door waited at the far end of the corridor. He shouted, "Open!" in English, and the door crumbled as he struck it, dissolving into splinters and powdery, throat-choking dust. Behind the door was a landing, with stairs up and down. Jeremy clattered down, found some vilorgs hard at his heel, and spun in his tracks. Three sweeps of the sword cut the beasts down and blocked the stair; then he was flying down again.

He passed another landing, and then the stair ended at another closed door. Jeremy wielded the sword like a baseball bat, and the blade cleaved through the wood as if it met no resistance at all. A kick cleared the way.

Jeremy found himself in the dripping garden, walled on all sides. A colonnade led to his right, and he fled down it. He kicked a door open and hurtled into a

kitchen. Vilorgs, smaller and thinner than the warriors—
these are the females, he thought—gaped up stupidly from
stove and table. Jeremy ran through, found an outside
door, and went through it.

He stood in a woodlot piled high with cord upon cord
of firewood, surrounded by a ten-foot wall broken at the
far side by a great wooden gate. Behind him came the
noise of pursuit. Hesitating only a moment, Jeremy clambered up a pile of wood, dislodging several chunks of it
and almost toppling backward, leaped to the wall, narrowly escaped falling, and then let himself down. He
landed in miry ground, but he was outside the Hag's
castle.

Something splashed in the muck a few feet beyond
him. He ran, this time hearing the whizz of the arrow
before it narrowly missed him. Voices again, behind him—
the guard coming out of the castle, no doubt.

His mind was working furiously. Already the sodden
ground, clammy and chill beneath his bare feet, was
slowing him. He flourished his sword as a great dark
shape loomed out of the fog ahead—and then realized he
had been about to assault a tree. It was a bent and black
tree, but a few wan leaves sprouted from its twigs and its
gnarled branches bent low before sweeping back upward
again. Jeremy climbed.

He got as high as he could and rested in the crotch of a
great branch. He panted from exertion, but there was
another feeling too, a kind of pins-and-needles tingling,
the aftereffects, he supposed, of the Hag's spell. His
mundane immunity had not kept the full force of it away
from him, but at least he had not been struck down like
the others. He began to doubt the value of the tree as a
hiding place. The little spring leaves were not dense
enough to conceal him, though he had at least some hope
of escaping notice up here. A twig right by his face,
sprouting directly from the trunk, boasted four pathetic
leaves, pale green, like the unluckiest four-leaf clover in
the universe.

Struck with a sudden thought, Jeremy plucked the
twig. "Everyone," he recited quickly, softly, and in his
own language, "occasionally wishes not to be seen. The
four-leaf talisman is the answer. Yes, as long as you have
this incredibly lucky charm about you, you will not be
seen. Only YOU will know where you are!"

Something happened. For a moment the twig seemed alive, galvanized and twitching, and Jeremy had the same feel of some current flowing around and through him. Closing his eyes, he thought to himself that such an ad wouldn't have gone over very well at a staff meeting. But here—well, he could at least hope. He swallowed hard and tucked the twig safely inside his belt. A moment later, he winced as an invisible searchlight glared at him from the gloom. The Hag had *felt* his magic, and now she was seeking him. He swung down from the tree and landed with feet spread.

Something else was happening: a wind had sprung up, and the fogs were stirring, thinning. Jeremy had the eerie feeling of great magic at work: the Hag wanted her warriors to see him. In moments the air began to clear, and a watery sun, already low in the sky, showed over a dismal world of slime, water, mud, and ruin.

Vilorgs, a dozen of them, came pattering over a hill. Behind them, grim and shadowed even in the light of the sun, the stone castle of the Hag, its towers squared, its stones streaked and discolored, reared against the northern sky. Jeremy raised his sword.

The creatures bypassed him entirely, snuffled and gabbled around the tree for a moment, then tore off southward. Jeremy took a deep breath. His incantation had worked. He toiled to the top of a rise and looked about him. It was a bleak picture. Beyond the forbidding pile of the castle was a vast circular body of black water, Illsmere itself, he guessed. To the east, toward the river, the landscape slumped away to barrens of mud, broken stubs of trees, rutted bare hillsides, occasional moss-grown stones. To the south, more meres glinted, and there away off was a party of vilorgs, either the one that had passed him or another. Squinting to the west against the low sun, Jeremy could just make out a dim, jagged line of purple mountains, the Wolmas range. If he could cross those and continue due west, he would sooner or later come to the River Ap; and if he followed that south, then he would arrive at Langrola, the fishing town where Nul and Kelada had rested.

But that would take days, and help was by no means certain in Langrola. He shook his head. His task, whatever it was, lay here in the Haggenkom, the Hag's Vale—and, what was worse, in the castle of the Hag herself. He turned north and made his way back to the brooding structure.

He came right up to the walls, seeing now that they were manned by vilorgs, the one nearest to him definitely a three-eye. The courtyard gate seemed to be a great drawbridge in the eastern wall, crossing not a moat but a veritable quagmire; or at least, if it were open, it would have done so. Invisible or not, Jeremy had no illusions about walking on that liquid surface, and he skirted it, moving away from the walls as he made his way north. Before long he stood on the edge of the great mere, a mile or more across, utterly still, dark, and forbidding. He glanced into its waters and saw something stirring there restlessly, as if waiting to get out, some large shadowy shapes, as of circling sharks well below the surface. He shuddered, reminded suddenly and strongly of the shadow-rider, a thing seeming as much dead as alive.

On the mere side, the castle wall dropped bleak and unbroken straight down, a hundred feet he estimated, into the water. There, somewhere on the north side, would be the little room with the mirror in it. Jeremy pondered trying to put together a transportation spell of his own, but his mind touched barriers that told him it would be impossible.

He took a deep breath. It was through the gate or nothing, as far as he could see, if he intended to reenter the castle from this side. It was not a prospect that pleased him, and he started back. What he saw before him froze him in his tracks, literally.

He had left a trail plain for anyone not blind to follow: a set of deep footprints, unmistakably human, impressed in the mud. The vilorgs might not see him, but to miss that—inconceivable. What was worse, he found almost no firm ground where he didn't leave traces, at least not until he reached the south wall of the castle again. There, close against the wall, he found that he could walk, carefully, without leaving footprints.

And not a moment too soon, for from the south came more vilorgs, or a smaller detachment of the same party, stooping low and babbling as they followed the track he had left. Jeremy eased to the west as they disappeared around the corner of the castle.

He paused when he neared the woodyard wall, for now that the fog was gone, he could see something he had not noticed before: in the distance a body of water, too straight-sided to be natural, led to a short, broad, paved road, and this in turn led to the gate to the woodyard in the southwest corner, which was open, probably left open when the pursuers had come after him. The water was clearly a canal, leading west and south and glinting in the last light of the sun. Indeed, far down the watercourse he could make out the dark speck of a sizable boat, and smaller boats seemed to be tied at the pier that formed the far end of the paved course. For a second he contemplated stealing one and fleeing, but the memory of his task, and of his friends, pulled him to the open gate instead. He slipped in, stepping gingerly over a generation's supply of splinters soft and springy underfoot but sharp for the unwary, until he reached the flagstones outside the kitchen door. This, unfortunately, was closed. Jeremy sat resting with his back against the wall, pondering his next move.

The sun had not been down long, for the western sky was still silver with its last light, when he heard a clopping of horses outside the wall. He carefully stepped across the yard again and peered into the twilight. A wagon had come from some entrance off on the western side of the castle, and two huge horses were pulling it down toward the pier. There the boat had tied up, and men labored to throw bundles and packages off. Jeremy darted out and caught up with the slow-moving wagon easily. The driver, a slack-faced man, turned round to stare over his shoulder, as if he had heard Jeremy's approach, but he turned back again almost at once. Something about him—Jeremy squinted: the shape of the head—of course. It was not a man at all, but a vilorg carrying an illusion spell. If he concentrated, Jeremy could see the form lurking beneath the appearance, could even make out the color of the third eye.

But the boatmen were genuinely human. "Here it is," one of them said in a gruff, strangely accented voice. "Ought to hold her ladyship for another week or two."

"Load it," the driver said, and Jeremy felt his flesh creep, for he knew it was the Hag's voice speaking through her tool.

"We brings the stuff. We don't have to—"

"Load it!"

The boatman looked at his crew and shrugged. "Put it

on the wagon, boys," he said. "Sooner that's done, sooner we're out and gone. That's five golders for the lot, food, wine, and all."

The disguised driver tossed a small sack down, and the boatman snatched it out of midair. He bent close in the dying light to count the coins, grunted his satisfaction, and dropped the sack into a pocket. Meanwhile his crew had loaded crates, kegs, and sacks aboard the wagon. None of them seemed to care for the driver, and they took a good many more steps than they needed just to avoid him. "That's it, chiefey," one of them called as he leaped back onto the boat, a flatboat, Jeremy could see now, that the men moved by poling.

"Same next week, then?"

"Sssame."

"All right, then. Give her ladyship a kiss for me." The man stooped to untie, tossed the rope aboard the boat, and jumped on himself. The crew leaned into the poles, the flatboat backed away from the pier, and in a few moments all was lost in the deepening dusk.

The driver sat motionless until the boat was out of sight. Then he shuddered, softened, and slumped into his true form. He twitched the reins, turning the horses, and as the wagon swung wide, Jeremy clambered aboard. This time the vilorg didn't even look back. Jeremy crouched over a sack of onions, or something very onionlike in aroma, and braced himself against a dark, oil-stained keg that gave off a fishy smell. A dim yellow light burned ahead, showing him the gateway in the western wall through which the wagon had come, guarded by a portcullis. The wagon rumbled through, the portcullis dropped with a crash, and Jeremy leaped down.

More vilorgs came slouching out to unload the wagon. It had come to a stop in a cramped courtyard, with storage rooms on the right, a blank wall on the left, and what seemed to be stables straight ahead, though in the gathering dark Jeremy could not be sure. He had to step lively to keep from colliding with one of the work detail, and at last when the wagon was empty, he just managed to slip inside a door before the last of them came back into the castle.

But once inside he was lost. He wandered, trying to find the stair, or any other way up, for a long while, stumbling along badly lit corridors and freezing like a statue at every noise along the way. Once he opened a promising door onto an overpowering odor like a heap of decomposing fish. Here too a few dim torches flickered, and water made yellow reflections dance on ceiling and walls. At first he thought he had looked into a cesspool filled, inexplicably, with floating heads of cabbage; then his eyes adjusted, and he realized he saw a vilorg dormitory, with dozens of the creatures crouched on their bellies in shallow water, heads and buttocks showing. He closed the door very carefully and retraced his steps.

At length, in a room that seemed disused, huddled in a corner, hugging his knees—it was *cold* in the castle—Jeremy let his head sink forward. If only he could dream a solution, as he had in the Between. He let his mind reach out, seeking his friends.

And in sleep he found one. "Jeremy?" Barach's voice, or his mind.

Yes. Where are you?

"A room, with Gareth and Syvelin. You?"

Somewhere in the castle.

"The Hag is planning something terrible."

I know.

"Get out. Get away, and warn Tremien."

No.

"Go, I tell you! No magic can reach him from here. Something damps it out, keeps it from operating properly. He must be warned."

No. I have to save you and the others.

"The soldiers are dead, except for Gareth and Syvelin. I don't know where Nul is. I think the women are somewhere near; faintly I can sense Melodia's aura. But we have no way of escape."

Then I will find one.

"I think I did make a wizard of you, young man."

Am I only dreaming this?

"Who can say? They tell a story of a king who once dreamed he was a butterfly. The butterfly flew in the sun until nightfall; then it rested with folded wings on a blossom. It slept, and in its sleep it dreamed it flew to the palace of the king, to see him sleeping. It fluttered to a casement ledge and paused there, looking into the throne room. And the small wind it made with its wings wakened the sleeping king, whose eyes immediately fell upon the small blue butterfly. The king crept close to the window, lifted his hand, and brought it down sharply, as if to crush the insect. With that the butterfly awoke, and the king and castle vanished to nothing."

It's you, all right. I am coming.

"Jeremy? You had better hurry. I think the Hag is up to something terrible. Whatever it is—I think it will happen at dawn."

Jeremy jerked awake cold, hungry, and strangely heartened by the dream. He arose, found his legs and back stiff from his cramped position, and cracked open the door. The hall outside was empty, and he slipped once more into a maddening maze of corridors, small rooms, large rooms, and rooms where vilorgs turned to stare mutely at doors that opened themselves. Most of this floor seemed to be deserted, but the few vilorgs who lingered here and there had an air about them of waiting, of anticipation. It was contagious, for Jeremy felt threat building, heavy as a sky before a thunderstorm. He began to wonder just how big the castle was and how anything this massive could keep from sinking into the mire of the swamp.

At last he found a way into the square garden, colorless beneath the light of a nearly full moon overhead. The flowers gave off a rank odor, like cabbages well past their prime, as he brushed past them. He spotted the long colonnade. The broken door of the stair was then easy to find, and he slipped past the three-eyes who guarded it with no trouble. He half expected to find the door on the throne room floor intact but for the form of a running man, like a door in an old Bugs Bunny cartoon, but it had been cleanly blasted away and lay in fragments on the stone floor of the landing. Another three-eyes there sniffed the air as he passed, but gave no other sign of recognizing his presence.

Jeremy found no ward at the entrance to the throne room—but neither had he found one there earlier, upon entering. He suspected the wards worked in one direction only and that his passage there would surely arouse the Hag. The only alternative he could think of was to bypass the door by climbing out the windows, but those were far too narrow for him. He paused in the corridor to think, staring hard at the space in front of him.

Presently he became aware of a gauzy kind of light,

but when he looked directly at it, it vanished. Experimenting, Jeremy found that from the side he could indeed see a faint glow in the doorway, webbed and strung as if woven by a spider—but a web of light, not of silk. That, he thought, must be the ward spell.

And it began about a foot above the floor.

He crept closer, still turning his eyes aside, and even when he crouched near the door, the space just above the floor seemed clear of any trace of magic. In the gloom he became aware of more lines of force, lying flat on the stones of the walls, the ceilings, the floors. The castle seemed to be held together by them. That, he believed, supported the structure and kept the swamp from claiming its stones. But if the ward spell indeed had a space limitation, he could, if he were careful, slip through without detection.

Jeremy lay on his back and squirmed under the invisible barrier. When he was well within the throne room, he stood. The room was not quite deserted: two more three-eyes stood on either side of the throne. They appeared not to notice him as he studied the opening to the northern passage. Here the web of light was brighter, pulsating: and from down the corridor came darts and flashes, auroralike displays that portended more and stronger magic. The eastern passage, though, was warded no more thoroughly than the western one, and Jeremy wormed his way beneath that spell too.

He began to sense something, presences not cold like the vilorgs but warm, human, from down the corridor. He hurried along, came to a place where a stair led upward—the corridor continued to the left of the stair—and, recalling Kelada's description, he climbed to another level. Then straight ahead, down a windowless passage with rotting tapestries hung on the wall, to another stair. At the bottom of this one, a door had been boarded up. He was on the right track, at least to the cell where Kelada had once been kept. When he turned a corner and saw two more three-eyes standing guard outside a door, he realized that he had found at least some of the prisoners.

He slipped closer, tiptoeing on bare feet. The nearest guard turned his head, peered down the corridor anxiously, then turned and mumbled something to his companion. The other looked, too. Both of them shifted nervously back and forth.

Jeremy reached for his sword. His right hand felt the hilt. He could draw it, attack invisibly, and the guards would be dead before they knew they were threatened. It would be the work of a moment. Possibly he could even kill them before they could alert the Hag. Certainly now the Hag did not possess either of them, for both vilorgs were nervous and frightened. The blade could taste their blood before they realized their danger, could kill both in the wink of an eye.

The blade could. Jeremy could not.

He took reluctant fingers off the hilt. Somehow he could not bring himself to kill these grotesques, these cold-blooded, froglike beings. Mentally he called himself seven kinds of a fool; he totted up reasons why the creatures had forfeited all claim to mercy, to pity. It was no good. He could not see himself striking from the dark, striking with such advantage, and being the same Jeremy Moon afterward.

All right, he thought. They wouldn't put Kelada in the same room she had escaped from. What had the Hag said? "The deepest hole in the castle." Yet Barach had the feeling that Kelada was nearby. Barach, Gareth, and Syvelin presumably were imprisoned here. That would mean that Kelada and Melodia were somewhere beyond. He flattened his shoulders against the wall and slipped past the guards. They continued to look with evident apprehension down the way he had come.

He turned a corner. Now there was a door on his right, unguarded, and farther down the corridor, a guarded door on the left. He paused, sent out mental feelers— and felt the presence of Melodia certainly, and Kelada. They were somewhere near now.

For a long time Jeremy pondered the problem. He could think of no way past the guards except to chance the use of magic. He tried to think of a small spell, a spell that would not attract the attention of the Hag. At last he whispered in English, "You are asleep, but you will not fall."

He crept closer and closer. The guards stood, not exactly at attention but at least fairly straight, on either side of the door. Their eyes were open, he saw. The spell had not worked.

Trying hard to think of something else, Jeremy slipped nearer and nearer the guards. He was only an arm's length away when suddenly both of the creatures' throats ballooned alarmingly, making him start. They were only breathing, he realized. He watched them for a long time before the throat pouches inflated again, for so long, in fact, that he began to wonder about them. The breathing was so slow—on a sudden suspicion he looked closer at the huge eyes.

He almost laughed aloud. They had no lids. The guards were standing entranced. Jeremy looked hard at the door. Some magic hung about it, an extremely pale web. But it was kept closed by lock and key, not by magic, and one of the guards wore a ring of keys at his belt. Carefully Jeremy lifted the ring and tried the keys in the lock. The fifth one fitted, and he opened the door very slowly, wincing at each tiny groan of the hinges. He passed through the web-shimmer, feeling nothing but knowing that he had broken some ward of the Hag's. He left the door ajar and stumbled into a very dark room.

Very dark and very empty, a cubicle of stone with only the one door. But the sense of Melodia's and Kelada's presence was most intense here. Where could they have gone? Jeremy thought. "The deepest hole in the palace." He dropped to his hands and knees and felt his way around the floor in narrowing concentric circles. Yes, there, beneath his hands: a ring of cold iron. He grasped it and pulled. A heavy stone grated, pivoted open, and warm air rose against his face.

Lying on his belly, he reached down into the opening. It was about three feet square, and seemed to drop indefinitely into the darkness. He could feel no ladder, no way down. "Is anyone there?" he whispered as loudly as he dared.

Something rustled far below. An answering whisper, indistinct. "Who is that?" Jeremy called.

"Kelada! Jeremy?"

"Yes. Where are you?"

"Down here under you."

"Where's the ladder?"

"They took it. How did you find us?"

"Tell you later. How deep?"

"I don't know. Three times as tall as you, maybe."

Jeremy sat back on his haunches beside the trapdoor.

Say fifteen to eighteen feet: too much to jump, certainly. He sighed, unbuckled his belt, and said in English, "Stretch."

The spell must have been used many times before, in many different languages, for the belt remained only a belt. Jeremy thought for a few moments before coming up with: "The Wonder Belt! The amazing belt that can be a rope just long enough to rescue your friends! Something every adventurer wants—and it's yours TODAY!" Lord, he thought to himself. When I get back to Taplan and Taplan, I'll be good for nothing but writing TV ads for Oriental knives and bamboo steamers.

But the spell worked. The belt twisted in his hands, rounded, and became a rope. He heard the tiny sound of the end of it striking many feet below. A second later he felt a chill. The Hag had sensed the latest magic, and she searched for him.

The invisibility spell works against magic too, Jeremy thought fiercely to himself. *She can't find me.* He hoped that was true.

"Find the rope," he whispered aloud.

An instant later he felt a tug from below. "Pull away," Kelada whispered.

Jeremy stood and hauled hand over hand, straining against the weight. In a few seconds he heard someone struggling against stone, and a second later the pull on the rope slackened as the person scrambled out of the trap.

"Help me." It was Melodia. Jeremy found her in the dark, helped her untie the rope from her waist. Her arms went quickly around him, and she kissed him. "Now Kelada," she said. "Hurry."

Jeremy dropped the rope down again. Kelada was lighter, and with Melodia to help, they had her up in no time. The rope twisted again, flattened, and was only a belt. He threaded it through the scabbard and buckled it on again. He felt on the floor for the ring of keys, then found Melodia's hand. "Here, carry these, and keep them from clanking. Kelada, you lead. Don't worry about the guards. You won't be able to see me. I'm invisible right now. Magic. I'll explain later."

Kelada led them from the dark room to the doorway. Jeremy, sword in hand, opened the door. The two vilorgs still goggled at nothing, still breathed in the peaceful rhythm of sleep. "Come on," Jeremy whispered. Kelada frowned at him and slipped through. "How did you get out last time?" Jeremy asked.

"I thought you were invisible?"

"Yes. I have this talisman under my belt—" He had taken the belt off in the cell, in the pitch dark. He grimaced. "Forget it. Where's the way out?"

She pointed to the door at the other end of the corridor. "This cell has a window we can get through."

He paused to take off belt and scabbard. The scabbard he dropped; he gave her the belt. "Take this. It will become a rope when you need it. You and Melodia get out and get away. I'm going to try to find the others."

The door of the cell swung open easily—the lock was either broken or rusted—and the three slipped inside. The room was not quite dark, for through the eastern casement came the twilight preceding dawn. Jeremy remembered the warning Barach had given him, or that he had dreamed, of some dire event to come at dawn, and he moved a little faster. The unglazed window was easily wide enough to allow the women to escape. "Just a second," Jeremy said, now daring to speak a bit louder. "I think I know where everyone is except Nul. I want to try to find him."

He gathered his strength, took a deep breath, and thought of Nul. He was conscious of crying out, not loud but groaning. Then all was darkness until he felt soft hands stroking his face. "What is it?" Melodia's voice, urgent but quiet. "What happened?"

"Nul," Jeremy gasped. "I—my God, I think he's dying."

The pain racked his entire body, as if every joint were on the verge of bursting. Nul's mind was there, a blank but for the white-hot glare of pain, pain, pain. Jeremy tried to give some thought of comfort, but could not bear the agony and the knowledge of his friend's suffering. He slipped back into himself, lay gasping.

"Are you well?" Melodia again, a silhouette in the gloom.

"Yes. I've got to find him. Go."

"No."

"Yes! Go with Kelada, now!"

"Kelada has already gone."

Jeremy raised himself on his elbows. "How long have I been unconscious?"

"Not long. A few simi."

"Why did Kelada leave without you?"

"I told her to go. Come, we must find Nul."

"But—"

Melodia's soft hand covered his mouth, stopping his words. "Hush. I am a healer. Come."

"I don't know where he is."

"Now that you have brought his pain into my presence, I can find him. It is a sense I have, as unerring as Kelada's direction talent. You clear the way, and I will save Nul if I can."

Jeremy got to his feet. "It's dangerous. I think the Hag knows I'm in the castle."

"I could not call myself a healer if I did not at least try."

"Come on, then. I think I'll have to kill two guards." Jeremy, now beltless, grasped his sword, and its light flickered pale against the stone walls. "All right. Let's go."

At the corner, Jeremy motioned Melodia to stay behind. He tensed himself, gathered his strength, and sprang. The sword did not fail him: one guard had fallen before the other even moved, and the second was down an instant later. Quick thrusts made the killing certain. Jeremy did not like the victory, or the feeling of excitement it gave him.

This door was of flat, woven bars of iron, with a larger, heavier lock than the others. Only three of the keys on the ring Melodia carried looked as if they might fit. The last one did, turning easily. Jeremy pushed the door open. "Barach?"

A jingle of chains in the dark. "Here! Jeremy? Then it was not a dream at all!"

"Where are you?"

"Here, chained to the wall."

"A moment," Melodia said. She stepped into the hall, over the fallen body of one of the guards, and came back almost immediately with a lighted torch.

Barach, Gareth, and Syvelin lay manacled hand and foot, shackled to rings set in the stone. "Hold still," Jeremy said, and with quick strokes of the sword he severed the iron. "Can you move?"

"Well enough to fight," Gareth said grimly. "Syvelin?"

"Stiff but unwounded."

Barach got slowly to his feet. "I fear the Hag knows we are out. I feel her anger even now, but distant, divided."

"Dawn has come," Jeremy said. "She has her attention elsewhere. There is a way out."

But none took it. Gareth and Syvelin each picked up a sword from the fallen guards, and in a body they went down the stair, back toward the throne room. At the foot of the second stair Melodia suddenly stopped. "Nul," she said, turning to look past the stairway down the corridor. "He is there somewhere. I feel it."

Barach laid his hand on Jeremy's shoulder. "Day is breaking. We must try to end the Hag's evil, and soon."

Unbidden, a picture came into Jeremy's mind: snow-crowned Whitehorn Mountain, Tremien's stronghold at its summit. The white snow lay in the sun blotched and streaked with red. Blood, human blood, ran down from the top in rivulets, spreading and staining. Unwillingly he said, "We can't help Nul now. We have to stop the Hag's magic."

"He is dying!" Melodia cried.

"One life or many," Jeremy said. "I'm sorry."

Gareth seized Melodia's arm. "I'll take her. The rest of you go on, and quickly. Here, the torch should be yours, for your way is the darker. Lead the way, Lady."

Jeremy nodded, Barach took the torch, and the two fled down the corridor. Syvelin, Jeremy, and Barach took the other direction toward the throne room. They did not pause at the entrance, but burst through the ward. The guards inside were ready for them. As the three charged, spears flew. One seemed ready to skewer Jeremy, but missed by inches—and Jeremy remembered the spells Tremien had placed on him. Then he was on the guard, his sword swinging. Three blows ended the battle. He whirled to face the other guard, and found the vilorg already stretched on the floor, Syvelin's sword thrust into its torso. Syvelin himself was crouched on his knees at the thing's feet. Jeremy touched his shoulder. "Come on."

The soldier fell sideways, and only then did Jeremy see the shaft of the spear. The point had pierced Syvelin's mail, and some fell magic crackled about the shaft still. Barach bent over the fallen man. "There is nothing to do."

"Then let's find the Hag."

They entered the northern passage side by side, and Barach stiffened immediately. Jeremy felt it, too: powerful magic, more concentrated than any he had known, bristling invisibly from the walls, ceiling, and floor of the passage. They waded against a thick tide of it, found themselves invisibly held back as if they were yet in the bog fighting for every step. They reached the doorway and the magic held them, encased them, let them go no farther.

Inside the chamber the witch stood with arms folded and bony chin sunk on her breast. Light streamed from the mirror to illuminate her. "You will die," she said without looking at them. "You will die, as Tremien's other helpers will die. You will die, or worse. And Whitehorn shall be mine."

Jeremy heard Barach attempt to speak, heard him produce only a hoarse, croaking sound. His own throat felt constricted. "A silence spell is on you," the Hag said. "You will approach."

A sluggish tide pulled them into the room and toward the Hag. Even when Jeremy resisted, he felt his bare feet being dragged over the stone floor, inch by inch. It was easier to take step after leaden step toward her. He concentrated on the sword, but he could no more wield it here than he could have if submerged in molasses. Invisible fingers pried at his own, loosened his grip, and as if from a distance he heard the sword clatter on the floor.

Barach and Jeremy came up beside the Hag. The mirror again held the view of Whitehorn, this time of the mountain itself, and dark shapes climbed its slopes. "They come from the Meres," the Hag said. Jeremy recalled the shapes he had glimpsed in the lake the evening before, the dark, circling, hungry shades of the dead. "Their substance is the slime of the swamps, their will my own. Look!"

The slouching dead were halfway to the stronghold. A wave of fire swept down the mountain toward them, a fierce yellow wall of flame, and Jeremy sensed in it Tremien's magic. It rolled over the shapes, and none faltered, none slowed. They continued on. "They cannot be halted. They cannot be turned. Magic will not touch them, for the Dark One has given them a shield from another world. And they cannot be killed, for they are already dead."

Something cold and foul spilled into the room from the passage, not an odor but a *feeling*. "Take them to the throne room," the Hag said absently. "When my attention here is no longer needed I will deal with them."

Clammy hands closed on Jeremy's arms, and he felt himself dragged backward through the door, down the passage. Not until he reached the throne room and was pushed roughly to the floor did he see his and Barach's captors: walking skeletons packed with the ooze of the swamp, dripping with it, arms and legs articulated with twisted grass and ropes of green slime, mud dripping endlessly from eye sockets and jowls, ribs clenched over heaving, stinking blobs of filth. Barach had lost his hold on the torch. One of the foul things picked it up in skeletal hands and set it in a sconce behind the throne. The other stood over Barach and Jeremy.

Jeremy tried to move and felt as if he weighed tons. Invisible weight pressed on his chest, making each breath a struggle. The Hag's magic held him in a giant's grip, and he could hardly think, much less articulate a spell. Turning his head was an agony, but he managed it. Barach lay facing him, his face above the gray beard red with pain. But the mustache fluttered, and Jeremy realized that the old mage was trying, *trying* to whisper a spell of magic.

The fist squeezed tighter and Barach's eyes rolled. Jeremy closed his own eyes, found himself alone in the dark with pain. He had felt something like this when in Nul's mind. Nul. The thought of the pika shamed him: Nul had endured torment like this for who knew how long, perhaps endured it yet. Jeremy could not fight the pain, could not face it.

Instead he went away.

His mind fled to some deeper part of himself, some distant part where it looked on helplessly as the body suffered. This is nightmare, he told himself. This is all bad dreams made into one reality, all evils ever visited on humans in sleep coming to me at once, incubus and succubus, vampire and ghost, ghoul and hobgoblin. This is black night and no morning, dogs stirred and howled by the moon, dark woods and cobwebs across your face. This is the dead come back to drag you down, worms crawling deep in your flesh, the stench of corruption coming from your own wounds. It's a rat nesting and gnawing in your belly, it's the whistle of the black train that screams on hell-bound tracks, the bodiless hand that comes in the night and presses your mouth and nose closed and will not let go.

Despair closed on him, colder than the hand of the Hag and more powerful. He huddled even deeper in himself and found there, in the heart of his darkness, a spark, a tiny flicker.

He found a thought.

It's only a dream.

For a timeless period he paused in that private darkness, willing the spark to grow, just as long ago he had willed the spark to catch in the tinder when he had to make up the fire. It is only a dream. There is no reality here, nothing to fear: it is dream and nothing more. As the thought grew in him, Jeremy began at last to stir, to move, to test the strength of the spell that seemed to hold him. Like a god in an ancient myth, he put his hands on the darkness and thrust it away, rolled it back, pushed it before him. It was a dream, and he would wake and be free of it, be free of it all.

It was like rolling a great stone up an endless hill, like swimming from the deepest floor of the ocean to an impossible surface. Jeremy fought every inch of the way, reached beyond his reach, strained his mind and spirit more than he thought possible, until—

He woke up.

He woke up in his own bed, in his own apartment in Atlanta, in the middle of the night, sheets damp and tangled around him, red digits of his clock-radio reading 4:22 A.M. Lights from the apartment complex parking lot outlined the window dimly. Against the panes he could hear the steady tapping of light rain or sleet. The room was cold. No sooner had the thought hit him than he heard the sigh of the air register, felt the first puff of warm air from the furnace. He took in a deep breath; his chest was free and unconstricted. In a moment he would have to get up, go into the bathroom, the tiles cold underfoot, for his bladder was tight in his belly. In just a moment, but not right now. Somehow Jeremy knew that it was December 22, the day after he had taken the sleeping pills, the day after the whole dream had begun, and he had nothing more adventurous to do than deal with Escher and Taplan the younger in a conference this morning. He was free, it had all been a dream.

Except that far down, somewhere away below him, an old magician held in a spell of dire power writhed in pain on a cold stone floor, a witch stood before a mirror and directed a weird battle, a sad and gallant little creature named Nul lay broken and dying, and that was real, too.

Something told him, some inner voice, that he could go back to sleep, could wake up in the morning, go to work, and never be burdened with nightmare again. It would take so little: close your eyes, drift away, forget the dream, forget the nonsense, forget the fantasy, forget, forget.

Or.

Or not. Or accept the other reality for the reality it was. Jeremy seemed to pause above the alternatives, wavering, undecided. Like a timid man who had climbed to a high diving tower and then had looked far below to see the water distant, hardly existing, Jeremy hesitated. Melodia. Kelada. Nul. Barach. Gareth.

Cassie. Escher. Taplan. Brother Bill.

Risk and safety, unknown and known, death and life.

Stepping off the tower was the hardest thing Jeremy had ever done in his life, the hardest thing he could imagine doing, but he did it. He plunged down toward dark waters, toward the castle of the Hag, toward blood and death.

And as faster and faster he plummeted downward, he screamed, screamed in anger, screamed in defiance, screamed in triumph.

CHAPTER 13

JEREMY SANK BACK into his body, back into agony. The Hag's spell, a vise tightening without mercy, gripped his chest, squeezed hot red anguish into his mind, obscuring thought, feeling, everything but the knowledge of suffering. Jeremy faced the knowledge, examined it, knew it for all it was, and thrust it behind him. He ignored it, became conscious instead of the power filling the room, flowing under and about him. He visualized it as a net of pulsing red light, real but impalpable, holding him caught in its meshes as a fish might be trapped in a fisherman's seine. But he was not as defenseless as the fish, for another current flowed in him, his own *mana*, which he saw as a pale white shimmer pounding lighter and darker with every pulse beat. Use it, he told himself. Use your own magic to fight back.

His throat felt clogged, closed, plugged by the Hag's will. He had no voice, could speak no words. The pressure allowed him no hope of speaking, of using an oral spell. His mind went back to his earliest lessons in sorcery, to the three-step path. Formulation, visualization, realization. He could do all but the last, and that one was beyond his ability, a cloud full of water floating high above a man dying of thirst on the ground. *It doesn't matter*, he told himself. *The spell must be spoken only if you believe it must be spoken. Say it in your mind. Say it here, where the Hag cannot come, inside your own head.*

It was hard even to think in English, but he tried. Without using vocal cords, throat, mouth, or tongue, he told himself that the grip of the Hag was growing lighter, that her force around him was weakening, and he willed himself to believe that it was true. He could not realize, but he formulated and visualized for all he was worth, and then put the wish into English, all inside his head.

231

He used the language that no one else had ever uttered
on this planet, the one that, being fresh, had the property
of tapping deep into the flow of Thaumia's magic, deeper
than anyone else's abilities, deeper even than the Hag's.
Her hold on me is slackening, he thought. Her grip is
growing feeble. Her strength is nearing an end. Whether
he was right or not, he found a breathing space, a time to
think, and his thoughts turned outward, to others.

Nul.

Darkness only, void. Where was the little pika? Jeremy could not find his thought or his spirit, could find
not even his pain. There was simply nothing to connect
with Jeremy's questing mind. Nul was gone. In his mind
Jeremy saw Nul tumbling spread-eagled, as from a great
height, hurtling into depth and emptiness. Nul has fallen
into death, Jeremy thought. Grief welled inside him for
the little creature. He turned the grief to anger against
the Hag, blew on the embers of that anger, fanned it to
fire, and warmed himself by it. If Nul was dead, his
death would not go unavenged.

Melodia.

Yes, somewhere, very faint, very sweet, like the faraway song of the bells she wore. Melodia, who could not
be untrue to love, who could not let a cry of pain go
unanswered. Where are you, Melodia? Can you hear
me? You give of yourself, healer. You are brave, though
you do not think you are. Your courage is not the valor
of arms. You could never take a life, even if in taking it
you saved your own. No, yours is not the courage of the
soldier but the will to wrestle with death itself, to taste
despair sour and bitter on your tongue and yet still breathe
sweet hope. O Melodia, Jeremy thought, brushing that
dim presence with his mind, teach me to give, too! Show
me the way to hold back the blackness, to send what I
can of myself to the aid of my friends! Out of all the hope
in your heart, give me a portion to sustain me! The
curtains of consciousness trembled, and Melodia was gone.

Kelada.

Clever thief, hardheaded waif. There she was, like a
bright flame on a dark night, stealing silent through stone
halls, evading notice, coming ever closer. That flame
burned hot, and only death could extinguish it. Kelada,
you are lovely, you are starlight, you are warmth. Take
no notice of your broken nose, of your narrow chin, of

your body thin as a boy's. Oh, Kelada, you should see
the fire that burns inside you, fierce and bright and pure!
Men will sing songs of your deeds when the mountains
have been washed grain by grain into the seas, and their
remote descendants will remember you when the last
embers of magic flicker and die in a universe gone
mundane.

Gareth.

You, soldier. You have a laugh for death and a taste
for action. With fear in your bones but strength in your
arms, you grin and go forward; with death screaming
your name, you hear only the call of duty. I see you,
soldier, doorkeeper, sword at the ready, and at your feet
I see the work of your hands, the enemies you pulled
from Nul, and those you kept from Melodia when she
bent over the still and broken body. Give me your courage, Gareth! I have such need of it.

Barach.

Talker, teacher, weaver of spells. I feel your throes of
torment, I know your fear of defeat and what defeat will
mean: the dying of the light, the passing of all fire, all
warmth, all happiness. Old man with the young heart!
For your parables and your wisdom, thanks. Now take
from me what I can give you of strength, of comfort, and
do not give in to hopelessness, for it comes from the
mouth of the Hag, and she is a mumbling liar. Be ready,
teacher! and your pupil will show you something. Yes, I
believe you may learn a trick or two yourself today,
teacher, and not be ashamed to call me student.

Jeremy relaxed, slipped away, was himself again and
only himself, alone in the dark behind his eyelids but
calmer now and more hopeful. This time there was no
mistake: the pressure on him had lessened. He opened
his eyes. The ghouls raised by the Hag still stood over
him, the muck between their bones glistening in the light
of the flickering torches. They trembled and swayed,
held up by the will of the witch, sustained by her power
and that flowing through the mirror. He could sense that
too, an alien magic, different in texture from anything
except what he sensed in himself. Magic drained from the
earth, he thought, from our world that has so little to
start with, so little that for all my life there I missed it,
passed it by, never looked to see it, never reached to
hold it. And now it was being dragged here, to Thaumia,

turned to evil purposes, and made to serve the ends of those who despised the light and sought the darkness. Yet he felt stray currents of the magic in the room, spilling from the corridor, seeping into him. For what it was, the earthly magic was his magic, and he concentrated on absorbing it, using it, feeling it gather bit by bit inside himself.

Jeremy lay on his back, sprawled before the iron throne, his head lolled back, his arms and legs spread. Beneath him the stone was hard, cold, rough. He tried to speak but could not. He tried to move, willed himself to break free of the magic holding him, telling himself silently in every language he knew that he could do it. In his mind he pictured a million tiny strands holding him down, saw himself as Gulliver staked on a beach by tiny imps, and he imagined their strongest ropes were only cobwebs to him. Oh, there were many of them, a million of them, but each thread was a slender one. There, he had broken one, though he could not move. One thread doesn't make a lot of difference. There, this time two had broken. Now four. Eight. Sixteen. He multiplied in his head, imagining the bindings of the Hag's magic to be flying apart in geometric numbers. Two hundred fifty-six. Five hundred twelve. A thousand twenty-four.

One finger moved.

It was like a pebble slipping from under a boulder teetering at the summit of a cliff. An instant later the rock itself bowed forward in ponderous acknowledgment of the pebble's motion and began to roll. As if invisible bands were breaking, Jeremy felt the lines of magic releasing him one by one as he strained against them, stretched them, and tore them apart. With a shout he rolled, pushed himself up, got to his knees, then his feet. The shambling ghouls were almost on top of him. He retreated before them down the long length of the throne room, and still they came. He snatched a dead torch from its sconce and swung it hard, aiming for the nearest ghoul's head and striking it.

The apparition reeled sideways, slime and mud spattering from the skull. Jeremy smelled its fetor, and for a second he was sure he had destroyed the thing. Then it found its footing again, turned on Jeremy, and plodded forward, the lower jaw broken and hanging by the right socket only, filth drooling from the gaping mouth. Jeremy again tried to speak, to send a magic spell against his foe, but found he still could not. He struck at the second apparition's legs, hit solidly, felt both bone and torch break from the impact. The creature's left knee was shattered, and the foot spun half around, but the grinning skull gave no indication of having felt pain and, lurching and flailing, the ghoul limped on implacably.

This is what Tremien faces at Whitehorn, Jeremy thought. *The ghouls fear no attack and are unaffected by magic; and they will be the old magician's defeat.*

Jeremy had backed all the way against the far wall. The animated hulks would fall on him as soon as they found an opening, and he had only the broken stub of a torch, a pitiful stick perhaps a foot long, to use against them. Again he tried to draw on any reserve of magic left in him, and still he found he could not speak.

But he could hear, and from his right he heard a woman's voice: "Jeremy! I'm coming!"

He whipped his head around. Kelada had just slipped through one of the narrow windows in the western corridor. She flew toward him now, a spear in each hand. Beyond her two of the vilorgs lay in crumpled heaps. Jeremy worked toward her, scraping his shoulders against the stone wall. When the undead creatures lumbered forward, he hurled the broken torch at the face of the nearer ghoul, and held out his hand behind him. Kelada slapped the cool shaft of a spear there.

Her own point went into the eye socket of the skull with the broken jaw, carried it back, smashed the skull against the stones of the throne-room wall, shattering bone and splattering mud. The ghoul slipped down to a sitting position, reached to jerk away the spear, and then tried blindly to rise. Jeremy swept his own spear through the legs of his limping opponent, sent the thing crashing to the ground. Kelada fell on it, getting her hands under the edges of the rib cage, bracing, pulling herself up, spreading the bones.

The thing cracked open like something rotten, spilling the contents of the chest cavity in a liquid wash of putrefaction. Across the room, the headless creature still stirred feebly, trying to rise, to walk, to fight. On the floor even the scattered bones of the ribs seemed to twitch with a mockery of life, to attempt to crawl back into the ruined nest of the body. Jeremy grabbed Kelada's arm and dragged her into the throne room.

Barach lay quiet, his eyes open. His glance darted to Jeremy's face, urgent with meaning, and then rolled toward the northern corridor. Jeremy dropped to his knees. He knelt, touched the old man's forehead with his own. *Take what strength I can give you, father in magic*, he thought again. A picture, a dream of his grandfather came to mind: the old man as Jeremy had last seen him, threaded with tubes, hooked to bottles, gasping out his life in a hospital bed. Once as Jeremy had sat with the old man, all alone—it was just before Christmas, he recalled now—his grandfather's mind had cleared, and he had spoken Jeremy's name quite plainly. Then, reaching a wizened hand up to clasp Jeremy's, he had said his last farewell. What had the old man said? Something Jeremy could never understand: "Son, you have to sit here with me. I'm sorry for you."

Something happened. Barach stirred, groaned, tried to sit. Kelada helped him up. Jeremy almost fell, drained suddenly, feeling like a marionette whose strings had been cut. Power had surged from him, he knew that. He could only hope that it had passed to the old teacher and that it was enough to sustain Barach. The old magician struggled to his feet. He was already speaking quickly, harshly, in a language Jeremy did not know, but one that somehow sounded ancient, arcane, complex. The magician took a step forward, another, making for the northern passage. He almost glowed with magical energies, but within the glow the old body looked frail and shaken.

In the doorway to the passage Barach straightened himself, spread his arms wide, and threw his head back on his shoulders. The magic fairly sizzled around him, and his voice suddenly cracked out, a whip slashing toward the Hag. The stones of the castle seemed to vibrate to the sound, and for a second Jeremy felt the power of the Hag slip away from him entirely, and he could talk. "Barach has the power," he gasped in his own language, hoping that the wish carried the force of a spell and that the spell would help.

Then a blast of malignant force like nothing Jeremy had felt or imagined swept down the corridor, exploded into the throne room, smashed Barach aside, filled the room with the Hag's power and her hatred. It passed like the hot breath of a detonation, leaving Jeremy dazed, sunk to his knees, clinging to the iron throne. Kelada sprawled not far away, and Barach had been tumbled thirty feet, a third of the way down the length of the throne room. Jeremy staggered toward the old man, fell, and crawled the rest of the way. He found Barach lying on his back, eyes wide under their birds' nest brows, gray beard pointing stiffly at the ceiling. The old man's chest heaved when Jeremy laid a hand on it. "Are you hurt?" Jeremy asked.

The mouth twitched under the sweeping gray mustaches. "What a question."

"Can you move?"

"Ah. A better question." Barach stirred his head, his arms and legs. "No bones broken. Yes, I can move. But I am blind."

Jeremy passed his hand across the eyes. They did not focus or blink. "Barach, we have to get away—"

The old head rolled from side to side against the stone floor in weary negation. "Go if you can. It is better for me that I remain. I have failed, and Whitehorn will fall. And after Whitehorn, the whole land and the whole world."

"But we can try again—"

"Not I, my son. I have no magic left." In the instant of his speaking, Jeremy felt the truth of what his teacher said. Barach had put everything, every last reserve of *mana* that he could call on, in that last mighty spell, and it had almost been enough to quell the witch and quench her power—almost but not quite. Now the old man lay an empty vessel, one that could never be filled again.

Jeremy felt his own forces growing within, like a fire that had burned almost to ashes given new fuel. Somewhere he at least was finding new strength. "Where there is life, there is magic," he said. "You taught me that, Barach. You of all people should know that the Three Laws are immutable, even for a stubborn old man." Kelada came to kneel beside them. Jeremy reached for Barach's hand, put it in Kelada's. "Get up, my teacher. Kelada will be your eyes. Our business here is not finished."

The blind eyes wrinkled into a semblance of Barach's old smile. "Once a man fell off a high cliff, and a little bird noticed him smiling on the way down. 'How can you smile?' the bird demanded. 'You have no feathers or wings, and death awaits you in seconds!' 'Who knows,' the man replied. 'I might land in a haystack!' "

"Jeremy," Kelada said. "The Hag comes."

Barach slowly got up. Kelada helped him, and they limped down the western passage—no wards at all blocked the way now, Jeremy saw. He sensed that the Hag's forces had been tested to their utmost limits, that she too now had to rest, to build up her strength again. It would be a long time coming, he thought to himself, taking small comfort from the thought. The Hag had all the seeming of a dry husk, a body without a spirit, save only the spirit of her anger and hatred. He turned to face her as she tottered into the room, supporting herself with a hand against the stone wall. "The Dark One knows of you now," she said, glaring at him. "He will have you!"

"Bogey tales! Save them for the nursery." Jeremy took a step toward her, trying hard not to betray the weariness he felt. "Your death was in that spell, Hag. You spat out your life with the venom you sent against the old man. You have burned yourself out like the guttering torch behind you."

She did not look at the torch but edged sideways until she could grasp one arm of the throne, then the other. She lowered herself down, and she looked more than ever like a living skeleton, like one of her own creations. Even the deep-set eyes had lost their glitter and looked flat, like a doll's eyes, or like the eyes of the dead. "I will recover, youngster. My armies have halted, but they have not retreated, and no magic of Tremien's can dislodge them so long as the Dark One supplies them with power. Power, young fool! It flows into the castle even now. Can't you feel it? A day, two days, and I will be strong as ever, or even stronger, and then Tremien will know my anger."

"You have the droppings from the Dark One's table, Hag, such stale crumbs as he cares to give you. He will use you as long as he finds you convenient, then kill you. You are the fool, not I."

The bony fingers clenched and unclenched atop the skulls, and in the Hag's face the lips drew back, white and bloodless, over the cracked, broken, brown teeth. Spittle dripped over her chin, and she wiped it away with the back of her hand. "You speak big. Show me your magic, if you have any left."

Jeremy shook his head. "No. I will not waste it on you. I have enough power to harm you, but not enough knowledge, and you cannot trick me into squandering what I must use for the defense of Tremien."

Behind the Hag the fire in the guttering torch flared and smoked, turned a dull orange. Jeremy furrowed his brow. There was something that he should recall, something he had learned or had been told. What was it?

"The Dark One is calling you," the Hag said. "How will you feel, I wonder, when he brings you before him? You call me evil? Wait until you find his hand upon you. You will curse the day of your being born, and your mother for having borne you, before that one is finished."

"And how will you fare, witch, when he learns of the secrets you hid from him?"

She shook her head, but her eyes were frightened in the dark caverns on their sockets. "He needs me. It does not matter. He cannot work his will here in the northlands without the mirror, and only Sebastian Magister had the power of their making. Now only this one is left, and the Dark One cannot control or use it without me."

"I think not," Jeremy said. "He has drawn power from my world, the Dark One has, and it has made him stronger than even you can guess. I think you will find yourself facing some wickedness beyond your control or warding when you face him."

She cringed inwardly. Jeremy *felt* the wards now, shrunk to protect the Hag herself, gathered about her in a small globe, pulled back from all the rest of the castle. They were strong in place there, too strong for him to penetrate with his own power so low. He examined his own *mana*, and he pictured it as a dwindled glow, like the dancing flames on the torch behind her. The Hag had pulled back, and yes, she was afraid. But to Jeremy she said, "The Dark One is a mortal, long-lived though he be. He has no magic beyond my holding and my wards, not in my own place of power. I do not fear him as long as I am in my castle, for, learned as he is in the ways of magic, yet he is no spirit, no elemental."

And then the knowledge Jeremy had been groping for moments before was in his mind. The torch had been kindled by Melodia back in the passageway; by Melodia, who carried with her an innocuous tinder box. Jeremy looked more closely at the torch and saw shape there too definite for fire alone. Yes! "Smokharin!" he shouted, so loudly that the Hag started up, thrusting her hands before her as if to turn him away, to hold him off. "Smokharin, the Hag!"

An orange spark gathered and leaped in a yellow arc from the torch to the throne. The Hag had begun an incantation that broke into a shrill cry of fear. She threw her hands wide, then beat frantically at the yellowed, dry gown she wore. Smoke puffed from the skirt, and a moment later she exploded in flame, fire so fiercely hot that Jeremy had to back away and turn his face. She shrieked in a voice that hurt Jeremy's ears, then cried aloud in great, wordless howls. A commotion at the back of the room, and another skeleton shambled in, muck squeezing between its ribs as through the fingers of a clenching fist. It made for the Hag, then, twenty feet from her, began to jerk and twitch.

The Hag was a wailing, tottering, living torch encased in the flames, skin crisping away from flesh, eyes clouding, wisps of flaming hair and cloth rising from her, whirling aloft, carried in the hot breath of the fire that consumed her. Great black billows of smoke boiled up from her, streaks of soot drifted and swirled in the light the pyre gave off, and the air became acrid and biting with the stench of burned hair and seared flesh. The figure inside the flame fell to its knees, bent slowly back. The arms contracted, drew up in front, as if the Hag were a boxer trying to defend herself against the blows of death. The body toppled sideways, and at the same instant the ghoul simply fell apart, collapsed into a heap of slime and disconnected bones. The fire began to die, leaving behind a shrunken black skeleton flaking to ruin already. A fine rain of oily black soot, droplets small as baby spiders, commenced to fall in the throne room. One smoldering fragment of the dress came to rest on the dead torch that Jeremy had used as a weapon, down beyond the Hag's body and the ruin of the ghoul, and in a second red sparks began to appear on the head of the torch.

Jeremy went to it. Smokharin was there, small, bright. "The Hag is finished," the salamander said.

"Yes. She will trouble Melodia no more."

"A victory for you."

"For you, you mean."

"No, mortal. Your thought gave me the power to slay the Hag. We cannot deal thus on our own."

"Together, then. Will you be all right on the torch?"

The little salamander flared even brighter. "I can burn stone if need be!"

Jeremy lifted the torch and fit it into a sconce. "Then I will leave you. My task is not yet done."

"I know, and I can help you no more. But I think the better of you, mortal magician, for the love you bear Melodia." The torch smoldered to a low flame. Jeremy turned and walked toward the north passage and the mirror.

The stones in the walls shuddered. From somewhere below him a wrenching, grating sound began and went on and on. The floor sagged as the stones of the castle settled one upon the other. The Hag's magic had perished with her, and now the castle had to stand under only its own strength, the strength of stones and not of magic spells. But in the room of the mirror the old enchantments held firm, perhaps even stronger than before. The blanket had been cast aside, and the oval mirror stood unshrouded in the center of the room. Jeremy reached for it, knowing that he could not bring himself to touch it, that some force more mighty than he would keep his hands off, and he felt invisible resistance, as he expected, a foot or more away from the mirror. The sword he had forged in magic lay on the stones, its light low, but the only light in the room. He stooped and retrieved it. In his hands the sword flashed brighter, giving him hope, and he swung the weapon at the mirror as hard as he could.

He felt a wrenching shock, numbing his arm and shoulder, and in the close confines of the mirror room his ears sang with the noise of a tremendous crash.

For a moment Jeremy thought that he too had been blinded, as Barach had, by some malign curse. He stood stunned, his ears ringing, his eyes seeing nothing but blackness. But then he felt the dull weight in his hand, not much of a burden but heavier than it should be, and feeling somehow mundane. He ran his fingers along the blade of the sword, feeling rough spots and patches of rust, then a jagged edge of metal where the blade had snapped eight inches from the hilt. The mirror was whole, but the sword had shattered, and its magical light had vanished. Only the far-off glow of the torch shed any light at all in the room, and that was too little to see by.

"What are you afraid of?" It was a voice, though not a sound.

"I don't know," Jeremy said aloud. "Where are you?"

"In my own place." It was a calm voice, not deep but clear and soft, a man's voice; yet he heard it in his mind, not with his ears. "You are afraid and do not know what you fear? Not a position for a wise man! Let me see you."

"Here I am," Jeremy said.

"No. Come before me. Here." Silver light streamed from the mirror, illuminating the rock wall to Jeremy's left in a shimmering oval. The light seemed to transform the stone, to soften it almost and show the flecks of shining mica the rock held, to transform dull gray building stones into a brilliant, shapeless constellation of minute stars. "Come and stand here, in the light. What are you afraid of?"

"I am afraid," Jeremy admitted, "of looking in the mirror."

A silence, and then the voice again, smooth, indulgent. "You are wise beyond your years. Mirrors and love are detestable, for both multiply the numbers of men. But that is not what you mean, is it? You are afraid of what you might see in the mirror, what it might show you of yourself."

"Yes."

"Hmm. A fear like none I have ever heard of before, especially from one supposed to be so terrible. Is this the hero? Is this the one who came into my world, thrust by a fate he could not control or understand, who summoned all his courage, who took his destiny into his own hands and fought to make himself into something he had never dreamed of being? For shame, visitor to our world! Come. Come see the hero."

"No," Jeremy said between clenched teeth. "No. I am no hero."

"You are, you know. You have it in you. Or if you are not yet the hero, you might be. You could rule in place of old fools with long white beards and no thought but

fear in their bald heads." The voice rose into a senile
crackle of apprehension: " 'Oh, my dear, is that a witch
stirring? Alas, alas, the portents from the South are evil!
Oh, our power on the foolish peasants will be shattered!
Who shall we send to do the work we dare not do?' "

"Shut up!"

A sound like hollow laughter. "You did not ask for
this, mortal. Do you feel heroic? Or do you not feel
used? Where is Tremien? Did he come with you? I think
not. I think he sits safe on his mountain and thinks of you
and laughs at how he fooled you. Or think of those who
did come with you, who were duped, like you, by an old
wizard. Look around you. Where are your friends now?
Gone, fled. Do you think they waited while you dealt
with the Hag? Perhaps long enough to be sure her wards
were down, until they knew it was safe to leave. Now
they are gone, run away. Do you think they'll make their
way back to Tremien? What story do you think they'll
tell of you there? That you alone stood and fought when
they ran, that you of your own resources killed the Hag?
Or that *they* did that work after you had failed? Who will
be the hero in that tale, I wonder? The unknown visitor,
or the brave captain of arms who was nowhere to be
found when you needed him; or the wise old man of
magic who fell through his own pride; or the gentle,
hypocritical healer who glories in the name of charity
others give her while privately she sweats in a bed of lust,
her body spread open for an outlaw; or the determined
thief who deserted you as soon as she could? They de-
spise you, you know. You showed them how weak they
were, how impotent and false, and they hate you for the
faults you show them in themselves. You are their mirror, and they fear to look into it! I expect you will play
some small part in the tale they tell, and it will be
forgotten by the next time spring comes to Thaumia."

"Who are you?" Jeremy yelled, setting up a clattering
echo.

"You know. I am you."

"Sebastian?"

Laughter again. "What ignorance, and what an insult!
But ignorance can be remedied, and the insult was not
meant, I know. No, I am not Sebastian, not the ambitious boy. No, not him, good tool though he was, faithful

servant for a time. Look in the mirror if you really want
to know who I am."

"The Hag is dead," Jeremy said. "Her creatures have
fallen to pieces. Whoever you are, you know that your
plan has failed."

"The witch's poor mindless creations, her pretty little
puppets, have dissolved. Yes, and on Whitehorn old
Tremien scratches his brown, bald pate and wonders what
has happened. He may even glory that his magic van-
quished them, old fool that he is. He is wrong. True, the
legions of the Hag have vanished for a time. But they
have only gone to ground. When I turn my attention on
them, they will rise again and march, and this time they
will not stop until Whitehorn itself has fallen. The Hag
was but my servant. Wait until the master strikes! And
the power is building, building. I will not send them
today, and not tomorrow, but soon they will rise and
march, stronger than ever. And no one can stop them as
long as the mirrors remain intact. But I forget; that was
your quest, was it not, to learn about the mirrors that
Sebastian wrought so well? I can teach you all about
them. Come, boy, and look into the mirror."

The voice held something compelling in it, something
perverse that made Jeremy think it was taunting him to
do something the speaker really feared. Was that the
case, or was the tone a clever trick? Jeremy licked his
lips. "I will look into the mirror—when I can break it."

"Oh, but you *can't* break it. Of all the people of
Thaumia, you alone are perhaps the only being of whom
I can truly say that: you will never be able to break the
mirrors. Don't you understand that now? The spell is a
very special one, for it has touched the world from which
you came. You are part of it, and it is part of you. Have
you never considered the magic of a mirror, never truly
looked into a mirror? Don't you see yourself in it whenever you look? You look in one mirror, and then you go
away, a hundred thousand paces, and no one knows
where you are. Then you look into a second mirror, and
whom do you see but the person you fled? There you
are, caught, entombed forever behind the glass. Look in
the mirror, and look closely. You are only looking into
yourself. What do you see today? A new wrinkle on your
face, a gray hair that yesterday was dark and lustrous
with youth? Your double has them, too. You see time in

the mirror, don't you? Time, and death waiting to swallow you at the end, picking away at you day by day with bony fingers. A blemish here, a balding head, a tooth out that will never grow back. Don't you know the person in the mirror hates you? He's killing you, boy, killing you by moments. How would you like to strike back? How would you like to see him grow old, and yourself grow younger, as young as you like? It's a great magic, boy, one not many know. I can show you how."

"You're lying," Jeremy said.

"Perhaps I am. Yes, I am a liar. Or am I? If I lied when I told you that, I'd be telling the truth always, would I not, except when I lied to tell you that I lie. But if the mirror is a liar, I suppose that I am, too. Like the mirror, I turn right to left and left to right, I render what you find in all your books backward and unreadable. Do you know how you really look? I wonder. A mirror cannot show you, for a mirror tells lies. If a book is backward in a mirror, so is your face! A picture cannot show you how you look, for by the time you see the picture the person in it is gone, drifted away down the river of time itself. That's why you don't dare to look in this mirror, whether you know it or not. You cannot bear to see the way you really look."

Jeremy did not answer. He knew, or at least he felt, that if he did not listen, did not speak, if he saved his energy, he would grow stronger, for the alien magic filled this room, drifted in it lazily and hung in the air like an invisible smoke. He seemed to draw it in with every breath, and when he concentrated on it, the magic seemed to gather and grow in his chest.

"What are you doing now?" The light was silver and soothing on the stones, soft light like moonlight on a fine summer evening back home. The stone looked almost soft, like a beach, and Jeremy found himself recalling a hotel balcony, a full moon, with luminous waves rolling in to die on the dark and glittering sand. The voice purred on, insinuating: "It's a shame about your companions, isn't it? Did you feel the travel spell a moment ago? They're on their way to Whitehorn right now."

Jeremy blinked, all thought of moonlight and beaches out of his head. "I felt nothing."

"Ah, so you *are* still there. Do you know why you felt nothing? Because there was nothing to feel. No, no one used a travel spell. I am a terrible liar, as you said. You find that contemptible? You scorn me? What about you? Have you ever told a lie? Made a living from telling your lies? I sense that you have, though I do not understand how." After a long silence the voice added, "Not talking anymore? Too bad. It's a pity, isn't it, that not all your companions will return to Whitehorn. Not the soldiers whose bodies lie in the mud outside the castle, or the one struck down inside on the stones. And not the little skulking black rat of a creature that the Hag played with."

"Nul?"

"Is that its name? Nul? Null, nothing. A good name for such a sneaking thing. The Hag gave it to me, you know. I swallowed it quite up, and barely noticed that I had eaten it. It's here still, somewhere. Let me look. Ah, here we have the beast, yes, barely alive. I think it has no mind left. Look, its arms and legs are all broken."

A sound split the quiet of the mirror room: a hopeless gurgle, a ratchetlike groaning cough, a moan. "Oh, I think it's dying right now. Look at the blood coming from its nasty mouth. I could save it, you know. But such a filthy, beastly thing should die—"

"Nul!"

"Oh, look, it heard you. It must be a pet. Look at it! Oh, it's so funny to see, you'd love this. It's trying to crawl toward you. Look at how its broken arms flap, at the bloody splinters of bone sticking through! Oh, you would laugh—"

"Nul! Are you there?"

A wrenching little cough. Jeremy could stand no more. He stepped in front of the mirror and saw—

Darkness only.

"I am such a liar," the voice purred. "I'm quite ashamed of myself. And there you are. You are very like Sebastian Magister, our beloved pet, aren't you? And now, of course, you cannot move."

The silver light pressed against him, held Jeremy against the wall as tightly as shackles. "I'm looking," he said. "I see nothing."

"You see yourself. You *are* nothing. You will be nothing."

"Then show me something different. Show yourself!"

"Oh, my dear boy, I'll do much more than that. I'll

shake your hand, I'll embrace you, I'll have a chat with you face to face. After all, we are going to be very close, you and I. Come toward me now."

Jeremy felt himself being dragged forward, toward the mirror. Now he could make out a figure in its depths, a wizened man-sized figure, a mere silhouette against the deeper blackness. "Yes, that's good," the voice said as he stopped inches from the mirror's surface. "Oh, you do have some magic about you, and a very interesting type. I've never seen it before, not even in Sebastian. I wonder what it is and how I'll like having it when I am you." The figure had come closer, too, and now was almost like Jeremy's reflection standing just behind the glass, its head tilted just as his was, its attitude mocking his own.

He remembered a nightmare he had had—when? Ages ago, in another life. In that dream he had been facing a mirror, just like this one, when—

Hands came through the glass, grasped his shoulders, pulled him forward. He screamed. It was happening, just as he had dreamed. He was being pulled into the mirror, falling into nothingness, caught in the clutches of his own reflection.

And this time it was real.

CHAPTER 14

JEREMY FELL AS he had fallen in dreams, with what seemed to be terrifying speed. An instant after he screamed, he crashed through a round opening, landed on his feet—and realized he was unhurt.

"There," the old man said, grinning at him toothlessly. "You came through safe enough." He stepped back, a bald, ancient mummy of a man, his nearly fleshless arms projecting from great, floppy sleeves. He wore a robe like the one Sebastian had worn in the Between, but this one was of no color Jeremy could name. It seemed darkness gathered rather than fabric, and the old man's head floated above it like a death's-head moon.

Jeremy took a step forward. "No," the old man said. "I'm afraid you cannot hurt me. As a matter of fact, I am not even here. This, you see, is illusion." He vanished. "Look around," his voice said in Jeremy's mind. "This will be your home, for many, many long years, I hope. Even for centuries, if you respond well to certain spells we have learned in our time. Look around! I am busy with other thoughts and more powerful enemies, but I will spare you enough light to see by. I do without light myself."

Light came from somewhere at that, though not from the sun or the moon. Jeremy stood in the open, on an enormous flat platform of stone, of a single stone, as far as he could tell, hundreds of yards across. Behind him was the oval mirror—no, not the Hag's mirror. This one, in a plain frame of ebony, was a bit larger. He took a step toward it and found himself held in place. He would not be allowed to touch this mirror either. Its surface swirled with layers of black within black, and it reflected nothing, not even his face. He walked away from it, a hundred steps, to the edge of the platform and looked down. He was three hundred feet high at least, the stone dropping away in a sheer, unbroken wall. He paced to a corner of the platform and discovered that he stood on a gigantic cube high above an arid land.

It reminded him of the Between, and of the Hag's domain too, in its desertion, but it was different. Overhead the sky was dark, not with night, but simply darkened, as if clouds too thick for the sun to penetrate hung heavy over the countryside. They had lifted a little from the far horizons, Jeremy saw, and that was where the light came from: a bare rim of clear sky all the way around him. He could see mountains on one side, tapering away to hills on his right. Behind him a plain stretched far away, and to his left he saw deep cracks and fissures branching as if a river had once run nearby. Nothing stirred and nothing lived here, and the only sound was the stony lament of the wind as it fingered the sands far below.

Relas, Jeremy thought, and knew he was correct in so thinking. The southeastern continent of Thaumia, once a land of fifty kingdoms, a land of men and women, now the empire of the Great Dark One. It was an empire of desolation. He walked all the edges of the great platform and saw no way down. Impatient, thinking of the rope he had conjured from his belt, he began to work a spell but then stopped. No, he told himself. That's what he's waiting for. He wants to see what I can do, and how I do it. The cure for that was simple enough: Jeremy would use no magic. He contemplated the landscape again. Not even on the gray plain of the Between had he seen anything so utterly forlorn, so empty.

Jeremy thought, This has been a home for people. That's the difference. The Between is no one's home, and those you encounter there aren't really *there,* no more than the Great Dark One was here a minute ago. In the Between, people are only visitors. There the dreams live and the dreams are real, but the dreamers themselves touch the land only in mind and are themselves illusions. But here people lived once upon a time. Water flowed in that river and children swam in it. Boys climbed the trees that once grew on those hills, and little girls ran barefoot through the grass that grew there. Husbands buried their wives in this soil and wept at the parting.

The people are gone, dust long ago, but they were here, and the land remembers.

He walked back to the center of the platform, circled the mirror, trying to find some weakness in the wards around it. Again he felt he could almost see the magic: deep-colored this time, purple, the hue of a black light, and solid rather than meshlike. A stronger spell than any the Hag had at her call, surely. If he could push the mirror to the edge, topple it over, it might break. But he could not even approach the mirror.

Now wait. He had come through the mirror, that much he knew. The experience was nothing like the travel spell, but he had traveled, had been pulled from the Hag's castle to Relas. And that meant that he had been inside the ward at least once. He swept his hands over the all-but-invisible shield of the spell, feeling nothing under his palms except air, yet unable to press his fingers through the barrier, to move one centimeter toward the mirror. But there was a way. Something told him there was a way.

He thought. The mirror was not of the Great Dark One's making, that was the first thing to remember. There had been only one maker of mirrors in Thaumia. The mirror from the Between, Melodia's mirror, the Hag's, and now this one. They had been shaped by Sebastian—and why?

Because the Great Dark One could not make a mirror like this. That had to be the reason. Jeremy raised his voice: "Are you here?" Nothing answered him but the wind, and it seemed only to sigh. Relas, alas. . . .

"You could not make the mirrors," Jeremy accused. "You had not the knowledge or the power to create a simple mirror. For that you had to use Sebastian." Still no answer, though somehow Jeremy sensed a listener now. "Oh, you taught him techniques, I'm sure. You gave him directions and watched as he worked. But you lacked the talent, didn't you? And now you can only use the mirrors, not create more. What did you do? Supply some of your *mana* to Sebastian, as I gave Barach my power? For much of your magic *is* tied to the mirrors, Dark One. Through Sebastian you have put some of yourself in each of them. How much less would you be without the mirrors?"

Nothing. Anger boiled in Jeremy. If only the Great

Dark One would come out of hiding, if he would purr and sneer and mock as he had done in the witch's castle, then Jeremy would have an enemy to fight. As it was—ah.

As it was, the Great Dark One was still probing, still studying. He did not know Jeremy's powers, could not guess what threat the Earthman might bring. When the obvious temptations the voice had suggested failed, the Great Dark One simply moved to more subtle temptations: let's bore him, let's make him decide to act on his own. We'll see a sample of his magic, and then he's ours. Then we'll know how to handle him. That's why the Dark One did not seem to be here. He *was* here, of course, concealed somewhere. Jeremy could almost feel his gaze.

"The devil's best trick is to pretend he does not exist," Jeremy said. The words died on the dead air. He sat cross-legged before the mirror, chin on hand, gazing at it. Jeremy was prepared to be as patient as a brass Buddha if need be. Nothing that he had thought he needed at first proved to be important, really. He did not need to escape; he did not need to fight. He needed only to think.

Now. Sebastian made the mirrors because he had some talent, some quirk, that the Great Dark One lacked. Jeremy had seen that in Thaumia: Melodia's specialized healing talent, working on animals but not on humans; or Barach's ability to see the magic in a person, something that even Tremien could not do without his enchanted spectacles. Talent in magic, it seemed, chose definite pathways sometimes, like streams meandering to a sea they all reached eventually but by different routes.

Sebastian's powers must have run in a similar course. He could trap magic, put it into material things, mirrors especially, and hold it there. But alone, Jeremy was sure, Sebastian could never have created mirrors with so much power. Possibly he could have made them into speaking devices, communicators, but surely not into transportation devices, or devices to transfer magic from one spot to another. No, that had the stamp of the Great Dark One on it. Sebastian had forged the tools, but the ancient magician had used them.

Sebastian and mirrors. Sebastian was Jeremy's mirror-image, his dark twin. Jeremy Sebastian Moon Magister. Words chased themselves in Jeremy's thoughts. Then he laughed. He had it: he sensed the connection, and he thought he had a chance of breaking the mirrors and escaping the Dark One; a chance, should the opportunity present itself and should inspiration strike. A ghost of a chance, in fact.

"Dark One! I grow tired of waiting for you!" Jeremy called. After waiting perhaps half a minute, he yelled again: "Come and let's have that talk you promised. You could tell me much that I want to know!"

Silence and darkness. It takes a specially baited hook to catch a very old fish. Jeremy decided to give back what he himself had had to take earlier in the Hag's castle. "What? Afraid, you? The magician who juggles skulls like rubber balls? Who wallows in evil as a pig wallows in mud? You, the all powerful, the omnipotent, the conqueror of a continent? Where are you hiding, brave one?"

No answer. Jeremy got up and began to pace the platform, began, in fact, to strut. "I am here, Dark One! Where are you? Who are you? No answer? I'll tell my name, my whole, full, and secret name. Are you listening? I am Jeremy Sebastian Moon, Dark One! Do you know what my power is? Do you? I reach up into the sky and pull down the lightning to light my way. I speak in one corner of the world, and my voice is heard continents away. I ride horses that no one can see, that drink but never eat. My brothers have leaped off the face of the world and into the dark sky. They have walked on the moon, Dark One! And I do more: I speak with the dead. I hear their words and know their thoughts. My own words have lives of their own and will go on after me. I have left my world for many months now, and yet the force of my words has not failed. Can you say the same, O Dark One? And do you know the greatest wonder of all the wonders? Can you guess the secret within my secret?"

Jeremy felt something, a tension in the air. *So, you crafty old cat, some curiosity still lives in that shriveled brain of yours.* Still, no voice answered him. "I will give it to you as a present, O Great Liar. And you know I am not myself lying, don't you? You can sense that, I know. Yes, you realize that I speak only the truth, don't you? Are you ready for my secret, you great dark fool? Here it is:

"I did all these wonders *without magic!*"

At last an answer, booming from all around in a voice like an earthquake: "Impossible!"

Jeremy threw his head back and laughed. "Is it? Is it not true? Can you not tell?"

He thought this time there would be no response, so long did the silence drag on, but at last it came: "You speak the truth. But how? How can you do these things without magic?"

"Show yourself. And not in illusion but in person; ward yourself as well as you please, but I will not speak to the air any longer."

"Wait."

He came through the mirror and passed through its ward. Jeremy walked over to the ancient man, looked into bleary, red-veined eyes. "Welcome," he said.

The Great Dark One smiled. "You are impertinent! I welcome you, for this is all my land, my possession. I have been here all along, as you guessed. You are a canny one, aren't you? Our Sebastian fancied himself clever, oh yes he did, but you have him all the way across and six from the bottom, don't you, Jeremy Sebastian Moon?"

Jeremy shrugged. "I do have my moments," he said.

"Oh, modest, modest, we are. A silly virtue, boy, one you should learn to master. Modesty will be the ruin of you yet if you let it run untrammeled. And now you will tell me how you perform these wonders without magic, I have no doubt."

"Possibly. If you will answer me, question for question."

"Who are you to make bargains?"

"You know who I am. Oh, come on, G.D."

The Great Dark One blinked. "What did you call me?"

"Well, you won't tell me your name, and Great Dark One is so melodramatic. Stuffy, don't you think? You don't strike me at all as a stuffy person, you know. Will you tell the truth, just once? If I ask you an innocent question? Never mind, I'll ask it anyway: you enjoy this, don't you? You find me a puzzle, and trying to solve me stimulates you and makes you feel alive. Confess it."

The old man wrinkled his forehead, though he had no eyebrows left to raise. "You are a character," he said.

"By Gadfrey, sir, so I am," Jeremy returned. "Will

you meet my terms? Question for question, lie if you like, but give me answers at least?"

"I ask first."

"Done."

The old man's eyes lost whatever look of bantering they held. He leaned forward, his face earnest, almost pleading. "How do you speak to the dead?"

Jeremy said, "I read."

The Great Dark One sighed. "A trick."

"Not at all. Why do you think language was invented? It holds thoughts, puts them into words. Writing puts those words on the page, and reading liberates the thoughts again, butterflies coming to life right off the paper. Do you think a book is dead? It isn't. I can pick up a book written a hundred years ago, or a thousand, or five thousand, and I hear the voice of the dead speaking to me. I speak back. 'Why does your character do this?' I ask, and the dead writer says, 'Watch, pay attention, and I'll show you.' "

"Words, words," the Great Dark One scoffed. "In our world, and I'm sure in yours, the dead go elsewhere—or they simply cease. All I am and all I have I would give to pierce that last mystery, were it in my power."

Jeremy looked down at the man. "Now answer my question," he said. "Who are you and why do you want me?"

The old man sighed. "Let us sit," he murmured. "I tire of standing." They sank to the surface of the platform together, wary of each other. An evil Gandhi, Jeremy thought with surprise as the ancient mage settled cross-legged, his gown of thunderstorm-color settling around him. The withered mage shook his bald head. "You cheat. That is two questions. Never mind; I like a cheater. First, who am I? I am many people. I am, or will be, you."

"Explain."

"Oh, I shall. On this very spot, some two thousand and seventy-four years ago, a man was born. This little plaque that we sit on is my sentimental gesture to that historic occasion. His parents called him Jilhukrihain, "Lake Blue Sky" in their language, for his eyes were of that color. He grew to be a powerful magician, and he studied many deep and ancient spells. But increasingly as he grew older he feared death, and hated it, for it would put an end to his knowledge and to his learning. He bent all his skills and all his talents to learning how to cheat death. And when he was very old, he found a way. He devised a spell, this Jilhukrihain: a spell that would copy his memories, intact, and his will into another person. He tried the spell with a young student of his, a wonderfully talented young man named Yawivonne. Jilhukrihain lived a few months more and then he died, but in Yawivonne all his memories up to the time of the spell were saved, and his will was growing, like a fetus in its mother's belly. The time came when that spell conquered the student, and the student became Jilhukrihain.

"But not completely. This was a new person, a person with the memories of both. The old person, the 'real' one, was dead. Still, just as the former Jilhukrihain had, the Jilhukrihain that had come to be desired endless life, immortality, and the cycle was begun.

"There have been many hosts in the two thousand and more years. I have the memories in me of seventeen different men and women, and sixteen of us are dead. Still I recall the first memory of Jilhukrihain: I was sitting in the shade as my mother picked lentils, and a red bird cried out overhead in the tree and frightened me. That happened two thousand and seventy-one years ago, but I remember."

Jeremy nodded. "I think I see. You are an incarnation of the Great Dark One; your will is the will of the original Jilhukrihain, but your memories include the memories of all the people you have come to possess."

"Yes. I have not yet learned the secret of immortality. I, the man sitting before you, will die. But first I will plant a seed in you, and it will grow. It is an interesting sensation. Days pass, and you feel only a mild discomfort, a feeling that you are changing. Then one day your left hand will not respond to your mind's command. Then your right hand, perhaps, or maybe your legs. Soon you are just a dwindling spectator tucked in a corner of your own mind. Your consciousness fades like a candle flame guttering. A little puff of wind comes along one day, and then the flame goes out entirely; then you are nothing, a collection of memories, no more."

"And that has answered my second question," Jeremy said. "I am to be the next Great Dark One. Why me, if I may ask an extra question?"

"It could have been anyone. I have always tried to choose magicians, for when I take their bodies and minds, I gain their talents as well. Oh, I am powerful now, Jeremy Sebastian Moon, for I am the inheritor of all the special people whose bodies I have taken. Mostly magicians, as I have said; though on one occasion, when my enemies thought they had seen the end of me, I was growing in secret inside an illiterate, deaf-mute peasant girl. That was horror! I could force the mouth to speak but could not hear the words, and so could not be certain that the next incarnation would even happen. It did; I took the body of a young man, a mediocre talent, who had come to sleep with the girl one drunken evening. The memory of that woman so tortured me that I sought her out and with my own hands put her to death, while the part of me that was still in her struggled to croak out a spell of defense." The old man shook his head. "I wax garrulous in my old age. It has been long since I had someone to speak to. To answer your question more directly: your talent intrigues me. You pull *mana* from another reality, and with it, I might even defeat death."

"But you haven't yet."

The eyes hardened. "No, and that is bitterness and gall to me. I am tired of these long lives with death waiting at the end. But if I cannot live forever, I will live beyond the span of Thaumia! I will live to see the whole world empty and sterile, as quiet as Relas, and as barren. Then, when I alone am left alive, when death itself is all but dead, then I will laugh at fate and magic and the tired, sick joke of life, and I will truly die. I will die in the knowledge that I have outlived all, and that will be my triumph."

Jeremy leaned back, his hands thrust out behind him to support his weight. "I do not think you are such a liar."

"You will find out."

"But you will die." Jeremy smiled. "You think no one understands you, but you're wrong. Someone told me about you: he said you desire to swallow all life, to eat it, to make it part of you, and then when you've made Thaumia a desert you will stand in it at night, look up, and curse the stars because you cannot have them too."

"Well, well." The little man smiled again, too. Just two friendly magicians sitting on a giant stone cube in the middle of nowhere passing the time of day. "Perhaps your friend is right. We all have our failings."

Jeremy squinted. "Your magic field is weak, old man."

"I have used much strength in the war. Yes, it's true, I am not what I was three hundred years ago. Why, I could scarcely lift this cube that we're on with one hand. I am a shell, a pitiful wreck."

"Then how do you plan to pursue your war against the magi of Cronbrach? Surely your cause is lost with the loss of the Hag."

"Not at all. You should really see this; it's most interesting. Here, watch. Will you help me up?"

Jeremy got up and held a hand out. "Here you go."

The Great Dark One rolled his eyes. "You are a fool, aren't you? I've just told you I could move this cube, and you believe that I'm weak enough to need your help? Don't you know I could begin to change you if I touch you?"

"You wouldn't. I'm your prisoner. I think I know you well enough to see that you'll be very sure to tell me when you begin the spell."

"You are right. I think I will enjoy being you." The Great Dark One put a papery, dry hand in Jeremy's, and Jeremy pulled him to his feet. "You are a young man. With the spells I know, you might live four, five centuries. Tell me: do you fear death?"

"I don't welcome death. I don't think man was meant to die calmly, or in resignation. But fear it? No, not in an abstract way. I will not die easily, when the time comes, if I can help it. But I will not find terror, I think, and for whatever comes afterward—well, I can hope."

The Great Dark One shook his head. "You are too young."

"Maybe. But just before my grandfather died, he told me he was sorry for me. I think he was sorry because he knew how I felt about his leaving me. I think he was sorry for me because he was getting to die and I was not. Death may be something wholly different from what you think it is."

"You are completely crazy. It is refreshing to talk with you."

"Thank you. And you're even loonier than the Hag was, you decrepit old son of a bitch, but at least you're civil when you want to be. Now, I think you were going to show me something."

"Yes. How I will wage the war against the magi of Cronbrach—or if I die first, how you will do it. Observe the mirror."

The Great Dark One positioned himself before the oval of glass and spoke a word. The cube shivered beneath Jeremy's feet, as if an earth tremor had disturbed it. The mirror flared briefly, light swirling within it. Then it cleared. Jeremy looked into his own bedroom back on Earth, though it was dark and indistinct. From the mirror poured a stream of light, converging as if focused on the old magician's chest. He spread his arms, the roomy sleeves of his gown falling down to his elbows, and absorbed the power.

"Magic?" Jeremy guessed.

"Yes. Sebastian knew nothing of this. It was a great chance for me to take as well, for I had no way of knowing whether it would succeed or not, but only Sebastian could have done it. I saw to it that he was exiled to the Between, you know. Yes, I betrayed him to the stupid magi, and I put it into their heads to thrust him into the dream-world, something they could do but I could not. You see, I hoped he would create a mirror there, and that through it I could drink in some of the raw creative power of dreams. I did, for a little while. Then he went on to another reality, and I found that it too had its powers. I haven't really tapped it yet. That pleasure will wait for you, my sweet morsel! But you, or rather the part of me that will become you, will soak, and soak, and drain, and grow more powerful until nothing on Thaumia can stop me."

Jeremy put his hand in his pocket. Something small, sharp, and cold was there. He pulled it out. The Earth magic shed light across the top of the great stone cube, a warm golden light. In it Jeremy turned over his find.

It was only a tooth.

Jeremy came close beside the Great Dark One. He held the tooth up in the light streaming from the mirror. "Do you know what this is?" he asked. His hand felt warm, and the warmth flowed up his arm and right to his heart.

"I have no idea."

"It's a souvenir of the creature your Hag killed. Nul, my friend. Do you know what it signifies?"

"You exasperate me with questions. What do you think this fragment signifies?"

"Your failure, Great Dark One. You old fool! *I AM THE MIRRORS!*"

He felt the ancient mage's cold anger and fear flashing out at him, but Jeremy was light, flowing back into the mirror, following the path that the beam on his hand had forged. Then he was *in* the mirror looking out, seeing the Great Dark One pronouncing some horrible spell. No, Jeremy thought. Not any more, you evil bastard. I can't kill you, but I can ruin you. I am on Earth.

He was on Earth.

Jeremy hung in an indeterminate space behind the mirror that Sebastian had placed in his apartment. The mirror drank magic, though Sebastian did not know that, and magic poured all around Jeremy in a flood, a flow of unimaginable force. He absorbed it, swelled almost from the glut of it. He willed to see into the room, and instantly began to perceive outlines, forms, shapes.

Two figures in the bed, one dark-haired, one blonde, sleeping like nested spoons beneath a pale blue sheet. A stir in the faint light from the window, a click, and the bedside light came on. Sebastian Magister sat up against the pillows, all tousled hair and gasping mouth, his chest bare, his eyes wide. Jeremy could not hear him, but he saw the word form on the beardless lips: "You!"

Cassie, nude, sat up beside him, her eyelids thick with sleep. She asked Sebastian a question, touched his face. Sebastian spoke to her, smiled, but his eyes darted sideways, drawn by the bearded apparition in the mirror. Cassie followed his glance, stared for a puzzled moment directly into Jeremy's eyes, and screamed.

"Sebastian," Jeremy howled. "Sebastian, you bastard!"

He could climb out now and throttle the magician who started all this, and he ached to feel Sebastian's throat constricting under his grip—but not now, not when he had to do what he had come for. "It's all a dream, Cassie," he said, willing her to believe it. Out in the bedroom she had buried her face against Sebastian's chest, and he had spread the sheet over her, hiding her face from Jeremy. He could still see her hair, though, and he concentrated on it: "You've had a nightmare, Cassie,

and now you're going to sleep again. It's all a dream."
He pushed his fingers through the glass, felt them pierce
the surface, curl around in the sweet air of Earth, grasp
the outer plane of the glass itself in their grip. Nothing
could make him let go, not Sebastian's frantic gibbering,
not the memory of Cassie's horrified eyes. Not even the
promise of home would release that grip, not the keen
desire he felt to come through and end the whole impossible fantasy by waking up from the nightmare that was
no nightmare. Not death itself, he knew with certain and
grim knowledge.

"Now," he yelled. Already at his back he felt the Dark
One's spells coming after him, strong and fuming with
anger, with hatred, and, yes, with fear, trying to dislodge
him or to change him. "Now I'm coming through. Hear
me! Mirrors, all mirrors—*break!*"

He hurtled backward as if he had been struck by a
truck, but his fingers had locked onto the glass, had
become a part of the glass, and the glass shattered,
following him. He saw it dancing through space just in
front of him, sharp and beautiful and deadly, glittering
and flashing in the last beams of magic ever to reach
Thaumia from Earth. His back hit the Great Dark One's
mirror, but he had given the command, and that too
broke. The oval frame hung empty. A snowstorm of
broken glass whirled between Jeremy and the frame, but
through it he had glimpses of the wizard who wished to
live forever stretching out his clawed hands in impotent
fury. Then the Great Dark One was gone, left behind.
The Hag's next and last, and then release.

I will not die easily.

Dark One, can you hear me? I'm laughing.

The mirror—crash!—and then the wall, knocking the
wind from him, and a deadly shower of all those daggers
striking him, raining all about him. He felt the cuts as
cold spots, striking him like the first fat drops of a spring
rain, and he saw the blood not red but black. But deep in
his mind he was warm, ready for sleep. There, he thought.
That's done. At last that's done and now I can rest.

Except for the woman. She hauled him most damnably
over rough stone. She yelled in his face and slapped him.
"Go on," he said. Get out of here, he thought. Leave.
Go without me. I don't want to come out of this warm
place into the cold anymore, not ever again. "Go."

Kelada would not go on without him. She screamed something in his ear. "What?" He had to listen. What a bother.

"The whole castle is falling into the mere! Help me! Walk, can't you?"

"No," he said. "I'm dying."

"Then I'll drag you every step of the way!"

"Kelada," he said. "I am sorry for you."

Tumult and confusion. Darkness all around him, and the sounds of toppling stones. The unnatural lake of the Hag's making was claiming its own. He looked to his left, and Nul lay there, his orange eyes pale, his mouth open, his gums showing almost no color. "Nul," Jeremy said. "I'm glad you're going with me. Listen, do you know what the magic was? It was friendship. I thought of you, and the ward wasn't there anymore. Your damned old tooth I knocked out. The ward kept out anger and attack, but it couldn't keep out friendship. The Great Dark One doesn't know the meaning of the word. Of course he can't defend against it. Am I talking? Doesn't matter. You look afraid, Nul. Don't be. It isn't so hard to die."

There was something he wanted to do. He opened his eyes again. A moment had gone past, or an hour. The sun was in his face. Hot and bright, like the magic stolen from Earth. The old fool. That magic was in him and of him, and he shared its essence. He *became* that magic for just an instant, for just long enough to flash into the mirrors and beyond all reach. But there was still magic in him, some work of magic left to do. Kelada stooped over him. "I'm trying to bandage you," she said. "Hold still."

Jeremy moved his left hand, held it close before his eyes. An inch-long triangle of glass had embedded itself in the base of his thumb. He grasped it with his right thumb and forefinger, and pulled it out. Tip downward, it dripped blood. "For the woman who wants to be beautiful," Jeremy whispered.

Kelada was weeping. "Stop."

"Can't stop, it's a spell. In English. Wish I could have taught you English, Kelada. Here goes. The one and only elixir of loveliness. Only one drop will make you just as beautiful as you ever wanted to be."

"Oh, God, stop!"

"Guaranteed for a lifetime. And in a bottle . . . to match . . . your true beauty."

He held no longer a shard of glass but a tiny bottle, a clear, flashing crystal shaped exactly like a teardrop. Deep in its heart was one precious golden drop of liquid. "Take," he said. "Drink it."

"Jeremy! Damn you, don't die!"

"Take."

She took the bottle and clenched it against her. Her face was twisted into a mask of despair, and tears spilled from her eyes, dripped from her ridiculous elfin chin. He tried to give her a reassuring smile, but he was too tired. "Sorry," he wanted to whisper, but it came out "Soft," and he let it go. Now, he thought. Now I can die.

He closed his eyes and all was peace.

CHAPTER 15

NUL WAS WITH him. "Did you suffer much?" Jeremy asked, surprised that his voice worked even now.

"Nah, nah, not so bad. You want something to eat?"

"I still hurt. That can't be right. What did you say? Eat? But—"

"What?"

"The dead don't eat."

Nul looked puzzled. "What dead have to do with it? Where you think you are?"

"Heaven? Or—"

The pika gave his urfing laugh. "Nah, nah, you not dead. You resting in own bed. In Tremien's palace on Whitehorn. Open eyes again and look."

Jeremy did. He was in the old tower room again, on a deep, soft bed, a sheet drawn almost up to his chin. His arms lay on top of the covers, and they had been wrapped with many bandages. He tried to move his right arm, and, to his surprise, it moved. "How long?" he asked.

"You really awake now? Not talk-talk in sleep, in strange language anymore?"

"I'm awake. How long has it been?"

"Since Hag's house fall into water? Three weeks, a little more, few days more."

Jeremy brushed back his hair. It felt oily and dirty beneath his palm, and he realized the room was warm enough to make him sweat a little. "I don't remember anything. I thought you—" Jeremy turned his head to look at Nul. The little pika sat in a chair stuffed with cushions, and on a low stool before him his legs, both splinted and wrapped tightly in bandages, were carefully propped. The left arm too was splinted and in a sling. Nul's face had shrunk in on the bones a little, and the orange eyes will still a little paler than they should have been, but his grin was as roguish as ever, and the gap in it was now completely closed. Jeremy smiled back at him. "How are you?"

"Healing. Melodia pull me back from doors of death. Strange, you know? At first I not want to come."

"I know," Jeremy said.

"She say I always walk with little limp. But otherwise, good as ever, same old Nul. Pika-man hard, like bones of mountains. Good thing for me. How you feel?"

"Sore. What happened to me?"

"Lots of little glass-glass. Your mail shirt protect you mostly, but many in arms, some in face. Miss eyes, though, and that good. And you hit wall hard. Kelada bring you out of castle, you know?"

Jeremy frowned. "I think I remember that."

"Yes, whole castle begin to fall into mere, one stone, two, then all stones. We all safe on hill outside curtain wall, and Kelada go back in. She pull you out window somehow, into garden of castle. Then all stones begin sinking into swamp, she left finally on island. She pick you up. Yes! The little woman pick up you, walk across swamp on top of sinking stones. Then try to bandage while Melodia called Tremien. Tremien put travel spell on all, we come here, healers work with you. Close, they said. Not loss of blood so much as—what word for great strain, tiredness?"

"Shock?"

"Ya, ya, shock. But you getting better now."

"The others?"

"All well. Melodia, Gareth, Barach, Kelada, all well. They see you pretty soon."

"Is this the hospital wing?" Jeremy asked.

"Hospital? Nah, nah. But I get tired alone in 'nother room, nothing to do but sit. Think if I come and wait till you wake up, you maybe tell more stories."

"I will," Jeremy smiled. "I promised."

Nul grinned at him, then grew more sober. "I sit and think much these last days. Everyone treat me good, very kind, but in sickness I still feel all alone. Now I want ask your opinion. I think, Nul, it time to seek family. Must be some trace of pika-people left. Now Hag gone, Wolmas Mountains safe again, and caverns under them. I think maybe I go try to find if any pikas left alive, you know? You think that a good thought?"

"I think it's a wonderful thought," Jeremy said.

"Not great quest, but important to me." Nul looked away. "Would like to have magician along, maybe, for company. Maybe could help out little bit."

"Nul, I would be honored."

"Not expect much. Dirty old caverns."

"Nul."

"What?"

"I think I am hungry."

Two mornings later, Gareth and four soldiers came to carry Nul and help Jeremy downstairs. Jeremy was alarmingly weak—he had to stop and rest every few feet, and Gareth practically bore his whole weight down the stairs—but he walked into Tremien's study under his own power. Still, he was grateful that Tremien had set a large chair directly across the desk from his own, and he sat down with a sigh. He looked from face to face: Melodia, unusually solemn; Gareth, honesty and concern shining in his countenance; Barach, strangely quiet; Nul, his white legs thrust stiffly out ahead of him; and old Tremien, seeming more withered and ancient than ever, but his eyes still bright. "Where's Kelada?" Jeremy asked.

"She did not know if you wanted her to be here," Tremien said. "I will send for her."

One of the soldiers at the door turned and went on the errand. Barach winked at Jeremy. "You can see," Jeremy said in surprise.

"Oh, yes, my eyesight returned." What was there in the voice? It was something new, a serenity that Jeremy had never heard there before. "It was a spell of the Hag's, you see, or tied up in the one that she hurled. When she perished, my vision came back."

"Your magic?"

The warm brown eyes smiled. "No. I am no longer a magician, or will ever be again."

"But he is still a teacher," Tremien said. "If the old fool would admit it."

"Who would wish to be taught by a mage who can no longer do the least magic?"

"I would, Master," Jeremy said. Both Barach and Tremien looked hard at him. "The mirrors are broken," Jeremy went on. "I have no path now to lead me home. I have to stay here in Thaumia. I don't know what will happen—my original *mana* came from Earth, and was tied somehow to the mirrors—but I've been exploring my feelings for the last two days. I still have magic in me, and if I'm not mistaken, it's growing."

"You had better look," Barach told Tremien.

The old mage fumbled for his spectacles, hooked them around his ears, and studied Jeremy through their lenses. "Bless my soul. It seems you are right, Jeremy. Your emanations are growing stronger—and stranger. There is still much there of Earth, and much of Thaumia, but something yet different from either, and very beautiful. I don't know what you'll make of these powers, but powers you possess, beyond any doubt."

"Then I will need a teacher."

Barach looked at him for a long moment. He is so fragile, Jeremy thought, yet so tough too; if he stood before a candle in a dark room, the light would shine through him. "Jeremy, if you stay with us, I will certainly teach you what I can," he said at last.

Jeremy frowned. "If?"

"Hush," Tremien said. "Enough of that for the moment. Kelada, Jeremy has asked for you."

Jeremy turned in his seat. For an instant he was breathless: Kelada stood just inside the door, her hair longer than he remembered it and more golden, her eyes downcast. She wore a dress of palest blue that left her arms bare, and on her feet were blue slippers. When she looked at him, her eyes held more beauty than anything he had ever seen. It wrenched his heart to look at her. She came forward slowly and shyly.

"Well," Tremien said, "here we all are at last! Each of you has asked me at one time or another various things, and it is better to answer with you all together, so I will not have to repeat myself. First, I hope, in your hearts is concern for me. I am fine. Like Jeremy and Nul, I was wounded—more through loss of magic than anything, though, and in spirit only, not in body—but I am fast mending. In fact, I believe that with the turning of a year I shall be stronger than I have been for a long time, for the Hag is no longer here to darken my spirit and trouble my mind. For that, Jeremy, all of us in Cronbrach must thank you.

"Second: the Great Dark One lives still, but the council have felt his power diminish greatly. In fact, if I could be permitted a small jest, I privately think we should change his title to the Lesser Dark One immediately. He lost more than we had dreamed possible when the mirrors were shattered, and it will be many years before he could regain enough strength to be a threat to anyone outside of Relas. But the council are debating measures to be taken now, and it may be that while he is trying to recover from the blow Jeremy gave him we will wish to move to erase his evil for once and all. Again, Jeremy deserves all our thanks.

"Third: the Hag is dead, and her spells are utterly broken. Already my messengers tell me the Haggenkom is cleansing itself: the river running sweeter, the meres beginning to clear, even a little greenery peeping through the soil here and there. It will be weary long years before the valley is whole, but a time is coming when humans will once again live there and call it home. We will have a problem to deal with, however: the vilorgs."

"No problem," Nul growled. "Kill them."

Tremien shook his head. "No. The Hag used them for evil, but the vilorgs are not evil in themselves. They fled the collapse of the castle, but now they are drifting back to its site. Creatures of habit, they try to resume such duties as they knew, but they are not bright enough to live on their own. And they are harmless now, pathetically grateful for food and shelter, I hear. They cannot revert to being mere animals, for the Hag made them more than that, yet they will never be human, or as intelligent as the pikas, say. But they did not make themselves, and I will not have them killed for something that is no fault of their own."

"Mage Tremien," Melodia said, her voice tentative.

"Yes, Melodia?"

"Gareth and I have spoken together of the valley. We would go there, if you will allow us, to bring healing and protection. Such aid as my magic will give the vilorgs shall be given to them, and such comfort as my healing powers can bring to the valley shall be bestowed there, with your permission and the council's."

Tremien regarded her intently. "I have talked of this with Gareth. Is it truly the decision of your heart?"

Melodia would not look at Jeremy. "Yes, Mage."

"So be it, then. Gareth, I name you and Melodia Protectors of the Valley—and let its name be no more the Haggenkom, the Witch's Vale, but rather its name of old, the Arendolas, the Place of Many Lakes." Jeremy saw Gareth take Melodia's hand, and his heart twinged with jealousy. "Now," Tremien resumed, "what have I left unanswered?"

"What happened to Smokharin?" Jeremy asked. "I left him in the throne room, in the flame of a torch."

"When the castle fell," Gareth said, "a fire broke out in the wrack amid a pile of tapestries, splintered timbers, and even of vilorg bodies. Smokharin manifested in that, and Melodia was able to recall him to his tinderbox. He is safe."

"We fared better than I could have expected," Tremien said. "Yet we have many dead to mourn. Five of your party, Jeremy, and nearly a hundred who fell in the defense of Whitehorn. It is meet that we celebrate, yet we must not forget them, either. Now. It is time for you to heal, to gain your strength back, and to look ahead: for the council are discussing your great gift to us and your great accomplishment, and we may have something to surprise you with before the summer reaches its height. In the meantime, Jeremy Sebastian Moon, I name you mage. You are truly one of our brotherhood now, and one day before long we will ask you to sit with us at council. But for now, rest, grow strong, and heal the hurts of your heart as well as those of your flesh."

Jeremy bowed his head. "Thank you, Mage Tremien."

"No, Mage Jeremy. Thank *you*. Thank you for saving our lives and our world."

Almost another week passed before Jeremy was able to speak to Melodia. The snows of Whitehorn Peak persisted even into the summer, though they diminished and were too much melted to walk on, but within the courtyards the ground was free of snow, and in one pleasant spot the cooks grew herbs, vegetables, and a few kinds of flowers. Jeremy, walking for the sake of exercise, had grown tired in the garden and had settled on the low wall of a stone pool full of darting red and blue fish. Melodia came to him slowly, wearing a gown with tiny bells on it. "Gareth and I leave tomorrow," she said. "I wanted to say good-bye."

Jeremy moved over, and Melodia sat beside him. "Are you certain that you want to go?" he asked.

"No. How can I be? But Gareth loves me, he says, and I care for him a great deal. Do you remember a time in the Hag's castle when you touched us all with your mind? Gareth felt you, knew you were there, but I was *in* you for just a moment, and I knew all your heart, all your secrets. You love me, I know, but I also know now that your love is different from mine. Believe me, this is better for us both."

"You can have anything in my gift that you would name," Jeremy said.

"I know that. But there is something else. Something hard for me to say."

"What is it?"

"I give life, I do not take it, ever. And you have killed."

"But so has Gareth!"

"I know. But I was not *part* of him, as, for just a moment, I was of you; I did not feel his joy in killing, or his wrath, or his sorrow. And I did not gain his memories of the ones he had slain. I am very sorry, Jeremy, for in some sense I love you still, but never again could I look at you in the same way, or feel the same feelings as once I did."

"Will you kiss me?"

"In farewell."

Her lips were soft, her breath warm on his face. Then she rose and walked away without a look back. Jeremy lingered in the garden until the sun had dropped below the western walls, and then he too got up and slowly walked back to his room.

Nul remained in Jeremy's room, sleeping propped in the chair, chatting with him during the long days of healing. And he had stories from Jeremy, yes, as many as Jeremy could recall. Nul's eyes shone at the witches in *Macbeth*, and he rolled their chant over and over his tongue for many days after hearing the tale: "Double, double, toil and trouble . . ."

He sympathized with Othello, but stubbornly maintained that the whole tragedy was a result of human stupidity. "Pika-mans not have just one wife. Pika-Othello, he say, 'You want Desdemona? You take, I have plenty more.' Why human-mans so selfish about wives?"

But most of all, Nul enjoyed Jeremy's fractured recollections of *Paradise Lost*. He seemed to regard Satan as one of the incarnations of the Great Dark One, and in the archangels he clearly saw the magi of Cronbrach. He sighed at the ending, but cherished the hope of good coming from evil. "Always the way," he assured Jeremy. "Bad happen, think all over. But look close, close, see some little seed of good left. Evil never finish ahead, never; it seem that way, but little good still growing, put little root under rock of evil, one day split rock apart. Always the way."

"Nul," Jeremy said seriously, "I wish I had your conviction."

A day came heavy with thunder and thick with rain that lashed the valley below, sent gray fingers to break and dwindle the snows of the peaks. Jeremy, sitting in a chair and staring out a window, heard someone come in. It was Barach. "Are you better?" the old man asked.

"I don't know. I have times when I feel as if I am, and then times when I wish I had died in the Hag's castle."

"It's all in the way you look at things, you know," Barach said.

Jeremy smiled. "Have you a story about that, teacher?"

Barach pulled up another chair and sat with him. "Let me see. Not a story exactly, but I do know a riddle that touches the matter. It is called the riddle of the inns. Shall I tell it?"

"I would like to hear you talk again," Jeremy said.

Barach laced his fingers across his stomach and began: "Once there was a small inn nestled between two tall trees not far from a bridge that spanned a broad river. One summer evening, two travelers stopped there, one going south, one north.

"The traveler heading north was returning from a city where he had sold some goods in the marketplace. They had brought him less than he thought they should, and he looked forward to a bad-tempered greeting from his shrew of a wife when he returned. But the traveler going south was a young man who had long been in love with a young woman of the city, and only yesterday he had received a letter from her father consenting to their marriage.

"The two travelers arrived at the same moment, put their horses in adjoining stalls, and went together into the inn. They sat at the same board, ate the same food, and at the coming of night went into rooms alike as two scales on a fish.

"They awoke at the same hour next morning, ate breakfast at the same table, and prepared to go their different ways. The northbound traveler paid his score with ill grace. 'The stable boy nearly killed my horse, not rubbing him down before he put him in a stall. The slop on your tables would not be fit provender for my pigs. Your rooms are dear and filthy, and I have never slept in a harder or more verminous bed. Never shall I lay my head under your roof again!' He counted the coppers out grudgingly to settle his bill and he left, throwing a curse back over his shoulder.

"But the southbound traveler paid what he owed with a smile and a good word for everyone. 'You have cared for my horse as if she were a prince's steed!' he cried to the ostler, and then gave the man a silver coin above what he owed him for taking care of the mare. The traveler then burst into the kitchen, smacked two resounding kisses on the fat cheeks of the cook, and declared, 'You are a treasure! You make bacon and potatoes a feast for the gods!' And to her he gave another silver piece. And last, he called the innkeeper the best of hosts, extolled the cleanliness and comfort of his rooms, and gave the man two silver pieces to make sure that the man would hold vacant a suite of rooms for the traveler's honeymoon in two weeks' time. Then, riding away from the inn, the southbound traveler prayed blessings on the inn and its owner.

"Now, apprentice, here is the riddle: there were two travelers. Where there not also two inns?"

Jeremy looked from the rain to the bearded old man. "Welcome back, teacher," he said softly.

On still another day, one of those bright days of summer when the sun climbs high and the clouds are small, white, and puffy, Kelada and Jeremy took a meal down into the valley and found a pleasant place beside the river for a picnic. The water rushed white over stones, and now and again a fish leaped. The only other sound was a drowsy, distant chopping as foresters trimmed away last year's dead trees and prepared firewood for the coming winter. After they had eaten, Kelada and Jeremy waded in the cold water, felt it clutching and tugging at their bare legs; and then they sat beneath a tree, close together.

"You have ruined me," Kelada said. "I will never be a thief again."

"Liar," Jeremy said. "You will steal men's hearts."

"There is only one that I care to have."

"It is yours already."

She traced his scars, now unbandaged and healing. "Your poor face. These will go without a trace, I think, but this one here on your right cheek will leave a mark. And your beard just here, below it, is growing a white streak."

"I could spell it brown again."

"No. I like it." She kissed his cheek.

He pulled her to him and gave her a longer kiss. Her arms went around him. Next to them the water sang, and far away the chop-chop-chop of the woodsmen went on uninterrupted. There came a time when he looked at her body and marveled. "I'm a better magician than I know," he said.

She crossed her arms. "Don't stare at me that way."

"Once you didn't mind."

"Well—now I do."

"Then come closer, so that I can see only your eyes."

Later that afternoon, Barach met them as they came back through the gates, after Jeremy had settled a squabble between the stone guardians Fred and Busby. Fred maintained that the Hag's castle had been built from marble quarried in the southern part of the Wolmas Mountains, while Busby held that the material was northern granite; when Jeremy and Kelada described the stones, Busby grinned fiercely, even for a gargoyle, and Fred lapsed into stony silence. Barach stood just within the gates, his hands behind him. "Well," he said, smiling. "And did you young people have a good day?"

Kelada looked down and blushed. Jeremy said, "A fine day, Master. A perfect day."

The council came when apples were still green on the trees but beginning to show a hint of red about them, when the bees were still fat and lazy, droning from flower to flower as if the burden of pollen they bore were almost too much for them on such a warm and pleasant morning. For days they closeted themselves alone, and at great length they sent for Jeremy.

The atmosphere in the Great Hall was decidedly warmer than it had been on Jeremy's first visit. Jondan, the youngest of the magi, rose and held a chair for Jeremy this time, and as he sat he felt all eyes warm upon him. Barach, across the table, beamed and winked. "They come late, young man," motherly Mumana said, "but all of us wish to add our thanks to those of Tremien. You did not know it, but the Dark One had other curses, and lesser ones, at work in our lands as well as here, and when the Hag failed, so did the Dark One's spells."

Altazar of the high-pitched, querulous voice smiled at him. "You honor our council by being one of us. And if you decide to stay, from henceforth your seat will be among ours at every consultation."

"I have little choice." Jeremy smiled.

"Not so." Imperious Wyonne looked to Tremien. "Tell Jeremy of our decision."

Tremien clasped his brown hands before him. "Jeremy, some months ago I devised a spell that communicated with your world. Not all its virtue is gone, and I could reopen the pathway. In view of your services to Thaumia, the members of our council have agreed to use their powers to hold the passage open and to send you home. But you must send Sebastian back to us in exchange."

"Why? What will you do to him?"

"It is not vengeance, Jeremy," Barach said. He held his hands out, palms up, as an illustration. "It is a question of balance. You and Sebastian are mirror-images. It is right that one of you be in your world, one here in Thaumia. What would happen if the balance were broken, we do not know, but we cannot chance upsetting the natural laws of either universe."

Jeremy blinked. "But I had just resigned myself to living here for the rest of my life. I—could I have some time to decide?"

"Unfortunately, you cannot," Altazar said. "I have made some study of what we know of your world, and of Sebastian's spells. He chose a time of exaltation to enter your universe, our day of midwinter. I believe it is the twenty-first day of one of your months."

"Yes. December 21."

"And now we approach the day of High Summer. In the scraps of lore that Sebastian left behind him, he has identified June 23 as the equivalent day in your part of the Earth. That day is tomorrow. It is another time of exaltation, and if we do not make the exchange then, we will never be able to do it. Tremien cannot hold the virtue of his spell for much longer, and after that has gone, we lose all hope of sending you home."

"You must decide," Barach said gently. "The magi must begin preparations at once."

For long moments Jeremy sat in silence. At last he looked up. "Send me back home," he said. "The Earth is my world, not Sebastian's. I should go where I belong."

A sigh went up around the table, of mingled relief and regret.

"I hate to break a promise," Jeremy told Nul.

The pika, his legs still heavily splinted but now able to hobble about with the aid of two short crutches, shook his head. "Nah, nah. Of all here, I know how you feel. I lost my world, too. Well, go with my friendship. Think of Nul now and again."

"I will. And I hope you find your family."

Nul sniffled. "Pika-man cannot cry," he said. "No water in eyes for it. But my heart cry."

"I know," Jeremy said. "Mine too."

To Barach, Jeremy said, "Find yourself a student, teacher. Find yourself a young man with power that he cannot control or understand. And tell him every one of your stories, even if he doesn't get the point of any of them."

"I will never have a student like you, Jeremy. But I will do what I can."

"And will you say my farewells to Gareth and Melodia? Tell them I wish for them every happiness."

"They know already. But I will tell them."

Jeremy embraced the old man. "Grandfather," he whispered, too softly for Barach even to hear.

"How can I leave you?" Jeremy asked Kelada in the depths of the night.

She kissed him. "You will do what is right. I know you now." The bed creaked, and she was gone. In a moment she had returned. "Here. Take this with you, if you can." She put something small into his hand.

"What is this?"

"It is the potion you made for me. I never took it."

"You never—but you—"

"The potion did not transform me. You did. Your love did. Before, I never loved myself, but now I do, because you do. Not all magic is to be found in potions and spells." She sobbed. "Damn. I never thought I'd have to cry about you again."

He held her until the sun turned the sky outside the arched windows rosy with dawn.

The Great Hall had been cleared of all but the magi of Cronbrach. Again a five-pointed star had appeared in the center of the room, on the stone floor, and a mage stood on each point of the star: Altazar, Wyonne, Mumana, Jondan, and Tremien. From the corner Barach, bereft of his magic, watched quietly. Jeremy, as he had been bidden to do, dropped his robe and walked naked to the center of the star.

The magi began to sing then, a song wordless, or else in a language older than song. Jeremy clutched in his right hand the tiny teardrop vial that Kelada had returned to him: otherwise he had nothing to take back with him.

The room faded from his eyes, and he had the impression of rushing through untold distances of space, of cold and heat, light and dark, and of galaxies dancing to the silent music of time. Then he was behind a mirror once more, looking out, but this time the mirror was the one behind the sink in his own bathroom back in Atlanta. He leaned forward, felt the glass become soft, and slipped through.

Once in his apartment, Jeremy unclenched his hand. The vial and the potion were no longer there. He turned: his naked reflection faced him, bearded, hair long and unkempt, eyes somehow older than they should be.

"Sebastian," he said under his breath, "I'm coming for you."

But Sebastian wasn't at home. Jeremy padded naked through the whole apartment, and on the dinette table he found a disarranged newspaper, the remnants of eggs and toast, and thirty-five cents. The paper was the Atlanta

Constitution for Tuesday, June 23. The clock on the kitchen wall said it was 10:15 A.M. Sebastian was at work already.

Tremien had warned Jeremy that he had only about four hona—that would be roughly four and three-quarters hours here—to send Sebastian back and be sure of his arrival. Jeremy went back into the bedroom and opened a bureau drawer. He expected underwear. What he found were socks. He grabbed a pair, tossed them onto the bed (neatly made, a habit he had never formed), and opened the next drawer. There, beneath a fresh layer of red, blue, and even wilder-colored nylon bikini briefs, Jeremy discovered some plain white J.C. Penney undershorts, size 34. He pulled them on. From the closet he took a familiar old pair of lightweight gray slacks, a blue shirt, and a new navy blazer. The shoes were mostly new, but in the back of the closet he found a battered pair of L. L. Bean boat shoes, old companions, and he slipped them on.

Sebastian didn't seem to have disturbed his junk drawer. He found his old wallet there, empty except for oddments, but in the back of the drawer was an envelope from the bank, and in the envelope was his spare magic card. He stuck it into the wallet and went downstairs.

The branch bank was nearly six blocks away, and overhead the sky was dark with clouds grumbling thunder at him, but he made it into the computer kiosk before anything hit. The automatic teller accepted his card. As a precaution, he first asked for his checking balance. The computer pondered for a minute, then told him he had $8,291.43 in checking and wished him a nice day. Jeremy clenched his jaw. He had never had that much in checking. But he withdrew $200.00, the maximum limit. It came hissing out at him as ten twenty-dollar bills, crisp and so new that he half expected Andrew Jackson to have dark hair.

Jeremy telephoned for a cab from the bank, using the change he had found on the breakfast table. It came for him only twenty minutes later, an ancient vehicle smelling of stale sweat, decomposing foam rubber, and rusting seat springs. The driver warned it would be a fifteen-dollar fare, complained about having to take him north of the perimeter, complained about the weather, complained about the city. Jeremy didn't mind. The cab rattled so much that he could hardly hear the man's voice.

Outside of Taplan and Taplan Jeremy climbed out of the taxi. He opened his wallet and gave the driver two twenties. The man scowled at them. "Hey, is these things real?"

"You're welcome," Jeremy said, turning on his heel.

Charlie, sitting his tour of duty out behind the front desk, looked up and nodded as Jeremy turned the visitor's sheet toward him. Charlie was working on the Jumble word puzzle on that morning's comics page. With a pencil he was pushing the letters G-I-C-M-A this way and that. Jeremy hesitated, signed the register "Sebastian Moon," gave his own office as his destination, and turned the sheet back around. "It's 'magic,' Charlie," he said.

"Huh," Charlie said. "So it is." He looked at the register. "Mr. Moon? You a relation, huh?"

"A cousin," Jeremy said.

"Down for the weekend, I guess. Go right on up. Elevators over there."

Jeremy wondered why he was down for the weekend. The elevator stopped on the fourth floor, and he made his way to his own cubicle. Glenda was away from her desk, which suited Jeremy fine. He walked in and said, "Hello."

And a bespectacled young man looked up with an absent expression. "Can I help you?"

"Uh—I'm looking for Jeremy Moon. I thought he worked here."

"He does. Mr. Moon's office is on the other side. Number 412."

"Thanks."

Number 412 was the office of the department head. According to a discreet name plate on the door, it was also the office of Jeremy Moon. Dixie, the chief's private secretary, smiled as he came in. "Yes, sir?"

Damn the beard, Jeremy thought. It doesn't change me *that* much. But of course the people at Taplan and Taplan *knew* what Jeremy looked like. "I'm here to see Mr. Moon," Jeremy told her.

"Do you have an appointment, Mr.—?"

"He'll want to see me." Dixie smiled her barricade smile at him, and he added, "I'm family."

At that moment Sebastian opened the door, looking

down at a sheaf of papers. "These will do fine, Dix. Copy them and—" He looked up.

Jeremy smiled. "Hi, cousin," he said. "Didn't expect to see ol' Sebastian around today, did you?"

Sebastian blinked once. "Ah—no. No. Here, Dix. Well—Sebastian. It's been a while."

"Sure has." *Sebastian, how would you like to return to Thaumia as a toad? I wonder how much* mana *I have left.*

"Well—ah, Dix, what's on for the rest of the day?"

Dixie consulted a calendar. "You have a meeting with the department at one-thirty to talk about the new Moss account. Then at three you wanted to confer with the artist on the Pinella spots. Mr. Bush of Creative Consultants is due at four."

"Yes, well. Ah, postpone the department meeting until tomorrow, it'll hold. And can you call the artist, ah—"

"Lakie."

"Right, and Bush, and reschedule? I think I'm taking the rest of the afternoon off."

"Surely," Dixie said.

"Come on, cousin," Jeremy said, throwing his arm around Sebastian's shoulders. "We've got a lot to talk about."

In the parking lot, Jeremy stared in disbelief at the red Porsche. "Why?" he asked.

"Cassie liked it," Sebastian said. "And you could afford it. You had enough in savings to pay cash for it."

"But my Civic—"

Sebastian smiled sheepishly. "I broke it. I didn't know driving was so difficult."

"Get in," Jeremy said. "Let's see how your driving is now."

"It's better," Sebastian said as he slid behind the wheel. "I used my magic to learn it."

"And the language, and my job?"

"Yes. But it's gone now. I've lost all of it. Spells are hard to work in this universe, and it took tremendous power." Sebastian started the engine. "Where to?"

"I don't know. Just drive for now. Downtown."

Sebastian grimaced. "Making me drive in downtown Atlanta. You must really be pissed off." But he pulled the car out of the lot and headed south. "What happened back in April?" he asked suddenly.

"When?"

"You appeared one night, remember? Then my mirror exploded, and Cassie had hysterics. I finally convinced her she'd had a nightmare and blamed the broken mirror on a sonic boom."

Jeremy looked out the window. "It's too complicated to go into right now. But the Hag is dead, and the Great Dark One's power is broken." He shook his head. "Jesus, do you realize how crazy that sounds while we're driving past the Doraville GM plant?"

"How did you do there?"

"Well enough. I was the one responsible for killing the Hag and breaking the mirrors."

Sebastian gave him a look of frank respect. "There was more about you than I suspected."

"Good Lord," Jeremy said. "What's that?"

"Oh, they finally finished the new interchange." Sebastian turned off onto I-85. They merged with steady traffic and headed in toward the city. "So what happens now?"

"I'm supposed to send you back in my place."

"Bob Escher was fired, did you know that?"

"How could I?" Jeremy demanded in a querulous voice. "You seem to have made out well yourself."

"Uh-huh. Just took a little drive and determination, that's all. People here are bizarre, Jeremy. They'll believe anything. You should see the package of ads I put together for this rinky-dink wine company. Tripled their sales in the last quarter! And I got an award for the ads, too. That cinched the promotion, I think. Oh. You've been head of copywriting since April first."

"No fooling."

"No, honest."

Ahead of them the towers of Atlanta showed suddenly, etched against a background of dark clouds. Lightning ripped through the sky. Three miles farther south, Jeremy sat up very straight. "Turn here. This exit."

At the top of the ramp, Sebastian said, "Which way?"

"Left. Turn in over there."

Sebastian looked aghast at the sign, red letters on a white background, and at the restaurant under it. "What?"

Jeremy glowered at him. "I want a Varsity chili dog, french fries, and a large Coke. It's been a long time."

After lunch (Sebastian didn't eat; he just looked on in horror, once muttering, "Do you know how much cho-

lesterol is *in* that junk?"), Jeremy checked the time on the
car clock: 12:17. "Drive some more," he ordered.
"Downtown."

Atlanta had not changed very much in six months. The
wind still whipped dust and stray newspapers high in the
cross streets off Peachtree, and the MARTA buses still
went anywhere they wanted while smaller cars cowered
away from them. "Do I have any money left?" Jeremy
asked.

"What do you mean?"

"I saw the suits in the closet. And this car. I was saving
up in case—"

"Don't worry about it. Mom—your mother, I mean—is
living with Bill now, in Baltimore."

"What?"

"Look, your brother Bill—"

"Bill and Mom never got along! They'll tear each other
apart!"

"No, no, you don't understand—"

"My God! Bill's a bum, but I wouldn't wish Mom
on—"

"Jeremy!" When Jeremy fell quiet, Sebastian said,
"Look, Bill's been in the wrong job all his life. He was
never meant to be an engineer, I don't care what Georgia
Tech said. I've got some investments in a sporting-goods
company, and they needed a sales rep for the D.C. area.
Bill was out of work in February, and they took him on,
on my recommendation. He's going great guns. He's
always been a salesman; he just didn't know it. And all
Mom wanted was for him to settle down, which he has.
You should see them together. You'll want to vomit."

Jeremy stared at Sebastian. "When did I invest in a
sporting-goods company?"

"It's a new account. And I'd already paid for the
Porsche, and there was some left over. It's a good return,
believe me, especially after I analyzed their demographics and showed them— "

"You can't do that!"

"I did it." They stopped at a red light on Peachtree.
Sebastian chewed his lip. "Look, if you don't send me
back, here's a proposition. Nobody at the office is to
know about it, but on the side I've set up a little consult-
ing outfit. I need somebody good to run the place. Just
front for me, really. If you wouldn't mind being my

cousin, it's a great opportunity. Say forty K to start, then—"

"You bastard!" Jeremy laughed. "You love it, don't you? And you were the great magician!"

"No so great." Sebastian turned right. "I'm going over to Techwood, okay? Less crowded in the middle of the day."

"Fine."

"I wasn't so great. I could do the magic, but it never felt good, you know? But this, God, what a kick. And it's so easy! People just don't see how easy it is when you learn a few angles. So, what do you think? Would you run the consultancy for me?"

"No. I'd hate it."

"Then I have to go back?"

"You got it."

Sebastian pulled into a parallel parking spot on a side street. "There's something else you should know. Now, don't get mad."

"What is it?"

Sebastian looked long and hard at him, then blurted: "You're marrying Cassie on Sunday. Then you're off for two weeks' honeymoon in Vail."

Jeremy went dead cold inside. "That's why you have so much in your checking account. *My* account, damn it! We'll just have to call it off."

"Four hundred guests. You're supposed to pick up Mom and Bill at Hartsfield, five o'clock Friday."

Jeremy stared at his own image. "You don't love her."

Sebastian swallowed and averted his gaze. "I didn't know what love was until I met Cassie," he said quietly. "You can believe it or not, and to hell with you." After a long silence he added, "I have no magic left. I'm burned out. What will I do back in Thaumia, assuming they let me live?"

For ten minutes they sat there. Then Jeremy cursed. "Come on. We have to get back to the apartment. That's where the spell will work. Wait, though. Stop at Rich's. You'll have to get back to Peachtree and turn south—"

"I know where Rich's is. What do you want there?"

"A backpack of some kind."

They drove to the department store, and Jeremy bought a bright blue nylon knapsack for twenty dollars. Then,

back in the car, he said. "Home. But not right away.
Take Ponce de Leon east to Highland, then north."

"What's there?"

"Bookstores," Jeremy said. "Mark's first, then all the
way up to the used textbook store near Emory. What's
the matter? Don't you read fantasy and science fiction?"

"I read *Fortune*," Sebastian said.

Kelada came into the Great Hall, and behind her Nul
stumped in on his crutches. "Is it happening?" Kelada
asked Barach.

"It is beginning."

"I want to see him," Kelada said, her voice cold. "I
want him to know what he caused."

"Give me ten simi alone with Sebastian," growled Nul.
"Bandages and all."

"Look."

In the center of the star a golden mist coalesced, shimmered, shrank—and became a man. "Well," he said,
hefting a strange blue package. "The spell I put on it
actually worked. The knapsack came through whole."

Kelada ran forward, and Nul whooped, waving his
crutches so hard he almost fell on his face. Laughing,
Barach picked up the cloak Jeremy had discarded early
that morning and went to throw it over the shoulders of
the naked, bearded man. It was hard work, for first he
had to pull Kelada away. The man put his hand on
Barach's shoulder. "You still have one pupil, old teacher."

For once in his life Barach could not speak. Nul had
clumped over to the knapsack that the traveler had
dropped. "What in this?"

"Stories, little friend. All the stories I will write. After
all, my magic may not last forever."

Nul had opened the pack. "Pretty pictures," he said,
looking at the covers of compact paper-covered books.
"Writing strange. You can read this?"

But Kelada had thrown her arms around him again,
and for the moment, at least, Jeremy was not able to
reply.

AFTERWORD: OF THAUMIA AND ITS MAGIC

IN WRITING THE tale of Mage Jeremy Moon and his quest to destroy the mirrors created by his dark double, I have dealt already with the world of Thaumia and have told of many of the ways this world differs from the Earth. Still, any world is commodious enough to contain more than can be kept between the covers of any single adventure, and there may be a few readers interested in knowing more about the alternate universe of Thaumia, its origin, and its relation to our universe. While not exhaustive, this afterword may help explain some riddles that would trouble an analytic reader. In any case, it does not further the story of Jeremy's experiences in Thaumia (that must wait for another tale), but it does shed a bit of light on the reality in which those experiences happened.

First let's consider the origin of the plural universes. Kelada, admittedly unschooled, was by no means uneducated (there is a difference, even in Thaumia). Her account to Jeremy, though not couched in the academic phrases beloved by magi and full professors, was correct in its essentials. Back at the beginning of things (or rather before, since without space there could be no time), at the commencement of the Big Bang, the cosmic egg which contained all that was to be burst open, not like a real egg to hatch one chick but rather like the bud of an incredibly complex flower. From the multi-dimensional point which was the origin of all universes, and which the Thaumians know as the Between, petals burst in many different dimensional directions. Each petal comprises one universe.

Now, our universe received a great amount of what we call energy and only a little of what the Thaumians call *mana* (we'd know it as magic). As a matter of fact, our universe *is* energy and space—nothing more, if one excepts the minute quantities of magic that fill the interstices and are hardly noticed in our day-to-day life. All matter is simply solidified energy, energy standing still in one place for a short time. This book is energy, the chair you're sitting in is energy, and *you* are energy. This is all a much more verbose way of saying what a wise and gentle mage of our own world once said much more succinctly: $E = mc^2$.

In the Thaumian universe the reverse obtains: there magic is the primary stuff of creation (though energy does exist there as magic does in our own universe). There, should Tremien or one of his peers enunciate it, the equation would be expressed as $M = mc^2$. Or maybe not, for the speed of light is a function of physical law, and physical laws are unique to their own universes. There is a universe, for example, where the speed of light is in our terms about twelve miles per hour. The inhabitants of one world on the outermost fringes of a galaxy there only began to see other stars about a week ago. Prior to that time, the sky had been dark except for their sun (actually an image of what their sun was like 19.41 years ago, since it takes that long for its light to reach them). They still don't know what to make of these new lights popping into their sky, and rather regard it as a celestial fireworks display. But they do think it is very pretty, and they stand outdoors through most of the night now, gasping "Ooh!" as a new star appears and occasionally bursting into spontaneous applause at the debut of a new red giant. But this is in another place, so back to Thaumia.

Thaumia is full of potential magic, just as our world is full of potential energy. Here we must use physical means to liberate and use energy: muscles swing a bat that sends a ball over a distant fence; gasoline unites with oxygen to drive pistons that move a car; friction warms a match and produces combustion. In Thaumia, mental energies can release magic and use it to do work. However, the user of magical energies must be very certain of what he or she wishes to accomplish. You would not (I hope) attempt to cook a steak by inserting one end of it into a light socket. On Thaumia an untutored person attempting to use magic is in exactly the same position. Thus the three-stage ritual of using magic—formulation, visualization, and realization—really is just a safeguard against unhappy accidents.

The Thaumians, with their study of the mind and its influ-

ence on magic, have learned more than we about the earliest
blossoming of the universe. It is true that the Between
unites all universes still, like the heart of the flower in
my metaphor. It is also true that the Between is both
finite and infinite (Earthly logic does not apply here)
and that conditions of existence in this primal place
are different from anything found anywhere else in all
the universes. We visit it in our dreams, and it is literally
such stuff as dreams are made on. However, all the
dreaming races of all the other inhabited worlds of our
reality (and there are billions upon billions of them) also
visit the Between, and the same holds true for all the
other unthinkable numbers of universes and their inhabitants. As it happens, though, there are harmonies within
discord. Earth and Thaumia are examples of that.

Earth and Thaumia, first of all, inhabit neighboring
universes. Both planets were formed, each by means
peculiar to its universe, at exactly the same relative time
(simultaneity is possible between universes, though not
within our own universe), occupy the same relative amount
of space, and have on them the same forms of life. There
is an unusual sympathy between these two sister planets,
one that creates conditions that do not otherwise exist.

For one thing, it is very clear that in the past there
were more "windows," either intentionally created or
spontaneous, through which traffic between worlds was
possible. The humans on Thaumia are genetically identi-
cal to the humans on Earth; in fact, they are descended
from common ancestors. The fact that the human population of Thaumia currently stands at seven hundred million indicates that the Thaumian ancestors came from
Earth, and not vice versa. The same is true of many
plants and domestic animals: horses, dogs (rare in Thaumia
but they exist), cats, cattle, chickens, swine, a variety of
wheat the Thaumians call sheaf, and dozens of other
food crops and useful trees all came to Thaumia with
human colonists. The major colonization presumably occurred during the Neolithic period, since except for only
a few fairly clear-cut examples, the languages spoken on
Thaumia bear only remote resemblances to such ancient
Earth tongues as primitive Indo-European.

Certainly there were succeeding exchanges (perhaps
the mischievous pika people, once much more numerous,
ventured into Europe in the Middle Ages and earlier,

planting the seeds for legends about the wee folk, bogles, goblins, and pucks), attested to by the presence of Asian, African, and Native American strains of plants and animals; however, these movements must have been smaller ones, and the Earthly folk taken into Thaumia were assimilated, their languages lost (though any inventions they carried in their heads or their hands might have survived and spread). Sad to say, in our time the exchanges seem to have ceased, except for very rare and exceptional cases like Jeremy's. No authentic cases of changelings, for example, have been reported in something over two hundred years.

The Thaumians by now have their own culture, history, and literature, and a little of it came out in this story. One note on the language: it is, like English, a language primarily of nouns and verbs, but the syntactic order is different. By a minor enchantment Jeremy acquired the language intact and spoke and thought it without effort, so until he actually noticed what he was saying and thinking, he believed himself to be speaking and thinking in English. This is not surprising. You, for example, are not aware of your own breathing—well, *now* you are.

Anyway, a book written in the Thaumian language would be fascinating but would sell only to people who had a table with one short leg. I have accordingly translated all the speeches and thoughts, and indeed all the place-names where it mattered, into English. To give you a few examples of the Thaumian equivalents (and I must pause to note that on Thaumia, too, there are many distinct languages and language families; the primary one used in the book is Presolatan, and from this tongue all the examples are taken): *Whitehorn* really is *Duap,* a worn-down combination of *duli,* cone, used also to refer to the horns of cattle, and *aphin,* white; *Haggenkom* is a version of the Presolatan *Sregukivi,* literally "witch's vale." *Ivi,* however, is an antique word, with no one using it except the scattered population of Lofarlan in the far northwest. Originally it meant a small hollow on the side of, or at the base of, a hill, but as the Hag's influence grew, the word grew to encompass her devastation. Furthermore, the ending has worn off the word, which should really be *ivirn.* The closest analogue of the word in English is the almost obsolete Old English term *coomb;* the Witch's Valley becomes, in my version, the Haggenkom.

Some peculiarities of our tongue have their equivalents in Presolatan. Nul, who naturally spoke Pikish as his native tongue, had some trouble with niceties of Presolatan involving articles, declensions, and linking verbs, and so, sensibly, he ignored them when he could. None of these existed in Pikish, and it was a chore for him to have to recall them. The quibble he engaged in with "longtooths" and "longteeth" as alternate plurals is genuine and neatly paralleled by the tooth/teeth singular and plural in English. The name of the beast in Presolatan, however, was *krasibor,* "fang-cat." Two of the beasts would be called *krashibor,* while two common cats would be called *kresh.* The liberty taken in translation was not great, and, I hope, conveyed something of poor Nul's problem in learning a strange language.

Perhaps it should be remarked in passing that one indication of a migration of Europeans to Thaumia in prehistoric times may be found in the name of Nul's people. In his language they called themselves *pwyktwa,* which simply means "the people." The humans who first encountered them called them something very like *piksa,* with a short "i." This looks a great deal as if it comes from the Indo-European root *pik-,* "black" (we can see a modern descendant of this root in the English word "pitch"). The term must have been purely descriptive at first, referring to the dark fur of the pika; however, the sound of the Pikish word, coincidentally echoing the human one, no doubt assured the survival of "pika" as a name for the creatures. Whether or not the term bears any relation to the much later English "pixie" is unknown.

Much more remains to be told of Thaumia: Jeremy, for example, had almost no contact with the genuine wild animals of the countryside, for the travel spells got him past the wilderness areas. He would have been astonished to see some of the forms of animal life, since they parallel most of the fabulous beasts of Earth (more accidental cross-world leakage in times past, no doubt). One exception, of course, lay in Jeremy's numerous encounters with the vilorgs. However, since the vilorgs had been radically changed by the Hag's magic, forcibly evolved from the large, lethargic, subsentient amphibioid creatures they originally were, they hardly count. From all

indications, the Hag's first experiments with them created exceptionally strong, malignant, and feral creatures.
By the next generations, those Jeremy encountered, the
vilorgs had become tamed and were almost totally dependent on the Hag's will for their own decisions.

Another problem left unresolved in the present story,
of course, is the fate of the Great Dark One and his
subsequent moves against the magi. For he did find a
way of continuing himself, with devious and evil intent,
and his next actions were subtle, determined, and pointed
in many ways directly at Jeremy. But since Jeremy knew
no more at the conclusion of his adventure with the
mirrors than you do (actually rather less since you've
read this far in the Afterword), all that was best postponed.

Jeremy failed to discover many other facts about
Thaumian life during his first half-year there: he never
really learned much of the complicated system of govern-
ment, the religious sects of the planet, or the economic
system and its total lack of advertising. But then he was
at first fully occupied with the problems of the moment.
He learned much more as time went by, and while it
would be too much to say that he and Kelada lived
happily ever after, they certainly did live *interestingly*
ever after.

However, the account of that belongs not here, but in
other songs, other tales, and other books.